Books by Gregg Hurwitz

The Program
The Kill Clause
Do No Harm
Minutes to Burn
The Tower

And Available in H___

Trou___hooter

GREGG HURWITZ

THE
PROGRAM

HarperTorch

An Imprint of HarperCollinsPublishers

This is a work of fiction. Names, characters, places, and incidents are products of the author's imagination or are used fictitiously and are not to be construed as real. Any resemblance to actual events, locales, organizations, or persons, living or dead, is entirely coincidental.

HARPERTORCH
An Imprint of HarperCollins*Publishers*
10 East 53rd Street
New York, New York 10022-5299

Copyright © 2004 by Gregg Hurwitz
Excerpt from *Troubleshooter* copyright © 2005 by Gregg Hurwitz
ISBN-13: 978-0-06-053041-9
ISBN-10: 0-06-053041-3

First HarperTorch paperback printing: September 2005
First William Morrow hardcover printing: September 2004

HarperCollins®, HarperTorch™, and ♥™ are trademarks of Harper-Collins Publishers Inc.

Printed in the United States of America

Visit HarperTorch on the World Wide Web at www.harpercollins.com

10 9 8 7 6 5 4 3 2 1

For Delinah,
the purest heart

There are only two things in the world—nothing and semantics.

—WERNER ERHARD

THE PROGRAM

Prologue

*T*o the bemusement of the tourists and a third-grade class shepherded by a portly teacher, the woman crouched naked near the fourteen-foot mammoth and urinated. Her hands gripped the kinked-wire fence encircling the vast Lake Pit, the La Brea Tar Pits' main attraction. Her face was smooth and unlined; she could still have been a teenager.

A few of the children laughed. A stout man in a white Vandyke and a pinstripe shirt ceased his lethargic tapping on a set of bongos, gathered up the bills he'd accrued in an over-turned boater, and scurried off. A golden-years tourist clucked disapproval, clasping her strap-held camera to her side. Her husband gazed on, mouth slightly ajar, as if unsure whether the vision before him was real or a preview of senility.

Heedless that her ankles were getting splattered, the young woman stared through the fence at the fiberglass family of Columbian mammoths, life-size props for the prehistoric death trap. The baby mammoth stood in its father's shadow on shore, watching its mother mired in the hardened surface a stone's throw out. The mother stayed snapshot-frozen in her sinking terror, her upper legs midflail, trunk extended.

Farther into the lake, the tar crust gave way to a murky brown liquid that fumed and bubbled with eruptions of methane. The sludge beneath the surface housed the world's richest deposit of Ice Age fossils. A thick, oppressive smell pervaded the area—equal parts sulfur dioxide and baked Nevada highway.

The woman turned to face the crowd, and it froze, as if this rail-skinny girl were wired with explosives. Her inside-out panties lay where she'd kicked them off, crowning the heap of clothes to her left. The backs of her arms were purple, contused from elbow to shoulder.

"Why isn't anyone helping?" the naked woman implored the onlookers. "Can't you see? Can't you see what's going on?"

The teacher blew into the whistle dangling around his neck, withdrawing his class to the picnic area near the rest rooms. A two-man security team motored up on a golf cart, cutting through the thickening mass of gawkers. The driver hopped out, face shiny with sweat. His partner stayed in the cart, fingers drumming nervously on the security decal; dealing with a naked woman pissing on county property was a far cry from tending to sunstrokes and graffiti.

Backhanding moisture off his forehead, the driver spoke into his radio. "Is LAPD on the way?"

From the burst of responding static resolved a few security catchphrases. *". . . backup en route . . . crowd control . . . detain the perpetrator. . . ."*

He plucked at the front of his blue shirt. "Ma'am, please put your clothes back on. There are children present."

An appeal to common decency wasn't the shrewdest approach when facing a naked crazy person.

Cars had backed up on Wilshire Boulevard, parallel to the fence on the lake's south side; spectators were standing on top of a bus shelter for a better vantage. Onlookers streamed over to the scene. At the west edge of the park in the café of the neighboring county museum, the windows were all but blotted out with faces wearing blank expressions of morbid curiosity. A KCOM cameraman tripped over a cable and went down, cracking his lens and bloodying his palms.

The girl's head pivoted frantically as she suddenly became aware of the commotion. Her chest heaved. When she spotted the four blue-uniformed officers cutting through the crowd, she sprinted along the fence, to a proliferation of gasps and shrieks from the crowd. At the south edge of the lake, a break in the fence accommodated a low cast-iron bridge. She vaulted deftly over its side, landing on the strip of dirt, and scurried back near her previous post, this time just inside the enclosure.

Three of the cops froze on the other side of the fence; the fourth followed her route and paused with one black boot up on the bridge's rail. The girl's eyes darted, terrified pupils held in crescents of white. "Can't you help? Why won't you help?"

One of the cops, the oldest, eased forward, gesturing down the fence line for his partner on the bridge to stay put. "We're here to help."

She walked down the slope to the father and baby mammoth at the shore's edge, treading on yellow flowers.

A note of alarm found its way into the veteran cop's voice. "Ma'am, just hold up now. Please don't go any nearer."

The girl rested an arm on the baby's side, staring out at the doomed mother who remained sunk in the sludge, rocking slightly in her perennial grave. The girl was crying now, shoulders heaving, wiping tears off her cheeks with the back of a slender hand. The air was filled with an electric charge, the anticipation of something horrific about to occur.

The other officers were fighting to calm the spectators, who were shouting advice to the cop and demands to the girl. She remained lost in herself.

"Get them back!" the veteran cop shouted. "Get up a perimeter. Let's get this girl some space."

His hand was still extended, holding his partner on the bridge in place. He tried to keep his voice calm and reassuring while speaking loudly enough for the girl to hear him over the commotion. "My partner there, his name is Michael. He's gonna wait right there until you're ready for him to come down. Then, when *you decide,* we can come help you take care of that mammoth."

A burst of bubbles broke through the thick tar near the female mammoth, creating a momentary pool before the crust re-formed. The girl turned back to the lake. The cop on the bridge tensed like a retriever at the edge of a duck blind.

"Wait!" the officer shouted. "Talk to me. Tell me what I can do."

She stopped and gazed at him. Her face held a sudden calm, the calm of determination. "The Teacher says to exalt strength, not comfort."

She turned and strode out onto the lake's tar surface. The cop on the bridge leapt down, but he was a good thirty yards away. The older cop was yelling, veins straining in his neck, and the spectators went mad with a sort of frenzied, hypnotic motion, like concert viewers or soccer fans. The girl's bare feet slapped the black surface, which started to give as she neared the enormous female mammoth twenty yards from shore. The crust gave with a wet sucking sound under her next step, and she screamed. Her arms shot up and out, and she struck the thin layer of congealed tar with her right knee and elbow, both of which immediately adhered to it.

The crowd surged and ebbed, drawn and repulsed.

The girl tried to pull herself up, a gooey sheet forming between her trapped arm and the lake's surface, but then her hip stuck and she rolled to her side, the tar claiming her hair. One of her legs punched through the crust into the brown liquid below, and her body shifted and started a slow submersion. Still she struggled toward the mammoth.

The cop from the bridge was standing on shore, and the veteran cop was still shouting—"Get a rope! Throw her a goddamn rope!"—both meaty hands fisting the wire rectangles in the fence so tight his fingers had gone white.

The girl strained to keep her face free and clear, pulling against her entangled hair so hard it distorted her features. Aside from her panicked eyes, she seemed weirdly calm, almost acquiescent. Both of her arms were mired now, her lower body nearly lost, and the crowd watched with horrified apprehension as she sputtered, a quivering, sinking bulge. Her face, the sole oval of remaining white, pointed up at the midday sun, sucking a few last gasps before it, too, filled and quieted, enveloped beneath the surface.

The crowd was suddenly silent, deflated. From the throng emerged the sound of one person sobbing, then another. Within seconds a chorus of cries was raised.

The veteran cop was on the radio, sending for an aerial ladder truck from the fire department, shouting across the receiver between transmissions for security to locate a garden hose. He'd sweated through his undershirt and uniform, the dark blue turning black in patches. When his partner reached him, he was still staring at the dented ring of tar where the girl had disappeared.

His lips barely moved when he spoke. "What the hell could make a person do something like that?"

The tar slowly constricted around the spot where the girl had sunk, until it again formed an oblivious, smooth sheet.

One

Dray walked briskly through the kitchen and entry, wiping barbecue sauce on her olive sheriff's-department-issue pants, which she still hadn't had time to change out of. She pulled open the front door, and the image hit her like a truck—husky detective in a cheap suit thumbing a bound notepad, dark Crown Vic idling curbside behind him, partner waiting in the passenger seat, taking a pass on the advise-next-of-kin.

The detective crowded the door, imposing and cocky, which further added to her disorientation. "Andrea Rackley? Mrs. Tim Rackley?"

Ears ringing, she shook her head hard. "No." She took a step back and leaned on the entry table, displacing a tealight holder that rolled off the edge, shattering on the tile. *"No."*

The man's forehead creased. "Are you all right, ma'am?"

"I just talked to him. He was in the car, heading home. He was fine."

"Excuse me? I'm not sure what you . . ."

He lowered his pad, which she saw was not a detective's notepad but a PalmPilot encased in fine leather. Her darting eyes took in that his suit was not cheap but a fine cashmere, the car was in fact a maroon Mercedes S-class, and the partner was not a partner at all but a woman with a wan face, waiting behind like a well-trained dog.

The flood of relief was accompanied by a torrent of sentence fragments even she couldn't keep up with. "You don't come to the door of a law-enforcement family all somber asking for a next-of-kin ID already lost someone in the family my *God*—"

She leaned shakily against the wall, catching her breath. A draft sucked the doorknob from her grasp. Startled, the man skipped back, lost his footing at the step, and spilled backward, landing hard on his affluent ass.

Dray had a split second to note the pain and alarm register in the wide ovals of his eyes before the door slammed shut.

*T*im stifled a yawn as he pulled into his cul-de-sac, the starch-stiff security-guard monkey suit itching him at the collar and cuffs. His baton sat heavy on his equipment belt, along with a low-tech portable the size of a Cracker Jack box, which seemed like a toy company's idea of a radio rather than the thing itself. A big comedown from his beloved Smith & Wesson .357 and the sleek Racals he'd used as a deputy U.S. marshal before his own shitty judgment in the wake of his daughter's violent death had forced him from the Service.

Yesterday he'd chased down a teen vandal at the facility where he worked on the northern lip of Simi Valley. The pursuit represented the second time he'd broken a sweat in the eleven months he'd been guarding RightWay Steel Company's storage warehouses; the first had been unglamorously instigated by a roadside-stand enchilada *mole* he'd injudiciously wolfed down on a lunch break. Eleven years as an Army Ranger, three kicking in doors with the U.S. Marshals Service warrant squad, and now he was a locker-room commando with a diminished paycheck. His current coworkers got winded bending over to tie their shoes, which seemed to come undone with such alarming frequency that he'd spent the majority of the monotonous morning debating whether to volunteer proficiency training on the matter. The old man's groan he'd inadvertently emitted while stooping to pick up a dropped key outside Warehouse Five had leached the superiority right out of him, and he'd spent the afternoon valiantly refraining from doughnuts.

He was reminding himself that he should be grateful for *any* work when movement on his walkway drew his attention. A man stood appraising his suit, dusting off the pant legs as if he'd just taken a spill.

Tim accelerated sharply, almost clipping a parked Navigator with tinted windows. He pulled into his driveway and hopped out as the man smoothed his clothes back into place. A woman had climbed out of the Mercedes at the curb and was standing meekly at the end of the walk.

Tim approached the man, keeping the woman in his field of vision. "Who are you? Press?"

The man held up his hands as if conceding defeat. He still hadn't caught his breath. "I'm here to . . . speak with . . . Tim Rackley. Marshal Tannino gave me your address."

The mention of his former boss stopped Tim dead on the lawn. He and Tannino hadn't spoken for the better part of a year; they'd been very close when Tim worked under his supervision, but Tim last saw him in the midst of a storm of controversy Tim had brought down on himself and the Service.

"Oh," Tim said. "I'm sorry. Why don't you come in?"

The man patted the seat of his pants, wet with runoff from the sprinklers. He glanced at the door nervously. "Truth be told," he said, "I'm a bit afraid of your wife."

*T*he kitchen smelled sharply of burned chicken. Dray had forsaken her corn on the cob for a three-finger pour of vodka. "I'm sorry. Something about it—the knock, his expression—put me back there, the night Bear came to tell us about Ginny." She set her glass down firmly on the stack of overdue bills at the counter's edge.

Tim ran his fingers through her hair and let them rest on her shoulders. She leaned into him, face at his neck.

"I thought my heart would just give out there at the door. Good-bye, Andrea, hasta la vista, sayonara, I've fallen and can't get up."

Her voice was raised and, Tim was fairly certain, audible to the couple sitting on the couch one room over.

"He's a friend of the marshal's," Tim said softly. "Let's sit down, see what he wants. Deal?"

Dray finished her vodka in a gulp. "Deal."

They shook hands and headed into the living room, Dray refilling her glass on the way.

The woman sat on the couch, a gold cross glittering against her sweater. The man stood at the sliding glass doors facing the backyard, hands clasped behind his back, his stoic posture undercut by the moist patch of trouser plastered to his rear end. He pivoted as if just taking note of their entrance and nodded severely. "Let's start over." He extended a big, rough hand. "Will Henning. My wife, Emma."

Tim shook his hand, but Dray stood where she was, arms crossed. Copies of *The Lovely Bones,* gifted eight or so times by well-intentioned acquaintances, occupied the shelf behind her, the bluish stack accentuating her light hair. "What can we help you with?"

Will pulled a fat wallet from his back pocket, flipped it open, and withdrew a snapshot from the fold. He gestured impatiently for Tim to take it, his face averted as if he didn't want Tim to read the pain in it. A posed high-school-graduation photo of a girl. Pretty but awkward. A bit of an overbite, front tooth slightly angled, mournful green-gray eyes that were almost impossibly big and beautiful. Straight, shoulder-length hair that shagged out at the edges. Her neck was too thin for her head, lending her a certain fragility. Understated chin, full cheeks. The kind of face Tim had seen described as "heart-shaped" on fugitive identifiers; the term had stuck because he'd never before found it to make sense.

Tim's eyes pulled to the much-publicized school photo of Ginny on the mantel. Her second-grade year. And her last.

"I'm so sorry," Tim said. "When was she killed?"

Over on the couch, Emma made a little gasp. Her first peep.

Will took the picture back from Tim abruptly, casting a protective eye over at his wife. "She's not dead. At least we hope not. She's . . . well, sort of missing. Except she's eighteen—"

"Nineteen," Emma said. "Just turned."

"Right, nineteen. Since she's not a minor, we have no legal recourse. She's gotten herself in with one of these cults. Not like the Jehovah's Witnesses, but one of those creepy, mind-control, self-help deals. Except more dangerous."

Tim said, "Have you tried—"

"The goddamn cops have been useless. Won't even file a missing person's. We've tried every law-enforcement agency—FBI, CIA, LAPD—but there are virtually no resources devoted to cults. No one cares unless they turn Waco."

"Her name," Tim said.

"Leah. She's my stepdaughter, from Emma's first marriage. Her real father died of stomach cancer when she was four."

"She was a student at Pepperdine." Emma's voice was brittle and slightly hoarse, as if she had to strain to reach audibility.

Tim's eyes returned to Emma's cross pendant, this time making out Jesus' tiny hanging form.

"Three months ago we got a phone call from her roommate. She said Leah had dropped out. She said she was in a cult, that we'd better find her or we'd never see her again."

"She came home once," Will said. "March thirteenth, out of the blue. My men and I tried to reason with her but she . . . uh, escaped out the bathroom window, and we haven't seen or heard from her since."

He was the kind of man who had men.

"I'm sorry," Dray said. "I don't mean to be rude, and I understand how painful this is for you, but what does this have to do with Tim?"

Will looked to Tim. "We're familiar with your . . . work. Marco—Marshal Tannino—confirmed that you were a brilliant investigator. He said you used to be a great deputy—" He caught himself. "I'm sorry, I didn't mean it that way."

Tim shrugged. "That's okay. I'm not a deputy marshal anymore." The edge in his voice undercut his casual tone.

"We need our daughter back. We don't care how it's done, and we won't ask any questions. She doesn't have to be happy about it—she just needs to be home so we can get her the help she needs. We want you to do it. Say, for ten grand a week."

Dray's eyebrows raised, but she gave Tim the slightest head shake, matching, as usual, his own reaction.

Tim said, "I don't have a PI license, and I'm not affiliated with any law-enforcement agency. I got myself into some trouble about a year back, with a vigilante group—maybe you read about it in the papers?"

Will nodded vigorously. "I like your style. I think it was a great thing you tried to do."

"Well, I don't."

"What would make you say yes?"

Tim laughed, a single note. "If I could follow the trail legally."

"We could arrange that."

Tim opened his mouth, then closed it. His brow furrowed; his head pulled to the side. "I'm sorry, who exactly are you?"

"Will Henning." He waited for recognition to dawn. It did not. "Sound and Fury Pictures."

Tim and Dray exchanged a blank glance, and then Tim shrugged apologetically.

"*The Sleeper Cell. Live Wire. The Third Shooter.* Little art-house flicks like that."

"I'm sorry . . ." Dray said. "You wrote those movies?"

"I'm not a *writer.* I produced them. My films have grossed more than two billion dollars worldwide. If I could get fifteen Blackhawk choppers landing in Getty Plaza on three days' notice, I certainly think I can orchestrate your redeputization." His steel gray eyes stayed fixed on Tim. A man used to getting his way.

"The marshal probably has his own opinion on the matter."

"He'd like to talk to you about some creative solutions in person." Tannino's business card magically appeared in Will's hand. Tim took it, running his thumb over the raised gold Marshals seal.

On the back, in Tannino's distinctive hand: *Rackley—to-morrow a.m. 7:00.*

Tim handed the card to Dray, who gave it a cursory glance, then tossed it on the coffee table. "Tell me about the cult," he said.

"I don't know a goddamn thing about it, not even its name. Considering the amount we've paid for information . . ." Will shook his head in disgust.

"How do they recruit?"

"We don't know that either, really. We talked to a few cult experts—deprogrammers or exit counselors or whatever they're calling themselves this month—and they coughed up some generalities. I guess a lot of cults prey on young kids, in college or just out. And they recruit rich kids." He grimaced. "They get them to turn over their money." He ran his hand through his hair, agitated. "Leah gave away a two-million-dollar future. Just gave it away. That money was for her first indie film, grad school, a house someday. I even bought her a forty-thousand-dollar car before college so she wouldn't have to dip into it. Now her money's gone, she's alienated her friends, her family"—he nodded at Emma, who sat passively, hands folded, forehead lined. "She has nothing, nowhere to go. I've sent her letters begging her to come home. Emma has sent articles about cults, what they do, how they work, but she's never responded. I tried to talk some sense into her when we had her that day, but she wouldn't listen." His face had colored; his tone was hard and driving. "I told her that she'd given away her whole future."

"You told a girl in a mind-control cult *that?*" Dray said.

"We're not here for family therapy. We're here to get our daughter back. And besides, what was I supposed to say? You try dealing with a teenage daughter who's got all the answers."

Dray took a gulp of her vodka. "I would love to."

Tim squeezed her hand, but Will just kept on talking. "Leah's trust fund is irrevocable—I set it up that way to maximize tax benefits. It turns over money to her every year, and there's nothing we can do to stop it. She gets another million when she turns twenty, another million every year after that until she's thirty. Those people are stealing my money."

"The car," Tim said. "She still has it?"

"Yes. It's a Lexus."

"Is it registered in your name or hers?"

Will thought for a moment, eyes on the ceiling, fingers fiddling with the catch on his gold watch. "Mine."

"Okay. When you leave here, file a report that it's been stolen. The cops will put out a BOLO on the car—a Be On the Lookout. If they pick her up, they can hold her, and we'll see about getting her released into your custody."

"Jesus." Will looked excitedly to his wife. "That's a brilliant idea."

"Did she tell you anything about the cult?"

"No. No names, no locations, no matter how hard we pressed."

"So how do you know it's a self-help cult?"

"From her buzzwords. They weren't religious. More about how she learned to 'tap her inner source' and 'own her weaknesses' and crap like that."

"She didn't mention any names?"

"No."

"What did she refer to the guru as? She must have mentioned the leader."

Will shook his head, but Emma said, "She called him the Teacher. Reverently, like that."

Her husband regarded her, brow furrowed. "She did?"

"You mentioned the cult was dangerous. Did you get any death threats?"

Will nodded. "Couple. Some punk called, said, 'Back off or we'll slice you up like the lamb you served for dinner last night.'" Emma raised a wan hand to her mouth, but Will didn't take note. "Creative little threat, letting us know they had eyes on us. I'm used to threats and bullshit—thirty-four years in Hollywood—but I don't like being pushed around. I didn't realize how serious it was until our investigator went missing. Then we got another call: 'You're next.' They probably figured if they hurt Leah, they'd be killing the golden goose, but us, hey. We're expendable."

"Who was the investigator?"

"A PI. Former chief of security for Warner. My men hired him out of Beverly Hills."

Tim's mind reversed, drawn by the pull of a buried instinct. "The same men parked up at the mouth of the cul-de-sac in a Lincoln Navigator with tinted windows, license starts with 9VLU?"

Will stared at him for a long time, eyebrows raised, mouth slightly ajar. He finally sat. "Yes. The same men."

Tim crossed the room and grabbed the pen and notepad by the telephone. "Go on."

"Short little nervous guy, the PI was—Danny Katanga."

"And he was killed?"

"Disappeared. Last week. He must have been making some headway." Will let out a grumbly sigh. "That's when we decided to go to Tannino."

"We've had no word from Leah at all since she left," Emma said.

Will said, "I keep writing letters, hoping, but nothing."

"How can you send her articles and letters when you don't know where she is?"

"She left a P.O.-box number on our answering machine right after she first disappeared, so we could forward her mail—probably so she could keep getting her financial paperwork. We figure it's a holding box for the entire cult."

"Do any of your letters get returned?"

"No," Emma said. "They go through. To somewhere."

"Where's the post office?"

Will said, "Someplace in the North Valley. We tried to look into it—do you have any idea how difficult it is to squeeze information out of the United States Postal Service? We talked to some postal inspector, he acted like he was guarding the recipe for Coke or some horseshit. We finally sent Katanga to stake out the box, but the post office crawled up his ass about invasion of privacy, so he had to watch from the parking lot. He sat in his car for a few days with binoculars, but she never showed up. The cult's wise to it—they probably send someone different each time to pick up the mail. If they pick it up at all."

"I'll need that address."

"I'll have my assistant call Marco with it first thing tomorrow. Watch yourself with that postal inspector—I'm not kidding. He'll open you up a new one."

Tim jotted a few notes. "Did you record any of the threatening phone calls?"

"No. We managed to trace the second call back to a pay phone in Van Nuys. Nothing came of it."

"I'll want that information, too." Tim flipped through his notes. "What's Leah's last name?" Off the Hennings' blank stares, Tim added, "You said she was from Emma's first marriage?"

"She has my name. I adopted her legally when she was six. She's my stepdaughter, but I make no distinction between her and my own daughter." Will cleared his throat. "I may have progressed a bit foolhardy out of the gate. Wasn't sure what we were dealing with, so I came out swinging. In retrospect that may not have been the best plan of action." He had a habit, Tim observed, of holding his own conversation, undeterred by interjections. "I had my men post these around town. We got nothing but a bunch of nowhere leads." He pulled a flyer from his back pocket and smoothed out its folds on his knee before handing it to Tim. The same photo of Leah, beneath which was written *$10,000 reward for information on the whereabouts of this girl, Leah Elizabeth Henning. Persons wishing to remain anonymous should tear this flyer in half, transmit one half with the info submitted, and save the remaining half to be matched later.* Leah's identifiers and contact information followed.

Tim thought he detected the faint tracings of pride in Will's face, probably from the *Dragnet* wording on the flyer he and his men had cooked up.

Tim turned the flyer over, unimpressed. "So now everyone in the cult knows you're after her, that you're the enemy. That's quite a mess."

"That's why we need you to clean it up. And why we'll pay you well to do it." Will enclosed one large fist in his other hand, bringing them to rest against his belly.

"We have to back off now." Emma shot a loving look at Will, which he returned. "We just had our first baby together. I won't have her be put in harm's way."

"And we're very concerned for Leah," Will said. "Who knows what they'll do to her? If they let her go, she can reveal secrets about them, maybe even try to get her money back. They need her either loyal or dead." He rubbed his eyes, wrinkling the skin around them. "They've convinced me they mean serious business. That's why we need you to poke around, quietly. Someone who can't be traced back to us or to her this time."

"What made Leah take off? When she came home that day?"

Emma rustled uncomfortably, and Will looked sharply away. "They're inside her head. She was insane, convinced we were persecuting her. She played around on my computer and managed to find all the e-mails I'd been sending out to cops and the like."

"She's a whiz with computers." Profound sadness undercut Emma's proud smile. "She was studying computer science. A straight-A student before she . . ." The scattering of pale freckles across her cheeks was visible only if the light hit her the right way. "To go through something like this, as parents, you have no idea."

Dray stiffened. Taking note, Emma shifted, noticing the framed picture of Ginny on the mantel. Mortified, she flushed, her eyes moistening. "Of course you do. I am . . . so terribly sorry."

She dug in her purse for Kleenex, tears running. Tim located a box and offered it to her. Will laid a thick arm across her shoulders and gathered her in. He kissed the top of her head gently. The two couples sat quietly in the room as Emma dabbed her eyes.

"It's terrible for me to cry here, after what you've been through," she said. "It's just so awful knowing she's out there, with these people. She wasn't herself when we saw her. It was like she'd been replaced by another person. She wore a filthy T-shirt, and she had a rash across her chest, bruises up the backs of her arms, open sores around her ankles. God knows what they've done to her. God knows what they're doing to her. Day after day." She pressed the balled tissue to her lips to still them. "How are we supposed to live with that uncertainty? As parents?" She made a strangled noise deep in her throat, something between a gasp and a cry.

Dray's face reddened with emotion; she looked away.

Will gazed tenderly at Leah's photo before leaning forward and setting it on the coffee table. "She was a damn good kid."

Dray said, "Maybe she still is."

Tim studied the picture, noticing for the first time it was worn around the edges, one corner faded by Will's thumb from being removed countless times from the billfold.

"I'll help your daughter," Tim said.

Dray lay curled beneath the covers, facing away, the sheet hugging the dip of her waist. Through the bedroom window, the moon threw a patch of light that angled along the floor and climbed the edge of the bed like a kicked-off blanket. A light rain spit at the glass—the first three weeks of spring had been unusually wet.

Tim slid into bed beside her, resting one hand on her hip and flipping through his notepad with the other. Dray was incredibly fit at thirty-one, her body tuned from self-defense drills and weight training. Three years older, Tim could no longer rely on his work to maintain his lean build; he'd started running early mornings and lifting nights with Dray.

"What a character, that guy." Her voice was slow, tired. "He's mostly frustrated that he hasn't got the upper hand. Typical Hollywood asshole. Thinks he can buy everything. You, the Service, his daughter. 'Her two-million-dollar future.' 'A forty-thousand-dollar car.' I felt like I was on *The Price Is Right.*"

"He's hurting, though. You see how he looked at that picture of her?"

Dray gave a little nod. "My heart goes out to her, and to

them as parents, but . . ." She twisted, regarding him across the bulge of her shoulder. "Call me callous, but if some girl wants to join a cult and fuck herself up, so what? It's not being forced on her. She chose it."

"During Ranger training, they put us through some paces in Psy-Ops. There are ways to break people down, play around in their mind. They don't always have a say in it."

Dray made a noncommittal noise of acknowledgment—the one that meant she needed to give something more thought. "What if she's already dead? What if they killed her and dumped her body somewhere?"

"Then I'll find it and give the parents a burial. End their uncertainty—that's something we were spared."

She nodded slightly and turned back over. "I want Sleep Hold."

Tim slid down in bed, spooning her, and she responded with a lazy arch of her back. She raised her head, and he maneuvered his left arm beneath her neck. His cheek rested against her hair, his lips just touching her ear.

Her voice was faint now, skating the edge of sleep. "Tell me something about Ginny."

Tim stared at the darkness. He squeezed her instead.

Two

Tim strode down the hall leading to the marshal's office, his steps hushed by the carpet, his head numbed by the 6:00 A.M. wake-up and the deadening hum of the air conditioner vents overhead. His first return to the administrative offices, located behind the Federal Courthouse downtown,

was proving to be even more uncomfortable than he'd anticipated. Shame had overtaken him when he drove past the imposing, wide-stepped expanse of the courthouse, dogging
him as he walked this familiar path. He could have spent the
past year and the rest of his life as part of this institution. Instead he was stuck patrolling steel warehouses, sipping Big
Gulps, spitting sunflower seeds, and knowing every minute
that it was entirely his own fault. And knowing that the rent-
a-cop job itself was a kind of penance.

Entering the lounge, he sat beside the antique safe with its
faded rendering of a stag—a relic from an 1877 marshal's
stagecoach escort team. The marshal's assistant nodded at
him formally through the ballistic glass, but her eyes seemed
to glitter in anticipation of the lunchtime gossip she'd be able
to impart.

The infamous ex-deputy dropping in for the first time
since his release from jail. Since the plea bargain he had resisted but taken.

"He's expecting you." She punched at her computer keys
with long-nailed fingers. "Go right in."

Tannino rose from behind his sturdy desk to greet Tim.
They shook hands, Tannino studying him with dark brown
eyes. At six feet, Tim had about five inches on him.

Of the ninety-four U.S. marshals, Tannino was one of the
few merit appointees, having served his street time before
rising through the ranks. The marshalships, one for each federal judicial district, had traditionally been sinecures, though
Homeland Security concerns were changing that rapidly.

Tannino gestured to the couch opposite his desk, and Tim
sat.

"What's his pull?" Tim asked.

Tannino got busy polishing an already spotless picture
frame.

"You might as well come clean now," Tim said. "Save me
the time."

Tannino set down the photo—his niece wearing confirmation white, drenched in creamy angelic lighting. His sister's husband had died a few years ago of a heart attack, and Tannino had taken over paternal duties, which seemed mostly to involve interrogating prospective dates and delegating boyfriend background checks to his less industrious deputies. He laced his hands behind his head and leaned back in his chair, his coiffed salt-and-pepper hair looking even more dated than Tim remembered. "He's a big political donor—helped raise four mil for Senator Feinstein's campaign in '98."

The trail of obligation wasn't hard to trace—Feinstein, as the senior senator, had recommended Tannino for his position. Though Clinton had rubber-stamped Tannino through, it was Feinstein to whom he owed his career, and the feelings of loyalty and respect ran both directions.

"So you redeputize me, put me on the trail unofficially, keep the donor's purse strings loose, and maintain plausible deniability. If I stumble upon the girl and haul her in quietly, no one has to ask questions and a blue-chip case is tied up with a bow. If I screw up, I'm a perfect cutout operative. Tim Rackley, loose cannon and known assassin—shit, he just went off on his own, we weren't really sure what he got himself into. Mobs rally with pitchforks and shovels, and you help stoke the blaze."

"You're getting cynical in your old age, Rackley."

"It's been a long year, Marshal. I lost my stomach for circumlocution."

"I heard Kindell went away for life. I thought that might have lightened the load."

Five months ago, Roger Kindell, the thirty-six-year-old transient who had killed and dismembered Ginny, had pled to life-no-parole to keep the lethal injection at bay. Black-and-white photos depicting him in the act, stained with Ginny's blood, hadn't left the defense many alternatives. At long last, Kindell had run out of loopholes to slip through.

"Rackley? Rackley?"

Tim looked up, regained his focus.

"You're right on one count. We can't go after his kid because she's an adult. Nothing illegal has happened. What we can do is open a quiet investigation on her disappearance and see what options that presents us. If you locate her, maybe you take her into custody quick and quiet and we all get back to more important matters."

"Henning's got money. Why doesn't he just hire a witch-hunter to kidnap her?"

"First of all, it's illegal. Second, those guys are all ex-military machos. Henning can't risk that visibility. He's got political aspirations—he's not feeding money into senate campaigns for the shiny plaques. He's half retired from the business now, a big name around town, there's a congressional seat opening up, maybe the governor's office from there. A botched kidnapping would kill him. You've seen firsthand what the press can do."

"And it's a lot harder to campaign with your daughter off spinning in robes at the airport. We wouldn't want an ally tripping over that hurdle."

"It's not all politics in this room, despite what you may believe."

As much as the bureaucratic back-scratching chafed Tim, he had to respect the marshal's no-bullshit approach to the intricacies of the situation. Tannino was a straight-thinking street operator who'd found himself promoted to a political position; he had to whistle along occasionally, but that didn't mean he liked it.

"You were one of the best deputies I've ever had. Hell, that I've ever *seen*. And I went to bat for you when the chips were down. I had certain limitations, but I did go to bat for you. Don't make this all neat and simple and stick a black hat on me." Tannino took a deep breath, held it a moment. "It's about time you did something more than guard sheet metal and throw a shadow. Let's get you redeputized. Our two-year window hasn't closed, so I can give you a pass on going back to the academy. You can have full reinstatement rights—hell, you and Bear can even go back to swapping lipstick like the old days. I can offer you your appropriate pay grade, GS12, plus availability pay, of course."

"Am I back permanently?"

Tannino sighed. "I'm not gonna lie to you, Rackley. Trying to get you on full-time after the stunts you pulled last year would be like trying to shovel ten pounds of shit into a five-pound bag. We can see how things play, but this is probably a temporary arrangement." He removed a badge and a Smith & Wesson .357 revolver—Tim's preferred, if outdated, duty weapon—from a drawer and set them on his desktop. Tim looked at them for a long time.

"Why didn't you call me first?"

"You would have said no. I needed you to meet the parents."

"Because Will Henning has such a glowing personality?"

"No, because they're real people in real pain."

"So you're willing to forgive me my trespasses as long as the donor deems me useful."

"Exactly. You still want in, though. Why?"

"It may sound trite as hell, Marshal, but I love the Service."

"It doesn't sound trite to me, Rackley. Not at all." Tannino rooted around in his file cabinet for an oath-of-office form, then stood. "Raise your right hand and repeat after me."

*G*ripping his holstered .357, the badge weighing heavy but comforting in the back pocket of his khaki cargo pants, Tim headed to the Roybal Center's Garden Level. After numerous delays and endless bitching, the deputy offices had finally been moved from the shoddier Federal Building next door. It was another temporary arrangement, until the Service took over the third floor from Secret Service, its final step up the ladder of budgetary recognition. The neat lines of desks—cheap, dark wood with shiny faux-gold pulls—and the two waist-high barriers segmenting the room added to

Tim's disorientation on his return. A row of windows to the south overlooked the gardens.

Maybeck went red in the face when he spotted Tim, but Guerrera covered for him nicely with a nod. Across the room, Denley leaned over and wisecracked to Palton from behind a cupped hand. Tim kept his eyes forward as he walked, pretending his peripheral vision was inoperative. The past year had provided him plenty of opportunity to exercise the oblivious-yet-dignified skill set.

The top explosive-detection canines, Precious and Chomper, whimpered at Tim's scent, tails wagging, but they'd been put on a sit-stay, so they didn't run to greet him. Reacting to his dogs, Supervisory Deputy Brian Miller stood to look over the barrier. The others followed suit, rising to their feet and staring, curiosity overcoming tact. A few new faces made Tim's hiatus all the more acute.

A current of whispers followed him to his new desk, empty save a faded blotter and a crumpled Doritos bag. The wood partition provided him momentary respite from the stares. He set the S&W on the blotter and stared at it, weighing for a moment the significance of putting on a weapon again.

Then he looped several rubber bands around the fore end of the grip, just below the hammer. He slid the gun in the back of his pants above his right kidney, the grip out, ready for the draw. The rubber bands kept it from slipping beneath his waistband.

He removed the Marshals star from his back pocket and studied it. Last night he'd called to quit his security gig. His supervisor's only interest had been getting back the uniform and baton. That Tim was so eminently replaceable was apt commentary on the worthlessness of what he'd been doing over the past year.

A massive thunk hit Tim's back, startling him from his self-loathing. Bear's voice boomed over his shoulder. "You know why they put a circle around that star?"

A faint smile crossed Tim's lips. "So it's easier for them to shove up your ass."

He turned to stand and was swept up in a turbulent hug. Until last year Tim and Bear had partnered on the warrant squad's Escape Team and served together on the SWAT-like Arrest Response Team. Though he was nine years older than Tim, Bear looked up to him and Dray like older siblings. A loner with many friends and few intimates, he'd been an uncle to Ginny. Tim had once saved his life and been awarded the Medal of Valor for it. Bear had returned the favor by being the most unerringly loyal friend Tim had.

Over by the coffeemaker, Denley muttered something and Bear shot him a hard stare over the top of the barrier. "Fuck off, Denley. You got something to say, get your ass over here and say it."

Denley held up a sagging coffee filter. "Actually, Jowalski, I was just complaining that some numbnut left the old filter in."

Some of the noble indignation leaked out of Bear. "Oh," he said.

Tim smiled for the first time since entering the building. "I really appreciate you easing my transition here."

Bear lowered himself into a nearby sliding chair, spilling over it in all directions like a rhino on a unicycle. "Tannino briefed me yesterday. I already followed up the ground-ballers. There's nothing on the PI, Katanga. Just vanished."

"The girl?"

"Ran the usual suspects on Leah Henning—phone, gas, power, water, and broadband. All last-knowns trace to an apartment in Van Nuys. Here's the address. I spoke to the manager—cranky old broad. Leah skipped her lease March fifteenth, left the security deposit behind."

Two days after her visit home.

"No forwarding info, no new bills in her name. She just blinked off the radar." Bear coughed into a fist. "What do you have?"

"Not a damn thing."

"Well, that's why you're here. To make magic outta moleshit." Bear wiped his hand on his pant leg. "The P.O.

box checked out to the San Fernando office, just north of Van Nuys, where the girl lived. I guess if we get desperate, we can sit someone on it, but I'm not sure Tannino'll give up the manpower for a low-odds angle this early in the game."

"The PI already gave it a go with no luck. Let's save that for a last-ditch."

Bear flattened the chips bag with his hand and seemed disappointed to find it empty. "These cults pull some intense shit. Didn't you do some mind-control mumbo jumbo in Ranger training?"

"Biofeedback stuff mostly, to teach us to control our thoughts, balance our emotional responses, mediate our pain reactions."

Bear wore the dubious expression he generally reserved for discussing political correctness and tax hikes. "How'd they do that?"

"They stuck us with needles and put probes up our asses. We'd joke that we got lost at the Blue Oyster Bar from *Police Academy*."

The white coats had taught him to focus on his breathing, his heart rate, even his body temperature. Eventually he could lower them at will, even when the techs were giving him mild shocks or pricking his fingertips with needles. They'd kept cardiac leads all over him, hooked into a computer; his task was to lower his blood pressure and make pink dots disappear from the screen. The aim, one walleyed tech bragged, was to regulate his adrenaline response, to disconnect the wiring of his fight-or-flight instinct. Four twenty-minute sessions a day, seven days a week.

When Tim finished, his core body temperature stayed at ninety-seven degrees.

"There *is* a shadow government." With effort, Bear pulled himself up off the chair. "Page me if you need me. I gotta chase down some jackass who walked out of an Inglewood halfway house after banging a cohabitant. Remember, it ain't all glamour."

He thundered off, hefting his pants by his belt.

Tim sat for a moment, elbows on his knees, head lowered. It took a while for the juices to get flowing, but the instinct returned like a remembered melody. He plucked the phone from the base, called the *L.A. Times: Valley Edition* and then the *Weekly,* asking for Classifieds. Newspapers were notoriously fastidious when it came to confidentiality, so he introduced himself both times as Lee Henning and complained that he'd been overcharged for a moving-sale ad he'd placed in the papers a few weeks ago. He was additionally pissed off because they'd misspelled his name. Neither paper could locate an ad. He came up blank at *Pennysaver* and *Recycler* but got a hit at the *New Times*, a lower-circulation rag that catered to students and the younger set.

"Yeah, right here," the clerk said. "L*eah* Henning." A hiccup of a giggle. "Bet that confused the buyers, huh? It just ran once. You should've been charged thirty-five bucks."

"If memory serves, I was charged fifty."

"Nope." The sounds of fastidious keyboard clicking. "Got the bill right here."

"Can you fax me a copy of it? And the ad, too, while you're at it?"

He waited, fingers drumming on the desktop, until he heard the fax machine whirring across the room. Reluctant to ask his way around the new office, he followed the noise through the maze of desks. The papers awaited him in the tray.

A notation on the bill showed that Leah had paid the bill with cash, which struck Tim as odd and inconvenient. Tim had run through some specifics with Will last night while walking him and Emma to their car, and Will had mentioned he'd cut off Leah's credit cards. But she still, presumably, had a bank account with a checkbook. Unless she'd signed that over to the cult in addition to her trust fund.

Leah's ad, which had run nearly a month ago, offered a bureau, two nightstands, a bookcase, a mattress and frame, her bicycle, and an array of computer equipment. The sell-off fit-

ted the profile of either a fugitive preparing to go under-
ground or someone moving overseas. The latter, a distinct
possibility, worried him. He didn't want to have to inform the
Hennings that their daughter was hoeing fields in a cult
colony in Tenerife.

More focused now, he headed out, mumbling to himself
and drawing a few glances from his colleagues.

Three

Tim worked the phone on the drive up the coast, net-
working through contacts and eventually placing calls
to the Leo J. Ryan Foundation, the Cult Information Service,
and the American Family Foundation. When he informed the
phone counselors that he needed to bring his teenager in for
postcult therapy in Los Angeles, the same name topped all
three referral lists: Dr. Glen Bederman, a UCLA psychology
professor, one of the country's foremost cult authorities.

Tim dialed the number, keeping an eye on the winding road.

"You've reached the office of Glen Bederman. If this is a
harassing phone call, please leave all slurs and deprecations
after the beep. If you're suing me, please phone my lawyer,
Jake C. Caruthers, directly at 471-9009. Process servers
looking to locate me, here is my calendar for the week. . . ."
Listening to Bederman's lecture schedule and office hours,
Tim couldn't help but smile. "I'd like to close with Articles
Five and Eighteen of the Universal Declaration of Human
Rights: No one shall be subjected to torture or cruel, inhu-
man, or degrading treatment or punishment, and everyone
has the right to freedom of thought, conscience, and religion.
Good day."

After the prolonged beep that indicated a surfeit of messages, Tim introduced himself briefly and mentioned he'd try to catch up with the professor later that day.

Next he reached the postal inspector in charge of San Fernando—a nasally voiced fellow who introduced himself as Owen B. Rutherford.

"Yes," Rutherford said with thinly disguised irritation, "I recall fielding questions about this particular already."

"I was just wondering if you'd consider—"

"You should know better, Deputy. Bring me a warrant and I'll arrange a time to see to your concerns."

"Look, work with me here a little. I don't have enough for a warrant—"

"Not enough evidence for a warrant, yet you want me to root through privileged billing and registration information?"

Rutherford's prissy tone was surprising, but his vehemence was not—postal inspectors were 1811s, investigators who toted guns and tracked leads hard. They had a near-fanatical regard for the mails, which Tim respected though found difficult when it inconvenienced him. Realizing he lacked good reason for his frustration, he held his tongue.

"The mails are sacrosanct, Deputy. I'd like you to consider something for a minute. . . ." Rutherford's voice, high and thin, took on the tone of a rant. "People only *complain* about the mail. When it's late, when it arrives damaged, when some unwashed misanthrope uses it to deliver anthrax. Think about the fact that for thirty-seven cents—*thirty-seven cents*—less than the price of a pack of gum, you can send a letter from Miami to Anchorage. Thirty-seven cents can buy one ounce a *four-thousand-mile* trip. This country has the finest mail system in history," Owen B. Rutherford continued, seeming pleased to have secured a scapegoat for what Tim could only imagine was an elephantine bad day. "We move forty percent of the world's mail, seven hundred million pieces a day, and—unlike you big-budget DOJ agencies—we're entirely self-supporting. This country runs on its postal service. Taxes are paid, votes are tallied, medicines delivered in our mail system. And that system has got to be an asymptote approaching the line of perfection. Imagine if your paycheck arrived only two times out of three. Imagine spending your last minutes on your deathbed hand-penning a draft of your will that had only a fifty-percent chance of making it to your attorney. Imagine, for that matter, a confidential P.O. box that you establish for the receipt of documents or personal items, only to find that some knuckle-scraping federal employee with an inadequate grasp of civil liberties called in favors from a corrupt postal inspector so that your political petitions, or inflatable sheep, or letter from your dying ¡Kung aunt"—this complete with tongue click—"in the Kalahari is suddenly a matter of illegal government inquiry!"

"I, uh . . ."

"Good *day,* Deputy Rackley."

Tim sat for a minute, a dazed grin touching his face. He couldn't recall being so effectively and summarily told off since Ms. Alessandri benched him in fifth grade for supergluing the donkey tail to Tina Mindachi during end-of-year festivities. He tossed the phone in the passenger seat, deciding to enjoy the rest of the ride.

The Pacific Coast Highway hugged the coast to Malibu, affording a continuous panoramic view of the gray-blue ocean. The best lawn in Los Angeles stretched back from the intersection of PCH and Malibu Canyon, steeply inclined acres of grass above which the campus rose like a fortified city. After contending with a militant parking attendant, Tim wound his inferior Integra through the main drag lined with Beemers and Saabs. He asked a gardener—the sole person of color he'd glimpsed on campus—for the Sigma dorm.

A remarkably attractive blonde answered the door. Her face was structured like a model's—high cheekbones, generous jaw, abbreviated ski jump of a nose. The orange-and-blue scrunchie holding her hair back in a ponytail matched her Pepperdine sweatshirt; the pullover itself featured King Neptune looming with trident and flowing beard, the school's umpteenth stab at personifying its banal mascot—waves. She tilted her head slightly so she could look up at him through her lashes, a well-practiced move. "Who are *you?*"

"I'd like to speak with Katie Kelner."

The girl rolled her eyes and leaned back, letting the door swing open. Inside, three surfers were sprawled shirtless on a futon with another girl, an equally attractive redhead. Tim felt as if he'd stepped into a Gap ad. One of the guys tossed a beach towel over a bong smoldering on the coffee table.

"That's me," the blonde said. "What do you want?"

"I need to ask you some questions about Leah Henning."

"Again? It's been, like, three months. Aren't you people over it?"

"Your concern is touching. Weren't you friends?"

Two of the surfer boys snickered, and the redhead cracked up, a lungful of held smoke bursting out of her.

"Yeah," Katie said. "We were *real* close."

More laughter from the stoned peanut gallery. "Man," the most tousled surfer said, tugging at the protruding band of his boxers, "that chick was a serious *buzzkill.*"

"Hey, Gidget." Tim flashed his badge at the kid, and the smile dropped from his face as if someone had pissed on his wetsuit. "Your towel's burning. Why don't you take it and your controlled substance and go hang ten."

The three surfers hurriedly cleared out. The redhead leaned back on the futon and indulged a long, sleepy blink.

"I'm sorry, Officer," Katie said with a pert smile. "I didn't realize you were here, you know, *officially.*" She raised her foot, bare to the toes, and swung her knee out, slowly, then back. She wore an anklet with tiny letters on cubes: WWJD.

"Can I speak with you in private, please?"

"Absolutely." A game smile.

They went to her bedroom, and she closed the door behind them and sat on her bed, legs pulled up to her chest. Her shorts were riding up, giving Tim a pretty good eyeful of inner thigh.

He rose and opened the door. The redhead had passed out on the couch, potato chips across her chest. From the TV an inane cartoon discharged piano-tinkling and boinging sounds. Thirty-five thousand dollars' tuition put to good use.

"I thought you wanted to speak in private."

"This will be fine." Tim sat on the bed opposite her, a sheetless mattress. "Was this Leah's bed?"

Katie nodded. "When you get dropouts or suicides, they let you have your own room for the whole year. It kind of rules."

Makeup bottles blanketed one bureau; the other was blank. Katie's bed was covered with flowery pillows and teddy bears. A single window overlooked the well-kept track with its rubber runway and lush grass oval. Beyond it the hill dropped away steeply. A line of palm trees reared up in the distance, the bursts of fronds silhouetted against the back-drop of the Pacific like fireworks.

"Tell me about Leah."

"We sort of got stuck with Leah. Assigned roommate. She was pretty sweet when we first got here, but she wouldn't rush the sororities, and we sort of left her behind, you know? Socially." She cupped a hand by her mouth and stage-whispered, "She was, like, the big V."

"The big V?"

"A virgin. Which is cool, but we tried to bring her around guys, and she was just so . . . I don't know, geeky. Playing on her computer all day and stuff—total code monkey. And her clothes—her clothes were *bad*. And then she started acting weird."

"Weird how?"

"She sort of turned her back on her friends—what friends she had. These dorky kids from her classes, they stopped calling. And she got really anal. Like, on time to the *minute*. And really neat—lining up the edges of her notepaper and stuff. When we first started as roommates, she was way more casual. I never would have lived with her if she was like how she ended up."

"When did you notice this change?"

"Like, maybe a month to six weeks before she split."

"How did you know she got in with a cult?"

"She kept asking us to come to meetings with her. Stuff like that."

"Where were the meetings?"

"I don't know. Off campus, I'm pretty sure. We didn't listen, really."

"What did you do?"

"Laughed at her mostly." A flicker of remorse in Katie's sea-green eyes. "Hey, I'm being honest."

"Did you meet anyone in the cult?"

"No."

"Notice her with anyone new?"

"No."

"Do you know the names of her friends? Here on campus?"

"Like I said: What friends?"

"Did she mention the names of anyone in the cult with her? Or refer to someone as the Teacher?"

"No."

"Have you heard from her? Or has anyone seen her?"

"No." Katie smiled. "No. No, no, no. I don't know anything about where she is. I just know she's gone." She checked the tag on her inner wrist with a shrug of her hand.

Tim jotted down his cell-phone number on the back of a generic Marshals Service card with the Spring Street address and main phone line.

"If you think of anything else, give me a call."

Katie relinquished her hug hold on a big white bear and took the card.

Tim stood, giving a last glance at Leah's half of the room. Bare mattress, empty shelves, empty nightstand.

The thought of growing up in the house of Will and Emma Henning left Tim cold. So did the thought of living here with these veiled bullies, painting their lashes and nails and talking in code like cackling hens. Girls too pretty and rich and white to require empathy. Girls hell-bent on maintaining a status that required riding the top of a social hierarchy.

His first case since Ginny—he wasn't exactly keeping the misplaced protectiveness in check. He decided, staring at the left-behind Scotch tape on the blank wall, that if the empty rooms of girls hastily departed now struck a nerve, he would allow himself that.

He flipped his notepad closed. "Thanks for your help."

Katie scurried after him to the door. "What? I called. Her parents wouldn't even know she was missing if it wasn't for me. I did my part." The hard, pretty shell of her face shifted for a moment, and he saw the softer features of a girl who hadn't yet been trained in cruelty. "It's not my fault she went off and joined some cult." She reached down and scratched the skin beneath her anklet, the letter cubes bouncing on the leather cord.

"What does WWJD stand for?" Tim asked.

She lowered her eyes uncomfortably. "What Would Jesus Do."

*B*ear was correct in his assessment—the landlady was a cranky old broad. Tim might even have proposed a more canine term. Her apartment, from what he could see through the barely open door, housed a virtual conservatory of hanging plants. It smelled of stale coffee and cat piss, as did Ms. Adair Peters, sovereign of the Fleur-de-Lis of Van Nuys, a cracked stucco rise with smoked mirrors in the entry and ornate crown molding in the halls.

She emerged from her apartment, nightshirt trailing from the hem of a corduroy blazer she'd thrown on, breathing hard and clasping the lapels in a fist as if she'd been evicted in a blizzard. She ushered Tim into the elevator and slid the collapsible gate closed. The smell, in close quarters, was nearly blinding.

An interminable ride to the second floor.

At Leah's former door, Adair fussed in her pockets, withdrawing a ring of keys. She tried them each, muttering and overcome with the exertion. One finally turned, and she threw the door open, trudging inside. Tim followed.

A single room with a sidebar kitchen and a bathroom so small the open door rested against the toilet. The rusting coils of the radiator lurked under a sole window facing a Ravi Shankar billboard on which some mental giant had spray-painted OSSAMMA BEN LADEN IS A DUM SAND NIGGER.

Clearly, once Leah had moved from Pepperdine, she'd turned over the rest of her money to the cult.

"I was hoping you were a prospective tenant," Adair repeated for the fourth and, Tim hoped, final time. "I have to show the unit enough as is." She finger-teased her pink-tinted bouffant, glancing around. "Can't say I notice much of a difference with her being gone."

"The neighbors mentioned she wasn't around often."

"Barely ever. I only even *saw* her a few times. Sneaking out in the early morning, tiptoeing in at all hours. She had a full dance card, that's for sure."

"Ms. Henning advertised a moving sale at this address. Does that ring a bell?"

"She didn't have the common *decency* to inform me she was moving out, but I knew she was selling a few things. I remember telling the big fella to stop propping open the front door for anyone to walk in."

"The big fellow?"

"The lug who helped her with her little sale. No, more like he oversaw her. A weird name. Skip. Skeet." Her knobby fingers snapped. "Damnit. I can't remember. He wore a frayed shirt to show off his muscles, had some kind of chain around his neck, like that Mr. T fella."

"Gold chains?"

"Don't think so. Had beads."

"Do you remember anyone who bought stuff from them? Someone from the building, maybe?"

"Nope." Her lipstick was feathered around the edges. "Look, exciting as this is standing around an empty room, do you think you could move it along? You're not a tenant or anything, and I have responsibilities I have to get back to."

Including letting her cats resume their routine of pissing on her leg.

From the Hennings to the Katie Kelners to this sad box of a room, Ms. Adair Peters ruling supreme from upstairs. With these options, Tim would've hopped the first flight to Jonestown.

The pay phone from which Will had received the threatening call sat in a Lamplighter lobby six blocks up Van Nuys Boulevard. Was the caller a friend of Leah's or her guard? The big guy who helped her move? The P.O. box was in the neighboring town—maybe cult headquarters was in the vicinity.

Something scraped against the pane. Tim crossed the room despite Adair's labored sigh and opened the window, which gave with some reluctance. Duct-taped to the sill outside were three homemade vases, made from glossy cardboard rolled into thin cones. The wind had claimed the contents of the first two, but a dead carnation leaned from the third, its brittle bud half eroded from rubbing the pane.

Four

As soon as Tim entered Haines Hall on UCLA's North Campus, he heard a voice amplified off a lecture-hall ceiling. He followed the sound down a corridor and entered the arena-style room, standing with his back to the wall. Dr. Glen Bederman was pacing down below on a brief throw of stage, his hands clasped behind his back, bent slightly at the waist, studying the floor like a New England botanist on a stroll. A well-dressed man in his sixties, he walked gracefully, a microphone clipped to his oxford shirt.

A podium stood ignored, home to a second mike and a small bottle of mineral water. Bose speakers adhered to the ceiling piped out Bederman's voice a bit too loudly. The students attended his words diligently.

"In Jonestown, children were kept in a six-by-three-by-four-foot plywood box for weeks at a time. They were dragged out, thrown in a dark well, and told that poisonous snakes awaited them there. Husbands and wives were punished if caught talking privately. Do you know how? Their daughters were forced to masturbate in front of the entire population."

A few hushed exchanges among the students. A girl raised a tentative hand. "But the cult heyday has passed. I mean, they were all over in the seventies and stuff, but now they're kind of gone, right?"

Bederman scowled thoughtfully, as if considering her point. "How many of you have been approached at some point on this campus by someone ready to tell you about a wonderful way to take control of your life?"

Easily half of the students raised their hands.

Bederman drew his lips tight and gave the girl in the front a little nod. "There are more than *ten thousand* destructive cults operating today. The terrorist campaigns that have so changed our world were hatched inside groups where cult mind control is law. As we've just seen illustrated, countless cults still operate insidiously all around us in our community. And—even better—mind-control techniques and hypnotic inductions aren't even illegal. Literally millions of people are manipulated and indoctrinated *without giving informed consent* every year, and it's all completely lawful."

He walked to the edge of the stage. "Let's get back to Jonestown. Why did people obey? Why did they drink the Kool-Aid they knew would end their lives? Why did they squeeze cyanide from syringes down the throats of their own babies?"

"Because they were sociopaths?" a student called out.

"All nine hundred ten of them?" Bederman shook his head. "No. Because they were healthy."

A chorus of disbelief from the crowd.

"Stage hypnotists," Bederman said, "will choose the most ordinary volunteers. At all costs they'll avoid neurotics, who are all but impervious to suggestion. Con men and cult leaders go after similar targets. Statistics show that two-thirds of people who join cults are from normal, functioning families—whatever those are—and were demonstrating age-appropriate behavior at the time they joined. You see, the *healthy* remain attuned to the shifts around them, to suggestive cues in their environment. The human brain is a magnificently evolved tool, designed to adapt to an ever-changing—"

He stopped abruptly and shaded his eyes, squinting up toward the back of the hall at Tim. The students shifted in their chairs, turning around. At once Tim felt the discomfort of five hundred sets of eyes on him.

Bederman chuckled, and the students turned back to him, confused. "I just influenced the behavior of every last one of you. I indicated that there was key information over there—maybe a threat, maybe an opportunity—but something important enough to disrupt a lecture. Further, I am your professor, your authority figure. And if you believe you're not impressed with authority, permit me to impart one of my favorite facts: Students perceive professors as being *two and a half inches taller* than students of the same height. When I, your towering professor"—a self-deprecating grin—"looked to the rear of the hall, most of you followed my lead, bringing social pressure to bear on the rest. We are *wisely* influenced by information around us. That's what helps us function as healthy humans. Cults gain inroads to your brain by exploiting precisely such natural, unthinking reactions."

"Following your gaze is one thing," a serious young man in a wool sweater called out. "But it's not like we'd kill ourselves if you asked us to."

"Of course not. First I'd have to gain control over your thoughts, your emotions, your behavior. I'd get you off your turf and exploit the hell out of you." Bederman rapped the podium with his knuckles. "That would disrupt the key markers by which you understand your world. Your neuro-transmitters would reset at high levels, your stress hormones would burn out from continuous activation and stop secret-ing. I could traumatize you so greatly and repeatedly that your brain would be forced to call into question all it had ever learned. And then, everywhere you looked to gather informa-tion, I would present your new skewed reality."

The student shook his head, his long hair swaying. "There's no way you could argue me into a cult."

"Of course not. Arguing's not nearly seductive enough." A few students tittered nervously. Bederman continued to pace. "What's your name?"

The student tapped his pen against his notebook. "Brian."

"I would set out to create a new Brian. *Cult-Brian*. In his new world, Cult-Brian is rewarded for everything he says, does, and thinks by everyone around him. And True-Brian is punished for everything he says, does, thinks, or remembers. Pretty soon I'd have created a dominant cult personality much like everyone else's in my cult, trained to obey me. Why are you susceptible, Brian? You're a healthy, well-adjusted male, unburdened, I'd guess, by dire psychological problems. I need worker bees. I need bang for my buck. I wouldn't waste valuable time and energy indoctrinating someone who wasn't strong, caring, and motivated. Your ac-tive imagination, your creative mind, your ability to focus and concentrate—all the better to hypnotize you with, my dear. You're struggling to assert your individuality. Look at how well you've done so here in this forum. Wonderful. Come assert it with me and mine. We're rebels. We'll take on all of society, do things our own way, you and me and our nine hundred and nine friends. Your positive characteristics are merely tools for me to exploit. Within a few weeks, you'll think the cult's the greatest thing that ever happened to you. You'll never want to leave. You'd just as soon . . ."—he halted onstage, his momentum lost; the air seemed to go right out of him—"die."

A side door banged open. A man with a stocking over his head ran past the stage, screaming, "Fascist Nazi persecutor!" He threw a water balloon that exploded at Bederman's feet, spraying him with white paint. The assailant flashed out the emergency door, tripping the alarm.

Seemingly unfazed, Bederman pulled a handkerchief from his shirt pocket and wiped his paint-flecked spectacles, shouting to be heard over the din. "Okay. Here we go again! File out neatly and orderly! And remember to read Chapter Six for Thursday's lecture!"

Attaché in hand, Bederman made his way calmly up the stairs. Tim braved the outward rush of students. "Dr. Bederman!" he shouted. The alarm was so shrill it hurt his teeth. "I'm Tim Rackley from the U.S. Marshals Service. It's a pleasure to meet you."

Bederman nodded and took Tim's arm. They spilled out of Haines into the quad as several security guards trotted inside. "I would apologize for the ruckus, but I've grown accustomed to it. Its reliability is refreshing."

"This happens all the time, I take it."

"Paint balloons, fire alarms, bomb threats, files ransacked. Cults have an enviable amount of manpower at their disposal, especially for an old dragonslayer like me. They've canceled my hotel and airline reservations, sent fraudulent letters to the board of state medical examiners. Once, after one of my expert-witness testimonies, I received seventy-two hours of continuous phone calls. I've elected to find the attention flattering." He paused, sizing Tim up. "But let's get down to business. I'm so glad you got back to me."

"I'm sorry?"

"About my stolen mailing lists. They were encrypted, of course, but—"

Tim finally managed to slide in a sentence. "I think you have me confused with someone else."

"You're responding to my complaint? You're with LAPD, correct?"

"No, sir. I'm a deputy U.S. marshal. I contacted you because I need your help with a case I'm working on. I haven't received any correspondence from you."

"Oh." Bederman stopped walking. "Oh, oh, oh. How terribly disappointing." He studied his folded hands thoughtfully. "We see what we want to see."

"I'm trying to help a girl who got tangled up in a cult. I'd like a few minutes of your time."

"Let's see that badge."

Bederman examined it closely, then Tim's credentials. He handed them back and strode the path, Tim moving to keep up. "If you're making an effort to bust up a cult in a way that's real, I'll help you. If you're poking around, asking the usual questions to file the usual report that sits on the usual desk, I won't."

"My task is to locate the girl and get her out. I can't promise more than that."

"Can you promise me some turpentine?" He swept a hand through his white beard, and it came away spotted with paint. "That was a joke."

"Pretend I laughed politely."

He halted and looked at Tim. "I like you. No tough-guy routine, no unrealistic promises, no polite laughter. And you could have taken advantage of my misunderstanding about your identity."

"I've been taken advantage of too many times in my life."

"So you feel bad for others?"

"I don't like the feeling it gives me when I do it to others."

"Very good, Deputy Rackley. Very good." Nodding at a passing faculty member, he hurried down a set of stairs. "Tell me about this girl."

Tim had mostly filled him in by the time they entered Franz Hall. He couldn't help but think of the horrible evidence he'd discovered in this very building a year ago in William Rayner's office. With some effort he refocused on Bederman's words.

"The good news is, there are signs that this girl is receptive to leaving the cult. The timing might be good. You say she went home for a day. Even if she fled, that shows she's at least open to other options on some level. She's probably just too afraid to seek them—she's likely been programmed to believe that her life is worthless outside the group. Did she have any new allergy problems, asthma, or ailments when her parents saw her?"

"Her mother mentioned a rash, yes."

"These are ways the body makes cries for help when the mind won't. She might be ready when you find her. But if you come into any contact with the cult, you'll have to be extremely careful. Mind-control techniques are very subtle and coercive."

"I can handle myself. I've had military countertraining."

A slight smile played upon Bederman's lips as he opened the door to a corner office on the second floor. "You have, have you?" Papers and files covered the entire room, taking up virtually every horizontal surface. Tim noticed a piece of almost comical hate mail on the assistant's empty desk, its jagged little letters cut from magazines. LEAVE US ALONE OR DIE. A framed poster on the wall showed a herd of cows being driven into a slaughterhouse. In black lettering across the bottom: *Safety in Numbers.*

"It appears messy to the untrained eye, but it's actually a highly sophisticated filing system. Be careful not to move anything. Would you mind sitting up on that counter?" Bederman pointed to a clear stretch of water-stained countertop in the corner.

"I'll stand."

Bederman settled into his desk chair, fingers resting on his cheek. "Right. Maybe the coffee table there would be more comfortable. Take care not to wrinkle the papers."

Tim sat awkwardly on the low table.

"As I was saying, do not underestimate mind-control techniques."

"I'll be fine. I have an eye for that stuff."

"I'm sure you do. Military countertraining and whatnot." Bederman's eyes twinkled. "But I just got you to sit on a coffee table."

Tim looked at the two chairs in the office, which were unburdened by paperwork.

"Reciprocal concessions," Bederman said. "I conceded that you didn't have to sit on an uncomfortable countertop. You then made a concession to match my concession, never mind that there are two perfectly fine chairs at our disposal, never mind the fact that if I'd asked you first to sit on the coffee table, you almost certainly would have declined."

Tim took a moment to remind himself he should be impressed, not irritated.

"You're neither weak nor foolish for doing this. Reciprocal concessions are a key aspect of living in a community. If there were no social obligation to reciprocate a concession, who would want to make the first sacrifice? How would society function? Mind control can begin with simple, innocuous 'suggestions' like these." He winked. "Get a flower, give a dollar, right?" He gestured at a chair with a hand that, Tim noticed, trembled slightly. "Please."

Tim moved to the chair.

"I'm not trying to make you feel foolish. I'm merely trying to show how insidious these techniques are. Do you have children?"

Tim felt the familiar ache in his chest. "I did."

Bederman nodded sympathetically, assuming divorce or estrangement, as they always did. "Well, you remember the annual Christmas-toy crazes, then? Cabbage Patch Kids, Beanie Babies, Nintendo GameCubes?"

"The hot holiday toy that every kid absolutely must have."

"Precisely. Children extract promises from their parents that they'll receive said toy, but toy companies purposefully limit the supply. Panicked parents have to buy *other* holiday gifts to appease their tyrannical youngsters. The toy companies wait until late January, then flood the market with the desired toy. Parents have to fulfill their prior obligations to their children and—*bam*—toy companies have managed to double their sales. Literally millions of families are duped into buying dumb, unwanted crap *and* helping promote the über-toy every year and are not the least aware of it."

"So once you *do* what they want, you're more inclined to *think* what they want."

"Exactly. How were you suckered? Tickle Me Elmo?"

A chuckle escaped Tim. "Furby." He remembered trekking around town for weeks trying to locate the damn thing for Ginny, enduring endless jokes from Bear that a deputy U.S. marshal trained in hunting fugitives couldn't locate a mass-produced talking hairball. A My Pretty Pony had arrived under the tree instead, the Furby in February. "I'd never claim I haven't been made a fool of, probably more times than I'm aware."

"There's more to mind control than meets the eye, Deputy Rackley. That's all I'm cautioning. In fact, it's all about what *isn't* perceived, what *isn't* thought. You'll have to watch your back in ways that—even as a federal officer—you aren't accustomed to."

"Given I'm on your turf here, do you have any *specific* advice on how to do that?"

"It's game theory, really—mind games. All cults work by a finite number of truisms. You'll want to crack the code. What are the twelve steps? The seven habits of highly effective zombies? The Ten Commandments? Once you know what kind of cult you're dealing with, then you can figure out how to protect yourself."

"Does anything I've told you about this girl's cult ring a bell?"

"Yes. All the bells." Bederman smiled. "Does anything you've told me indicate one particular cult over another? No. The particulars you have are almost universal."

"I was told you treat a lot of cult survivors in your clinical practice."

"Hundreds. They're often programmed to self-destruct when they leave the cult, so they're rarely in good shape."

"Have you counseled anyone in the past few years who was recruited off the Pepperdine campus?"

He thought for a moment, finger pressed against his beard, then nodded. "About a year and a half ago, a family contacted me. Their son was a cult castaway, living on the streets. His parents enlisted my help, but he was too far gone. A schizophrenic mess."

"Where is he now?"

"I'd imagine still in the Neuropsychiatric Institute, busy with the voices he's tuning in through his dental work."

"Where's the institute?"

"Right here—UCLA Med Center. I helped get him admitted."

"I'd like to speak with him today if that's possible. Could you help me?"

"If he's still there, I'm sure I could. Though I didn't do much, his family feels indebted to me. I don't know what good it will do you. He's nearly catatonic—not your usual cult survivor. More a cult victim."

"I'd appreciate that very much."

Bederman flipped through an old-school Rolodex, its cards written in code, then punched a number into the phone and spoke briefly with the charge nurse. He hung up and regarded Tim. "Even *if* you can locate this girl, there is a very specific skill set you'll need at your disposal. You'll need incredible patience. She won't have access to the thoughts and feelings you'll expect her to. If you push, you'll cause her to retreat further or melt down altogether. If you try to reason with her, she'll likely fight the process with meditation or thought stopping."

"I'm not planning on reasoning with her."

Bederman rocked forward in his chair, arms resting on his blotter, his voice warning of impending outrage. "What do you mean? How do you plan on getting her out?"

"By any means necessary."

"Oh, no, no, no. Abducting her would be a grave mistake. You law-enforcement types have three approaches—force, force, and more force." Bederman seemed unnerved by Tim's silence. "You can't show someone that coercion is wrong by coercing her in the opposite direction."

"She's clearly not thinking for herself. What if a recovery operation is the only way to get her the help she needs?"

"It's *never* the only way." He'd come up out of his chair with the exclamation; he took a moment to ease himself back down.

"What matters is getting her out."

"It's not that simple. The process by which a person gets out from under the cult's dominance is essential. She'll be crippled by implanted phobias about leaving. You might wreck her in the process of trying to save her." Bederman cocked a snowy eyebrow. "Force may work when tracking down crooks in stocking caps, but it doesn't stand a chance when you're up against mind control, psychological coercion, phobias. Take it from me, Deputy. You can very easily, very quickly get in over your head here."

Five

The institute's bleached tile, white walls, and the antiseptic chill of fluorescent overheads all contributed to the serene mood. Tim drifted down a corridor past a bank of windows looking in on a cluster of people in gowns, twisting, bending, and extending their arms in slow motion, a sculpture garden coming sluggishly to life. A social worker with sharp, attractive features and shiny black hair met him at the reception console, wielding an immense visitors' log. After he signed in, she led him to her office, where she called Ernie Tramine's father and confirmed approval for the visit.

"Ernie hasn't spoken in weeks. I'm not sure what you hope to accomplish." Her voice was pleasant and observational.

"It's part of an investigation." Tim immediately regretted sounding like an uptight TV cop; her polite interest in his badge at reception had made him feel like a kid showing off a tin sheriff star.

"Take a seat behind my desk. I'll bring Ernie right in."

The office's single window overlooked a treetop canopy six stories below. A prepackaged Zen garden on the desktop tirelessly cycled water. Tim sank into Ms. Liu's chair, which tilted accommodatingly under his weight. He pushed "redial" on her telephone, and a number popped up on the Caller ID screen as it dialed. He punched the number into his own cell phone to save it and hung up the receiver before the call rang through.

A few minutes later, Ms. Liu entered again, guiding Ernie in front of her. Tim was struck immediately by how young he looked—he couldn't have been over twenty-one. His chiseled features and dark eyes had probably served him well in the past. He looked like a kid whose biggest concern should have been how many girls were showing up to the next three-kegger, and yet here he was, rocking and mute, his feet encased in paper slippers. He wore a few days' scruff and an incredibly blank expression, as if his facial muscles had atrophied.

Ms. Liu steered Ernie into the interview chair facing the desk, and Ernie immediately began to rock. "I'll be right outside," she said.

The door clicked behind her. Ernie's eyes focused on his tight-clasped hands.

"Hi, Ernie. My name's Tim Rackley. It's nice to meet you." Ernie swayed rhythmically.

"I have a few questions I'd like to ask you." Tim might as well have been talking to a watercooler, a fire hydrant, his father. He realized how foolish he'd been to ignore Bederman's and Ms. Liu's hesitations.

"I'm looking for a girl who joined up with a group of people. I think she was recruited off campus at Pepperdine. You went to Pepperdine, right?"

Ernie leaned forward in his chair, zoned out. Tim drew nearer in an attempt to engage him, resting his elbows on the desk. He brought his face within a few feet of Ernie's, but still Ernie didn't look up to meet his eyes.

"What was the name of the group you joined?"

The lulling whisper of the trickling water.

"Do you remember joining a group?"

Ernie's gentle rocking continued, regular as a heartbeat. Tim studied his eyebrows, his pupils, the occasional flicker of his lids.

"Can you tell me anything about the Teacher?"

Ernie snapped forward violently, screaming, his face inches from Tim's. Tim jerked back, elbow striking the Zen garden and sending it crashing to the floor. He rolled back until the chair collided with the wall. Ernie paused only to suck in a deep, screeching breath and then continued. Ms. Liu burst through the door, looking uncharacteristically flustered, and Tim heard the pounding footsteps of approaching backup.

Ernie continued to scream, so loud his voice was already flattening into hoarseness. He bobbed fiercely in his chair but made no move to attack Tim or Ms. Liu.

Two burly psych techs skidded into the room, followed by a jogging doctor.

One hand raised calmingly toward Ernie, Ms. Liu glared at Tim. "I think you should leave."

When one of the psych techs grabbed Ernie's arm, he threw himself off the chair, thrashing on the floor. As Tim stepped out into the hall, he heard the doctor calling for a Haldol cocktail.

His heart still pounding from the scare, Tim headed toward the exit, moving against the stream of responding workers.

The reception console stood vacant. Giving a glance in all directions, Tim slipped behind the reinforced glass, locating the overburdened visitors' log beneath the front counter. Ernie's screams continued to echo up the corridor.

Tim flipped through the sheets, finger scanning down the "Patient Name" columns. Where *Ernie Tramine* appeared—a few times on each page—Tim cross-referenced the "Visitor Name" box. *Jennifer Tramine. Pierre Tramine. Pierre Tramine. Mikka Tramine.*

Footsteps approached, several sets.

"—never seen him that agitated—"

"—Haldol should take the edge off—"

Tim moved furiously through the last few pages. *Jennifer Tramine. Pierre Tramine. Reggie Rondell.* He stopped at the last name, checking the corresponding date—2/05. About two months ago.

Tim tossed the log beneath the counter and stepped out of the console just as the charge nurse rounded the corner, flanked by psych techs. Passing the patients' disrupted yoga session, he fished his cell phone from his pocket and hit "send."

A male voice. "Yes?"

He shoved through the door, exiting the NPI. "Pierre Tramine?"

"Yes?"

"Hello. My name is Tim Rackley. I'm a deputy U.S. marshal." The flush of pride he felt at announcing himself as such evaporated when he remembered his temporary status. "Dr. Bederman directed me to your son."

"Yes, Janet mentioned something about that. Listen, anything you can do to find the bastards who did this to Ernie . . ."

Tim thought about how many times Pierre's name appeared on the visitor clipboard. What was it like for this parent to see his child—his adult child—in that condition, week after week?

"I'm doing my best, sir."

"Anything I can do to help. Anything."

"Well, I do have a few questions. What was the name of the cult Ernie joined?"

"We don't know that. Getting him to talk about it at all was like pulling teeth."

"Did he ever mention the name of anyone in the cult?"

"No. He'd decompensated pretty badly by the time we found him. He admitted to getting caught up with a group of people, and we sort of pieced together it was a cult. But no names, no locations, nothing like that. He would melt down when we pressed him on it, so we finally stopped."

"Your son had a visitor some time ago—a friend called Reggie Rondell. Is that name familiar?"

"No. Hang on." A rustle. "Hey, Mikka. You hear of a Reggie Rondell, one of Ernie's friends?" Tim waited patiently by the elevator. Pierre's voice came back regular volume. "No. He was no friend of Ernie's, at least not through his time at Pepperdine."

"Any chance he might be a friend you and your wife hadn't heard of?"

"No. We're a very close family." He caught himself. "We *were* a very close family. We knew all of Ernie's friends up until he disappeared."

"Doesn't someone need your approval to get on the visitor list?"

"Now they do. But until recently Ernie could make phone calls, put his own visitors on the list. He took . . ." Tim waited patiently through the pause. When Pierre spoke again, his voice wobbled a bit. "He took a turn last month. That's when I became his conservator."

"I'm very sorry to hear that, sir."

"It's like there's something inside my son's head, eating him. Eating the boy we raised and knew." The muffled sound of Pierre blowing his nose. "How old are you, Mr. Rackley?"

"Thirty-four."

"Kids of your own?"

The elevator dinged open, and Tim stared at the vacant interior. "No."

"Well, when you have them, you watch out for them. You don't know who's out there."

It took Tim a moment to find his voice. "I'll do that, sir."

Six

The comm center, buried in Cell Block on the third floor of Roybal, hosted a panoply of security screens showing various suspects pacing in cells. Bear hunched over the computer at Tim's side, smelling of the Carl's Jr. he'd just denied eating, offering in place of an admission the implausible claim that he'd filled up on a salad. A chronically unhappy dater, Bear was recounting his latest travails while calling up DMV info on the state computer. "So we get rerouted, laid over in Vegas for the night. Instead of lying on a beach in Cancún, we're stuck at Westward Ho—which by the way is the shittiest joint on the Strip. And to make matters worse, the hotel is having a short-people's convention."

"A short-people's convention? Like dwarves?" Tim pressed his lips together to avoid smiling. The women Bear dated weren't exactly ballerinas—the couple must have terrified the petite attendees.

To Tim's left, two court security officers were embroiled in an argument about the relative attributes of Mexican-mafia tattoos versus those of the Higuera Brotherhood. A third regulated radio contact with deputies in the field.

"No, just *small people*." Bear's wide fingers moved across the keyboard with surprising fluidity. "So me and Elise, we can't go anywhere without stepping on 'em. We rode elevators with guys who couldn't reach the top buttons. People threw us the stink-eye at the all-you-can-eat buffets. They were selling T-shirts you couldn't fit on my hand. It was very unsettling. Elise lost a cool grand on the tables, and some Danny DeVito look-alike kicked me in the shins for accidentally sitting on his wife at the slots. What am I gonna do? Hit him back?" He pulled his glasses—another addition to his life as a forty-three-year-old—from his shirt pocket, and a Carl's Jr. ketchup fell on the desktop. Mortified, Bear swept the offending packet into the trash can.

Tim's eyes didn't move from the screen. "The salad souschef accidentally drop some Carl's Jr. ketchup in your shirt pocket?"

"It's from last week. Anyways, me and Elise had a miserable time, haven't talked since we've been back." Bear exhaled theatrically. "Shit, I think you grabbed the last good one off the market, Rack. I'm never getting married."

"Do you *want* to get married?"

Bear chewed his lip, breathing hard. "Nah. I prefer to direct all my hatred at myself." The photo of a skinny kid popped up on the monitor, and Bear pointed at it, his ham hand blocking the screen. "So there he is. The fifth Reggie Rondell."

"The fifth?"

"Five Reggie Rondells in the greater Los Angeles area, believe it or not. That includes Reginalds and Reginas, just to be safe. Reginald Rondell Jr. is a crusty white guy from Orange, moved to Philly in January, hasn't traveled west since, at least by plane. Regina Rondell, age seventy-five, God rest her soul, kicked in June. Our third Reggie Rondell is enrolled at Marquez Elementary School in the Palisades. I got the parole officer of the fourth on the phone about ten minutes ago—homie had a dealing problem, was on the inside two months ago. Which leaves us with the fifth Reggie Rondell."

Tim checked the identifiers—five-seven, 135 pounds, hazel eyes, brown hair, twenty-three years old. Reggie had no outstanding traffic tickets, and he didn't legally drive a motorcycle or commercial truck.

Tim pointed to the listed address. "Let's go."

"It's not that easy, my simple friend. The driver's license is two years old, and the only current info falsely lists him as an inpatient at a Santa Barbara nuthouse."

Tim noted Bear's pleased little smirk. "Oh, no," he said flatly. "Whatever are we to do?"

A proud finger shot up. "Have no fear. I called my hook at the IRS, turns out RestWell Motel in Culver City filed a W2 for a Reginald Rondell. RestWell central payroll in Bakersfield—believe that shit?—confirmed he's a current employee. His shift started"—Bear consulted his watch dramatically—"twenty minutes ago."

All this in the hour since Tim had called to fill him in from the road. On Arrest Response Team raids, Tim was the number one on a door-kick entry stack, Bear at his back. During intense fugitive roundups, they sometimes hit as many as fifteen dwellings a day. Trigger time like that went a long way toward fire-forging a friendship.

Tim rested a hand on Bear's shoulder. "It's good to be back."

Bear studied him, his face shifting into a smile.

They rose to go, Tim readjusting the .357 in his waistband, Bear humming the theme to *Baretta* as they passed through both security doors into the tiled corridor outside. The wall abutting Cell Block hid a foot of concrete and reinforced steel.

The snickering approach of a few deputies soured Tim's mood. A prisoner between them, Thomas and Freed eyed Tim as they stopped to slide their weapons into the gun lockers outside the Cell Block entrance.

"Hey, Rack?" Thomas's voice was edged and nasty. "I seem to have misplaced my Charles Bronson video. Maybe you've seen it. It's—"

"I know," Tim said. "*Death Wish.* Why don't you two go sit in Isolation Three and see if you can work up some fresh material?"

Their prisoner, a heavyset Latino in wrist and ankle cuffs, sniggered as the court security officer buzzed them through. Thomas mumbled something to Freed as they steered the suspect brusquely through the door.

Tim and Bear continued down the hall in silence. Bear punched the elevator button a little too hard. The car arrived, and they stepped on. Bear's face kept its pissed-off cast for a few floors, then loosened. "I would have gone for *The Stone Killer* myself."

Seated in Bear's Dodge Ram in the parking lot, they watched Reggie at the motel front desk. As Bear had promised, they'd found him on shift, elbows on the counter, fists shoving his cheeks skyward. He was entranced by the hatchetfish and platies circling listlessly in the fifty-gallon aquarium next to the blotter. Gray bags rimmed both eyes, raccoon-defined against his sallow skin. A flannel shirt, standard red and black checks, hung over his rail-thin frame, his wrists poking from the sleeves. Had Tim not known Reggie's age, he would have put him near forty.

Bear said, "Tell me why you like this guy?"

"A new friend, maybe from Tramine's time in the cult."

"You don't even know it's the same cult as Leah's. Just because Tramine was recruited off Pepperdine . . ."

"He did freak out when I mentioned the Teacher."

"The shape he's in, he might have freaked out if you'd mentioned the Pillsbury Doughboy."

"No, he actually responded warmly to the Pillsbury Doughboy."

"Oh," Bear said. "Well, that's cheering."

They climbed out together. Bear took up a post outside, and Tim entered, the top of the door smacking the obligatory dangling bells. Reggie tensed up. His eyes, mud brown and piercing, darted constantly—he took in Tim with abbreviated sweeps and climbs. Tim stayed focused on Reggie's right hand, out of view beneath the counter.

"Help you?"

Tim stepped up to the counter. "Are you Reggie Rondell?"

He worked his gum a few chews, then swallowed hard. "Yeah."

"Friend of Ernie Tramine's?"

"Never heard of him." His forearm tensed, indicating his hand had just grasped something.

Bear had run Reggie, and he'd come up clean, but there was no telling what crime he might have just committed, what visits he was fearfully anticipating.

"Listen. I'm only here to ask some questions about a cult—"

The hand pulled up, gripping a metal flashlight. The instant the silver handle cleared the counter, Tim's vision tunneled, the scene slowed. Tim shuffled back two steps, the

.357 up and sighted on Reggie's chest before the flashlight finished its arc.

Reggie swung the shaft into the aquarium. The glass popped and avalanched down, the water holding its rectangular form for an instant before following suit. Reggie shot around the counter. He threw the door open, but instead of daylight there was just Bear's hulking form all but filling the frame. Reggie hollered. Bear spun him effortlessly and proned him out on the carpet, his cheek pressed to soggy gravel, fish flopping next to his face.

Reggie had frozen up. "Don't kill me, man. Please don't fucking kill me. I won't say anything. I won't talk to anyone, I swear."

Tim crouched, helping Bear frisk Reggie. "Be careful of the glass."

Short of a wallet holding the same license that had graced the Cell Block computer monitor minutes earlier and a bulky ring of keys, Reggie's pockets were empty. Bear hoisted him to his feet and leaned him against the counter. "You gonna be cool?"

Reggie's eyes widened a bit as he took in Bear. He nodded.

"We're not here to kill you," Tim said. "We're deputy U.S. marshals, investigating a cult."

"Lemme see your badges." Reggie crossed his arms and squeezed them to his chest. "I'll know if they're fake." He was trying to play cocky, but his tremulous hands gave him away.

Tim and Bear laid out their stars, and Reggie took them, holding them under the dim desk lamp as if checking for watermarks.

"They check out there, Mr. Ashcroft?" Bear asked.

"Okay if I look back here?" Tim asked. Reggie nodded, and Tim walked behind the front desk, making sure there were no hidden weapons.

One of the hatchetfish quivered on the counter, drawing Reggie's attention. He watched it, head cocked like a dog eyeballing a squirrel. A good thirty seconds passed.

Bear's blue dress shirt wrinkled over his crossed arms.
"'Scuse us."

Reggie started, as if he'd forgotten they were there.

"Done with the badges? Or are you waiting for forensic
analysis?"

Reggie blinked, concentrating hard. "Right, right." He
leaned away from Bear as he handed him his badge. Bear
started to say something, but Tim shook his head slightly.

"I . . . I don't know anything about a cult."

"Sure you do," Bear said. "You were in a cult with your
buddy named— What's his name, Rack?"

Tim opened a cabinet, revealing a tray full of key rings.
"Ernie Tramine."

"We'd like to—"

Reggie held up his hand, fingers spread, his face drawn.
"Wait a minute. Wait. I can't do this with him here. You. I'm
sorry. You're one of my triggers."

Bear's finger went to his chest. "I'm one of your . . . what?"

"A trigger, you know. A trigger. Like the queen of diamonds in *The Manchurian Candidate*. Something that triggers the mood they put into you during indoctrination. A
paired stimulus. Three blasts of a trumpet. It puts you back,
right back in it. One of my triggers is big fucking muscle.
Like you. It takes me out. I can't . . ." Reggie rocked autisti-
cally, squeezing his right pinkie in a fist.

Bear's scalp shifted with his expression of disbelief. "You
shitting me here?"

Tim said, "It's fine."

With his eyes and hands, Bear made a stage-worthy appeal
to heaven before exiting.

"Did your cult have big guys guard the doors?"

Reggie recoiled, lost in memory, a snail shrinking from
salt. His voice came like a child's whisper. "All the time. You
couldn't leave the room during meetings or Oraes."

"Oraes?" Tim asked. But Reggie was scurrying around the
small office, shoes crunching gravel, peering out the win-

dows and closing the blinds. Pausing from his search of the drawers, Tim watched him closely. "Are you more comfortable talking to me with my partner gone?"

"I'm not talking to anyone. If I cause any trouble, they'll find me. What if you were followed?"

Light seeped in between the slats, cutting the shadows into wafer-thin planes. The dying fish flopped and shuddered, the delicate crunching of gravel encroaching on the silence. It sounded like thousands of insects feeding.

"We weren't followed."

"It's too dangerous. Why should I stick my neck out?"

The hatchetfish flipped itself over on the counter, staring up with one bulging eye.

"I'm trying to help a girl get out of a cult. I believe it's the same cult you and Ernie were members of. She's a young—"

"I don't give a shit. I've made my peace. Moved on. Put it behind."

Inside the last drawer sat a brown paper bag, top crumpled over. Tim set it on the counter and opened it. He grabbed the top orange bottle, reading the handwritten label. Xanax. His eyes skipped to the ten or so other bottles in the bag—peeling labels handwritten in Spanish and English. Klonopin, Valium, Ativan.

"Okay, great. So I've got some Tijuana meds. You gonna use them to leverage me?" Reggie slapped his forehead with his hand. "Fuck. I *knew* I shouldn't have let you back there."

"No," Tim said. "I'm not."

"No?" He tugged on his pinkie. "Look, I'm not gonna relive all this for you. I just can't do it."

Tim felt the hard edge of instinct rise—the need to squeeze an informant, to press an unwilling speaker—but he seemed to have misplaced the strength to resist empathy. His own pain this past year had softened him, blunted his imperatives. Too old to be headstrong but still well short of wise, he merely nodded.

He remembered Dr. Bederman's cautions about the fragility of cult members. He'd have to give Reggie his space. For now.

He handed Reggie his card, complete with penned-in cell-phone number. "This girl's in trouble."

Pausing at the door, he faced Reggie.

"I'm sorry for what you got put through. I bet it was horrible."

He walked out, and the door clicked quietly behind him.

Seven

When Tim arrived home, Dray wasn't at the kitchen table or on the couch, her usual postwork sprawls, and the house was dead quiet. If it weren't for her Blazer in the driveway, he might have thought she'd decided to clock a P.M. after her morning shift.

He called, and she answered from down the hall. She was sitting on the floor of Ginny's old room, back against the wall. Same flowered wallpaper, same Pocahontas night-light. In the middle of the room sat a heavy-duty garbage bag, stuffed with diminutive clothes from the closet. Hangers scattered the floor.

Dray's face was blank, her forehead unlined—the impassivity of shock relived. "Sorry I didn't wait for you. I know you've been ready"—she gestured to the empty closet—"for a while now. I just wanted to . . . I guess with my reaction last night at the door, it made me realize . . . maybe it's time to move through it, like you've been saying."

He bobbed his head.

She blew a wisp of hair off her forehead. "It's so damn exhausting. It shouldn't be, this stuff, but it is." She extended an arm, and he pulled her to her feet. They kissed, Dray wrapping her arms around the back of his neck. She hadn't been as demonstrative or as emotional before Ginny's death, though Tim didn't mind the change a bit.

She moved to the bed and began pulling off the sheets—Powerpuff Girls flannels that had been dutifully washed weekly for over a year. Ginny's motifs were relics in the fast-paced world of children's trends. They'd grown outdated and unhip, an ignominy Ginny would never have permitted. Tim had learned, step by step, how to live again without a daughter, but he still missed toy stores and zany cartoons and Olivia the naughty pig. There was a time he could distinguish *Beauty and the Beast* songs from those from *The Little Mermaid*. He thought of Bederman's diatribe about the Christmastime ploys of toy companies and realized he would do anything to be conned into buying the latest and greatest girl's novelty right about now.

He started to help, emptying the desk drawers into a fresh bag, careful to handle Ginny's former belongings with care. When he realized he was treating a SpongeBob pencil eraser with reverence, he let go and started scooping and dumping. Dray's voice pulled him from his thoughts. "I don't even know if this makes me sad. Or guilty." She held a tiny T-shirt in each hand; they drooped like dead kittens. "We see so much of this shit, this heavy symbolic shit, in movies, on TV, but maybe this isn't the time and place for it." Her voice was flat like her eyes. "Maybe we should try not to think and just get this done."

At the end of the hour, Ginny's possessions—the sum total of her physical grasp on the world—were bound up in seven Hefty bags bound for the Salvation Army. Tim hauled them to the porch, then took apart her bed and her desk—doing his best not to let the crayon marks, the Kool-Aid stains, the glittery Dora stickers reduce him to uselessness. Once the furniture also made its way outside, he came back in, sweaty and hot in the face. Dray was standing in the entry, looking out at the sad assembly of goods on the front walk, a broken-down convoy.

Dray said, "I think I'm going to cry now."

Tim started to say okay but caught her as her knees buckled. He held her, stroked her hair. He pressed his face to her head, rocking her on the floor, her legs kicking and sprawling. He worked to control his own reaction, because the unspoken deal they'd arrived at through trial and error was that they'd only let go like this one at a time.

The crying stopped, then the tight sobs accompanying her inhalations. Her hair, normally razor straight and straw-colored, stayed pasted to her sticky face in brown swirls. Her eyes—honest and strong and magnificently green, as always. She coughed out a brief, exhausted laugh. "Guess I figured out what to feel, huh? Hell."

"Let me take you out. How about Nobu?"

"Nobu?"

"What the hell, I'm making the federal bucks now."

They'd been only once to the upscale Japanese restaurant, located over the canyon from their Moorpark house. On their post-Ginny wedding anniversary, a grim evening in May, they'd sat stiffly among second-tier movie stars and Malibu divorcées, pretending not to notice the three well-groomed girls at the table to their left or the empty chairs at their own four-top.

Dray changed quickly, even putting on a touch of eyeliner and blush. Makeup, which she rarely and reluctantly wore, didn't suit her—her looks were so natural and healthy she could go without—but Tim didn't mention it because he prized the intent behind her effort. He threw on a pressed shirt, and soon they were on their way in Dray's Blazer, Tim at the wheel, holding hands across the console. Dray blinked against the sting of the mascara. "In Your Eyes" wailed from the speakers, seeming an added contrivance to the impromptu romantic outing. When they reached the 23/101 interchange, Dray finally snapped down the visor and started smearing off her makeup. "You know what? This is too weird after everything tonight."

Tim let out a relieved laugh. "Thank God. How's Fatburger sound?"

Dray smiled as he exited the freeway. "Divine."

Eight

*T*he insistent bleating of the cell phone pulled Tim from sleep. Buried in blankets, Dray made tired noises and shifted around. A spout of hair across the pillow, the sole trace of her, had gone red in the alarm-clock glow—2:43.

Tim sat up before answering, feet flat on the cold floor—a habit that forced wee-hours lucidity. "Yeah?"

"Tim Rackley?"

"Who is this?"

"You tell me."

He rubbed an eye, running through the options. Since he was working only one case, it didn't take long. "Reggie Rondell."

"Just might be."

"It's two-thirty in the morning."

"Is it really?" No hint of sarcasm. Some rustling. "Holy shit, look at that—you're right. I don't keep track of the hours so good anymore."

"You want to talk?"

"Not on the phone."

"Okay. Let's set up a time, and I'll come see you."

"I got time now."

"Now's not the greatest."

"For who?"

Tim dropped the receiver from his mouth so his exhale wouldn't be heard. "Okay. Where are you?"

"Where you left me. I'm working back-to-backs."

"I'm gonna bring my partner. I can have him wait in the car if you'd like."

"I'd like."

Tim snapped the phone shut and blinked hard a few times. Dray surfaced, bangs down across her eyes. "I forgot about this part."

He crossed the bedroom, crouched, and spun the dial of the gun safe.

*B*ear gazed bleary-eyed through the windshield, one hand fisting the top of the wheel, the other holding a chipped mug out of which spooled steam and the scent of cheap coffee. "Here's where I wish I still smoked."

The headlights blazed a yellow cone between the asphalt and the morning dark, the truck hurtling toward dawn. Curled between them on the bench seat, Boston stuck his muzzle into Tim's side until Tim scratched behind his ear. Bear had reluctantly inherited the even-tempered Rhodesian Ridgeback, and the two had rapidly become inseparable. Tim had only recently begun to disassociate Boston from his previous owner, a plucky brunette who'd fared worse than Tim in last year's collision course.

"Kind of a shady meet, no? A nighttime summons to a by-the-hour motel the wrong side of Culver City?"

"That's why you're here," Tim said.

"And I thought it was my sunny disposition."

Road construction slowed them to a crawl at the 405 interchange. In L.A., even a 3:00 A.M. drive can't deliver you from traffic.

"He's got no wants, no warrants, for what that's worth, but his jittery-poodle routine doesn't fill me with trust. You think he's really scared of me or he's trying to sitting-duck my ass out in the parking lot?"

"I think he's really scared of you. Or what you represent in his cult conditioning."

Bear stared at him as if he'd shifted to Swedish. "Well, Dr. Phil, I still say we just haul him in and press the fuck out of him. Or are you gonna give me your bullshit about catching flies with honey?"

"We push too hard, the guy could melt down all over your fine vinyl seats."

The sky had lightened to slate by the time they pulled past the motel parking lot. Bear took the rig around the block once; everything looked clear.

The jangling bells announcing Tim's entrance sent the papers in Reggie's hands flying. "Sorry. I'm a little jumpy."

Though the carpet had been cleaned, it still squished beneath Tim's shoes. The place smelled like a bad sushi joint.

Reggie flicked the bent red plastic hands of a smiley-faced I'll-Be-Back-By clock to 6:00 and propped it on the cheap blotter. He pulled the brown paper bag from the drawer and carried it out with him, tucked under an arm like a clutch purse. "I don't take them, the downers. I don't need to, as long as I know they're here with me."

Reggie led them down the walk running along the lot's edge, key dangling from a plastic medallion with 5 stamped on it in flaking gold. Tim noticed he kept his eyes on Bear in the truck, only glancing away briefly to navigate. Through the reflections off the windshield, Bear offered a cheery wave, which turned to a middle finger when Reggie rotated to jiggle the key in the knob. Bear made his trademark "what the fuck?" head dip about the locale switch, aped by Boston beside him, but Tim gave them both the flat hand, indicating everything was okay.

A few more tugs and pushes and the door swung open. An index card hanging from a length of yarn affixed to the ceiling slapped Reggie in the face when he stepped inside. It read: *Lock Door Behind You.*

"Right," Reggie said, speaking to the card. He stepped aside, letting them in, then bolted the door.

They were literally ankle deep in clothes and trash. The floor was likely carpeted, given the slight yield beneath Tim's feet; the bed and bureau he distinguished mostly by shape and location. A yellowed poster of the Department of Agriculture food pyramid sagged through its tacks, cheerfully declaiming, MEAT AND POULTRY—2–3 SERVINGS A DAY.

Keeping an eye on Reggie, Tim took a quick turn around the room, glancing into the bathroom and open closet.

Reggie pulled back the comforter, dispersing unopened mail and cheeseburger wrappers, and sat. "I think there's a chair over there."

Tim found it beneath a raincoat and a sweatshirt, which he set respectfully atop the TV before sitting.

Upsetting a glass of water, Reggie grabbed a worn spiral notepad from the nightstand. He flipped through it, finger tracing down the pen-marked pages. "Damnit. I forgot to deposit my check today." He squeezed the bridge of his nose. "But it's okay. I can learn from this. There's a lesson here."

"Reggie."

"Oh, right. Right." He propped himself up on some pillows. "Tell me about the girl."

"She's nineteen years old. Sensitive, vulnerable. A dreamer. Her parents are tougher than most but provided her more than the basics. A good worker—she was studying computer science at Pepperdine. She liked flowers, simple pleasures. Not the coolest girl in the dorm, maybe the last to get asked out, but the kind the guys'll regret ignoring when the ten-year swings around. Clean, pretty features, a touch goofy, but growing into herself every minute."

Reggie closed his eyes, leaning back against the wicker headboard. "God, I know the type. Ripe and willing. There are so many of them. You can choke the life out of them, just like that." A groan colored his sigh. "When you exit or get deprogrammed or whatever the fuck you want to call it, they say, 'At the time you were doing the best you could with the information you had.' I tell myself that when I think about all the kids I recruited, all the people tangled up and dismantled in there because of me. I tell myself that, but I'm also full of shit." He was gone for a few minutes, and then his head tilted forward. "How long's she been in?"

"Three months or so. Involved another month or two before that."

"There's still time. She could get out less damaged."

"Less damaged than who?"

His smile genuine but dead in the eyes, Reggie made a gun with his hand and pointed the barrel at his reflection in the spotted mirror on the opposite wall. "Nightmares, panic attacks, fainting, blackouts, exhaustion, difficulty concentrating, involuntary body shaking, episodes of dissociation, migraines. I'm a walking case study."

"But you're walking."

Reggie swallowed hard. "Look, the thing is, when you're . . . like *this*, it's hard to talk to anyone. It's embarrassing. To be seen, even."

"I'll be patient with you."

Reggie sniffed a couple of times and cleared his throat. Rather than look up, he flicked his hand inward—bring it on.

"Were you and Ernie in a cult together?"

A nod.

"What's the name of the cult?"

He snapped upright, eyes darting to the windows, the door. "I'm not talking specifics. No way, man. You can leave right now."

"Okay. Relax. We can take this at your pace. You won't give me any names? The cult leader, members?"

"They'll come after me. I'm the only one, you know. Me and Ernie, but what's Ernie anymore?"

"You're the only what?"

"The only nonsuicide. Not that I haven't tried." Reggie pushed up his sleeve, revealing a white worm of a scar on the underside of his forearm. "I slit my wrists, tried to hang myself."

"Both attempts since you've been out?"

"About twenty minutes apart, actually. I'm a fast clotter." He let out a shaky laugh. "Then the fucking knot didn't hold. The rope slid, left me dangling with my wrists scabbing up and my toes on the ground. I had to call for help. Isn't that the most pathetic fucking thing you've ever heard?" He leaned back and crossed his arms. "Whew. Haven't had a chuckle like that since I don't know when. Yeah, we all kill ourselves, pretty much."

Tim felt a stab of concern. "Did a girl join that group recently?"

Reggie waved a finger at him like a schoolmarm.

Tim wanted to see if Leah's name would draw a reaction, but giving it up entailed too many risks. "Why do you kill yourselves? Or try?"

"Shit, you're a babe in the woods, asking a question like that. Look around, man. You see anything appealing? I had money lined out—my dad's in land development. I used to drive a Porsche. Now I'm this. Here. My family's had it with me, and I don't blame them. They did their part already when I limped my ass back home fifteen months ago, so they can wash their hands of me now in good conscience. I want to pay them back for the cost of the deprogramming, but I can't even do that. It's all I can do to drag myself down four doors and work the counter. They're still in my head, man. They implant shit in your cells. They replace your identity. Problem is, once you're out, it's tough finding your old one. That's why no one leaves."

"You miss the cult?"

"Fuck, yeah I do. Part of it. It's like getting high. The meditation felt like melting into a river. You get hooked on it, that peacefulness, you know? Even when everything else is going to hell, you still felt like you were part of something special. And like it was a part of you."

He'd relaxed a little; Tim wanted to keep him talking. "How do new members join?"

"We find them. You have to bring in a certain number of Neos—that's what we call them—or you're a failure. I sorta had . . . sorta had a breakdown, under the pressure of it. I had a chronic 'need' to be weak and dysfunctional. You can imagine how that went over."

"What do you look for in a Neo?"

Reggie threw up his hands. "I'm done talking."

Using cult lingo back to Reggie was clearly a bad call. Tim had been trying to make Reggie talk to him like an insider but had only succeeded in putting him on guard by indicating how closely he was listening. Good job, Columbo.

"Listen," Tim said, "I'm not pressing you for any specifics here. I just need to know how it works. In general."

He regarded Tim warily. "I'll talk in general."

"So tell me how you pick new recruits."

"It's all about dosh, though no one says that directly. People 'reliant on money' are among those most in need of being liberated, you see. I was no good at picking them out. You'd think I'd be better at it, but every guy I thought was a big roller we'd find out was a poseur."

"Where would you recruit?"

"Anywhere you can catch normal people at a tough time in their lives. Airports are good—get them coming to a new city, out of their element. They're eager to connect. Funeral homes sometimes, catch them when they've just lost a parent—they've likely just come into some dough. You try to find them when they're looking for something. Singles services, church mixers, job fairs. We worked the high-end drug-rehab centers for a while, but that didn't pan out so hot. We had trouble with the snownoses—they were trust-funders, a lot of them, but they backslid too much, and the Teacher—" Reggie stopped, terrified by his slip.

Tim knew that recognition had shown on his own face, which probably wasn't helping matters for Reggie. He waited patiently.

Reggie took a moment to regain his composure. "And *our leader* hates messes. Oh, we also hit rich-kid schools like Loyola or SC."

Tim leaned forward. "Tell me about the schools."

Reggie smiled, his tongue poking in the space left by a missing incisor. "This one Pro had a great gig, working the registrar's office at Loyola for a few months. When kids came in to drop a class, she'd work them up: Having a tough time here on campus? Your parents don't understand why you can't keep up with your schedule? Things stressful? They were a needy bunch—smart and rich, too. More likely to accept an invite."

"An invite to what?"

"Shit, how'd you get put on this case? You have no clue how this works."

"Educate me."

Reggie stood and paced a few turns, stray papers crinkling underfoot. "It's a spiral, man, a flushing toilet. You snare 'em and drag 'em inward."

"What're the criteria?"

"If you have money. If you listen well. If you please him."

One male leader, Tim noted.

Reggie sat down, shoulders humped, exhausted. "He's real selective about who gets to move to the Inner Circle—that's why he's had so much luck with people staying on board. He'd never run the risk of people leaving and revealing him for who he is—he'd fucking kill them first. He's building a tight, loyal core to take on the world."

"You see any evidence of his killing anyone who betrayed him?"

"He never *had* to kill anyone. The couple of us he booted

out are such fucking messes there's not much threat anyone would listen if we *did* talk." Reggie picked at a button on his shirt. "Or that we'll survive very long. As long as I mind my own business, I'm safe from him." He snickered. "Not like Oprah's banging down my door anyway."

"So the recruits. What do you do with them?"

Reggie was up on his feet again, walking in circles. "We'd pick the best ones and try to get them to move into or near our house. We'd get the twenty-four-hour thing going, really start taking apart their minds and putting them back together."

Tim recalled the jarring difference between Leah's dorm room on an affluent campus and the dump in Van Nuys. Her "full dance card" after the move.

"How do they get you to sign over your money?"

"Oh, that trick he's got down. That's the whole point of it, really. Never mind that you wind up with nothing on the balance sheet but tens of thousands of dollars in gift tax you didn't know existed." Reggie smiled crookedly. "That's right. I'm a cool hundred grand in the hole. And since mind control *doesn't exist*—did you know that? Legally, mind control doesn't even exist, stupid asshole lawmakers—then what are you gonna do? It's not illegal to coax someone to give away all their money. Nothing to stop willing victims like me from ending up here."

"If I'm looking to find this girl and get her out, can I expect to run across muscle?"

"You can bet on it. He likes having big guys around. They help him feel taller."

Was the leader short? Tim didn't want to pry, since specifics seemed to set Reggie off. "The girl sold all her possessions three weeks ago and moved out of her apartment. No forwarding information. Do you think she's in the cult house?"

"Probably. The next step would be living with the leader, wherever he is now. Either way your nameless girl just entered a new world of trouble. They have their claws into her around the clock now. It's gonna be a rapid downhill from here."

"She get much time alone?"

He snorted. "No one gets much time alone. That's the whole point. You have a Gro-Par with you twenty-four/seven, group activities, le—"

"Gro-Par?"

A nervous glance around the room, as if invisible culties were in attendance.

"Growth Partner." Reggie ran his hand along the underside of his nose. "Yeah, no alone time at all. Why? You gonna try to nab her? Good luck. She'll fucking hate you for it. And she'll be right to." His pacing had taken on an agitated quality—he slogged through clothes and trash, hands jiggling, sentences running together. "Shit, you don't stand a chance anyway. They'll spot a Common-Censor like you a mile away. They're on the lookout, all the time. He sinks it into your brain to avoid outsiders. He says they come to kidnap you and take you back to your miserable former life. You gonna prove him right?"

"I hope not." He weathered Reggie's stare. "Anything you can . . . Anything you're comfortable telling me about the leader?"

"I'm not going there."

"Give me something, Reggie. Doesn't have to be his Social Security number. His tastes, proclivities, sexual preferences . . . ?"

Reggie rolled his head to one side, then back, lost in some internal debate. "He only fucks virgins. Or at least girls whose cherries he's popped—his Lilies. He won't fuck a girl if anyone else has."

Tim thought of Katie Kelner's sneering reference to Leah's being "the big V" and felt his stomach roil. "Does he rape them?"

Reggie's fingers pressed into his temples as he walked, as if staving off a migraine. "Define 'rape.' Define 'force.' Define 'free will.' No, he doesn't rape them, technically. He *convinces* them. But they don't have a choice."

"What does that mean?"

"If you don't get it, I can't explain it to you." Reggie's tone was so cold and definitive that Tim just stared at him for a few minutes. Reggie broke the standoff by falling back on the bed, pushing fists into his temples. "Look, I've got a massive headache coming on. I can't do this anymore."

"Where do they—"

"*I can't do this anymore!*" Reggie lay still, his breath coming in jerks—he was either crying or in intense pain. When he spoke again, his voice was apologetic. "I can't . . . I'm just done, man. I can't anymore. It puts me back."

"Okay. It's okay. Thank you." Tim rose to leave.

"Can you turn off the light?"

"The light's off."

"Wait. Can you . . . ? I can't figure out . . ." Reggie fumbled for the notebook, accidentally knocking it back between the nightstand and the wall. "Shit. That's my nighttime list. What should I do?"

Tim stared at him, nonplussed.

"What am I supposed to do? Like, before bed?"

"Brush your teeth?"

"Right, that's right." Reggie pushed himself up off the bed. "Hang on. Just stay a second. Please." Then, from the bathroom, "How much toothpaste?"

"Just enough to cover the bristles." This type of caretaking, while a bizarre variation, wasn't entirely unfamiliar to Tim. Two months ago, on Ginny's birthday—the year anniversary of her death—any movement had felt torpid and fatiguing. That night, as on a handful before, he and Dray had nursed each other through the rote movements of living.

"Can I go to the bathroom?"

"Yes."

The sound of Reggie pissing; he hadn't bothered to close the door. He came back and stood before the bed, staring at it, blinking. He'd remembered to remove his shirt, revealing a torso so wasted each rib was visible, but he was still wearing his jeans. He muttered to himself, confused, utterly backslid into dependency.

Tim flapped the comforter once, hard, scattering the trash to the floor. He pulled back the sheets. "Get in."

Reggie slid beneath the covers.

Tim pulled them up, dropping them so they fell across Reggie's chest. Reggie's eyes were bulging now. "Can I have the TV on? I need the light and movement."

"Yes." It took Tim a moment to locate the TV—it sat draped beneath a ratty bath mat. The antenna was snapped, so the picture came up a confusion of blurs and warped voices. Tim tried to adjust the stub, but Reggie called out, "It's fine like that. Makes me feel like I have a bit of company."

When Tim reached the door, Reggie said, "Hey, Sheriff."

Tim turned, resisting the urge to correct him. Reggie had pulled the sheets up above his chin; his eyes peered out, sunken and fearful. "You'd better get that girl out of there as soon as fucking possible."

Nine

Leah opened her eyes and felt a flutter of anxiety, as she had every morning for the last three months. And, as she had every morning for the last three months, she willed away her weakness, controlling her thoughts as she had been taught.

She told herself that her doubts were the last vestiges of her Old Programming.

That she could maximize her growth by minimizing her negativity.

That she needed to let go and Get with The Program.

It was a great honor to be invited to join the Inner Circle up at the ranch, just twenty-two days ago, and she wasn't about to screw it up. She'd sacrificed way too much for that. She stared at the cottage-cheese ceiling of her shared bedroom, the wrinkles of concern smoothing from her face, her heart rate slowing to normal. The space resembled a state-college dorm room—two beat-up wooden beds, drawers beneath, a single dresser, a closet with a splintering door that wouldn't close. Periwinkle paint covered the cinder-block walls, fading in patches where the sun hit it through the lone window.

Her Growth Partner breathed heavily on the other twin bed crammed into the space. Janie was a perky, attractive twenty-five-year-old; Leah found it hard not to envy her ready confidence and womanly curves.

The door creaked open, and the form of a man resolved from the dusty early-morning light. There were no locks on the doors up here, except, she had heard, in the Teacher's cottage. No phones, watches, clocks, TVs, or newspapers either. And no mirrors—Leah had learned to fix her hair without the aid of her reflection. Or, as was increasingly the case, she and Janie primped each other.

She had the luxury of working with computers, but always ancient ones with the modems excised or phone cords removed. Though she missed surfing the Web, it was unproductive to question and nitpick; besides, her computer skills landed her cushier specialized jobs that spared her Rec-Dute. The Recruitment-Duty shifts lasted eighteen hours or until one secured five sign-ups for a colloquium, whichever came first.

The man eased forward into the room. Leah pretended she was sleeping, but she heard the floorboards creak. A large hand came to rest on her thigh, protected only by a thin sheet. "Leah. It's your time to rouse the Teacher."

She opened her eyes. Randall, the bigger of the two Protectors, was sitting on the edge of her bed. He was almost entirely hairless—bald, no eyebrows, no chest hair—except for his arms; the dense mats of black hair caused the cuffed sleeves of his flannel to bulge.

"Let me tell my Gro-Par," Leah said.

But Janie was already up, fussing. Her bark-colored hair swayed with the effort; she wore it seventies style—center-parted and waist length. "Oh, my God. That's so killer. *I* can't be one of TD's Lilies because I'm married."

When it became clear Randall wasn't going to wait outside, Leah changed in front of him, made insecure by his beady eyes.

Janie preened her, combing her hair, which had been cropped in a shaggy pageboy her first day here. "It might be nice if you wore a sleeveless shirt instead."

"I'm a bit chilly. It's early."

"Cold is a state of mind, Leah. Don't indulge your Old Programming."

"I *like* this shirt."

Janie sighed dramatically, rolling her eyes at Randall. "See what I have to work with?" She covered up the slight with a nervous laugh and kissed Leah on the forehead. "I'm so proud of you."

Randall's throat rattled when he cleared it. "When you kiss someone on the face, you're sucking on a tube that's twenty-three feet long, the other end of which is connected to feces."

Janie shivered and busied herself tying Leah's shoelaces.

"I'll bear that in mind," Leah said.

Randall led her down the hall, past the cluster of closed doors. The cottage comprised two identical halves, each with four bedrooms and two baths, joined at a modest common room with a kitchenette. Cramped little structures with pebbles strewn across their flat roofs, the poorly insulated units were barely a step up from prefabs.

He headed outside, crossing the circular lawn around which the four other cottages were arrayed, Leah walking fast to keep up. At the edge of Cottage Circle, five enormous cypresses rose up, van Gogh shadows against the lambent glow of the horizon. The throw of land housing the little community was the sole stretch of flatness adrift on the thirsty brown mountains. The rest of the compound lay upslope on the precipice of a straight-drop cliff, except the Teacher's cottage, which stood to the west off a trail carved through chest-high brush.

As they turned onto the trail, Leah looked up at Randall, who had to stoop to get his six-three frame under the occasional branch. She spoke mostly to ease her own tension. "How did you find the Teacher?"

Randall kept on without pause. "He saved me."

The rest of the walk to the Teacher's cottage was silent.

Woods encroached on the rear of the building. Skate Daniels, the other Protector, tilted back on a rickety chair on the front porch, working at a hunk of wood with a hunting knife. He wore a boxer-style sweatshirt, the collar ripped and cross-threaded with a shoelace. The severed sleeves showed off arms massy with thick, undefined muscle. At his throat hung a crude necklace—two twisted copper wires threaded through tiny earth-tone beads, vaguely Native American in effect. Dangling from it like a pendant was the notorious tiny silver key.

Skate's two Dobermans bolted over to investigate, snarling and barking. Leah recoiled, terrified, but Skate backed them down with a snap of his fingers, and they scrambled off through the underbrush behind the narrow shed where Skate and Randall slept. Barely wide enough to accommodate two cots, the shed leaned like a wind-battered bait shack, exhaling a perennial spiral of smoke from a black pipe of a chimney. Once when Leah had to deliver a file to the Teacher, she'd seen Skate in there, shuddering against the cold and stoking the fire in the potbellied stove with a stick.

The shed, Leah had learned, was absolutely off-limits, as was the modular office a few paces behind it. The mod's door sported a profusion of locks, protecting its consecrated interior—the Teacher's private office space. Leah respectfully averted her eyes from the mod.

She stepped up on the porch. "What are you making there?"

Skate flicked the point of the blade against the wood, his flat eyes never leaving his task. "Jes' whittlin'."

Randall gestured to the door, and she stepped inside, nearly tripping over a white plastic tub brimming with mail. The ranch had been a bigwig director's retreat in the twenties; the Teacher's cottage was the only building not since supplanted by a lowest-bidder abomination. Beautiful stone exterior, slat-wood doors, a lazy fan overhead. Wagon wheels from a bygone movie shoot still lined the walk and framed the porch, sentimentalized by the adolescent residential treatment facility that occupied and further degraded the ranch before The Program acquired it.

Randall closed the door behind Leah.

Alone in the Teacher's cottage. She did her best to calm the storm of panic and excitement rising in her chest.

She prepared as she had been taught, first picking up and folding the Teacher's clothes, which had been left in the front room. She removed a ginseng mahuang smoothie from the tiny fridge, strained it into a glass to remove excess pulp, then arranged the vitamins in a grid on the serving platter. The napkin she folded into a crisp triangle.

After washing the hair from the shower soap, she ran the water so it would be hot when he was ready. She removed a fresh toothbrush from the cabinet and squeezed onto it a straight worm of Aquafresh. She plucked a premarked Dixie cup from the stack beneath the sink and poured mint mouthwash to the indelible-ink line drawn precisely an inch and a half from the bottom. She rested a new razor on the towel beside the sink and wiped the excess from the nozzle of the shaving-cream can.

You have been chosen, she told herself. You have been singled out. You are special.

The door to the Teacher's bedroom creaked slightly as she pushed it, balancing his breakfast tray with her other hand. His slumbering form lay beneath the king duvet. She set the tray on the nightstand and knelt at the side of the bed. She slid her hand inside the Egyptian-cotton sheets and gripped his erect penis.

"Wake up, Teacher," she said softly. Then she repeated herself, a little louder, barely recognizing her own voice. "Wake up, Teacher."

He stirred and stretched, arms shoving up against the massive headboard. He settled back, hands laced behind his head like Huck Finn. His facial skin was youthful, even taut, stretching his lips into thin strokes. A slender man with sharp, intelligent features, he had no wrinkles at all. His closely set eyes were hypnotic, captivating, prying; when he spoke to her, she tried to watch his hands or forehead instead. Now she kept focused on the task at hand, the silky duvet rising and falling a foot and a half in front of her face.

"Now, not too firm," he cautioned, his voice low and soothing. Then, a bit more sharply, "*Relax.*"

At once her mind went blank, her breathing smoothed, and her hand moved of its own volition, butterfly soft, doing what it somehow knew to do.

"There, now," he said. "There, now."

His hips rocked slightly on the cushioned mattress, and then he shuddered and it was done. She withdrew her hand, wiping it on the sheets. Still she avoided his eyes, but the en-

ergy coming off him was approving, and her insides went
warm with relief and gratitude.

Keeping her head bowed, she said, "Good morning,
Teacher."

He reached down and stroked her hair gently, forgivingly.
"Please," he said, "call me TD."

Ten

When Tim woke up half an hour later, Dray was on her
side, leaning over him, hand near his face. He jerked,
startled by her proximity, and she quickly rolled out of bed
and headed to the bathroom.

"What the hell was that?"

The shower flipped on. "Nothing."

Tim went in and leaned against the counter, arms crossed,
watching through the glass as Dray pretended to be absorbed
in the lathering process. Finally she glanced up. "Look, I put
my hand in front of your mouth sometimes when you're
sleeping to feel you breathing." She stepped back into the
stream. "So it's kind of freakish. . . ."

"You're worried I'm gonna die in my sleep?"

Furiously lathering a knee, Dray fought an embarrassed
smile from her lips. "No. Yes. I don't know."

"We have a deal, remember?"

"Die in our sleep when we're ninety. The same night."

"Right. So cut me a break until then, huh? You're over-
loading my pacemaker."

The shower door slid open, and a sudsy washcloth hit him
in the face before he could get his hands up to block it. He
pulled it off, laughing and coughing.

Dray poised her leg on the tub's edge and ran a razor up its slick length. "I wouldn't have to do it if you'd just snore like a *real* husband."

Dray, standing behind Tim, punched a fork into a hunk of his Eggo and mopped it through a pool of residual syrup. She had to angle her head to get the bite in and even still wound up dripping on his sweatshirt. Particularly after their morning runs, Dray ate like a Jurassic carnivore, but her current performance was more arresting than usual. Tim watched two links of sausage disappear in the same direction. He listened for chewing but heard none.

He'd freed up his morning to sit with the case file, but on his walk down the hall, the sight of Ginny's room empty had pulled him up short. He'd taken a moment leaning on the jamb, gazing in. He'd hoped to offset the shock with productivity but was having a sluggish go at it. Thus far he'd done little more than fail to defend his breakfast plate.

He glanced back down at his notepad, in which he'd listed the lingo he'd gleaned from his conversations with Reggie.

Pro, Neo, Common-Censor/Common Sensor? Trigger, Orae/Oray? Gro-Par/Grow-Par? Lilies, Inner Circle.

"You gonna eat that?" Dray's fork flashed past before he could respond. Staring at his sole extant sausage, he realized he'd better stop thinking and start eating.

"Sounds like it's gonna be tough to get to the girl."

"Yes."

"And then, when you do, she won't even want to be rescued?"

"Yes."

"No crime has been committed here, right? That you know of?"

Tim tapped his fork absentmindedly against his orange-juice glass. "No."

"And this would be a bad time for me to revisit why the hell you're doing this to begin with?"

"Yes."

Dray paused midchew. "Just checking."

Tim's cell phone rang, and he rose to grab it before it sambaed off the kitchen counter.

"Hi, Deputy, this is Katie Kelner, Leah's former roommate. Listen, you said to call if anything came up . . . ?"

"Yes."

"Well, I was going through one of my books—well, I *thought* it was my book, but I guess it got mixed up with Leah's, since she was taking Shit Lit, too."

Tim watched helplessly as Dray swooped down on his last sausage. "Uh-huh."

"She left a card in it, like an appointment card, for a bookmark, you know? And it was from the Student Counseling Center. I guess she was seeing a *shrink.*" This last word Katie whispered severely—odd that anyone in Malibu would believe the term required a lowered voice.

"Does it have the date of the appointment?"

"Yeah, it says December seventh at two o'clock."

A little more than a month before Leah had disappeared from campus.

"You said, you know, to call if I thought of anything."

"And I'm glad you did."

"Some of the stuff I said when you were here . . . I'm, uh, I'm not an awful person, you know."

"I don't think you're an awful person."

"What *do* you think?"

He thought that life hadn't smacked her around enough yet for her to realize she didn't know everything. "That's irrelevant."

She let out a dismissive little laugh. "Well, you don't know me. Who cares what you think?"

"To be honest, not too many people."

* * *

Getting information out of therapists was generally an exercise in futility, but since Tim was already planning to visit the Pepperdine registrar's office, he figured he might as well pay a courtesy call to the Student Counseling Center afterward.

He'd parked and was crossing campus at a good clip when the cell phone chirped.

A high male voice: "Mr. Henning wants to see you."

"Who's this?"

"He'd like an update on your progress."

"Who's this?"

"I work for Mr. Henning."

Tim had encountered enough Mr. Hennings in his life to recognize a power play shaping up. "If he wants to talk, have him call me himself. I don't deal with intermediaries." Tim snapped the phone shut. About a minute later, as he negotiated a river of students flooding from the Thornton Administration Building, it rang again. "Yeah?"

"I'm a very busy man, Mr. Rackley."

"You and me both, Will."

"Yet you insist on a personal phone call."

"This isn't a budget meeting. I'm protecting your confidentiality. And your daughter's. That's how this goes."

"Fine." The line went dead.

Tim's phone sounded a third time. "Hi, Tim, this is Will Henning. I'd like to see you."

Without the sarcastic tone, it might have been funny. "Where are you?"

"I work from home now." He added defensively, "I get more done here."

"I'll get to you sometime this afternoon."

"When?"

"When I get there."

Tim followed the signage to the registrar's counter only to find himself in line behind ten or so students. He waited with them so he could watch the proceedings. Dropping a class proved to be a protracted negotiation involving substantial paperwork. It took a good half hour for the line to dissipate, during which Tim noted nothing to indicate a recruitment ploy like the one Reggie had described.

The registrar, an octogenarian with a kindly demeanor and prodigious eyeglasses, informed Tim that she'd run the office for the past thirty-five years and assured him that no funny business had gone down under her tenure. For confidentiality purposes, she didn't permit student workers in the office, and the two women she oversaw had been there for years. A brief talk with both of them was enough for Tim to put the flimsy lead to bed.

He zagged back across campus in the car, following the blue signs. The Student Counseling Center proved to be a beige and brown modular home sandwiched between a parking lot and a scrubby hill. It seemed more like a school nurse's station in a welfare mountain-state town than the therapy center for a high-tuition Malibu university.

The potted plants lining the ramp brushed Tim's jeans on his way up. With its blue carpet and paneled walls, the interior typified modular décor. Seemingly out of place was the well-dressed woman behind the petite reception desk, whose cheery, first-name-basis nameplate announced her solely as ROBBIE.

Her pert face tightened a bit when he introduced himself. "Confidentiality is absolute here, Mr. Rackley."

"Please, call me Tim."

"We adhere to the guidelines of the American Psychological Association."

"Are all the therapists psychologists?"

"No, Mr. Rackley. Most are licensed social workers, but the same confidentiality guidelines apply to them."

"Do students need to be referred here?"

"They can come directly if they're an undergraduate or a student at the law school, GSBM—"

"GSBM?"

"Graziado School of Business Management."

"Would you be allowed to disclose when a particular student first came in?"

"Absolutely not."

A girl emerged from a back room, the floor creaking with her steps. She shuffled to get around Tim, but there wasn't much room. "I'm sorry to interrupt."

"That's okay," Robbie said. "We were just wrapping up. Maybe you could show the gentleman out." She busied herself clearing her desk.

When it was clear Robbie wasn't going to acknowledge him again, Tim followed the girl out. She held the door for him but stumbled over a potted plant when she turned. Tim caught her arm to steady her, and she let out an embarrassed giggle. "Sorry. I'm such a klutz. I get nervous, you know, when people see me here. I always think they're wondering what's wrong with me—" She blushed. "God, shut *up*, Shanna."

"You should see me waiting at the clinic for my results to come back."

Shanna stared at him, eyebrows raised, and then her face broke into a smile and she hit him lightly on the arm.

They walked down the ramp together. Two girls sat talking in a Range Rover parked in the first row of the lot beside Tim's Acura, not ten yards from the trailer's entrance. The therapy rooms emptied out directly into a major campus parking lot.

So much for absolute confidentiality.

"I just transferred in from Brigham Young this semester. It's kind of . . . not been the easiest transition, you know? Are you a student here? You seem old. I mean, not that way, but . . ." Shanna's face colored again, her hand over her mouth. Substantial diamond studs gleamed in her ears. "Just don't pay attention to me, okay?"

The front doors of the Range Rover opened simultaneously. The two girls climbed out and headed toward them, the long-limbed driver smoothing a paisley cotton skirt over her underlying bell-bottom jeans. Tim figured them for friends of Shanna's—they'd clearly been waiting, keeping an eye on the Student Counseling Center.

The shorter girl wore a red T-shirt under a pair of overalls, her hair thrown back in a ponytail. "Hey, there. How you guys doing today?"

"Good," Shanna said uncertainly.

"I'm Julie, and this is Lorraine. We're having a group gathering tomorrow night at our apartment, and we wanted to invite you guys."

They showed off perfect smiles.

"Oh," Shanna said. "That's nice."

Lorraine reached out and touched Tim gently, her well-manicured nails tapping his forearm. "We're gonna have a great talk and drinks and everything."

Tim's mind moved instinctively to intolerance, hardwired from years of dealing with pyramid schemers, religious zealots, time-share hucksters. He was about to open his mouth to issue his customary rebuff when realization struck.

Julie, voice lowered with compassion, patted Shanna on the side. "You seem a little down."

Tim turned with Lorraine, who was beaming brightly and strolling to his side, facing him flirtatiously across the ball of her shoulder. Her auburn hair was pulled back severely in a clip so it conformed tightly to the shape of her head. He strained to hear Shanna's response to Julie, but Lorraine, still circling, said, "You're a bit mature to be a student here, aren't you?"

He feigned bashfulness. Putting his hands behind him, he worked off his wedding band and dropped it in the back pocket of his jeans. "Well, I hooked up with a great counselor when I went to GSBM. She still sees me on the side now and then when I hit a bump in the road."

Lorraine's eyes fluttered wide. "GSBM? I *love* business. A lot of us do. We're going to talk about things tomorrow night that could really help your career."

Shanna was now out of sight behind his back; Julie and Lorraine had skillfully maneuvered them apart so they were facing opposite directions.

Isolating the prey.

Lorraine nodded at the Student Counseling Center. "Sorry to hear that things are kind of shitty right now." She stroked his forearm again, lightly. Smelling of a fruity, pricey skin cream, she stood to his side, lipstick glimmering moistly, torso swaying slightly so her firm breasts moved beneath the sweetheart neckline of her blouse. Since the girls had approached in a team of two, Lorraine's come-on felt not threatening, but friendly and flattering. A confused college kid wouldn't stand a chance.

Campuses teem with predators—rapists, muggers, stalkers. But this particular brand, so appealingly packaged, was all the more insidious for its harmless demeanor.

Behind him he heard Julie say, "Your haircut's the *bomb*."

And Shanna's nervous giggle. "Thanks. I just got it done at Frédéric Fekkai."

A whispered joke. The girls laughed together. Tim wanted to turn to look, but Lorraine was drilling him with eye contact. Though the two recruiters acted almost identically, Lorraine was less soft than Julie, the strings of her manipulation more visible.

Julie was the lure, Lorraine the closer.

"Anything you want to talk about?" Lorraine asked.

Tim chewed his lip, as if debating whether he should open up. "It's still hard for me to say, but I got, uh, divorced a few months ago—"

"That sucks. It must have been terrible."

"Pretty rough, yeah. And on top of it, work's been insanely stressful. I started up this little company a few years ago and grew it pretty aggressively. We were just bought out, which is great, but the ride hasn't exactly been relaxing, and now I'm sort of at loose ends about what to do with myself."

Her face held a predatory elation. "Having a company bought out? At your age? That's *incredible*." A warm smile. "What's your name? I want to remember it when I see it in the *Wall Street Journal*."

Tim fished out the last fake identity he'd used. "Tom Altman."

"We'd really love to have someone like you join us tomorrow. Will you come?"

"What kind of thing is it?"

"Just a lot of cool people hanging out, figuring out how to improve ourselves. That's important to you, isn't it?"

"I don't know." Tim shook his head. "It sounds a little weird."

"I bet you didn't get a company bought out by thinking inside the box."

"Nope. I did it by figuring out how to fit square pegs in round holes."

Tom Altman, dream Neo.

Lorraine said, "There ya go."

"Hey." Shanna was on her tiptoes, looking at him over Julie's shoulder. "What do you think? Are you gonna go? I'll go if you do."

Julie grinned. "It's gonna be really eye-opening, Tom." Even while working Shanna, she'd kept an ear out for his name. "What do you say?"

"Sure," he said. "I'll check it out."

Lorraine and Julie squealed with delight. "*Great* call! I promise it'll be worthwhile."

Julie wrote down the address for Tim. Lorraine offered Shanna a ride back to her dorm, and they all turned to the parking lot. Tim stopped short. Dinged and dented beside the Range Rover, the Acura Integra was not a car befitting Tom Altman. Not a car befitting a deputy U.S. marshal either— Tim had pulled it out of a junkyard last year when he'd needed an untraceable vehicle. He hesitated, not wanting to broadcast ownership.

The three headed to the Range Rover. It was new—no license plate to memorize.

Julie glanced back. "You need a lift to your car or something?"

"No. I think I left my keys inside."

As he started back toward the trailer, the Range Rover pulled out behind him, Shanna waving from the backseat.

Eleven

*L*eah spent the morning polishing the Teacher's shoes with another Lily, a plump, timid girl named Nancy. You had to be a virgin to be a Lily; in fact, only virgins were allowed in the Teacher's cottage. More than a hundred pairs of shoes were lined on shelves in the walk-in closet off TD's front room, each with its own jar of polish. A laminated sheet of paper tacked to the inside of the closet door held directions—counterclockwise circles, no excess polish, be sure to turn your head from the shoes if you sneeze.

Nancy kept applying too much polish to the heels, and Leah wiped it off for her, showing her how to apply the correct amount. Leah found the monotony of the task soothing, as the Teacher had promised.

Wax on, wax off. Perfection in the details, character through process.

The wisps of black-dyed hair sticking out at Nancy's temples were almost as baffling as the *Flashdance*-cut sweatshirt she wore off one fleshy shoulder. Nancy sat back on her heels, working a loafer, arms jiggling, her circles going clockwise. "Dr. TD says I have a need to infuriate men. He says he can tell from how I act."

"How do you act?"

"Difficult, I guess. I keep messing up the rules. I can't keep them all straight. He says I'm vengeful. I hold back a lot from male authority. I don't have the strength to Get with The Program yet."

They kept polishing, Leah's eyes darting between her own work and Nancy's. "Nancy. You have to do the circles the other way. Like this. It's an honor being able to practice on TD's stuff."

"I know, I know. Damnit. I'm sorry." Nancy's lips trembled. "There's so much pressure here I can't think, you know? Everyone's telling me what I do wrong all the time."

Leah's mouth moved with the answers before she even thought. "You want to take ownership of your choices. You know you're responsible for your own experience."

Nancy was crying now. "If I screw up any more, I'll be gone. I don't know what I'd do without Dr. TD, without The Program."

"You're only a victim if that's what you choose." Leah took up an oxblood loafer. "Nancy, stop crying."

Nancy sniffled and wiped her nose. It struck Leah that her pity felt more like empathy. Nancy's bad dye job tugged at her heart—like any superficial attempt at change, it would be met with customary disinterest from the world. Nancy would never get anywhere until she stopped setting herself up for failure. She wouldn't find strength in mirrors and the expectations of others.

Nancy touched Leah's shoulder, leaving a black smudge. "I'm sorry. You were right. I think I'm just emotional right now." She tried a smile, but her lips were still trembling.

The polishing took nearly two hours and left them with cramped hands and polish smeared up to their wrists. They each did their best to wash up in the bathroom. As they finished, TD entered. He'd been conducting a meeting in the modular with Stanley John, a young commercial-real-estate shark who was his second in command.

TD wore a polo shirt, untucked over a pair of pleated cargo pants that accentuated his slim, girlish hips. His freckles were pale, as if faded from childhood; they extended even to his ears and lips. Just below his mouth, a neatly trimmed patch of hair bristled. His head seemed slightly too small, even for his thin frame, a minor imperfection he'd brilliantly overcome by wearing his coarse brown hair puffed out. Leah had never experienced someone so capable of projecting his mood.

She kept her eyes lowered, as she'd been told. "Hi, TD." The privilege of using his nickname brought a flush of pride.

"Hello, Leah." He slid his hand into her hair, cupping the curve of her forehead. He wore no watch or jewelry; Janie had informed Leah that his energy sometimes conducted an electric charge, and metal could shock him. "Good morning, Nancy."

Nancy smiled, blushing. "Hi, Teacher."

He ducked into the bathroom, then backed out almost immediately. Leah and Nancy went stiff. He spoke very quietly. "Which one of you is bleeding?"

Nancy's knees buckled, but she caught herself before she fell.

Leah found her voice first. "I'm sorry?"

"There's a menstrual pad in my trash can." He placed a hand on the back of her neck, firmly, and guided her into the bathroom. "There," he said softly, almost lovingly. "Do you see?"

Leah nodded.

"It throws off my energy when I'm in the presence of a woman who's bleeding. We've talked about that. Now, which one of you is bleeding?"

Nancy's nose had gone red, presaging her tears. Her lips looked swollen and cracked.

TD's voice stayed perfectly calm. "Should we call Randall and Skate in here to help you look?"

Nancy was crying now, her terror contagious. She opened her mouth to speak, but Leah cut her off. "Mine."

TD nodded once, languidly, then walked to the door and knuckled it open. He called across the clearing for Stanley John and Skate, and almost at once Leah heard the mod door bang open. Footsteps sounded on the porch. The men halted dutifully outside.

"Skate, come in please."

Skate shuffled through the door. TD lifted the necklace off over his head, the beads knocking against the silver key.

Leah's mouth went dry; her voice came thin and high. "Oh, no. Please, no."

Nancy looked as though she might pass out. "Dr. TD, I—"

He held a finger to his lips and shushed her. "Nancy, I'm putting you on a word diet for the day. And I want you to leave. Do you understand?"

She nodded, mouth sealed, then exited. The dogs reacted to her violently on the porch, but Skate shouted out a command and they silenced.

Leah felt the blood rushing to her face. "Please don't put me in there. I'm sorry."

TD beckoned Stanley John with two fingers. He stepped inside, running a hand through his lank brown hair, which fell back perfectly along the part. He was the kind of guy the girls at Pepperdine had found attractive—strong jaw, perfect teeth, pronounced brow. He cast a concerned eye at the Teacher. "What's the prob, TD?"

"She's bleeding."

"C'mon, Leah. You know better than that. Now, don't you?"

She tried not to shake. "Well, actually, I was never told. I just finished my period, actually, so I wasn't really—"

"Oh, I think you know how to take accountability better than that, don't you?" Keeping his eyes on Leah, Stanley John extended his hand. TD lowered the necklace into his palm, the copper wires gleaming through the beads.

Leah studied her shoes, her face burning.

TD placed his ageless face before hers. "The Program ensures you'll have a steep learning curve, even if the learning isn't always fun."

Her head sank, her shoulders drooped. If she could have melted into the floorboards, she would have.

"You said last session that your parents think you don't listen. After your real dad died of cancer, you didn't fit in well with your new family."

She looked away to hide her welling tears. "Yes."

"Sound familiar? You not fitting in?"

Moisture on her cheeks. Shame burning like an infection. "Yes."

He placed his hands softly on her cheeks until she raised her eyes. "Your acting out like this isn't going to get you the kind of attention you're seeking."

"I know. It's my Old Programming."

"What do you feel?"

She wiped her tears. "That no matter what I say, you'll be disappointed with me."

"Don't you see that's a self-fulfilling prophecy? You're acting weak, crying like a victim. You're creating in me the very disappointment you're so afraid of."

Her thoughts pulled in ten directions at once. "I don't mean to do that. That's not what I meant to do."

"Don't worry, Leah." He stroked her face gently. "TD will break you of this habit. We'll get you fixed. Okay?"

Her head barely moved. Up, down, up.

Stanley John led her out. She felt dead inside, as if she'd withered away and her body was walking of its own volition. When they reached the oval of grass, the others stopped their gardening and playing and talking and stared, reading the situation from the expression on her face. When Stanley John started up the steep paved road toward the empty treatment wing of the preceding adolescent facility, there could be no doubt.

Two girls playing Frisbee stopped and called out admonitions. Janie's husband, Chris, the chubby Webmaster for The Program's incipient site, stopped flipping burgers in the barbecue pit and stared at Leah disapprovingly, one hand perched possessively on Janie's hourglass waist. Janie, looking even more youthful and pretty beside her balding husband, was shaking her head, knowing she'd face chastisement for Leah's failure. A group of people near the picnic tables whispered and pointed. Nancy stood among them, drunk with relief, seeming gleeful that the focus had been turned away from her. Her face still carried the pink stains of her earlier crying. Leah had lied to protect her, and she'd been repaid with derision. She felt too numb to hate Nancy. All she felt was her own shame at deceiving TD, at denying Nancy her rightful lesson. Clearly, Leah was getting what she deserved now.

The others started streaming over in twos and threes, following Stanley John and Leah up the hill toward the treatment wing. Leah could barely walk; her legs had gone weak with anticipation. Stanley John stopped her about thirty yards from the doors.

He walked ahead, fishing for keys in his pocket, as Leah felt the crowd swarm up behind her. The fabric of her shirt, pasted to her chest, fluttered with her heartbeat. Her rash, which stretched from her breasts to her clavicle, burned and itched. She closed her eyes against the snatches of conversation.

About thirty of them lined up on either side of her, forming a path to the front door, which Stanley John held open. Her breathing shallow and rapid, she started forward on tingling legs. The first girl on her right pinched her on the back of her arm, hard. Chris squeezed the soft skin of her left arm, twisting, a satisfied grin on his thick lips. Janie, fresh and vibrant, waited her turn beside him. Leah bit her cheek to keep from crying out as hand after hand reached out to nip the tender flesh at the back of her arms.

Janie leaned in close, her brown hair drifting like parted

drapes. "This is *your* experience. You can make of it what you want."

Leah tried to mouth her thanks, but the next sets of hands were on her, and she had to clamp her jaw to keep from crying out. She wanted desperately to break into a run, but if she tried to flee, she'd have to walk the Wellness Train all over again. She forced herself to step, pause, step, like a bride moving to the altar. Finally she couldn't help herself, and she started to pull away from the grasping fingers, elbows tucking to her waist. Her face was hot and slick with tears. Everyone was cheering and yelling. Nancy gripped her skin but didn't squeeze; her eyes were sad and horrified. Two new guys at the end eagerly awaited their turn. They grabbed the now-purple flesh and squeezed until Leah yelped, a small, throaty noise lost in the roar of the crowd. The guy on the right studied her face, an erection bulging in his shorts.

She stepped past them, her arms on fire, the rash on her chest seething beneath her sweat-drenched shirt. Stanley John took her by the shoulders and turned her around so she faced back up the aisle.

Everyone burst into applause for her.

"Way to go, Leah!"

"Atta girl!"

"No pain no gain."

Satiated, they dispersed, joking and talking about dinner.

Stanley John unlocked the door and led her in. She cupped the swollen backs of her arms in her hands. The pain continued to smolder within them, a deep-tissue burn.

"You'll have five hours of treatment."

A blast of denial hit her. "Five hours? I can't make it through five hours."

"You doubt yourself? You know what? I'm gonna prove to you that you can make it *six* hours."

They reached the Growth Room. He turned the key in the lock, guided her inside. "I want you to meditate on your negativity. We don't have room for it up here. And I want you to think about how self-impeding you were to question Teachings. Do you understand?"

"Yes."

"I want you to stay in there until you decline to exercise the option called weakness."

She heard the muffled thunk of the dead bolt as it slid home.

She sank to the floor and pulled her knees to her chest. Soon she was rocking, her back hitting against one of the padded walls. The caged bulb overhead threw a bluish light through the tiny cell, reflected in the small square of glass set high in the door. She was exhausted. Her arms throbbed. Her rash raged. Her head pounded.

The light clicked off. A few moments of silence. Leah's eyes darted about, her body braced. Static burst through hidden speakers at incredible volume, causing her to jerk back against the wall, hands pressed over her ears. It ended just as abruptly. The lightbulb turned back on. Hesitantly, she removed her hands from her ears, her heartbeat hammering, her eyes trained on the lightbulb.

She started to weep, her cries hoarse and desperate. Curled in the corner, she sobbed. Finally she closed her eyes, succumbing to exhaustion. After ten minutes darkness fell across her body. When the inevitable burst of static came, she screamed, scrambling around the padded room like a trapped rat.

At last it ceased. The pain in her head grew so intense it blurred her vision. She drifted in and out of sleep, snapping to and staring to make sure the lightbulb remained on. It clicked off at irregular intervals that made anticipation impossible. Eventually she started screaming in the dark even before the noise came. The deafening static lasted sometimes three seconds, sometimes five minutes.

She swore she couldn't make it. She was terribly thirsty and had to pee, but if she urinated in here, Stanley John would extend her lesson.

She lay on her side, hair across her eyes, a tinny ring vibrating in both ears. The room went dark, but she couldn't muster the strength to raise her hands to her ears.

Instead of the next surge of static, the door creaked open. TD appeared, backlit, a glorious vision. He crouched over her. Her lips barely moved.

"Please don't leave me in here anymore."

He gathered her up in his arms. "Have you united with your criticism?"

"Yes. God, yes. I'm so sorry."

He stroked her hair. "Sorry? To me? To yourself? You know why TD does this, don't you? Because I care so much about your growth. Being upset with me would be like getting angry at a surgeon for excising a cancerous growth. A good surgeon wouldn't stop if you cried out in pain. He'd keep going, no matter how much it pained *him*. He'd cure you."

Her head lolled in his lap. His petting hands felt divine.

"I know," she said. "I know you did the right thing. Thank you."

"You have to build up your psychological immune system. The Growth Room is sort of like a vaccination. You're a smart, smart girl. You know how vaccines work."

"Yes."

"My first memory is of when I was a baby in a high chair. My mother was stuffing my face with strained peas, and I threw up. She fed my vomit back to me with a spoon."

Leah's headache had subsided, but her voice was still weak. "God, that's awful."

"She left me at the side of a desolate highway in the snow. A trucker found me two days later. I was almost dead. Even when I recovered, I used to be cold all the time. Then I started going out in the snow without a jacket. I built up my immunity, just like you are now. Have you ever seen me wear a jacket?"

"No, never."

"That's right." He paused thoughtfully. "Your parents have made several attempts to kidnap you, to bring you back under their control."

". . . never . . ."

"I don't pray, Leah, but if I did, I'd pray you never make the mistake of forsaking the protection of The Program."

"I won't."

She let her eyelids droop. He caressed her face a bit more. "I know it's terribly hard for you to endure a lesson like this. It must remind you of when your stepdad used to abuse you."

"I don't remember him abusing me."

He rocked her gently, his eyes far away. "You will."

Twelve

Fully tacked up with vests and ballistic helmets, Denley and Palton fell on Guerrera, the youngest Arrest Response Team member, pounding him with expandable batons. Guerrera, his gestures slowed by the puffy red-foam body suit, skipped back, keeping to his feet, and flipped them off Italian style, one padded hand flicking out from under his chin.

The ethnic gesticulation was no doubt for Tannino's sake. The marshal had pawned off a visiting Justice Rehnquist on his chief deputy so he could sneak some time with his beloved ART squad in the mat room in Roybal's basement. Brian Miller, the supervisory deputy, stood to the side, his drills co-opted by the marshal not for the first time.

"You useless knuckleheads," Tannino said. "Two of you can't put him on his ass?"

Guerrera slapped his chest, looking like an ornery Michelin Man. "You *gringos* can't step to *papi chulo*."

"Fuck you and the raft you floated in on," Denley said in his thick Brooklyn accent.

Guerrera busted a few "Vida Loca" dance moves in the red-man suit, eliciting whistles and jeers.

From the door Tim watched the proceedings. In his jeans and collared shirt, he felt like a parent at a high-school dance. He'd been an ART member for three years; his operational skills, honed in the Army Rangers, had won him quick admittance to the squad. His subsequent actions had won him quick ejection.

Shaking his head, Tannino returned to his conversation with Tim. "You sure you need all this shit?"

"It's the best angle so far."

"Well, a vehicle's not too much of a hassle—I'll get you a list from Asset Seizure, and you can go to the warehouse and pick something that suits your needs."

In the far corner, Maybeck—who, like Denley and Palton, was decked out in gear to simulate street conditions—fired a laser gun at a fleeing suspect projected onto a movie screen. The unit made a woeful bleeping noise, and UNJUSTIFIED SHOOTING scrolled across the screen in red letters.

Maybeck lowered the gun. "Whoops."

Aside from Bear and Guerrera, who'd offered Tim a wink from the depths of his suit, Tim's former colleagues continued to show him a studied—however warranted—indifference.

"I'll also need you to build me an ID. The basics—credit card, driver's license, Social Security card. Name of Tom Altman, common spelling."

Tannino grimaced—Tim had used the name previously when eluding the marshals last year. "How about cash?"

"Ten grand."

"Don't push your luck. I can get you five. Does the money have to walk?"

"Probably."

Tannino pressed his lips together, thinking. "Okay. It comes out of Henning, but we still gotta keep the books tidy. We'll hit up the Asset Forfeiture Fund—I'll push it through the undercover-review board at the DOJ."

"I need it by tomorrow."

"They're a panel of attorneys, Rackley. It takes them twenty-four hours just to choose chairs around the conference table." He noted the resolve in Tim's eyes. "I'll get it done. But no more hoops. Just find the girl."

Palton came at Guerrera again, and Tannino shouted, "Goddamnit, Frankie, approach with your weak side so your weapon's not exposed. Look, look. Here." Tannino stepped forward, placing his left hand on Guerrera's shoulder. He hooked his foot behind Guerrera's heel and leaned in, letting his elbow rise to clip Guerrera in the throat. Guerrera flipped off his feet, striking the mat hard with his shoulder blades.

"Get me Johnny Cochran on line two," Guerrera moaned.

Tannino helped him up, slapped him on the back, and returned to Tim. "Good stuff, Rackley. The lead."

"It might not be the right group."

"And we might all die tomorrow if Salami bin Laden's henchmen uncork smallpox on us. I said good stuff, Rackley. Say thank you and go have a bourbon." Tannino threw up his hands. "Goddamnit, Denley, is it a takedown or a pirouette? Put some fucking balls into it!"

Tim watched them run drills a few moments longer before he retreated, the thuds of bodies pounding on neoprene following him down the corridor.

Thirteen

The dashboard of the Acura rattled when Tim hit eighty dropping into Simi Valley, heading for the Moorpark Station. An eighteen-wheeler dominated the parking lot. A white trailer with no markings, the mobile range drove from station to station, permitting sheriff's deputies to log required shooting time and complete their trimester qualifications.

Dray sat on the hood of her patrol car, a cluster of colleagues gathered around her. The sole woman at her station, Dray was the object of several unspoken crushes, the strongest of which was nursed by Mac, her sometime partner. As Tim approached, Fowler and Gutierez, with whom Tim had an uneven history, firmed up their postures—arms crossing, stances widening. For all the bluster, they returned Tim's nod.

"Hey, Rack." Mac flashed his handsome smile and extended a hand, which Tim shook. "Your gal here just qualified sharpshooter."

"Congrats." Tim raised a fist to Dray and she matched it, pressing her knuckles against his. "What'd you shoot?"

"Two-seventy."

"Best of the day," Mac added.

Gutierez smirked. "Mac squeaked by qual with a two-ten."

Mac's looks were not matched by his skills.

One of the trainees piped up. "I heard you're a helluva shot."

Tim said, "I can blow up a guy's head with a remote control, too."

Nervous laughter.

Gutierez showed off his target, poking his fingers through. "Why don't you give it a go now?"

"Okay. Whose head?"

"Come on, Rack," Fowler said. "We've heard so much grapevine about you, but we've never seen shit." His tone was joking but his smile tight.

Mac gestured grandly at the trailer. "We brought the range to you."

Dray pulled out her shooting card and pointed it at Tim. "You haven't broken in the new gun. Why don't you go shut these boys up?"

Tim generally avoided pissing contests, but the memory of watching from the sidelines while the ART squad dirt-dived their skills still stung enough for him to want to display prowess. There were likely more advanced ways for him to affirm his manhood than by flaunting his proficiencies on a mobile range in Moorpark, but none so user-friendly.

He snapped up Dray's card and headed for the trailer, the deputies crowding behind him, whooping and clapping.

The back door banged against the range operator's minuscule desk. The burly deputy nodded at Tim and punched out thirty rounds of ammo on Dray's card.

"Thirty-eight special," Tim said.

The operator tapped the rounds down on the desk like a brick of casino chips. The three narrow lanes, standard point-and-shoots, didn't quite stretch twenty-five yards, so deputies worked off smaller targets. Foam padding eliminated the ricochet factor but added to the suffocating feel of firing in a tight space. The bullets had to be range-issue, straight from the factory; given the tight quarters, no one wanted to risk some yahoo's toting in unreliable reloads.

Ignoring the chatter behind him, Tim rolled the foam earplugs between his palms, slid them in as they started to expand, and pulled on eye protection. He winked at his wife, who stood propped against the door with crossed arms and an amused smile. The target downrange, now turned sideways so it presented like a paper sliver, featured the archetypal floating silhouette, Johnny Critical Mass. Ever since 9/11, the establishment had sought to better acquaint its shooters with lethality—targets had become increasingly animated, sprouting faces and expressions, the bull's-eye going the way of the billy club.

The overhead fan worked hard to clear the smell of cordite.

Since Tim used a revolver, he prepped four speedloaders. Eschewing the convenient countertop at the mouth of the booth, he dropped the speedloaders into the leather pouch at his belt, where he'd need to find them in a real shoot-out.

The rules required he'd have to get off at least three rounds every six seconds. Most shooters fired autos, since the magazines held fifteen rounds—they needed only one reload per test. Tim would require four.

He held the .357 waist high and pointed to the right, both hands positioned on the stock, awaiting the swivel of the target. The interior dimmed until everything was dark but the floating silhouette, which remained semi-illuminated—low-light conditions to simulate night, when most shootings take place.

The target spun to face him. He'd sighted on the fist-size ring at the heart before it even finished its pivot, squeezing off six rounds. Thumbing forward the left-side lever, he released the well-lubed wheel, the spent casings sliding out as his fingers found a full speedloader in the pouch. Now he was in a tunnel—nothing existed except the weight of steel in his hands and the beckoning ten-ring. The gun barked six more times, and he tipped and reloaded, tipped and reloaded, casings raining at his feet, cordite spooling up from his booth in tendrils.

After firing off his thirtieth shot, he emerged as if from a daze, the overheads coming on, the target whistling uprange. A quarter-size hole penetrated the middle of the ten-ring, a few tattered chads dangling from the near-perfect O. A hushed murmur came up from the row of deputies at the wall.

Tim pulled off his glasses, thanked the range operator, and headed out with Dray into the blinding light of the afternoon.

They reached his car, Dray still squinting. "Show-off." She lowered the volume on her portable radio. "I have to get back out. What's the latest?"

She listened impassively to his account of the morning, then said, "And you lost your wedding ring?"

"Right." He retrieved it from his back pocket and slid it on.

She gave him a humorous scowl. "I'd better not find out you spent the morning cruising gay bars."

"The ones I go to, the wedding ring's a real draw."

"Cute." She held up an index finger to Mac, now awaiting her at the squad car. The trainee waved to Tim on his way back into the station. "Prowling a college campus for kids leaving therapy." Dray ran her hand through her hair, pinching a hank at the top so it arced forward in two wedges, brushing her cheeks. "They've got their system down, don't they?"

"It's a long con, really. They bilk kids out of their minds, then out of their money." Tim shook his head. "First rule of swindling—use people against themselves."

"Hitting a bit close to home?"

Tim pulled on his sunglasses and braced himself. "I'm thinking I might talk with him."

Dray released her hair, letting her arm slap to her side.

Tim waited. She added nothing to the disheartened gesture. "What?"

"I didn't say anything."

"He's got a pro's perspective on it all. Frauds, cons, scams, rackets, schemes."

"That's for sure." She stared at him through his sunglasses. "He's quicksand, Timothy. Make sure you keep one foot on solid ground."

Mac's piercing whistle snapped her head around, and she turned to start back to her patrol car.

*T*he old beige Cadillac Seville parked in the gravel lot told Tim he'd found his mark.

The shack had every order of car stereos and speakers embedded in its carpeted walls, a-thrum with the bass vibrations of the latest emissary for window-tinted low riders and Sunset club junkies. Spray-paint depictions of stereos dotted the plywood exterior, suspended in white clouds like the loot-filled imaginings of an acoustically minded cartoon burglar. A slight scan of the binocs brought the subject himself into focus, visible near the back door, his clean-pressed slacks and calm, pacifying gestures distinguishing him instantly from the animated, grease-stained mechanic and the flustered consumer.

He placed a hand on the customer's arm and steered him down into his vehicle, all the while his lips moving slow and steady. He waved as the car pulled out, the driver looking slightly confused but appeased.

Tim crossed Lincoln Boulevard in a jog and stole up on the shack. He tracked a man in a Nike jumpsuit to the door, then waited outside, hidden from view. The oppressive sound systems had been turned down, so Tim was able to hear the voices within.

"—six-and-a-half MB Quart component speakers," said the familiar voice. "You want to install it yourself, it'll void warranty, but I could let it go cheaper."

"How much cheaper?"

"Ricardo! How much are those new MB Quart separates we just got in?"

The mechanic's shout from the back was partially drowned out by the whir of his drill. "Five hundred."

"Four hundred dollars. You heard the gentleman. I can't do any better than that."

Tim leaned his head back against the cheap plywood, smiling. The man hurriedly paid and scampered out, the steal of the century boxed in cardboard and clasped beneath an arm.

Tim stepped through the doorway, and the man looked up. "Timmy."

"Dad."

"Nice deaf routine."

His father smiled and tilted his head gracefully. "I like to see people happy. And it does move product." He folded his hands, bringing them to rest at his waistline. "How'd you find me? Let me guess—you talked to my nanny."

Tim nodded.

"I'm sure my lowly parole officer couldn't dish the dirt fast enough for the great Tim Rackley. You came to gloat? Celebrate your old man's fifth release from the Crossbars Hotel?"

"I didn't know you were out. You been on paper a month?"

"Give or take. I got dinged on a 470 in November, trying to pass forged deeds of trust for these lots up Las Flores. I flipped on a schmuck up the ladder for a reduced sentence—six months custody, half time knocked it to three. I served it concurrent with the three-month parole-board-violation sentence. All in all, not a bad deal, except for my parole clock. It reset like an egg timer. Another three years."

Tim glanced down. His father was wearing the sleek gray pants he'd had tailored so the right cuff flared; it concealed an electronic monitoring bracelet.

"You were so close this time."

"Yes, but these were beautiful forges."

His father was, as always, dressed and groomed impeccably—not a wrinkle in his slacks, not a stray hair. He outclassed the cheap surroundings as he generally did, a ghetto-bound prince. He'd been born an unplanned child to displeased older parents—his mother forty-eight, his father sixty-one. His mother had died giving birth to him, his father six dour years later. He'd been raised by an abusive older brother who, as far as Tim knew, was still alive—a successful banker somewhere in the Midwest. Tim's father referred to him as "the VIP" so consistently that Tim didn't know his uncle's given name.

Of his own mother, Tim recalled only that she had soft hands and a melodic voice; she'd figured out before Tim was four that she'd be better off without either of the men in her life and was just gone one afternoon when he'd come in from the backyard. She had not been mourned or mentioned thereafter—neither was permitted—though Tim did remember standing in her abandoned work space, running his hands over her drafting table as if part of her still resided there. He'd been brought up by a man who regarded him as a curiosity—a resolute boy bent on lawfulness even as he was being deployed as a prop in one elaborate con after another.

"How are you doing?" Tim asked.

"Well, thank you. A bit tired. Picking up trash beside the freeway at six A.M. wears one out, but at least I get to wear a stylish orange vest. Now and then when the stars align, the Petty Ones bestow graffiti-removal duties upon me. It's great fun." He smiled a pastor's patient smile. "Is there something I can help you with? I'm quite busy. As you can imagine, car stereos do a brisk business in these environs."

"Yes. I need . . . I'd like your help. With a case."

"Back behind a badge, are we?" He turned to the abbreviated counter and tapped on a primitive computer. "I don't much care to contribute to the greater glory of law enforcement."

"I want to know how you picked marks. For cons."

He paused, his interest piqued. He gave a quick glance over his shoulder, but Ricardo was banging away on a dashboard in the back. "Depends on the con."

"How can you tell if someone has money?"

"A rich mark? I'm not sure. At this stage of the game, I just sense it."

"Well, think for a moment. If you had to break it down."

He nodded, a thoughtful frown wrinkling his face. As Tim had hoped, he couldn't resist showing off. "Well, you don't look at name brands. Not on clothes at least. Shoes sometimes, more with men—a woman will take out a second mortgage on her trailer to buy a pair of Jimmy Choos. Bulky-wallet guys are broke, generally. Money clips aren't. Mesh baseball caps—no money. White caps with curved bills—money. Check a shirt—has it been dry-cleaned? Are the lines crisp? Nice pens. Rich people have nice pens. Look for the snowy cap of a Montblanc, the cursive swoop of a Waterman. And watches, but not middle quality. Anyone can be gifted a Movado or a Tag for a birthday, a graduation. You want to look for Baume & Mercier, Breitling, high-end Omega, Cartier if they're nuevo."

"What else with new money?"

"They dress just wrong. A little too hip, like a divorcée in a singles bar. They reek of desperation. They've gotten ahead of themselves and see the long drop down."

"Other ways to tell rich marks in general?"

"Ask what their fathers do. I know—one of your childhood sore spots. Kids like you will cower from questioning. But those whose daddies are doctors and judges will perk their ears and bark. Richness begets richness, and affluent spawn may feign contrived humility, but if pushed right, they aren't afraid to own up fast and proud." He closed his eyes for a moment, lost in pleasant remembrances. "There's something in the movement, in the posture, that can't be taught—a smug self-assurance that's one of the many side effects of an entitled childhood." His eyes opened, held their gaze. "You move like a rich man, Timmy."

"Must have been my privileged childhood."

"Must have been." His father pressed his lips together, making them disappear. "The main trick to conning, I'd say, is circumventing people's thinking. You want them to respond instinctively, to salivate at the bell."

"Give me an example."

"Okay. A mark comes in here, he wants a stereo and speakers. What do I sell him first?"

"The stereo."

"The stereo. Why?"

"Because in contrast to it, the speakers will seem cheaper."

He smiled, pleased. "That's right. We sell him a two-thousand-dollar head unit first. After that, what's eight hundred for speakers? Besides, you can't enjoy the two-thousand-dollar stereo without them. Then you load him up with even cheaper accessories he doesn't need. It's all chump change now, Constant Buyer, in comparison. Just you try running a mark *up* the ladder. If you start with a thirty-buck CD-cleaner kit, the sheep are already thinking, 'My goodness. That's a whole dinner at Claim Jumper.' You don't want to climb that ladder. No, sir." He ran a hand across his clean-shaven face. "Of course, this sales scheme's old hat now—Christ, they teach it on Rodeo—but I knew it back when. I knew it like I know how to smell people. Like I know how to get into their brains."

"Or their wallets."

"There's a difference?" He paused, his posture flawless, his hands clasped behind his back. "Where do you think you got it? Your schoolteachers adored you. Your commander in the army took you under his wing. The marshal himself hung the Medal of Valor around your neck—you'd think you won the biathlon at Lillehammer. Do you think you got by on natural smarts and talent?" A smile warmed his features; even approaching sixty, he was still more handsome than Tim. "You know the angles. The well-timed favor. The chuck on the shoulder. Dropping heat-seeking flattery. You know how to read the river, just like me." When Tim didn't rise to the bait, he arched a silver eyebrow. "Why all this interest? Considering a career switch?"

"Background information."

"Mugsy and I used to run a lucrative ruse out in La Cañada that might be of interest. The mark can be anyone, really, but we had an easier go with elderly folk living alone. Widows are always good. I'd throw on a three-piece suit, and Mugsy would dress as a bank guard. I'd hit the mark around four o'clock, tell her I'm a professional bank examiner and her account has shown a few concerning irregularities. I have a culprit in mind, a crafty teller who's been doctoring transactions in certain accounts. I furnish him with a Jewish name. To be safe, would she mind going to the bank and withdrawing her savings so our team of highly qualified individuals can monitor the transaction as it crosses the culprit's desk?"

His tone, even now, exuded authority and reasonableness. "She pulls out her life savings and brings it home in a cab we furnish. I wait with her maybe a half hour, share some small talk over coffee. That's when Mugsy arrives. He tells her the culprit showed his hand and was arrested. Her account was straightened out, fortunately, and now it's safe from any future tampering. Our anxious widow is relieved beyond words. Since by now the bank is closed, I instruct Mugsy to return her money to the vault. We're back at the house splitting green before angina strikes." He moistened his lips with the tip of his tongue. "What's that face? Do I disgust you?"

Tim looked away, unsettled as always when confronted with his father's talent.

"Well, before you get too swept away in moral indignation, let me remind you of this: Those schemes fed you every meal of your childhood." His tone, as always, remained conversational, as calm as a flatline. "They dressed you, paid for your school supplies, afforded you the bed in which you slept every night. There's a little piece of me in you—in everyone, actually, but especially in you. It's in my DNA, packed into every one of your angry little cells."

Revulsion rose in the back of Tim's throat. A familiar flavor—the same he'd grown up with.

"Beware pride, Timmy. It's the most dangerous trait. We are low creatures. If we're foolish, we hold self-illusions. If we're smart, we use others' self-illusions against them."

"Fortune-cookie insert?"

"Need I remind you pride landed you in your own little quagmire last year?"

"My daughter being murdered might have had something to do with it, too."

"True. Quite true. How is Andrea?"

"Fine."

"Send her my regards."

"I will. We finally cleaned out Ginny's room . . ." Tim paused, stupidly anticipating some response but drawing only a slightly bored gaze. His capacity for expecting change in his father staggered him in its imperviousness to data. No matter how much he'd toughened into adulthood, some hardwired hope still flickered, the glow of a pilot light. He remembered, too late, Dray's warning.

His father's face sharpened, as if Tim's words had just sunk in. "You know what might go well in there? Your mother's old drafting table."

"You still have it?"

"Yes, but it's up in the rafters. A hassle to get down."

"I could take care of that."

"It's worth some money."

Tim took a moment to respond, his face burning. "I could pay you for it."

A pristine Lexus screeching into the lot drew his father's attention—more pressing matters at hand. The plate frames broadcast a Beverly Hills dealership. A tanned man in a crisp suit popped out and headed for them, a mascara-heavy girl-friend trailing in his wake.

To Tim's surprise, his father turned away from the approaching customer, absorbed in some paperwork. He slid a pair of eyeglasses from a drawer, an odd move given his 20/15 vision.

"Excuse me. *Excuse me.*"

Tim's father glanced up over the rims of the lenses. "Yes?"

The man stood with his legs slightly spread, suit fabric pulling tight at the biceps. The girlfriend arrived, a bit winded, and took up what appeared to be her customary post behind his shoulder.

"I'm looking for an Alpine ALD 900. The guy my dealer outsources to can't get his hands on one. Can you?"

Tim's father's eyes returned to the folder before him. "Pardon me for saying so, sir, but that's an extremely exclusive line. Perhaps I could recommend something a bit more . . . reasonably priced?"

Head bowed, Tim took his leave, heading out into the morning blaze. Behind him he heard the customer's raised voice. "Why don't you get it for me and let me worry about what I can afford?"

And his father, setting the hook with newly realized chagrin—"Right away, sir."

Fourteen

Tim asked Dray to join him for his six o'clock drive to Hidden Hills. They tangled in traffic at Thousand Oaks, lurching along beside a glossy red Ferrari with an Angels flag snapping from the rear window. Tim worked his lip between his front teeth, and Dray watched the scenery inch by, letting him muse. Between Top 40 hits on 98.7, Ryan Seacrest bemoaned his dating life.

Though growing up with a despotic father, an expended mother, and four older brothers hadn't been a breeze through the express lane, Dray had a perception about family matters that far exceeded his own—one of the reasons he wanted her with him at the Hennings'. Plus, as a sheriff's deputy, she had a stronger handle on state law.

The Hennings' house, an enormous Spanish colonial with pantile roofing, abutted an equestrian arena. The solid-core oak door, buttressed by strips of hammered iron, opened to a vaulting foyer and a displeased man with the size and bearing of a WWF grappler.

"Help you?" His nose, flattened and asymmetrical, suggested a history guarding club doors or encountering hockey boards. Black hair shorn in a buzz cut didn't widen his casting options. The Mickey Mouse voice, so discordant given his build, tipped Tim that this was the spirited caller he'd hung up on earlier in the day. One of Will's *men*.

"Yes, Tim and Andrea Rackley here to see Will." Tim's proffered hand hung in the air for a moment before he withdrew it.

The man stepped back, letting them enter. He walked with a slight limp, a cocker spaniel materializing to scurry alongside him. His body language suggested he was not a dog person. Tim and Dray followed him across a wide stretch of ceramic tiles into an expansive kitchen area. A wall of floor-to-ceiling windows overlooked an unrestrained lawn. Perched on two barstools pulled up to a granite-topped island, Will and Emma were finishing an early dinner. Though the meal seemed casual enough, Emma wore a conservative dress, stockings, and slingbacks. Perusing the *Hollywood Reporter,* Will foiled her in a velour jogging suit, royal blue with an embroidered *F* prominently displayed.

"Rooch Banner," Will said proudly, his game-show-host sweep of the arm acknowledging the low-grade butler. "Maybe you recognize him. He had a half season with the Rams."

Tim's apologetic shrug probably didn't help him with Rooch in the rapport department. Dray admired the photos adhered to the Sub-Zero—Will lying on his back flying the baby above him, the baby dressed as a sunflower for her first Halloween, a weary postpartum Emma snuggling the baby in a loaf of pink blanket.

Will drained a glass of vivid green liquid. To Dray's bemused stare, he said, "Blue-green algae. Antioxidants," then threw down his napkin and rose. Rooch set about clearing the plates as Will gestured them down a hall. They passed a palatial Pilates room and a home theater with rows of cushioned seats, finally descending into a sunken living room rimmed with couches and adorned with energetic one-sheets of films Will had produced.

Will sank down and patted the cushion. "C'mere, pooch."

The dog leapt up and curled under his arm. It yapped a few times, tail wagging. Emma snapped her fingers at it irritably.

Will rose and headed for a bar in the corner. A framed picture showed Leah in high-school-graduation garb, a pair of boxers and a smiley-face T-shirt peeking out beneath the gown. She was flashing the peace sign and smiling at someone out of the photo's span. It would take a strong-willed kid to argue that outfit past Emma. Tim wondered whether

Leah's unorthodox attire explained why the photo was consigned to the bar. His mind moved to the baby's pictures proudly displayed on the refrigerator.

Will dug into an ice bucket that Tim noted was kept packed. "Drink?"

"I'm fine."

"Vodka rocks," Dray said.

Will poured her an alcoholic's fill, which he matched in his own glass.

Emma took the opportunity to shoo the cocker spaniel from the couch. The dog took off, probably in search of Rooch, his reluctant playmate.

Will handed Dray her drink, then threw a glance at his Cartier. "Nice of you to make it."

Tim ignored the sarcasm. "No problem."

"Would it be rude of me to ask why your wife decided to tag along?"

"We want her brain on this. She's smarter than me."

A petite cry echoed down the tiled hall. Will and Emma tensed until the baby was soothed into silence by an unseen retainer. Mrs. Rooch?

Will sat back down on the couch. "Marco informed me you were reinstated. As I promised earlier, I'm happy to pay you an additional stipend on the side."

"Thanks, but I can't accept."

Will's eyebrows rose. He settled back with a faint grimace, regretting lost leverage or just upset at not getting his way. "Why don't you fill us in on your progress?"

Tim caught them up. Emma wept quietly for a few moments when he related the likelihood that Leah had moved into the cult home. Will let her cry on his chest as Tim finished.

"She needed more from me." Emma blew her nose into Will's handkerchief. "After her father died, I tried to be both parents—too indulgent, then too restrictive. For the past three months, I've replayed in my head everything we might have done differently. Sending her off to camp crying, and—"

"Emma," Will said gently, "you're making yourself crazy."

Because he would have preferred to address Leah's current position, Tim found Emma's self-flagellation to be wearing. It hit him that her reaction held up an unflattering mirror to his own manner of grieving.

Emma's exhale puffed out her cheeks. "I just wish I knew what could drive her to do something this foolish."

"We can address that once she's in our hands," Tim said. "Right now we need to focus on getting her back."

"How old is the baby?" Dray asked.

"Seven months."

Will said, "What the hell does that have to do with anything?"

Dray looked at him squarely. "Mrs. Henning is speculating about Leah's motivations. Leah's interest in the cult would seem to have followed the baby's arrival."

Will threw a glance at Tim. "What's the plan from here?"

"I'm hoping this is Leah's cult, but I'm still going off guesswork at this point. If she's there, I'll see if I can isolate her and persuade her to come with me. If she's not, I'll pump the others for information, get some names and leads."

"You'll find out who the bastard leader is. Can't you go after him? Cut the head off the beast?"

"It's not the quickest route, and time is of the essence. Plus, I'm not tasked with going after the entire cult. Just with finding your daughter."

Crunching ice, Will seemed to wrestle with his appetite for revenge. Finally he said, "Just get her home so we can take things from there."

Tim thought of Rooch Banner, Will's impatient rustling, the well-scrubbed tile of the kitchen. Not the warmest home to return to.

"Kidnapping our own daughter," Emma said tearily. "What has this come to?"

"I'm not kidnapping her," Tim said. "I'm taking her into custody. Think of it as a covert arrest."

Dray's head cocked. "On what grounds?"

"Grand theft auto."

"Pretty thin for a federal arrest. Plus, then what? You gonna charge her? Out of the cult and into jail? Sounds like a brainchild hatched in our fine federal bureaucracy, all right."

"We don't have to charge her, Dray."

"So just arrest her on trumped-up charges and violate her rights."

Tim took a deep breath, letting the mood in the room settle. "I'm hoping to come across something stronger. Evidence of Leah's being in imminent danger"—at this, Emma emitted a choked little sob—"or a 5150, danger to self."

"You can't make that determination," Dray said. "What, are you gonna smuggle in a psychiatric-evaluation team under your trench coat?"

Emma studied her through bleary red eyes. "How about abuse charges?"

"*Adult* abuse isn't illegal."

"What do you mean?"

"There's no adult-abuse statute. If there was, we'd have to run out and arrest anyone who's ever tried S&M. Whatever Leah's doing, it sounds like it's consensual. We've got assault and battery, but those require a victim pressing charges, which doesn't sound likely in this case." Dray shot Tim a glance. "This isn't news to you—you know how shitty conviction rates are when battered women back down."

Will smacked his palm on his knee. "So what *do* you propose? We just leave her in this cult?"

"Yes. I understand you're frustrated that you can't persuade her to leave, but she's an adult. Just because you have money doesn't give you the right to use other means to remove her." Dray moved her focus to her husband. "Come on, Tim. Let's call it like it is. I shouldn't have to remind you all that nothing illegal has taken place here." She gestured at Will with her glass. "There's a reason you're not sending Roach—"

"Rooch."

"—to do your bidding. There's a reason Tannino's using a freelancer for the job, and there's a reason he's using my husband." She softened her voice. "You're making some moves to get your daughter safe. Christ, with what we've been through, I can certainly relate. I'm not a saint, I'm not a priss, and I'm not a DA. I'm just recommending we all stay very aware of the game we're playing here. If my husband extracts your daughter, his ass is the one on the line when the spin doctors scrub in."

"That's not going to happen. Whatever you do, you won't have any legal problems. That I can assure you."

Dray was on her feet. "With all due respect, Mr. Henning, you can't make that promise." She set her half-full glass on the bar and left the room.

Will chuckled. "No shrinking violet, that one."

"No, sir."

"So how about the P.O. box? You make any progress with the inspector?"

"Let's just say he gave new meaning to the term 'going postal.' "

Will's hearty laugh filled the room.

"I'd like to implement some small, sustainable disguise elements, on the off chance someone in the cult recognizes me from the news footage last year," Tim said. "We usually pull a professional from the movie studios, but with the time frame—"

Will brightened. "I'll have the hottest new makeup-and-hair guy in town at your house first thing tomorrow morning. Nine o'clock okay?" He killed his vodka, plunked the glass on a side table. "When all this is through, I'll get you some Lakers tickets. On the floor. Right by Jack." He waited for Tim to stand. "Rooch will see you out."

Rooch had materialized above the steps, one hand clasping the other at the wrist. Tim paused on his way out, then turned back to Will. "Give me your watch."

"Nice line reading. I'll call you when we start casting."

"The Service issues replicas. The guys I'm swimming with might know the difference."

Though Emma made a displeased face, Will slid the Cartier off his wrist and tossed it to Tim. "That's a thirty-thousand-dollar watch. Keep your eye on it."

"I'll be sure to."

Rooch didn't speak to Tim on the long walk out.

Dray was sitting in the passenger seat. She winked at him when he got in. "I don't know about these freelance gigs, Timothy. Your track record is for shit."

Tim pulled out and drove a few blocks. "You're right. What you said in there."

They passed out of the community under a wood arch proclaiming ADIÓS AMIGOS.

"Their home should be beautiful, but it just feels cold and antiseptic. They want the dog on the couch, off the couch, in the room, out of the room—imagine how'd they'd be as parents." Dray let her breath out sharply through her teeth. "Emma's anxiety runs that house. It runs Will, too. Families portion out emotion—I'd say her whining wouldn't leave much room for a daughter to have normal growing-up difficulties. That would undermine Mother's martyrdom." Dray spoke bitterly—her own mother had enjoyed a familial monopoly on suffering.

"I'd guess Leah was an inconvenience to them."

"I'd bet her job was to be quiet, easy, and invisible. And I'd bet she didn't easily fit the bill."

The traffic had lightened significantly. As they drove north, Tim reflected on his visit with his father. He'd learned at a young age that opening up had its costs—it left too much of himself to protect. And so he'd learned to seek sustenance elsewhere, to generate it from within, to remain tightly and serenely wound into himself.

This strategy had aided him when he enlisted and was called upon to kill other men.

"These aren't people to be downstream from," Dray said.

"They have as much concern for you as they did for the late Danny Katanga. All they want is someone to bring in their daughter. Keep their house looking tidy. If that goes wrong, they'll be looking for someone to blame."

"But my reputation leaves me beyond reproach."

She laughed. "You're doing your Wile E. Coyote creep off the cliff right now. All I'm saying is, make sure you pack a parachute."

Fifteen

*I*n the back of the Growth Hall, Stanley John was beating the kettledrum, which sent a low, anesthetizing vibration through Leah's bones. It made her job—unstacking folding chairs—easier. She moved through her work rhythmically, like a dancer. The backs of her arms were purpling with the bruises.

Lorraine and Winona scrambled around on all fours buffing the lacquered wood. A converted gymnasium from the adolescent facility, the Growth Hall featured a high-tech lighting system, basketball court lines, and a stage. Rewarded for his progress on the Web site, Chris wielded a measuring tape to calculate the space between seating.

TD paced the growing aisles, his usual preshow warm-up, his eyes riveted on the checklist in front of him. He barked his shin on an out-of-line folding chair.

Stanley John stopped beating the drum. The tape recoiled back into the metal square in Chris's puffy hand. The gym fell silent.

TD glanced down at the wayward chair and then at Chris, who did not rise from his knees.

Dots of sweat rose on Chris's forehead. "I'm sorry. I take ownership of my incompetence—"

TD spoke with a calm, honey-coated intensity. "Maybe you can't step up to this task. Maybe measuring the distance between two chairs is too much for you."

"I'm sorry. I'm just a little distracted. I was up all night fussing with the hyperlinks—"

"Well, that's a ready batch of answers. Looks like we've backslid into excuse making. What's our friend Chris need to do, folks?"

"Negate victimhood."

TD brushed Chris's hair out of his eyes. "I think we need to reset your preferences for humility. You can start by unclogging the methane bleeders at the septic tank tomorrow."

Chris's eyes clenched shut. "Thank you, Teacher."

"Where's your wife?"

"Over here, TD," Janie called out with a smile. Her dark, stiff jeans, tight around her firm behind, struck a contrast with her baggy pink sweater. She finished dumping another five-pound bag of sugar into the vat of punch while another helper stirred away.

"Come."

Janie walked over and stood obediently before him, arms at her sides.

"Does your husband default to victimhood, Janie?"

She looked from TD to Chris, then back to TD. "He has lapsed Off Program a little lately."

TD nodded severely. "On the other hand, in the past few weeks, you've closed on"—he turned a half circle and raised his voice—"more Neos than anyone else." His applause was picked up by the others. Still on his knees, Chris clapped along with them. "Not like Sean and Julie, whose numbers have been down." Dark looks from all directed at the laggards. "Chris, give your wife the tape measure. That's it."

Chris raised it to his wife's waiting hands. TD cupped his palm on the ridge of Janie's hip, just above the back pocket of her jeans. Chris's eyes were riveted to TD's gently squeezing fingers.

Janie smiled, basking in TD's glow.

"Others have found it easier to work without a bulky sweater on," TD said.

Her eyes fixed on his, Janie pulled the sweater off over her head, revealing a fitted undershirt through which her nipples showed slightly. TD nodded, pleased, and resumed his pacing. The hall fell back into motion.

Chris rose and sulked in a rear corner, his eyes beady and small above his too-wide cheeks. Leah was relieved TD didn't take note, for something had changed in Chris's eyes, and it was a change he would not have liked.

She pulled the next chair off the stack and handed it to a young graphic-design guru whose name she'd forgotten; he snapped it open and slid it down the assembly line.

TD strolled beatifically through the flurry of activity, his focus never leaving his notes.

"Teacher, do you want the cookies arranged on the trays flat or stacked?"

His eyes stayed on his checklist. "Flat."

Another worker—"I cut my finger pretty good. Can I get a ride to the ER so I can get it looked at?"

"No. You can visit Dr. Henderson in Cottage Three after the Orae."

"TD, I really want to have sex with my wife. It's been almost three weeks."

"Fine. After the Orae. Missionary. In her cottage. Fifteen minutes."

"Thank you. Thank you."

"My father died. The service—"

"Stop crying."

"I'm sorry. The service is twenty minutes away. Can I have money for a bus ride?"

"Leave the dead to bury the dead."

"Will you let me grow a beard, Teacher?"

"Enough, please. I'm trying to prepare."

All talking ceased, the silence broken only by the quiet rustling of the workers.

Leah snapped a chair open, pinching her thumb in a hinge. She bit her lip so she wouldn't cry out, her eyes watering. The pain pulled her from her working trance, and she stepped outside. To her right alongside the building, three pay-phone handsets nestled in their hooks, severed cords protruding stiffly beneath them.

Down the curved road, lights twinkled in the cottages. To her left beyond a fence and a strip of fire-retarding ice plant, a cliff fell away. In the night the abrupt drop was a void. The cold bit her through the thin cotton of her jersey. She thumbed the fabric. Will had brought her the shirt back from location somewhere, a gift without an occasion.

"Leah? What are you doing out here?" Janie's voice yanked her from her thoughts. "You know better than to skulk around alone. Hurry now, or you'll throw off TD's concentration for the Orae."

Leah mumbled an apology and followed her back inside, where the five-foot stacks of chairs waited.

All sixty-eight Pros, stoked with candy bars and punch, packed the seats, riding out a sugar high together. Everyone held hands, swayed, and babbled excitedly. Randall and Skate emerged from outside, Skate's hands glittering with dog slobber, and took up posts at the base of the stage. The drum started beating again. Leah went under its spell.

The overheads dimmed, the footlights came up, and plaintive trumpet notes announced the Orae's commencement. As the music resolved into the opening motif of *2001: A Space Odyssey*, TD burst onto the stage, a Janet Jackson mike floating off his right cheek. The thunderous sforzando chords faded, and then there was just the slow, rumbling beat of the drum and the Teacher's words.

"Out there in the world are the Common-Censors. The human husks. The living dead. They're all stuck in the dead links of their *Old Programming*. They're like the three little monkeys—*deaf, dumb,* and *blind*." TD's eyes seemed to take in every face. "Now, some people may say *I'm* kind of crazy. Some people might call me a *weirdo*. But I like that label." His lips firmed in a wise little smirk. "They say we're a *cult*." He made spooky fingers in the light, his smile indicating this was of great amusement. A mocking rumble rose from the crowd.

Randall and Skate stood like Secret Service agents before the stage, hands clasped at their belt lines, all-knowing by proxy.

TD paced back and forth, never breaking stride, the heads of the Pros following his movement as if attached by invisible threads. "Anyone see any *brainwashed cult members* in here? Anyone see any *animals ready for sacrifice?* Anyone here against their will?"

Screams of repudiation. Scattered boos and derisive laughter. Protective cries of indignation.

"*We're* not brainwashed—they are. Obligation has been *pounded* into them, *pounded* into their cells since they were babies. They criticize The Program. Why? Because they can't *believe* we're this *strong*. That we're this *fulfilled*. They *have to* criticize us. In fact, their criticism is *proof* of how right The Program is."

A number of cries, the words wildly enthusiastic but unintelligible. Leah reeled, unsteady on her feet. The hall zoomed around her, a slow-motion tilt. She caught a glimpse of Chris in the back, crouching beside his chair, his sharp and lucid expression standing out from a sea of softened faces.

Shrieks of laughter. Her head buzzing with sugar, her eyes still adjusting to the dimness and the flickering lights, Leah felt her lungs inflate, her mouth open, her sides shake, and then she realized she, too, was laughing.

"Here"—TD's arms drifted out, shadows consuming the upward drift of the footlights—"we live in the Now."

Janie chattered next to Leah. "Living in the Now. That's so brilliant. It's so crucial to growth."

The drum continued its measured beat. Leah felt herself swaying with the crowd, with the cadence of TD's words. His sentences flowed into one another, rivers merging.

"We negate Victimhood. Those who *can't* need to—" He stopped abruptly, touched a hand to his ear.

"*Get with The Program!*" they roared.

"We are a *powerhouse* of resources. Attorneys. Investment bankers. Computer engineers. Recruitment is on the rise *every day.* Cambridge and Scottsdale will be ready to launch by the end of next month. All of our future ambassadors are *right here* among us."

Janie crossed her fingers, squeezed her eyes shut.

"It all starts here. Here in our *utopia.* This will be the model for all of California, then the U.S.A., then the world. But no matter how we grow, it all comes back to us here in this room. That's *you.* And *you.* And *you.* Why don't you all give each other hugs? That's right, stand up and embrace one another." TD waited, hands clasped.

A few of the wiser Pros remained seated, grinning knowingly.

"Come *on,* folks. If you want that self-help, feel-good crap, go to a Tony Robbins seminar and Awaken the Idiot Within. We don't *need* the Common-Censors. We don't need Deepak Chopra and his platitudinous spit-up. We each have within ourselves the potential to do *anything.* In The Program we don't even *need* each other. But we're stronger together." TD came to a halt onstage. "*Now*"—a darker tone—"in the past a few people have left the Inner Circle."

Murmurs. Leah was going hoarse.

"And they haven't had an easy go of it. Because once you've been *fulfilled*, once you've been part of this *great practice*, you can't turn your back on it. What's happened to those who have left the security of the Inner Circle?"

Leah's cheeks were wet; she couldn't stand the thought.

"They've gone *insane*, literally *insane*, stranded out there with the Common-Censors." TD's voice grew deep and sorrowful. "They've been *abused. Abandoned. Controlled.*" The footlights glowed through his hair like a golden hood. "Many of you remember Lisa Kander."

Boos and shrieks. TD's hand snapped up vigilantly, fingers spread, stealing five streams of light and shooting them to the ceiling. The noise ceased. "Let's be fair. She wasn't a *bad* girl. She just couldn't *make the grade*. She couldn't—"

"*Get with The Program!*"

And then, quietly, "I just found out she killed herself." A mournful pause. "She threw herself into the La Brea Tar Pits. Living out in the world, with *them*, was so hurtful, she asphyxiated herself with steaming tar."

Hushed silence, broken by a few gasps, even sobs. A row up from Leah, Winona was shaking so hard she seemed to be convulsing. One of the oldest Pros at forty-two, Winona had made sacrifices to Get with The Program, leaving behind a Common-Censor husband and infant twins. As a strong role model, she was accorded a special level of respect on the ranch.

TD fanned his arms, a gesture encompassing the entire hall. "None of you will ever have to feel that *emptiness*. That *loneliness*. That *abandonment*. Not as long as you stay On Program and with *The Program*."

A tidal wave of emotion. Squeaking chairs and undulating arms. A moment of disorientation as Leah's view was blocked, and then she rose to join the throng.

TD lifted his hands, and the sound ceased abruptly, as if a plug had been yanked. Everyone sat and held hands, rocking gently now in preparation for the Guy-Med. Leah's ears hummed.

TD's voice came calm and smooth. "Everybody close your eyes. Take a stroll back to your childhood. Remember your mind as it was. Free of your Old Programming. Empty of adult *cynicism*. Empty of adult *negativity*. Let TD guide you. Picture yourself at five years old. You're standing before your childhood room. Let's go inside. Go ahead—push open the door."

Leah felt her insides rear up as on a roller-coaster drop, then avalanche down and out of her, leaving her adrift in an intoxicating emptiness. When she came to, she felt drained. The formal part of the Orae was over. TD was sitting at the stage's edge, legs dangling, talking to the lucky Pros in the front row. She'd lost a lot of time, as she often did during meditation; Stanley John had told her it was a sign of her great sensitivity.

She never remembered what happened inside her childhood house during Guy-Med.

Squeezing past protruding legs, Chris made his way down the row, the others leaning sluggishly out of his way. Leah first thought he was heading for his wife, but the seat next to her was vacant; Janie was in the back replenishing the punch. Chris squatted in front of Leah, hands cupping her knees.

"Go away," Leah said. "You'll disrupt the Teacher if you're out of your seat when he's onstage."

Chris shot a nervous glance over his shoulder. "He's not looking. Just listen. I wanted to say I'm sorry for pinching you in the Wellness Train."

"You were right to. I needed it."

"No, it wasn't right." Chris's voice was rising. "It's not right for us to treat each other this way. It's not right to *be* treated this way."

Leah nervously regarded the others talking distractedly around them. "I don't know what you're talking about. It's our own growth."

He stood, flustered. "After TD scolded me, I thought about what you went through, then about my daughter from my first marriage. She's just a few years younger than you."

"It's fine. Chris, you're in a loop. Just sit down."

TD's voice boomed through the mike. "Yes, Winona?"

In the chair in front of them, Winona lowered her hand. Leah and Chris stared at the sprayed shell of blond hair in horror. "I experience Chris as undermining my time here tonight," she said.

Chris's whisper came garbled from his throat. "Please don't do this."

"I experience him as being negative about The Program, Teacher. And about you."

TD's voice, projected through the floor speakers, filled the entire hall. "That's okay. I'm open to criticism. Input, Chris?"

The certainty steeling Chris's posture just minutes before decayed. "No."

"Is that true, Winona?"

Winona's southern accent lent her words a haughty zing. "No. He's deflecting."

Leah felt TD's energy going away from her toward Chris and Chris alone. For a moment she thought the relief might send her unconscious again.

TD's voice assaulted them from the four corners of the room. "So you're willing to be negative to other Pros but not stand up for what you say. That's not a very *strong* position to take, is it?"

Chris shifted his weight, his eyes darting.

"I think I *angered* you when I took away the tape measure from you because of your *inability to do a job* and gave it to your beautiful younger wife. Did that anger you?"

The Pros pivoted in their seats.

"Answer him," Leah murmured, barely moving her lips. "Just give a response."

But Chris stood dumbly, legs shaking, watching some point on the floor between his shoes and the stage.

TD spoke so calmly Leah wondered why she imagined he was angry. "Control is your comfort, isn't it? You want to *control* how you're treated. You want to *control* this dialogue by not answering. You want to *control* your wife. This provides you *comfort,* but comfort doesn't interest us in The Program. *Strength* interests us. And you only get *strong* by rejecting *comfort.* I think you need some instruction in the matter. Janie? Where's Janie?"

Chris's flesh was a sickly, green-tinted hue, his face awash with sweat.

"Back here, Teacher!"

TD smiled at the crowd. "I think it's time we teach Chris about control."

Cheers of approval.

"I think Chris's unhealthy 'need' for his wife keeps him from maximizing his growth."

Clapping. Shouts. Boos.

"I think we should free Janie from his control."

"No." Chris's voice was barely a croak; Leah was sure she alone heard him.

"What do you say, Janie?"

"You know best, TD." She headed forward, her long hair swaying, brushing the back of her tight jeans.

"Stanley John, why don't you join Janie up here?"

Abandoning the kettledrum in the back, Stanley John strode down the center aisle.

TD helped them onstage and then stood between them, his arms spread across their shoulders. "Every time you confront a fear, you refuse to let it control you. That's the difference between your *Old Programming* and *The Program.* This, Chris, is for you." He kept his eyes trained on Janie's husband as he addressed the other two. "Go ahead. Undress her. Undress each other."

Leah felt delirious, drunk, hysterical with joy or terror.

She dropped her gaze as noises emerged from the crowd, sighs and grunts and shouts of encouragement. Everyone seemed to be breathing in unison. Chris staggered out into the aisle, barely making it before he dropped to one knee, his other leg bent behind him but not bearing weight.

When Leah glanced up, Winona's eager stance obstructed most of the spectacle, though she made out Janie's hands pressed palms down on the floor, the wispy sheet of her hair spread like a fan from her back to her extended arm. Stanley John labored behind her audibly, blocked from Leah's sight; she saw only the jeans and underwear bunched at his sneakers.

TD stood with his arms crossed, his eyes not on the scene before him but on Chris's crumpled figure in the aisle. Stanley John and Janie finished in a crescendo of gasps and then stood. Neither, Leah saw now, had fully disrobed. Janie rotated her jeans around the leg they'd tangled on, slid her other foot through, and pulled them up, her face red not with embarrassment but exertion. She stood unembarrassed, though a whole room had just partaken of her private, most guttural sounds. Through an evaporating haze of disbelief, Leah realized she was supposed to admire her for it.

Praise and affection rang out for Chris. Staggering up the center aisle, twisting one hand in the other like a limp kitchen rag, Chris bellowed something, his words lost in the ruckus and applause.

"You did it, man!" someone yelled. "You let go."

Winona was shrieking, her voice cracked and throaty. "You're both free now!"

TD twisted off his mike, smiled, and hopped from the stage.

Some of the viewers started to spill out of their rows. Others stayed, slumped and exhausted in the metal chairs.

Eyes narrowed, TD observed Chris's tedious progress toward the stage. Chris spotted him at the head of the aisle and yelled something else—Leah made out, ". . . people . . . the truth about you . . ."—then darted from the hall, banging through the doors into the night. Skate was already turning from his sentry's post at the base of the stage, his eyes somehow expressionless and inquisitive at once. TD nodded, a subtle dip of his chin. Then he turned, smiling. "The truth about me is what makes this work."

Skate moved to the exit. Before the door swung shut a second time, Leah saw the two Dobermans resolve from the darkness, black forms gathering around Skate's legs like the billow of a raincoat.

The celebration lasted until almost two. Leah chirped and giggled and ate candy, bouncing from foot to foot. Her memory went in and out. She remembered being pressed in a full-body hug by the muscular guy who helped unstack chairs—Chad—and she remembered it felt nice. She remembered holding hands with Winona, petting the sun-beaten skin of her forearm in sheer gratitude that she'd told only on Chris and not her. She recalled the remorse in Chris's eyes when he'd apologized to her, the way his features had seemed intent and broken all at once, and the image hit her so deep she felt the tears running even before she could remind herself she was crying with happiness.

After cleanup she walked back down to her cottage. Janie, flying high after TD's praise and her copulating with Stanley John, didn't even notice her solitary departure. The silhouette of a night bird drifted across the five spikes of the cedars. The smell of a distant skunk tinged the air. The night hummed with vitality, more than she'd ever felt in her nineteen years.

As she approached her cottage, a growl froze her stiff. Stretched in front of the door, one of the Dobermans raised his head, collar jingling, pupils iridescent with reflected light. Eyes trained on hers, he tipped his muzzle and resumed licking a moist paw. A sticky substance matted his legs, its color lost in the darkened fur. It was only against the pink contrast of the lapping tongue that she saw the ribbons of crimson.

The air felt at once inordinately cool. The dog groomed and rumbled, fixing her with his stare. She tried desperately to tamp down her spiraling fear, which she knew was radiating from her, an incitement to the dog. The sleek head pulled back on a muscular neck, ears on point. Flat, dead eyes studied her unblinkingly; the upper lip wrinkled away from the teeth.

She shrieked when an icy hand grasped the back of her neck. TD's voice purred over her shoulder. "Skate trained them to attack at the scent of blood." He chuckled. "Even the dogs around here don't like victims."

The Doberman rose, growling, but TD waved it back down. "Are you still bleeding, Leah?"

She shook her head, still too fearful to take her eyes from the dog.

"I think it might be nice for you to come back to my cottage."

*B*rambles crunching underfoot. The flutter of a bat overhead. Alone with the Teacher on a dark trail, weeds rising head high on either side of them.

Gathering her courage, Leah forced out the question. "Where did Chris go?"

"Chris couldn't handle The Program. Some people just aren't cut out for it. Like Lisa Kander."

"So . . . where did he go?"

TD turned to face her, still walking ahead, only a few inches taller than she was despite the lifts she'd found hidden in a box in the back of the shoe closet. She cringed, anticipating a burst of anger, but he just laughed. "What are you worried about? That I'd *injure* someone who didn't agree with me?"

"No . . . ?"

"Of course not. Skate just gave him a ride down the hill."

"Oh my God I'm so relieved I saw the dog and it was bloody around the muzzle and I should have known I'm so sorry for even thinking—"

"Sh-sh-shhhh. It's okay. I'm sure he just got into a squirrel or something. See how negativity can corrupt your thoughts?"

Her head nodded earnestly.

Nancy and Lorraine were waiting back at TD's cottage. They'd prepared his bed and laid out all his nighttime toiletries. He touched them each on the head, palm flat against their crowns. Smiling, Nancy scurried to the kitchen counter and presented a glass of mineral water and a tray laden with vitamins.

A former born-again and TD's first Lily, Lorraine shuddered, her plain features twisting. "Nancy, I *told* you vitamins were for the morning *only*."

Nancy's lower lip was already starting to tremble.

TD said, "It would be nice to have milk and strawberries."

Nancy scurried into the kitchen and emerged with a glass and another tray, strawberries arranged around the edge. TD washed down the first mouthful. Eyes on Nancy, he extended his red-stained fingers and dropped the strawberry's leafy hull. It hit the wood floor with a wet tap.

Balancing the tray, Nancy bent, wide knees cracking, and swiped at the floor with a napkin. As she rose, TD plucked another strawberry from the tray and bit into it. The hull landed about a foot from the last stain.

Tears started down Nancy's cheeks as she bent over. By the time she stood, TD had another strawberry poised before his mouth. A satisfied bite. She offered the trembling tray for his refuse, but he reached past it. Another wet morsel hit the floor.

Leah watched, her face hot.

Gasps escaped Nancy as she squatted again. She lost her balance and fell back, tray clanging off the plastic mail tub by the door. He extended the glass, gripping it with umbrellaed fingers at the rim, and released it. It shattered beside Nancy, splattering her with milk. Continuing to scrub with the dumb, repetitive gestures of a stuck pool cleaner, she started to sob, big blubbering cries.

TD said gently, "Negate victimhood."

Lorraine stepped forward and twisted the skin at the back of Nancy's arm. Nancy wept but made no effort to defend herself.

The door swung open, and Skate's broad shoulders filled the doorway, startling them all, even TD.

Streaks of sweat cut through the sheen of dirt covering Skate's arms. "Done."

"I think you're due for a reward." TD fanned his hand at the three girls. Having found her feet, Nancy picked bits of glass from the folds of the sadly outmoded denim dress that she'd worn so cheerfully to the Orae.

Skate's boots knocked on the wood floor. He paused beside Lorraine, eyeing her profile. She stared straight ahead, blinking hard. The color had left her cheeks. Another step brought Skate before Leah. A squint narrowed his brown eyes. He smelled of dirt and wet dog, and his knees were stained with soil. A sturdy finger rose from his fist, the knuckle caked with dried mud. It tapped her, leaving a stain on her shirt.

Leah felt no wave of revulsion, no horror, just the sucking of the void that had become her insides.

"No," TD said. "Anyone else."

Skate nodded, a thoughtful bounce of his head. He turned and studied Nancy's swollen face. His eyes dropped to her generous thighs, visible beneath the sweat-damp dress. He stepped to the side, a double tap of boot heel and toe, leaning to get an eyeful. He looked back at TD.

TD nodded at Nancy. "Go on."

Nancy's tears started again. Her voice was little more than a squeak. "I want to stay with you, TD."

"Go."

A meaty fist encompassed Nancy's considerable arm. Skate tugged, and she followed him out into the night. Her choked cries were audible all the way across the clearing. Then Skate's shed door slammed, and there were just the crickets.

TD stroked Leah's arm. "Come."

Lorraine sat down on an old love seat in the corner, pouting. On his way to the bedroom, TD told her, "I'd like my morning routine to go more smoothly than this."

He closed the door behind them and pressed a button on the wall-mounted stereo. A severed wire was all that remained of the radio antenna. As familiar music swelled, TD said, "Opera is one of four meaningful contributions mankind has made to the world."

She was too nervous to ask the other three.

He undressed by the side of the bed, his lean, sinewy muscles shadowed by the candles Nancy and Lorraine had dutifully lit before his arrival. He fell onto the bed, torso propped on silk pillows, an arm thrown back over his head just so. "You're stopped-up, Leah. Repressed. I've seen how you react to men. I want to lend you my body. You can experiment with me. Do anything that you want. TD wants to do this for you and your growth."

Through the speakers, a tenor moaned, "*La donna è mobil qual piuma al vento.*"

She felt impossibly small, a peasant girl before the throne. "I . . . I don't think I can."

"A normal woman would feel aroused. You're just holding back. Go on, give it a try. Put your mouth on me."

She shuffled forward, tiny steps on numb feet, but then doubled over clutching her stomach. "I can't."

His face creased. "It's this kind of behavior that got your dad killed from cancer."

"Wh . . . what?"

"You killed him by accident. I think you were always difficult and obstinate. I think dealing with you backed him up, stymied his development on a cellular level."

A dead weight tugged at her inside. "No. Don't say that. *No.*"

"If that makes you angry with me, too bad. Being nice doesn't interest me. I have more important responsibilities—to *reveal,* to provide *insight,* to *speak the truth.* If you want to stay with The Program, *listen, admit,* and *learn.* If you want to paddle around in your denial, go do it elsewhere. I can call Randall right now and have him take you back down the hill, just like he took Chris."

A flash of an image—the dog's moist muzzle—struck her.

"You can make your way out there if you'd like. Now, what's it gonna be? Well?"

Leah fought her lurching gut still. She crouched bedside and bent her head. TD leaned back among the opulent pillows and emitted the faintest of groans.

Sixteen

*W*hen Tim and Dray got back from their morning run, the light was blinking on the answering machine. Tim hit the button and lowered himself into a chair at the kitchen table.

Will's voice filled the room. "Listen, this stylist just got in from the Friedkin thing in Prague. Bill assured me he's the top of the A-list. He goes by Luminar—it's a one-name thing. Anyway, he'll be at your house at nine."

"Luminar," Dray said. "Top of the A-list. Christ help us."

The machine beeped again, presaging the second message. "Hello, Timmy. Listen, I gave some thought to our talk about your mother's drafting table. I thought perhaps we could have lunch and make arrangements. Give a call."

Tim stared at the quiet machine. "Maybe he does have blood moving through his veins."

Dray leaned on the counter. "When our child died, the man didn't send us a card. He left the funeral early, as if he had somewhere to be."

"I'm not putting him up for beatification."

"And besides"—Dray, once she picked up steam, was not easily derailed—"I don't want your mother's desk in there."

"The room is so . . . *empty.*"

"Maybe you shouldn't be so eager to fill it."

The doorbell rang.

"Goody," Dray said flatly. "That must be *Luminar.*"

When Tim opened the door, a dainty figure stood at the doorstep facing the street, one arm cocked in a V, cigarette holder and smoking butt leaning from a sharply bent hand. Porcelain skin, narrow shoulders, a sweeping kimono of some sort. The shock of red hair taken up in a silk scarf did little to provide Tim with gender cues.

"Nice neighborhood," a soft, decidedly male voice purred. "It's so *street.*"

Tim regarded the oversize metal box on the step distrustfully. "Luminar?"

"*Actually*"—the man swished around to face Tim, robe flaring, reddish eyes gleaming—"it's Lumin-*yae.*" He halted. His splayed arm dropped. He seemed to descend from tiptoes, lowering in his fabrics, the regality departing. In a completely unaffected masculine voice, he said, "Tim Rackley?"

Tim blinked to refocus on the spectacle before him. "Pete Krindon?"

"Oh, thank *God.*" Pete stormed past him, dumping his robe on the floor and snapping the cigarette from the holder. He sucked a deep inhale, eyes rolling with relief. "What the fuck are you doing, Rack?"

"You look like Liberace on the Zone and you're asking what *I'm* doing?"

Dray entered—a third baffled participant in the bizarre sketch. "Who's this?"

"Pete Krindon." Tim eyed him. "Or whatever name he's using this week. He's the surveillance guru Bear and I tap when we don't want to go through official channels."

"This guy? Luminar?"

"The *r* is silent," Tim and Pete said together.

Tim retrieved the makeup box and closed the front door. "What the hell are you into now?"

"Just doing this thing for this guy."

Pete Krindon, Master of Specifics.

"He wanted eyes on the inside. You'd be amazed the shit people tell stylists. Like, I really need to know who douches with Evian." Pete looked at Dray. "Sorry. Anyway, what better job for me? After working undercover all these years, I can run circles around the cosmopolitan-swilling pre-Stonewall stereotypes who call themselves makeup artists in Hollywood. They'd give their Jack Russell terriers for my skills."

Tim eyeballed his getup. "I'm doing some UC work myself. I've already made contact, so I can't show up a different person. I need some minor alterations, just enough that nobody I come across will recognize me from the media."

"Great shit, by the way," Pete said. "Last year. I was pleased to see you finally elected to pursue a more head-on means of conflict resolution." Tim couldn't adjust to the familiar voice issuing from the rouged face. "Okay. So we skew you a little. Who are you?"

"Thirtyish, earnest, wannabe hip, just came into some money."

Pete tapped a finger against his chin appraisingly. "Colin Farrell in *Phone Booth* meets Tobey Maguire in *Spider-Man*."

"Who are you working for?" Dray, occasional *Us* reader, had her interest piqued.

"That's not important." Pete's body suddenly transformed, limbs and joints angling to refashion Luminar's persona. "What *is* important"—a bored hand drifted out, finger swirling to spotlight Tim's sweats, T-shirt, year-old Nikes—"is that we get sister over here looking presentable."

Tim left the blue contacts at home and wore a baseball cap to hide his blond highlights and tweezed-back hairline, but his father's eyes zeroed in on the scruffy goatee right away. Pete had claimed that the facial hair would close off Tim's mouth and fill out his chin, and he'd shaped Tim's brows to alter the appearance of his eyes and forehead.

Tim's father rested his laced hands on the table, napkin in his lap, glass of water untouched, his stillness a mute criticism of Tim's three-minute tardiness.

Bracing himself for a put-down, Tim slid into the booth, nearly striking his head on a copper colander dangling from a ceiling hook. A clutter of wall-mounted black-and-whites showed hearty Italians sampling from tasting spoons, steering gondolas, whistling at girls. Franchise décor—Buca di Beppo by way of Pasadena. Tim's father had chosen the location, Tim assumed, to make convenient the retrieval of the drafting table from his nearby house.

They engaged in small talk until the entrées arrived, at which point his father steepled his fingertips over his steaming plate of linguini. "I'll tell you, Timmy. That community service is really wearing on me."

"I can imagine."

"You spoke to Carl. My P.O. That's how you located me, right?"

"That's right."

"How did you find him to be?"

Tim experienced the all-too-familiar sensation of getting lost in the labyrinth of one of his father's not-quite-hidden agendas. He answered warily. "Fine."

"He always liked you, didn't he?"

"I suppose so."

His father neatly cut up his chicken breast, drawing out the silence. "I thought maybe you could put in a word. You and he have some contacts higher up. I'd bet a few well-placed calls could get my hours reduced."

Tim pushed around his rigatoni with his fork; he'd yet to take a bite. "I don't think so."

"I see." His father took a sip of water, using his napkin to pick up the sweating glass. "You know, about that desk, I was thinking of holding on to it."

"Right."

"Memories of your mother." His father was studying him, his lips faintly curved to indicate the slightest touch of satisfaction.

Tim started to speak but caught himself. He shoved his rigatoni around some more until he could no longer contain the question. "Can I ask you something?"

"Of course, Timmy."

"Clearly you take some enjoyment in"—he gestured with his fork—"this thing we do. Like it's reprisal for something."

"That's not a question, Timmy."

"What did I do wrong to you? As a son?"

His father speared a cube of chicken breast and chewed it thoughtfully. "You acted superior. All the time. Like my brother. You and the VIP, birds of a feather. It was there, built into your personality"—his mouth twitched with remembered abhorrence, a rare show of emotion—"as soon as you could move or walk or speak. This indomitable superiority."

An affliction ancient to Tim arose from its buried confines. It enveloped him, tingling across his face, dampening his flesh, constricting his lungs.

"I endured enough of it for one lifetime at the hands of the VIP. I never thought I deserved to encounter it in my only offspring."

Tim's throat felt dry—the words stuck on the way out. "You weren't much of a father to me."

His father studied him intently. "You weren't much of a son to have."

Tim sat in silence as his father cut and chewed. When the waiter passed their table for the third time, Tim's father raised a single finger to him, then gestured for the bill. He crossed his utensils neatly on his bare plate and wiped the corner of his mouth with his napkin.

When the check arrived, he pulled his fake eyeglasses

from his pocket, set them low on his nose, and perused it. Removing the glasses and placing them beside his bunched napkin, he tapped his jacket pockets, then those of his pants.

Tim waited, knowing the routine.

"It seems I've left my wallet in the car. Would you mind?"

Tim may have nodded, he may not have. His father rose, administered a curt nod, and departed. Tim sat staring at his twinning reflections in the lenses of his father's forgotten prop.

Seventeen

A stack of hundreds money-clipped around a farrago of false identifications in the back pocket of his dark brown Versace corduroys, Tim eased up to the curb in a school bus–yellow Hummer H2. He left his wedding band in the glove box beside his .357—he couldn't risk revealing a gun beneath his loose-fitting Cuban day shirt. The pale line around his finger worked nicely for pitiable Tom Altman, who, despite a hairline that climbed high at the part, was striving fretfully to reclaim his youth in the aftermath of an unsolicited divorce.

It was a long step down before his light tan ostrich Lucchese roper hit pavement, and then he was strolling to the Encino apartment complex, a colossal stretch of building that took up the entire block. The outfit he wore, chosen by an embarrassingly animated Luminar from a variety of posh boutiques on Sunset, cost more than Tim's entire so-called wardrobe.

His genuine discomfort in the clothes, which were slightly too young and laboriously hip, contributed to the aura of susceptibility he was hoping to convey. His father's faux glasses topped off the ensemble, lending his face a nerd-banker's cast.

Winding through the endless halls, he came upon Shanna outside the apartment. When she saw him, she reached quickly for the doorbell, clearly self-conscious that he'd caught her standing by the door working up her nerve.

"This place is a maze. It's good to see a familiar face." She angled her head, taking him in. "You look good. New haircut?"

Before he could respond, Julie pulled the door open, her grin accompanied by a waft of scented candles. In the modest living room behind her, Lorraine and about ten others lounged on pillows and cushions on the floor.

No Leah.

Julie spoke in a hushed voice that connoted they'd interrupted something of great importance. "Tom, Shanna, glad you could make it."

Shanna picked up her whisper. "Hey, Julie."

Julie clutched their hands and tugged them inside, nodding at the stack of shoes on the square of tile that passed for the entranceway. Tim wordlessly removed his boots, Shanna her sandals.

"Excuse me," Julie said, her voice still lowered respectfully. "I'd like to introduce you all to some new friends. Tom is a *very* successful businessman"—a low hum of impressed voices—"and Shanna's a very cool girl we met."

The others, all in their late teens and early twenties, rose to greet them. Handshakes were coupled with lots of friendly touching—elbow grasps, rubs on the back by the girls, shoulder squeezes by the guys. They smiled continuously, enigmatically, as if sharing a secret.

Tim felt a keen disappointment that Leah wasn't there. A small group of kids this age was easy to control—he could've flashed tin, thrown around some copspeak, and hustled her out the door before anyone knew what was going on.

A sleek black-ash table against the wall housed a few of the myriad candles and trays of cookies and drinks. No chairs or couches—just a lot of blank carpet and colorful throw pillows. Tim noted the sole bathroom off a short hall that terminated in a closed door.

Everyone milled around, snacking and focusing on the newcomers.

"So, Tom, we'd love to know more about you."

"Shanna, are you from here?"

"You remind me of my older brother."

"*Great* new goatee. You wear change well."

"You have the exact eyes of this childhood friend who I *loved*."

When Tim or Shanna spoke, an awed hush filled the room. Lots of eye contact, sympathetic coos, encouraging exclamations. Tim couldn't readily distinguish between the other members—their intonations and facial expressions were remarkably similar. Though the responses were creepy and transparently manipulative, he had to confess there was also something pleasurable in being the center of such concerted attention. He felt buoyant and happy; his head hummed with a caffeine high.

His buzz was undercut by the sudden awareness that not only was he standing barefoot and mimicking the soft tones of those around him, but he was wearing a matching smile. He pictured Leah drifting into a room such as this, dissolving into the warmth and acceptance.

He excused himself to go to the bathroom, finding two crisp hand towels and three seashell soaps, all unused. On his way back, he peeked behind the closed door. A completely bare bedroom, as he'd suspected. Just a vacuumed square of carpet.

He returned to the group and mingled. When he tried to press Julie on specifics about the group, she smiled indulgently. "But we want to hear more about *you*."

Finally Lorraine interrupted the festivities, dinging a Cross pen against her water glass. She perched on her cushion with her flexible legs interwoven, a pose the others tried to mimic. When she faced Tim and Shanna, her entire bearing had changed. Her posture was tense, her facial muscles rigid, and her eyes had gone glassy, as if she were staring through them. Her speech was robotic, regurgitated, the intensity and volume lending a cadence different from her own.

"No matter how successful we are, we *all* have things in our lives that we're not happy with. Do you have things you're not happy with? Tom? Shanna?"

They nodded.

"Have you taken steps to change those things you're not happy with?"

"I guess not really." Shanna studied the floor, embarrassed. "I mean, I try things now and then, but none of them have really worked."

"Well, then you're giving those things the power to *control your life*. There's a colloquium that Julie and I have gone to that's given us some incredible insights. We'd really like your opinion on it."

Shanna fussed with a hangnail, her face uncomfortable.

"Do you want your insecurities to have power over you *forever?*"

Shanna kept her eyes lowered. "No."

"Well, by not going to this colloquium, you're doing just that."

Tim thought that a smart guy like Tom Altman might have a few objections at this point. "Is this colloquium the only way to avoid that?"

"Not at all. We just like you and want to share this with you. We're presenting a solution that could change your life and bring you a ton of fulfillment." She dealt with Tom's question but got right back to the script.

Julie picked up. "We figured you might appreciate a new option."

"I don't know. It just sounds a little like . . . I don't

know"—Tom Altman paused, fearful of alienating his new companions—"like you're recruiting us or something."

Flutters of laughter from around the circle. Not a hint of defensiveness.

"Like into a *brainwashing* cult?" Julie smiled.

"Well, I've heard those groups get people to go to seminars and stuff."

"And so do universities," Lorraine said. "That doesn't make them *cults*. And besides, if you look at it that way, *everything's* a cult. We all breathe air, so anyone who breathes air is in the *air-breathing cult*."

Tom Altman, wanting to be convinced, let the point go.

"This colloquium rocks. I'm telling you, it changed my life, gave me direction. You strike me as pretty worldly. We wouldn't waste your time—or ours—inviting you to something lame. You came here today, so obviously you're open to new ideas."

"I guess I am," Tom Altman admitted.

"So which colloquium do you want to go to? Tomorrow's or next week's?"

From the back—"I want to go tomorrow!"

The others scrambled to sign up for the next day.

Julie cast an eye at the clipboard. "Tomorrow's almost full."

Shanna nibbled on her nails. "I'll do it," she said in a rush. "I can cut classes."

"Tom? How 'bout you?" The clipboard was handed around the circle, landing in his lap. Thirteen sets of eyes fixed on him.

A glance at the clipboard revealed only one listed option. The proceedings began at five tomorrow morning, leaving recruits virtually no time to rethink their decisions and back out. His frustration rose—he still hadn't confirmed that this was Leah's cult, and he didn't have time to waste in an unrelated colloquium. "Can you tell me a little more about it?"

"It's *amazing*." Julie had an irksome habit of clasping her hands to her chest when she spoke.

"Who's gonna run the colloquium?" He received a round of confused looks. "Usually there's one person who steers the ship. An instructor or something."

"Well, we all participate together. What's really important is the experience you're gonna have. It's about you and your growth."

Too self-conscious to make eye contact, Tom Altman gazed down at the sign-up sheet. A single remaining blank line awaited his name. In less than an hour, someone with moderate Internet sophistication could uncover Tom Altman's $90 million portfolio, his hydrofoil in the Marina, his Lear at the Burbank airport, his recently sold Bel Air mansion, liquidated during the divorce.

"I'm just anxious about what happens if I go and run into problems. I mean, something someone ordinary can't solve."

"*Oh*." Lorraine grinned. "Don't worry. There'll be lots of Neos at your stage."

Tim leaned over and signed. "I think tomorrow works just fine."

Eighteen

"It's in a Radisson, Bear. How sinister can something in a Radisson be?"

"My date with Lenora Delarusso from Metro wound up there. That's how sinister."

At the wheel of his truck, Bear coasted about a half block behind Reggie Rondell, who was heading east on foot.

They'd pulled into the RestWell parking lot just as he'd struck out from the front desk, a little after 11:00 P.M. Boston rested his head on Tim's thigh, the warm drool just starting to work its way through Tim's pants. At Tim's respectful push, Boston aimed a baleful gaze his way, then curled around, redirecting his attentions beneath a flared hind leg.

"This won't be a roomful of easily cowed kids—it's a huge cult seminar. If the girl's there, you can't just flash badge and walk her out anymore. You've got adults, hotel staff, a shit-load of cult higher-ups. If you make a scene, *someone* is bound to inquire, and you've got dick to back up an arrest." Bear sighed weightily. "You can't risk that."

Keeping his eyes on Reggie's halting progress up the side-walk, Tim gave a little nod.

Bear, no enthusiast of pregnant pauses, glanced over at him again. "You're getting sucked in one step at a time. You didn't sign on for this."

"I'm just getting the girl out. No more, no less."

Bear adjusted his grip on the wheel, his face skeptical. "It *has* occurred to you that you're walking the same path they use to indoctrinate people."

"Yes. Did you check out the rental info for the space at the Radisson?"

"The International Ballroom was booked—no cheap af-fair, cost around seven grand. The check came in from TDB Corp, sources to an offshore bank account. I guess TDB holds one of these jobbies about every month. Up until now they've always used the smaller conference rooms."

"So there's either more money or more participants."

"Or both."

"Can we case it?"

"The events director says the clients have a crew there al-ready, prepping the ballroom. I wouldn't risk going by, could get eyefucked. You'll have to run it dry."

"Get what you can on TDB Corp, would you? I want a U.S. address."

"If we're tracking finances on that level, you know we're gonna have to call in Thomas and Freed."

Freed came from money—his parents owned a national furniture chain. He'd been groomed to take over the business but opted out at the last minute, electing to join the Service. He was the only guy on the warrant squad who drove a Porsche that he'd actually paid for, not borrowed from Asset Seizure. His persistence and quiet temperament made him a brilliant cross-agency synergist. One Christmas Eve he'd tracked down the vacationing secretary of the treasury on a Fijian Sportfisher for a telephonic consult on an international money-laundering scheme, a tale that had long calcified into Service lore. His abilities running down a money trail were unparalleled, and Thomas—his operating partner for five years—had evolved into an excellent collaborator. Charles Bronson comments aside, they were the right guys for the job.

Up ahead Reggie stuffed the ever-present brown paper bag into his coat pocket and ducked into a Blockbuster.

Bear pulled over and idled at the curb. "You wanna go talk to him?"

"No, he'll be more comfortable on his own turf. If he's getting a video, he's heading back home."

They sat in silence for a while, Tim flipping through his notepad and reflecting on the meeting at the apartment. Shanna had been glowing with anticipation on their walk out last night; he'd directed a few cryptic remarks her way discouraging her attendance, but she'd smiled, nonplussed, and chided him for being negative.

He reminded himself that she was a sentient adult who was capable of decision making. Spinning his wheels trying to tow her out would get him nowhere—she was one of maybe hundreds of recruits he'd come across. Why not rescue every participant he encountered? Or even Julie and Lorraine for that matter?

So what made Leah different? Merely the fact that he'd been tasked with her recovery?

". . . the small-people couple who stayed next door to me and Elise in Vegas said they'd met twenty years ago at a U2 concert," Bear was saying.

The small-people convention had really stayed with him.

"You believe that shit? People say they met at a concert twenty years ago, I'm thinking Bob Seger. We're getting old, Rack. Getting old."

Tim looked up from his notepad, glancing at the dash. Twenty minutes had passed. "What the hell is keeping him?"

"Maybe he slipped out the back."

"I'll go take a look."

"I'd offer to help," Bear said, "but I'm one of his triggers."

Tim found Reggie sitting on the floor in the middle of the Action aisle, videos scattered on the floor around him. Mumbling to himself, he appraised the cases like oversize cards in a game of solitaire. A passing father steered his two sons clear. The manager drifted in the vicinity, taking a gander from Special Interest and considering an intervention.

Reggie didn't seem surprised to see Tim. "There's *Rocky III* and *Rocky IV*. I like them both, but I can't decide. I've seen *Rocky III* more. And then there's classic Willis, you know, the *Die Hards*, *The Last Boy Scout*." He pressed his palm to his forehead and massaged it, swirling out a tuft of hair.

Tim made a reassuring gesture in the manager's direction. Administering a dissatisfied scowl, the man retreated to the front register.

"Which one should I pick?"

"I don't know."

Reggie's hand hovered tremulously over *The Last Boy Scout*. He looked to Tim for a reaction. "You can't just tell me?"

"That one's fine."

Reggie went limp with relief. "Really? You think so?"

"Yes." Tim crouched parentally, helping clean up.

Outside, Tim offered Reggie a ride, but Reggie took one look at Bear and said he'd rather walk. Tim went with him,

Bear rolling his eyes and shadowing in the truck like an inexpert kidnapper.

Reggie had been studying the video case, smoothing his hands over it as if it held great sentimental value. "I don't want to talk to you anymore."

"I'm going to a colloquium tomorrow morning. At the Radisson."

Reggie dropped the video, eyelids disappearing under his brow. "*Don't* do it." He snatched up the video and scurried down an alley, glancing around fearfully. Tim followed. Reggie slid up onto a Dumpster lid. He spoke with a whispered urgency. "He'll hook you. That's what he does. There have been others like you, always think you can handle it."

Tim wondered if Danny Katanga, PI, had liked what he'd found enough to join up.

"I seen the Teacher turn around angry family members, journalists, pastors, shrinks—man, does he hate shrinks—even cops." Streaks of sweat ran down Reggie's forehead. In his agitation he didn't seem to mind referring to the leader by title. "It's a black hole. It's—"

"*Reggie.* Calm down. He's not God."

A burst of laughter doubled Reggie over, ending in a hacking spell. "Clearly you haven't heard the hagiography."

"The what?"

"As a young boy, he had grand mal seizures. During one—when he was six or eight, depending on which version he's telling—he forced himself to stay conscious and gained untainted access to his Inner Source. After that he was a force of nature. He hypnotized other boys at school just by looking at them, left them to wander campus like zombies. Batteries discharge themselves in his hands. He touches books to his forehead and they're read. Lights flicker when he passes them." Reggie snorted up some phlegm and spit. "Don't tell me he's not God. He is whatever he thinks he is."

A few raindrops flecked their cheeks, then dissolved into a

wet breeze. Tim thought of Ernie Tramine's atrophied face and wondered how far gone Reggie's memory was.

Despite his puffy coat, Reggie was shivering uncontrollably. "He'll eat you alive."

"Tell me what to watch for."

A high, agitated whine. "I can't, man. If he fucking finds out . . ."

Tim held up his hands. "I just want to know what I'm gonna run into."

"Fuck knows. He's always improving, always evolving. He had a new set of tricks every time we ran another Orae."

"Like what?"

"*I don't know!*" Reggie's eyes darted back and forth as the echo of his voice bounced around brick and metal. It was a narrow alley, the tall buildings seeming to converge overhead. "I been out fifteen months. I've got no idea what kind of shit he'll throw at you now."

"How many recruits will be there?"

"Thirty, forty. The goal is just to hook three or four."

"Three or four what?"

Reggie looked away in disgust, his breath misting. A leaky gutter lent the asphalt a glossy sheen. "Did they love-bomb you? In your Prelim. The *meeting*. Did they love-bomb you? Touch you, hang on every word, tell you how fantastic you are?"

"Yes."

"Did you like it?"

Tim shrugged.

"Don't lie to me. Don't you *fucking* lie to me. Did you like it?"

"Yes, a part of me did."

"You'd better be goddamn honest with yourself when you're in there."

"Okay, that's one tip. You have more?" Tim took a deep breath and held it before exhaling. "Reggie. I've got to go do this thing in four hours. Help me out, man."

Reggie looked down. The laces of his left shoe had come untied, the tips tracing circles in the darkness. He mumbled to himself, holding up both sides of an internal argument. His lips stilled, then he said quietly, "Don't drink the punch. Watch the time. Pinch yourself." When he looked up, his eyes held a sharp focus. "Don't do it to her."

"Do what?"

"Kidnap her."

"I'm not really—"

"It was during a guided meditation at the Teacher's house. I'd been deteriorating pretty good for a couple of weeks. I blacked out. I couldn't stand up. My arms and legs were shaking. I couldn't get them to stop. I was lying on the floor in my own . . . my own piss." Reggie faced Tim unflinchingly, steeling himself like an AA member who'd toiled long enough to accept harsh facts. "My Gro-Par brought the Teacher over. I remember looking up at them. I couldn't talk, even. My Gro-Par said, 'Maybe we should get him to a doctor.' And the Teacher said, 'No, that'll just injure him more psychologically. He'll be better off on his own.' Two Pros came over, and they carried me out of the house. They set me down on the curb and went back inside."

He eyed the thin river of slate sky. "It was like falling deep in love, giving every ounce of trust I had only to find . . ." His hand rose, fluttering, then fell to his lap. "After working and slaving and signing over two and a half million dollars, I was abandoned the second I became inconvenient. I never get to decide for myself. I never get to walk out." His posture firmed, his head rising, his shoulders pulling back. For a moment he looked like a different person. Then he wilted, and he was Reggie again. "I never get to have that. *Never.* And now you're making sure this girl doesn't get to have it either. She's a ship in a bottle, man, and you're gonna throw the whole fucking thing against the wall so you can play with the pieces."

He rocked gently, heels striking metal. His sudden alertness vanished as quickly as it had appeared. His lips moved soundlessly.

Tim waited a few moments, but Reggie's eyes stayed unfocused and lifeless. Tim took a few backward steps, then turned, heading to the block of light at the alley's mouth, the Dumpster resounding like a kettledrum under the slow beat of Reggie's shoes.

Nineteen

*W*hen she finished this time, TD stroked her hair. "There, now, that was really great progress."

She slid off the bed onto the blanket and sheets laid out on the floor; the Teacher needed room in bed to sleep undisturbed. TD rolled to his side, and within seconds his breathing slowed. Leah lay awake as she had the night before, one hand clutching the butter-smooth sheets. Not wanting to disturb TD, she didn't move, even though her right arm was falling asleep. Split by the slatted blinds, the moon crept molasses slow up the blanket covering her.

She certainly had it better than Nancy, who had not reappeared from Skate's shed. All day Skate had patrolled the perimeter and shadowed TD with a satiated grin, disappearing at intervals. On the ranch, sex was a rationed privilege.

Leah was surprised to catch herself questioning the benefits of this aspect of TD's tutelage. She thought about her perverse need to be negative during a wonderful opportunity like this. Staying On Program, listening to the Teacher—that was how people grew.

A dying candle persisted on the nightstand beside her, next

to a telephone with its cord removed—TD called for the phone cord rarely and only for essential Program business. Tacked to the wall above the nightstand was TD's phone sheet, the schedule of hours at which he had set incoming calls. Callers, knowing they had a window of maybe five minutes to reach him, developed a discipline.

Her thoughts seemed a Christmas-light tangle, impossibly snared, granting flashes of lucidity at random yet somehow connected intervals. Nestled in the warm swirl of sheets, she reminded herself that she was privileged to be able to learn about her insecurities with the Teacher. She ran through Program precepts until they became thoughtless blurs. After an excruciating block of time, she heard the outside door creak open. The faint tap of a footstep. And then another.

Leah lay frozen.

A startled scream—Lorraine. TD bolted upright and rushed to the door, tugging his pants on, Leah trailing meekly for fear of being left behind in darkness.

TD hit the switch as Nancy shrugged off Lorraine's two-arm tackle. The misaligned buttons of Nancy's dress created mouths in the denim through which skin and bra peeked. The hem was ripped, the fabric marred by muddy groping. Her bed-swirled hair stuck out in all directions. Nancy began sobbing, her words barely comprehensible. *"Teacher, please, lemme back with you. Lemme be your Lily. Pleeease."*

TD calmly cinched his silk robe about his waist. "After you were with that filthy man?"

Skate was in the door, scratching his scalp, his fingernails giving off some good noise. "Guess she got away."

"Take her off the ranch. This one's not salvageable."

Nancy emitted a high-pitched moan, collapsed, and began crawling to TD. Skate pinned her beneath a knee and twisted her arm behind her back. Then Randall appeared, controlling Nancy's other side. They picked her up as if hauling a carpet and bore her out horizontally. Her hair whipped about her head, her screams so shrill Leah squinted against them. Her cries continued all the way up the trail. Somewhere around Cottage Circle, the wind finally carried them off.

TD went back inside and slid into bed. Leah followed and sat on her sheets, trying to sort her thoughts. Finally TD rolled over and said, "Yes?"

"Where . . . where will they take her?"

"Down the hill. Into the city. They'll leave her somewhere safe. But she's no longer my concern. Nor should she be yours."

"She'll"—Leah wiped her cheeks, glad the darkness prevented TD from seeing how shaken she was—"she'll die without you."

"She's dying already," TD said with finality. After another pause he sighed and shoved himself up against the headboard. "What, Leah? If you have something to ask, ask it. Don't just sit there radiating stress and fear."

"What do you mean, she's dying already?"

"She's decaying. Women peak reproductively at an early age, just after puberty. In primitive cultures and in the early days of this country, females got married when they were thirteen, fourteen years old. They'd bear several children and pass by twenty-five, maybe thirty. Women are designed to peak, breed, and perish. Nancy is twenty-four years old. Her eggs are old and stale. She looks forward to a future only because the artificial intervention of modern medicine has prolonged human life well beyond its natural range. But even medicine can't stop her body—that obese, jiggling mass around her—from slowly breaking down, from dying in minuscule increments as it has been for the last eight years. Her very appearance is indicative of a diseased way of thinking. Nancy won't figure her way out of her death dilemma. She'd rather be a victim. One of the dying. With her mind-set, she has nothing to look forward to but aloneness and the further putrefaction of her body."

He sighed and ran his hands over his face. "I know it might

appear cruel, but I have a responsibility here. I can't let someone like her infect the rest of you who are working so hard to grow past your physical and psychological limitations."

His indirect compliment warmed her, if only slightly.

"Before you go weepy for Nancy," he said, "why don't you reflect on the fact that this wake-up call is the best thing that could ever happen to her?"

Leah asked tentatively, "Do you think it was the best thing for Lisa Kander?"

She was worried TD might get angry, but he just laughed. "Now that you mention it, yes. She found life without The Program too much to bear. So she took her comfort in the soothing hiss of the tar pits. Beats living a lie. Beats being one of the walking dead. At least she took back some control in her death." He reached over and stroked Leah's head. "Good night. I need my sleep, and so do you." He smiled. "Big day tomorrow."

Twenty

*W*edged between a smoggy run of Sepulveda and perpetual traffic mainlining up Century Boulevard into LAX, the Radisson held its ground with a certain imperviousness and vanity, as if the recent renovation had fooled the establishment into thinking highly of itself. Tim pulled up and dropped a duplicate key in the palm of a youthful valet who all but Matrixed over getting an eyeful of the banana yellow ride.

"Keep it up front."

The valet nodded. "A-ight."

Standing erect amid streams of incoming attendees, Lorraine greeted Tim at the automatic glass doors, wearing a stewardess's polyester smile. "Nice wheels."

She took his arm, guiding him through the brochure-glossy lobby, leaving the others to progress unattended. Bill O'Reilly flapped about immigrants from a suspended TV in the bar area. A fountain nestled in the curving staircase's embrace burbled, the sound drifting with them up and around to a spacious second-floor landing. North-facing windows provided a view of a loading dock, a back parking lot, and an emergency exit.

A confusion of people sorted neatly into the International Ballroom through a set of double doors, the so-called Pros distinguishable by pressed blue polos and matching purposefulness. With a faint grin, Lorraine suddenly receded into the press of bodies, no doubt off to escort some other affluent convert.

Not only had event attendance grown exponentially since Reggie's day, but the target demographics had fanned out. The Neos, ranging from late teens to thirties, appeared to represent a variety of backgrounds. They hummed with nervous anticipation, picking up on the exuberance of the cult members. A few stragglers gathered near the back of the landing, staring longingly at a roped-off bank of pay phones guarded by an OFF-LIMITS! sign on a stout brass post. No one dared cross the velvet cord.

Tim scanned the crowd, looking for Leah's distinctive shaggy brown hair. The blue polos and flushed, youthful faces made the cult members easy to pick out as they darted to and fro completing their preparations, but there were too many for him to keep track. He barely had time to eyeball the ushers guarding the ballroom doors before a toothy young jock at a draped check-in table requested his name. Yes, Tom, there was a $500 fee. Wasn't his fulfillment worth spending a few bucks? No, they couldn't accept a personal check, but AmEx or Visa would be fine.

Another hand-off and he was whisked through the doors

by a robust young woman in a shapeless dress. Two segmented partitions divided the fourteen-thousand square feet of ballroom. Another brass-post sign identified the empty first section as ACTSPACE. Led by hand, Tim passed through a gap in the partition into a second area with about three hundred chairs positioned in a giant horseshoe, the open end facing a dais. The sign there, predictably, read HEARSPACE. The woman deposited him in the rear at a banquet table and vanished. Enya oozed, bass-heavy and forlorn, from hidden speakers.

Tim accepted a glass of punch from a female Pro and surreptitiously gifted its contents to a fake ficus leaning from a peat pot. So he wouldn't stand out, he held on to the clear plastic cup, carrying traces of the punch. He avoided the snacks but crumpled a napkin in his hand. As he drifted effortlessly through the clots of people, he grudgingly recognized that he owed his father much of his ability to work undercover. The others chatted nervously, strained alertness tightening their faces. The 5:00 A.M. commencement meant a four o'clock wake-up for most participants, giving them a head start on exhaustion.

"I can't really afford this whole deal," a burly guy in a jean jacket was telling a few uninterested girls and a tattooed Marine, "but the owner said he'd only hire me if I went through this thing." He tapped a passing Pro, who turned glassy pupils and a disarming grin in his direction. "Hey, what are we gonna be doing anyway?"

"You don't want me to tell you anything about today's work before we get to it. It would undermine your experience."

Tim stood at the fringe of the group, his eyes picking over the enormous room. Numerous light panels and thermostats, carpeted metal partitions and cloth-dressed walls, hideously patterned rug, equally offensive chandeliers like dimpled breasts. A service elevator briefly came into view when a stressed-out blue-shirt swept through a rear waitstaff door—Tim's favored extraction route.

Tim craned his neck to see through the fifteen-foot gap in the second partition, but the far ballroom section, labeled PROSPACE, was dark. He edged nearer, wanting a peek at Oz's command center. Cult members continued to stream out like diligent ants; he guessed there were sixty in all.

Easing away from the crowd, he neared the dark portal to Prospace, his advance going unnoticed. He shouldered against the makeshift jamb near a pinned velvet curtain, ready to slip through. Scurrying figures were barely discernible beyond, shadows against shadows.

A small orb in the darkness was suddenly illuminated— the glowing red dials of a sound board firing up—and there stood Leah, knock-kneed and soft-faced and taller than he'd imagined, bent over the apparatus like a pianist. Her slim fingers punched buttons and adjusted dials. Her competence and apparent collectedness made clear that the abduction was not going to be as simple as he'd imagined—carting off a zoned-out cult zombie. She looked up, burgundy suffusing her hair at the tips, and their eyes met and held. She smiled, showing off an angled front tooth, and he had just an instant to take in the absolute sweetness of her expression before a block of shadow took form and collided with him, a forehead striking the side of his face.

He fell back into the light. A squat guy was standing over him, shoulders drawn back so his arms bowed wide. A sweatshirt with ripped-off sleeves was pulled tight across his broad chest. A necklace—copper wires threaded through earthtone beads—was embedded in the V of chest hair visible beneath the shoelace stitching the ripped collar. He matched the description of the thug who'd assisted Leah with her move, bead necklace and all.

"Didn't see you," Tim said.

"Not allowed back here," the guy answered.

The thrill of finding Leah took the edge off the throbbing in Tim's cheek. A sharp pain pinched his hip where something hard and metal had struck him. A concealed weapon?

Tim pulled himself to his feet; no hand was offered. "Oh, I'm sorry. I didn't realize it was limited access. I'm Tom Altman."

The man stood motionless and unblinking. "You wanna be back over with the others."

The glow from the sound board had vanished, taking Leah with it.

"I didn't get your name." Tim smiled self-consciously. "I don't know anyone here."

"Skate Daniels. We're, uh, preparing back here."

A smooth voice reverberated through the speakers. "Let's all get seats now."

With a nod Tim retreated from the unbudging figure, finding a chair. Others trickled in, filling the horseshoe as "Orinoco Flow" continued to soothe. Sweat trickled down Tim's forehead; a raised hand to the overhead vents confirmed they were running full blast. He slid off his heavy winter coat and stuffed it under the chair. He'd made one arm of his long-sleeved undershirt detachable, Velcroed in place so it would give with a firm tug. The thick patch at the elbow doubled as a bit for the makeshift gag.

When the song ended, the low rumble of a drum replaced it, heartbeat steady. Tim felt tired already from the heat, and malleable, which was precisely the aim. Those around him seemed unnaturally relaxed, no doubt due to whatever concoction enhanced the punch.

Blond, fair-skinned, and slightly equine about the mouth, the couple who took the dais seemed peeled from a 1940s German propaganda poster. They gazed at each other with shared excitement, singers on the verge of a duet chorus.

"Hello, I'm Stanley John—"

"And I'm Janie."

Stanley John winked at the crowd, adjusting his head mike. "The Program was evolved by our teacher, Terrance

Donald Betters, through years of research and study. You're going to get the opportunity to hear from TD soon. But first we've got to lay down some basic practices for what will be the most transforming experience of your life. Number One: Don't destabilize our techniques. The Program is precise. Success for all is reliant on no one's interrupting the process. It's not fair to everyone else if you cut in and derail their forward movement. Make sense?"

Janie was nodding for him. "Number Two: No leaving before the colloquium is finished. No matter what. The instruction and group work go all day and night. At five A.M. when you graduate, you'll be different people. But before then you must not leave. Not if your mother has a heart attack and they're reading her the last rites. Anyone who can't handle this level of commitment should go now. This is your chance." A dramatic pause during which no one moved. "Good—but this is an *active* commitment. So everyone who's strong enough to see this experience through, stand up."

About 90 percent of the attendees, including Tim, rose. Slowly, the others joined them, pulled by discomfort or obligation, until only three remained sitting.

One of them, a weary thirty-something, raised her hand. "I'm an only parent, and my kids are with a sitter. What if there's an emergency and I have to leave?"

"If you're an excuse maker, then you'll never learn to take control of your life. Just leave now. No reason to stay and interfere with everyone else's growth."

"But what if . . . ?"

"Whoa, horsey." Stanley John chuckled kindly, Janie matching his Teutonic smile. Some scattered, nervous laughter from the crowd. "Ma'am, we explained the rules. We're not gonna take up everyone else's time holding your hand."

"Yeah, let's get on with it!" a plant shouted from the audience.

"If you want to be a victim of an emergency that hasn't happened yet, if you want to walk out on growth, the door's that way." Stanley John smiled benevolently at the woman, who wilted back in her chair, then pulled herself to her feet. He smiled even bigger, clapping, and the crowd slowly joined in. "Good for you."

During the applause one of the other dissenters stood, too, his face flushed. The last, an anxious-looking man in a bargain suit, scurried from the ballroom, shaking his head and muttering to himself.

Janie and Stanley John ran through the other rules in similar fashion. No questions during activities. No smoking or drinking. Eat only the food that's been provided.

"Why can't we take bathroom breaks without approval?" a frazzled woman wanted to know.

"Because TD found out it's too disruptive otherwise."

Tim began to rethink his plan for extracting Leah. Clearly he wouldn't have much mobility. He couldn't very well page her to a house phone or catch her on her way to the bathroom.

The recitation of the rules continued. Change seats now if you're sitting with anyone you know. Music will play between activities—get back to your chairs by the time it stops. You've got to participate fully.

The stifling heat, bursts of applause, and constant sitting and standing—enough to rival midnight mass—were working their magic, making the crowd at once obedient and lethargic. People with hesitations were mocked for being uncommitted, more people from the audience joining in each time.

Tim caught sight of Shanna at the far end of the horseshoe. Grinning dumbly, lips stained red with punch, she slouched in her chair, her head angled on a lenient neck. About five more people chose to leave before the lengthy introduction concluded, departing through a hail of hisses, boos, and—worse—sympathetic ohhs. The woman next to Tim, who wore a shell of egg-blond hair and no rings on her chubby fingers, appeared to be in a daze, humming to herself and nodding vehemently, her damp smock giving off an odor like curdled milk.

"All right!" Stanley John roared when the last rule had been summarily accepted. "Look around you. Everyone in this room has made the right choice. You've all chosen change and growth. From here forward, we're all in this together."

The room broke out in applause. Skate Daniels and the other likely knock-down man, a guy with a bald pate and a pronounced underbite, slid in front of the waitstaff doors and the Actspace partition gap—the only two exits. They stood like prison guards, arms crossed, expressionless. The herd was now corralled and Tim's extraction route blocked.

Jogging athletically around the horseshoe, Stanley John counted off the participants. More blue-shirts materialized to take control of the smaller groups. Tim looked for Leah to emerge, but evidently her technical skills were needed backstage.

"All right," Stanley John said breathily. "You twenty, come meet in Actspace."

Slipping on his jacket, Tim shuffled through the partition gap with the others. His neighbor introduced herself as Joanne, pumping his hand moistly. The gruff guy in the jean jacket was in their group, along with an appealing girl in a sorority sweatshirt who reminded Tim of Leah's college roommate. A gangly, thin-necked kid with comb marks gelled into his hair brought up the rear, his hands bunching the front of his Old Navy Swim Team shirt.

They formed a huddle of sorts, Stanley John in the middle, holding a plastic bin. "Let's put our watches in here. Cell phones, too."

Will's $30,000 Cartier disappeared in the heap.

They sat in a circle like kindergartners at storytime, filling out name tags that they were asked to wear at all times. Next a stack of forms magically appeared in Stanley John's hands. "These will help us keep track of your progress. Part of your job will be to look out for one another and provide feedback to me whenever you sense someone is getting Off Program."

Ben smoothed his name tag onto his denim jacket. "Big Brother's watching."

His joke was punished with disapproving silence.

"I'll do mine first." Tongue poking a point in his cheek, Stanley John bent over his form. He spoke the words slowly as he wrote. "My Program is: I experience empowerment as I follow guidance leading me to strength. My Old Programming is: I'm afraid to get angry." He looked up with a smile. "We want to stay *On Program* and reject our *Old Programming*. Get it? Now you guys go."

After everyone finished jotting, they went around the circle and read from their forms, the answers closely parroting Stanley John's examples. Blushing, Joanne read in a feeble voice, "My Program is: I experience fulfillment as I participate in my growth. My Old Programming is: I have a tough time standing up for myself."

Ray, the lanky kid, confessed that his Old Programming was that he was a bit of a control freak. Ben's was that he had a temper. Tom Altman confessed heavily that he often tried to solve his problems with money. The sorority girl, Shelly, admitted with obvious pride to using physicality to get a sense of self-worth.

"A consistent theme is an inability to express yourselves. Especially to express anger. We're going to do the Atavistic Yell to loosen up." Stanley John stood, the others following, and pointed at Joanne. "Go on. Yell at the top of your lungs."

She glanced around hesitantly. "What? I . . . Can't someone else go first?"

"Isn't your Program that you experience fulfillment as you participate in your growth? Are you participating in your growth by refusing to do the activity? Is she, folks?"

Several others chimed in. "She's Off Program."

"I think she's afraid to stand up for herself like she said!"

Her flushed cheeks quivered. She opened her mouth and emitted a tentative yelp.

"You call that a yell?" Stanley John was standing over her

now, screaming. "Get out of your Old Programming. Let's hear you *yell*. Let's hear you *stand up for yourself*."

She was shaking, eyes welling. The noise level rocketed around them as people in the other groups shouted and screamed.

"Look at you. A grown woman, you can't even open your mouth and make a noise. How weak. You're useless."

The ploy—boot camp gone self-help—might have been offensive were it not so transparent.

Joanne tried to scream, but it came out a hoarse gasp.

"We're all sitting around waiting for Joanne to scream so we can progress with our growth. *Everyone* waits for Joanne; is that how it is in your world? *Everyone* waits—"

Joanne leaned forward and screamed with all her might, arms shoved stiffly behind her. She sucked in air and bellowed again, screaming until she nearly hyperventilated. Stanley John was clapping, and the others joined in. Following his example, they administered the quaking woman full body hugs. Her top, now drenched with panic sweat, felt clammy beneath Tim's arms.

Her shoulders sagged with relief. "I've never done anything like this before. This is amazing. I feel all tingly."

"This is lame," Ben said.

Shelly turned a smiling plea in his direction. "Don't be so negative."

Stanley John chimed in with his beloved standby: "You're interfering with Joanne's experience. And everyone else's."

Ben looked away uncomfortably, no doubt weighing the costs of initiating his Old Programming. "I'm just saying this ain't my cup of tea. Especially not for five hundred bucks."

Janie, who'd been prowling the group perimeters, stepped in. "Group Seven is one man short. Anyone here who can go?"

"Seven's a great group, Ben," Stanley John said. "Why don't you join them?"

Before Ben could answer, Janie whisked him off, threading herself around his arm like an adoring date. Tim watched them make their way back to Skate's province near the door, where Janie introduced Ben to a cluster of other seemingly displeased customers—a dissenters quarantine. Skate nodded into the radio pressed to his ear, as if it picked up motion.

Becoming a behavior problem clearly wouldn't buy Tim a backstage pass and get him near Leah; for the time being, acquiescence was the only option.

Now that Joanne had broken the ice, Shelly carried out the exercise with a minimum of resistance, and Ray followed suit. When his turn came, Tim allowed Tom Altman to be briefly berated for holding back. Stanley John poked a flat hand into his chest where it met the shoulder. "You don't have your money to hide behind now, Tom. You have to yell just like everyone else."

The others chimed in with impressive vigor, Joanne the most aggressive in her exhortation. "Reject your Old Programming. You're being *weak*."

When Tom was finally able to let loose a satisfying yell, the praise was effusive. After being smashed in a sweaty group hug, Tim realized that the temperature had suddenly plummeted. The oscillation made him light-headed, and he felt his first flash of alarm—two hours' sleep and an empty stomach might not have been the wisest preparation for what was proving to be a marathon.

The lights suddenly dimmed, Enya pouring through the speakers. At once everyone sprang into action, people scrambling back to Hearspace and finding their seats. With the synthetic arpeggios and blasts of refrigeration, the space had taken on a certain unreality.

Tim noticed Group Seven being ushered out during the distraction—so much for the "no leaving" rule. He detoured by the waitstaff entrance and picked up Janie's calling the bald door guard "Randall."

The Pros stalked the center of the horseshoe, physically steering stragglers to their seats and yelling for silence. The people in the group adjacent to Tim's were talking and laughing. Stanley John pulled the leader aside. "If you keep choosing incompetence, you might need a visit to Victim Row."

The Pro blanched, then turned and chastised her charges with renewed energy.

The lights went out completely. Pants and gasps filled the perfect darkness. Despite his weariness, Tim debated making a run for Prospace, but he knew that his chair would be glaringly empty when the lights came up. Even if he could locate Leah, he was no longer sure what to do with her.

Three trumpet blasts scaled octaves to form the opening bars of *Thus Spake Zarathustra,* signaling the next leg of the space odyssey. Diffuse yellow light bathed the dais. A slender man stood in the center, head bowed. A voice boomed through the speakers. "In The Program there are no victims." He raised his head, the floating black egg of the mike visible just off his left cheek. A tiny rectangle of hair glistened high on his chin—his face was youthful and smooth, his age indeterminable. "There are no excuses. You create your own reality, and you live inside it. You can follow The Program and *maximize* . . . or you can stay mired in your Old Programming and be *victimized.* Those are the choices—the *only* choices."

The chandeliers eased up a notch, the room taking on the dimmest edge of dusk. Tim peered at the digital watch face he'd hidden in his pocket—8:03. Reggie's advice to mind the time had been crucial; with all the environmental manipulation in the ballroom, Tim needed to root himself in an external reality.

The participants gazed at the Teacher with adoration, all focus and veneration. Looking around, Tim couldn't help but feel as though he'd stepped into a dream. The Teacher began pacing the stage, and the white ovals of the faces pivoted back and forth, radar dishes keying to the same frequency.

"My name is Terrance Donald Betters."

The voices of the sixty or so Pros rose together. *"Hi, TD."*

"I've spent years and years and literally *hundreds of thousands* of dollars developing The Program. I do not exaggerate when I tell you it's going to change the world. It's a revolution. And guess what? You're ahead of the curve. You're joining in *already,* gaining access to The Program's Source Code. You're here to change your lives. And that change begins now." He stopped, breathing hard, looking out at the horseshoe's embrace. "Take sole responsibility for your life. You alone cause *all* outcomes."

Program Precept One was greeted by murmurs of wonderment.

"Your experience is your reality. You control *everything.* If you feel hurt, it's because you *decided* to feel hurt. If you feel violated, it's because of how you *chose* to interpret an event. The world is up to you. Make of it what you will. No experience is bad *in its own right.* I dare any person in this room to name an experience that is *objectively bad.* Well?" He scanned the masses before him, Moses considering the Red Sea. "Come on, now. I won't bite."

"Rape," a courageous effeminate male voice called from the back.

TD leaned back, laughing, his knees bending. *"Rape?* That's a good response." Again he began his hypnotic pacing, the steady, powerful movement of a caged tiger. "But take away *societal issues* around sexuality. Rape involves coercion—like lots of things in life. Getting pulled over and being given a ticket for an expired registration, for example. Paying our taxes. Submitting to having our shoes examined by idiots at airport security checkpoints. And yet we don't believe that those coercions are inherently evil. If you believe that rape involves some sort of objective, universal evil, you've been brainwashed. *Society* taught you rape was essentially evil. *Society* made you feel guilty if you entertained a rape fantasy. *Society* made rape fundamentally traumatic. And we bought it. Now, I'm not an uncaring guy. Nor a rapist. I'm not saying we don't experience *negative emotions*. After all, who among us hasn't felt *sad*? Who among us hasn't felt *depressed? Beat up? Kicked around? Put down? Violated?* We all have, haven't we?"

Shouts and exclamations. The lights dimmed until just TD remained illuminated. The heat was blowing again, mixing with the breath and perspiration of three hundred close-quarter adults to create a soupy humidity. Tim wiped the sweat fog from his fake glasses.

TD spread his arms. "You. Don't. Have. To. Feel. That. Anymore."

Somewhere in the darkness, a woman actually sobbed.

"A human being is the most sophisticated thinking machine *ever devised.* You work like a computer, but you know what? You're a lot *better than* a computer. You're the only computer able to run itself. Able to unplug itself and move itself around. The question is: Are you going to run yourself, or are you going to let others run *you?* The Program's not about how you *feel.* It's about how you *think.* Your Old Programming unconsciously *controls* how you think. Your Old Programming is everything your family and society *downloaded into you* that you've never considered critically. Your Old Programming is the part of your past that's *holding you back.* We're gonna take that, trash it, and teach you something that sets you free. You don't have to *empty* the trash. You can always recover lines of Old Programming code and use them again—they're always there. But we're gonna *overwrite* your Old Programming with The Program. And that, folks, is gonna set you free."

The second and third commandments.

Beside Tim, Joanne fumbled out an inhaler and sucked

twice on it. Her eyes glimmered with unshed tears. Tim glanced down the row—blank, neutral expressions, slack jaws, retarded blink and swallow reflexes.

"The Program works for *everyone* who's ever committed to it. *Every single person.* So unless you think you know better than *everyone* in this *entire room,* you'd better *commit* like you've never *committed* before. If it feels like it isn't *working,* it's only because *you're not working* hard enough. If you start having doubts, that's just your Old Programming talking. Maximize your growth by minimizing your negativity."

The Program Code was up to four tenets.

"The world around us has changed. Terrorists fly airplanes *full of people* into buildings. The news informs us daily as to what our level of *terror* should be. We march into war constantly. *Al Qaeda, Afghanistan. Iraq.* Pension funds suddenly evaporate. Everywhere we turn there's a new problem. *SARS. Global warming. Anthrax.* We're *scared.* We're *confused.* Well, *no more.* Say it with me."

"No more!" The chant filled the ballroom. Tim's eyeballs felt as though they were vibrating in his skull.

"Will we allow ourselves to feel shitty? No way!"

"No way!"

"Forget *common sense.* Do you know what common sense is? An excuse for *not thinking.* This is the *new* way to think. We're doing it *right here* in this room. The more you follow The Program, the more you are *free.*"

People were nodding along as if the doors to life's deepest meaning were flying open.

"It's time for our next activity. It's Going to a Party, and it lasts ten minutes. Your job is simply to get up and talk to one another. Do you think you can manage that?"

Happy-go-lucky smiles plastered on their faces, the Pros bounced up and began introducing themselves to Neos from other groups. Slowly the Neos joined in, mimicking the shiny smiles.

Onstage, TD let out a little laugh. "Who says The Program's *all* hard work? We have fun here, too." He pulled off his mike and hopped down from the dais, conferring with Stanley John and Janie, then laying the word on a couple of awed Neos. The others milled around, talking and laughing as cold air blew down on them. Tim passed unnoticed by Julie, who perkily badgered a shy girl, "Everyone else is having fun."

He sneaked a glance at his watch, timing the event. A guy with narrow features and a ponytail approached, sticking out his hand and jutting out his chest so Tim could read his name tag. "Hey there. I'm Jason Struthers of Struthers Auto Mall."

"Tom Altman. Unemployed entrepreneur."

"Huh? Isn't that an oxymoron?"

Tim sidled toward Prospace. "My company was bought out in January."

Jason fidgeted with his wedding band. "What kind of stuff did you do?"

"I can't really talk about it. Defense work. Nondisclosure agreements, classified projects. You know."

The guy nodded as if he enountered similar security protocol on the auto-mall circuit.

A redhead with bulging eyes and an excited smile stole Jason's attention, and Tim took advantage of the distraction to get away. Turning an occasional eye to Skate and Randall, he moved toward the partition gap through bunches of people chattering idiotically.

He peered through the curtain into Prospace. A computer monitor threw enough light to reveal five workers, Leah not among them.

He turned, and she was standing right beside him. "Hi." She extended her hand with mock formality. "I'm Leah."

Up close it was all the more clear that none of Will's hefty genes were in the mix. She'd yet to grow into her shoulders. Her tank top revealed the edge of a hidden rash. Her angled front tooth barely split her closed lips, lending them the faintest suggestion of a pout.

Her hand felt soft and fragile. She wore her hair pulled back in a clip, but it spilled from the sides, arcing forward in brown strokes around a slender neck. Her eyes dipped to his name tag. "You having a good time, Tom?"

She seemed kind and engaging; Tim had to remind himself that these were the traits she'd been conditioned to exhibit. "It's pretty fun. A little out there, though."

The sincerity vanished from her eyes and with it her allure. "I was put off, too, at first, but I learned to keep an open mind. Constant questioning will only take you out of your process. Don't be afraid to let go."

"I'm doing my best."

The life came back into her face. "I noticed you earlier."

"I noticed you, too. You deal with the equipment back there, huh?" Tim used the question as an excuse to brush aside the curtain for a protracted look. In the far back corner, he detected a faint green EMERGENCY EXIT sign—the iron staircase that led to the rear parking lot. Five Pros were positioned between them and it; TD had clearly set up the colloquium to guard against the abduction of Pros. "Pretty mechanically savvy to run a show like this."

She blushed a little, her head dipping. "Oh, I don't run the whole thing. I just handle lights and sound."

"Still, I'd bet that takes some skill. Last time I touched a lighting panel was at a high-school buddy's garage concert. I electrocuted his cat."

A giggle escaped her. "Oh, this is nothing. I used to—" She stopped, her features going blank.

"What's wrong?"

"Okay," TD boomed. "Our ten minutes are up. Now we're playing Going to a Zombie Party. You can talk all you want, but you can't use intonation. And you can't make any gestures with your hands, arms, or bodies. This activity will last ten minutes, too."

Tim turned and peeked at his illicit watch. As he'd suspected, only five minutes had passed.

The corners of Leah's mouth turned up ever so slightly. In a robotic voice, she said, "I had better go interact with others. You are monopolizing all my time at this festive occasion."

"Over and out, earthling. Go in peace."

A smile broke onto her face, which quickly turned into an uncomfortable scowl. She walked stiffly off toward the horseshoe, pausing once to look back at Tim.

The others grew giddy from their attempts to restrain themselves. When someone lapsed, the Pros only scolded in monotone, which added to the carefree mood. Soon laughter filled the entire ballroom. Ray, arms at his sides, looked dead ahead at a circle of other frozen Neos. They were all howling with laughter.

When TD called out that time was up, Tim confirmed that ten minutes had passed with a quick glance at the watch. The sweat trickling down his sides alerted him to another radical temperature shift. The lights dimmed a few watts, the change barely discernible.

"Now we're Going to a Silent Party, and I think we can all guess those rules. You can only communicate through eyes and touch. If you have to, you can make noises, but no words."

Enthusiastic silent shuffling. Two Pros mimed each other's movements perfectly. Shelly let her hand glide limply through the air, as if tracing something. Five Neos crowded around her, their entire bodies undulating with the movement. Joanne sat cross-legged on the floor, sobbing violently. A shoulder-massage train of twenty people—Neos interspersed with Pros—snaked around Hearspace before forming a ring. Other Neos looked agitated, darting frenetically like rats in a maze.

Through all his years of training, combat, and street operating, Tim had never seen so many people knocked completely off their bases. Shanna approached and spread her arms wide as if to hug him but hovered an inch from his body. He searched for Leah—she was tucked into a ball, arms wrapped around her knees, face buried, shaking despite the heat. Only TD, Skate, and Randall remained tranquil in their poses, calmly waiting for the activity to end.

But it didn't. It stretched on and on, the shrieks and laughter growing oppressive. His undershirt pasted to his body, Tim staggered through the swampy warmth, squinting in the dimness. People howled. Bodies fluttered on the floor. The last time he'd checked the watch, the session had been at twenty minutes. He saw flicks of static between blinks. He was about to sit down on the floor when the room flooded with Enya.

Neos jostled and crawled back to their chairs. The lights came up to reveal TD on the dais, grinning coldly. "That was excellent. You're my most advanced group yet! You folks aren't *afraid* to Get with The Program. Now, everyone stand up and take your neighbor's hand. That's it." He stepped down off the dais, extending inviting hands to either side as the two ends of the horseshoe closed around him. "Now, *squeeze* and *release*. Deep breath. *Squeeze* and *release*. We are all one. Can you feel it?" Propagating from TD, currents of hand clasping ran around the circle. "Can you *feel the energy* running through us? Running through *each one of us?* We are all going to be *successful*. We are all going to be *strong*. We are all going to be *happy*."

He laughed. "If you believe that crap, catch a magic bus back to the seventies. Affirmations like that are old-hat cult bullshit. Telling yourself something doesn't make it happen. *Making it happen* makes it happen. If you think you can *talk* yourself into who you want to be, you deserve est, and Ronnie Hubbard, and selling Amway toilet paper out of the trunk of a Corolla. We're not a religion. We're not *tax-exempt*. We're a *practice*.

"Some people might identify us as a cult. Are we? Here's my answer: *I don't care*. What *is* a cult? A belief system that the person using the word 'cult' does not like. Is AA a cult? *I don't care*. They've helped people—I hope I help as many people in my lifetime. Is the Marine Corps a cult? *I don't care.* I care about *effective.* And since I know The Program is *effective,* you can call it a satanic coven of witches if you want. The Program Source Code applies effectively to living your life. Judge us by what we do for you, not by some useless term you found in your Old Programming user's manual." He threw his hands up, and everyone else followed, the circle flailing. "Now reconvene with your groups in Actspace. You can bring one Pro friend you met at the party."

On his way back, Tim passed Leah, who was being admonished by Janie. "—should be back in Prospace. I think you might have to do some work on Victim Row."

Leah seemed to crumble at the mention of this duty.

Tim touched Janie lightly on the arm. "Excuse me. I met Leah during the party and invited her back to my group. I'm Tom Altman."

Janie's features loosened—clearly, Tom Altman had been designated a VIP. A glance at Leah. "That true?"

Leah paused, agitated, then gave a brief nod, her tufts of hair bobbing.

Janie's pert smile bunched her pretty cheeks into sinewy circles. "Okay. You kids have fun."

Leah trailed Tim back to the group, visibly upset by her conformity with Tim's lie. The others were crowded around Stanley John, an eager horde of informants providing "feedback."

"Ray was totally Off Program during Going to a Zombie Party. He gestured a *bunch.*"

"I experienced Shelly as being her Old Programming. She was using her physicality to draw people in so she'd experience self-worth."

"Joanne complained she was starving."

After administering a round-robin of reprimands, Stanley John walked them through several invasive "sharing" exercises, culminating in the Blame Game. Everyone had to share the most horrific event in his or her life, then reexperience it from the perpetrator's perspective.

Shelly, face stained with tears, was reliving a high-school rape. "I'm black. I'm poor. I don't have any money. I'm depressed. I live in a cardboard box, and a pretty young white girl walks by." Her chest started to heave, her words garbling. Tim noticed with a blend of pity and annoyance that she'd matched her hair clip to her socks. "I don't want to hurt her, I just want to feel good. She's wearing a low-cut dress and no underwear, and that makes it so easy."

"It's okay," Stanley John said. "You're doing great. We're all in this experience together."

They held hands in a ring, squeezing empathetically, and finally Shelly resumed her tale. "She's walking *alone,* she left a party on the Venice boardwalk *alone,* and is walking *alone* at three in the morning. I bet she wants it. Maybe she deserves it." She deteriorated into sobs, smearing her hair off her sticky face as the others clustered around to comfort her. Then Stanley John led her through confronting and telling off her rapist.

Joanne's teary performance as a breast lump that turned out to be benign was less rousing.

A woman nearby fainted, but a roving blue-shirt was waiting to break her fall. A group leader dragged an unconscious kid through the gap into Hearspace, probably to get him into cooler air—another procedure for processing the overwhelmed. Tim filed away this tidbit as a potential stratagem he could use later to move Leah's unconscious body from the building. Hot air kept gusting down; he added dehydration to his list of concerns.

Stanley John gestured to Leah. "Your turn to blame."

"Okay." Leah closed her eyes for a moment, as if gathering courage. "The last time I saw my stepdad was after I'd had a pretty tough run with him. My mom, too. I was going to see if maybe we could patch things up. You know when you do that? Try to talk to your parents as if they're actually going to listen this time?"

Tom joined the murmur of accord, which Stanley John cut short. "Quit whining, Leah, and tell it as your stepdad."

Leah took a deep breath and held it before exhaling. "You're always in need of attention. You get yourself into messes and expect me to clean them up for you, then you complain I'm too controlling. You're jealous of our new family, and you interfere with our happiness constantly. Then you complain you don't belong here. You indulge your fantasies of your dead father, reminding your mother of the pain of that past life—your very existence causes her suffering. It wasn't until you went to college that we could finally celebrate our new freedom by having a child—our *own* child. And just when we think you're out of our hair, you turn up again with another mess. I don't care if you're afraid you might have made a mistake. I don't even have to listen to you, because it's the same story every time. You deserved"—she pressed her lips together until they stilled—"you deserved for me to slap you across the face in front of your mother and your baby sister."

"*Great,*" Stanley John said. "Now, what do you have to say back to them?"

She took a moment to gather herself. "You punish me by taking a hostile disinterest in my life and friends and hobbies. You're cold and withholding, like you have to protect yourselves from me and what I represent, but that's nothing more than you stewing in your victimhood. Even though I love my baby sister, even though I think she's beautiful and precious, you've done your best to make me feel small by pouring your hearts and souls into her while reminding me every chance you get in some small, petty way how much you resent me. You want me to submit to your control, but I won't. Not anymore. It may drive you insane, but I'm finally learning to think for myself. And you know what I figured out? I don't need you anymore."

Whoops and applause. Joanne wiped her cheeks, shaking her head with amazement and envy. Tim blinked hard, seating himself back in character—he'd been drawn into her performance.

Leah's smoky green-gray eyes found Tim. "How about you? What's the worst thing that ever happened to you?"

"My daughter was murdered," Tim heard himself say.

Her mouth parted, but no sound came out. Stanley John stepped forward, shouting something above the deafening din and shattering the trance into which Tim had been lulled. At once he was back in the thrice-split ballroom at the Radisson with people sobbing and fainting all around him.

TD drifted to the periphery of the group, observing paternalistically.

A panic tingle ran across Tim's lower back as he fought for composure. He could practically smell the faint odor of baby powder and melted Jolly Rancher stored in the carpet of Ginny's empty room.

He started tentatively, "It happened about a year ago. Jenny was walking home from school. She never . . . never got there. They found her body that night." He was veering dangerously close to the truth. He wiped his nose, which had started to run, and became Tom Altman. "Even though I've had some financial success"—from Stanley John's expression, this wasn't news to him—"it's been a hard year. My wife and I split up."

"Tell it from the perpetrator's point of view," Stanley John said.

Tim sensed TD's eyes fasten on him. His mouth had gone dry. Sweat stung his eyes. He thought of Kindell's elongated forehead. The short, dense hair, so much like fur. "I, uh . . ."

"Go ahead, buddy," Stanley John urged. "This is about strength, not comfort."

Excavating a trick he'd learned in Ranger training, Tim imagined detaching from his body. He turned and watched himself, an interested observer.

Tom Altman faced the group, talking from the perspective of his dead daughter's killer. Tom Altman imitated the fictional killer, saying that he watched the girl walk home after school, but then suddenly Tim was back within his flesh, a seashell rush filling his ears. "One day she splits off from her friends and walks alone. I drive slowly behind her. I call her name. When she turns, I snatch her into my truck. I get tape over her mouth. I take her back to my place where I can have"—his body felt incredibly weighty, sagging on his bones—"privacy. I pin her arms down. I slice through her green overalls with a box cutter. She's very small and pale. She doesn't move. I don't think she knows what's happening. I don't want her to be frightened. But she is, and she gets even more scared when I cut through her underpants. They have different sizes of snowflakes on them. Later *I'm* scared when I cut her up with a hacksaw. I don't know how to dispose of what's left, so I dump the parts of her by a creek."

A clod of grief rose from his gut, lodging itself in the back of his throat. He coughed. The others' eyes were tearing up. Leah fixed him with a gaze that moved right through him. He kept his eyes on hers even as the others thumped his back and hugged him.

TD drifted back a few steps, keeping just within earshot.

"Jesus," Stanley John weighed in. "Great job. You can learn a lot by exploring your identification with your daughter's killer."

Staring at the genuine awe etched into Stanley John's face, Tim felt his hand twitch. He repeated to himself, *I am Tom Altman*, to help check his natural instinct, which was to ram his fist through that all-American jaw. Far more disturbing, he felt his mind open slightly to Stanley John's ugly suggestion.

"Now let's see you stand up to this guy. Tom? Come on, now. Your daughter's killer has spoken. Now respond to him."

Tim thought for a moment but came up with nothing except a feeling of sickness. "I have no response to him. He killed a random girl who happened to be my daughter. Telling him off would be like explaining to a rabid dog why biting is bad. He's just an animal. There is no answer."

Stanley John leaned in close. "The Program's going to give you that answer."

The ballroom fell abruptly into darkness. Trumpets vibrated the partition walls—*2001: A Space Odyssey* redux.

Mad, sightless movement as the crowd stampeded back to Hearspace. Tim used the confusion to sneak beyond the horseshoe, keeping Leah in sight. When she ducked through the curtain, he hid behind an amp nearby.

For once TD wasn't pacing; he sat on the edge of the dais, Stanley John and Janie perched on either side of him. His voice came low and smooth. "I'd like everybody to lie down flat on the floor for the first Guy-Med. Close your eyes. Make sure no body part is crossed over any other body part." A deliberate pause after each phrase. "Go still. Clear your mind. You're here for you. This is your moment. Now think about your breathing. Listen to yourself breathing. Feel the oxygen going into your body. Feel all your contamination leave you as you breathe out. Now concentrate on your toes. Take a deep, cleansing breath. Send the clean, pure, oxygenated blood to your toes."

TD moved soporifically up the body, repeating each command three times in rich surround sound. The lights waned until they held only the feeblest presence in the room. Most of the participants stayed eerily still, their brains autopiloting across a sea of alpha waves. The room went black. Crouching behind the amp, Tim felt his own eyelids relax, and he dug a thumb into a pressure point in his hand.

TD continued languidly, "You're six years old, standing outside your childhood door. You're going to follow me. Let me lead you. Let's open the door, you and me."

Tim pulled off his jacket and unzipped the heavy lining bit by bit, bunching the fabric over the teeth to cut the sound.

"Go inside. I'm going to leave you here. Don't be scared."

Tim freed the coat lining, tucked it under his arm, and belly-crawled the few feet to the curtain. When TD's voice changed intonation, Tim froze. He waited a few moments as the commands resumed, then continued.

"There are your favorite childhood toys. A beloved teddy bear—*discarded*. Your blankie—*ragged* and *torn*. Lie down on your little bed. Hold up a mirror, see what you look like. Look how *sad* you are. Look how *lonely* you are. *Confused. Insecure. Ugly.*"

Childhood images flew at Tim from the darkness, unleashed bats. His mother's bare drafting table. His father's entrusting him to a girlfriend's aunt when he left for a "business trip"—the woman hadn't gotten out of bed the entire three weeks except to empty her ashtrays and reheat frozen dinners.

"Why are you *weeping alone* in your bed? What made you a *victim?* Daddy forgetting to play with you? Mommy not kissing you good night? They're still there, those *broken promises,* tearing at you, controlling you."

Tim reached the curtain, blinking against the stream of light. Leah faced away from him, engrossed in the sound board. As hoped, she was alone.

He slithered into Prospace, rose silently, and unfolded the coat lining on the floor; it expanded into an olive-drab duffel. Another Pete Krindon perk—creative clothing design. He bent over, tugging up his pant leg and pulling the thin, handkerchief-wrapped flask from the top of his left boot. Presized strips of duct tape adorned the rise of the boot; using TD's sonorous voice for cover, he peeled them off and stuck them dangling from his arm. He slid the flask from its handkerchief. Using a rolling wardrobe as partial cover, he crept up behind Leah, holding his breath and dousing the paisley fabric.

He pictured it perfectly—one arm wrapping her torso, the press of the handkerchief to her mouth, the firming of the arm-sleeve gag. Working swiftly, he'd ease her unconscious body to the floor, crossing her ankles and weaving the duct tape through them. The thin strips he'd wrap around her thumbs so she wouldn't wind up with bruised wrists. He'd lay her in the duffel, hoist it over a shoulder, and shoot down the fire escape to the back lot before TD noticed a hiccup in his sound engineering. The Hummer held down a VIP space around front. The getaway key pressed against Tim's thigh through the thin pocket.

He moved forward, ether dripping on the carpet. Visible just over Leah's hunched shoulder, the EMERGENCY EXIT sign beckoned. He took a final silent step; he could have reached out and stroked the frayed edges of her hair.

TD's amplified voice continued its deadening cadence. "Look—there's your mother, full of life and *mistakes*. There's your father, with all his *shortcomings*. See him for what he really is. Why does he have a *need* to turn you into a *victim?*"

Tim lowered the handkerchief.

Leah spun and covered her gasp with a hand, unable to prevent a pleased smile.

"Oh," she said in a hoarse whisper. "It's you."

Her features transformed as she took note of the rag in his hand, the lengths of tape dripping from his forearm, the open duffel on the floor behind him.

One shout would bring a stampede of blue-shirts.

"You're here to kidnap me." She spoke with a sharp, wounded anger.

Tim stuffed the wet handkerchief into his pocket. "Not anymore."

"You lied. Like everyone else." Her face trembled, on the verge of tears. She edged toward the curtain, and he let her. She sucked in a breath, turning to scream, but then stopped and faced him. "Your dead daughter. You make her up, too?"

"No."

They stared at each other, the sound board humming beside them and throwing off heat. Tim barely had time to register the sudden silence when a burst of radio static issued from outside the curtain, followed by TD's unmiked growl.

"—what happened to my rear sound?"

Leah scampered back to the forgotten sound board. "Oh, shit. Oh, shit."

Tim dove behind the clothes rack, skidding on his stomach. He disappeared behind a veil of dry cleaning as Skate blew through the curtain with a flourish of his thick arm, radio pressed to his face. Peeking from the waistband of his sweatshirt was the gun-blued hilt of a knife—an odd tool for a hotel seminar.

He took note of the open duffel on the floor and, with a single expert movement, swept the knife from its sheath. He held the ten-inch bowie upside down, the blade out and pointed toward his elbow. "What's up?"

The ballroom, filled with hundreds of entranced Neos awaiting their next command, gave off a deafening silence. "Nothing," Leah finally said.

Skate toed the duffel. "The fuck is this?"

"It stores the mike cables."

Tim watched the exchange breathlessly through a screen of cellophane.

TD's voice spit again from Skate's radio. *"—there some issue back there?"*

Leah pursed her lips, stared at Skate's gleaming blade. "I . . . just zoned out. I got swept up in the Guy-Med."

Skate eyed her, probably picking up the slight tremble in her voice. Finally, he keyed the radio, sliding his knife back into its sheath. "She screwed up."

"Please explain to Leah that if she doesn't fix the rear distortion, I'm going to lose the entire group."

Head bent over the graphic equalizer, Leah fussed with the frequency levers. Skate stared at her for a long time, then withdrew.

"Get the hell out of here before the lights come back up," Leah said. "If Skate catches you, we're both in deep shit."

Tim found his feet. He hesitated, facing her.

"You've done enough already, okay. Just go. *Now.*"

"Mommy," a woman shrieked in a little girl voice. *"Moooommy!"*

Within seconds the ballroom reverberated with the screams of regressed voices, a chilling, insane-asylum chorus.

Tim crept over and gave a peek under the curtain. Skate had retreated to his post, but a few of the Pros were up, wandering the shadowy horseshoe perimeter, contributing malicious echoes. *"Mommy. Daddy. Where are you?"*

Stanley John and Janie patrolled the interior, leaning over the sprawled, mewling bodies, pouring it on. "We never wanted you!" Sweat dripped from Janie's forehead as she bent over a sobbing man. "You're worthless."

Tim watched the movement of the blue-shirts, then crawled out and rolled swiftly across the open carpet. He made it a few yards inside the horseshoe before Stanley John's voice rained down on him—"What are you doing over here?"

"Mom," Tim bleated, fluttering closed eyelids. "Where's my mom?"

"She doesn't care about you. She left you." Stanley John moved on to harangue someone else.

An overpowering voice cut through the commotion. "TD is here with you now. You're safe. Your guide is here." The clamor gradually settled, until only scattered sniffling persisted. "Now let me lead you out of your childhood room. Turn and say good-bye to me, your guide. I'm leaving right now, but I'll always be here, right inside you. *Always.* When the room grows bright, you'll come to, and you won't remember anything that you've experienced."

The lights came up, and they all stirred, then found their feet, battlefield dead coming to life. As the Neos groggily located their seats, TD pressed on as if nothing had happened.

"In The Program there isn't anything we despise more than a *victim.* I don't know about you, but I'm tired of living in a *victim society*. You can sue cigarette companies because you *chose* to smoke for thirty years. You can sue a TV show if your stupid kid lights himself on fire. Hell, you can sue Mc-Donald's because you turned yourself into a fat-ass. Better not pat a female colleague on the arm, or you might be *victimizing* her. Don't say 'Jesus Christ' in front of a Bible-thumper or you'll be *victimizing* him.

"In The Program we're *accountable* for our choices. We're not *excuse makers*. But some of you"—an Uncle Sam point of the finger—"still are, and your mind-set is contaminating. You need to *negate Victimhood*. Nothing is more useless than actions to *please*, actions to *gratify*, actions to *ingratiate*. They are the epitome of powerlessness. Your behavior should be for *you*. Don't laugh *courteously*. Don't call Mom because you feel *obligated*. Those actions have no place in The Program. Here we exalt *strength*—" He fanned a hand at the audience.

"Not comfort!"

"Comfort will make you weak. Only strength will set you free. We strive for *fulfillment*—"

"Not happiness!"

Tim mentally filed these additions to The Program Code.

"You don't want to be *happy*. Happiness is for idiots. You want to be decisive. You want to be *fulfilled*. Sometimes that involves *suffering*. Sometimes that involves *working hard*. Are you ready to *work hard?*"

"Yes!"

"I want each group to select their biggest victim to come up here and take a seat on Victim Row." TD rested his hands on the backs of two chairs in the line being assembled by diligent Pros on the dais. "Think of it as intense therapy." His voice dropped, taking on an edge of menace. "One Pro will be joining us onstage. You already know who you are." Leah emerged, head bent, and trudged to the dais. TD helped her up, eyes smoldering charitably above his tight smile.

Hearspace filled with the sounds of Neos fighting. A few Pros with trays strapped to them like vendors at a baseball game threaded through the bickering groups, tossing Cliff Bars and handing out Mountain Dews. People tore at the wrappers with their mouths, gulping and slurping, gulag prisoners in Levi's Dockers. Tim could almost hear the rising sugar hum. It took his last ounce of willpower to refrain. A woman screamed out that her bladder was going to explode; she was told to visualize it empty.

Back in Tim's group, Joanne, the leading contender for Victim Row, suffered a battery of buzz-phrase accusations. Her inability to stand up for herself only proved the charges against her. When Victim Row convened, she was seated beside Leah.

TD paced in front of the chosen ones. He laid into a nursing student first, working on her skillfully until she admitted she'd created her own diabetes when she was a little girl to get her daddy's attention. The prematurely bald teenager next to her divulged that he'd smoked pot twice and wrestled in high school; within minutes TD had him convinced he was a violent drug offender who'd never taken responsibility for himself.

Moving down the row, TD grew increasingly personal. The crowd contributed to the abuse during riotous interludes. After Joanne floundered on a few of his questions, TD produced a mirror and handed it to her. "Look at yourself." He spoke with an icy calm. "You're obese. You're disgusting. Why would anyone want to be with you? What? What, Joanne? Why are you blubbering? How am I making you feel?"

"You're making me feel inferior."

"*Wrong*. You *feel* inferior. Don't try to say it's my fault. Tell me I'm stupid. Go ahead, tell me."

She exhaled shakily. "I . . . I can't."

"*Can't*. My favorite word." TD's mouth became a dark slit. "Look in that mirror. Tell me what you see."

"I guess a woman who's trying to—"

"Trying to. *Trying to?* Let me tell you what *I* see." His eyes bored through her. "I see three-point-five billion years of evolution, drawing you out of the primordial stew, straightening your stoop, granting you opposable thumbs. I see the trillions of other faulty models with slightly different physical traits, perceptive systems, cognitive skills, who *died* along the way so you can sit here today. I see a two-and-a-half-pound cerebrum. I see thousands of years of cultural advancement leading to the crops and farms that produced the sustenance that's gone into your cells. I see the sunshine that fed those plants, the universe that created that sun. I see life, time, and space distilled into human form, into this pinnacle of existence. And you *can't* . . . what? Tell me I'm stupid?"

She was wheezing so hard she barely got out the words. "You're stupid."

"Guess what? I don't feel stupid. You can't *make me* feel anything. Do you know why, Joanne? Because I'm not a *victim*. And if you weren't a *victim,* you'd be able to take an insult or two. If you weren't a *victim,* you'd be able to endure a little criticism."

She fumbled for her inhaler.

"Oh, there it is. Your sympathy crutch. Did someone develop asthma so people would feel sorry for her? Where's your self-respect? Well, since you're so concerned with what other people think . . ." He faced the horseshoe. "Let's give it to her, folks."

The crowd exploded. Neos rose to their feet, shouting abuse at her. "Ugly pig!"

A shovel-spade of a woman, a good fifty pounds up on Joanne, stood on her sagging chair, hands clutching her buttocks as she leaned forward like a fan baiting an umpire. "Fat fucking cow!"

Joanne doubled over, head lurching. Janie stepped forward and produced an airsickness bag into which Joanne promptly barfed, eliciting another outburst of vilification from the audience. Her hairdo had collapsed like an angel cake.

"That's good," TD said. "Purge your self-loathing."

The torrent of deprecations continued unabated as Joanne

purged. At last TD raised his arms, and the crowd silenced instantly.

TD massaged Joanne's shoulders. "I'm proud of you, Joanne. By being able to sit through that, you've shown *incredible* growth. By the time you're done with The Program, you'll never have to feel that way again. Now, get up and take a bow."

Joanne's knees buckled when she stood. The crowd picked up TD's encouraging applause, drowning out her mumbled objections as she was guided off the dais.

Leah sat alone in the row of chairs, her hair over her eyes. Her fingers wound convulsively in the fringe of her shirt. The crowd was breathing together, a slow, forceful rhythm.

"Leah, do you still have your rash?"

"Yes. I've chosen a rash because it's a way to make myself a victim privately."

"You're still learning to escape your cycle of victimization, aren't you?"

"Yes. I am."

TD swirled in a magician's pivot. "Why don't you show everyone here your victim rash?"

She looked back at him with glassy eyes.

"You've learned to hide your urge to be a victim, not eradicate it. Hiding your victimhood gives you comfort. *So.* Why don't you show everyone here what a victim you are? In fact, why don't you take off *all* your clothes? You're not going to give these people the power over you to make you *ashamed of your own body,* are you?"

The audience began to simmer.

Leah mechanically began shedding her clothes. When she finished, her skin glistened with a fine perspiration.

The crowd went rigid with a kind of dark ecstasy. Despite the cooling drafts from the overhead vents, Tim's undershirt clung to him like a second skin. His stomach churned as he watched TD prompt Leah.

She bit back an energized smile and shouted, "This is my

body! And you can't make me ashamed of it! *I negate victimhood! I reject comfort! I exalt strength!*"

Uproarious applause. As Leah took up her clothes and stepped off the dais, TD said, "I wouldn't be surprised if that somatic manifestation of victimhood cleared up soon."

The activities and Oraes and Guy-Meds continued, an endless, torturous cycle, grinding down Tim's sanity until he longed to submit. But he fought every moment of the afternoon, evening, and night, upholding Tom Altman's plausibility while focusing, meditating, doing anything to avoid being swept away in the rush of lunacy. Using pain to guard against the ceaseless kettledrum and soft-fluttering lights, he twisted one hand into the other as if boring a screw through an obstinate plank. His palm was developing a blister from his thumbnail's grinding, a stigma he might have considered melodramatic had the discomfort allowed him room for amusement.

A flurry of scenes marked the final hours, glimpsed as if in the sporadic flash of a strobe light. Joanne standing on a chair, screaming, "I take on anger! I permit myself to feel anger because I stand up for myself!"

Shelly curled in the fetal position, sobbing, Stanley John leering over her like a barking drill sergeant. "Did Daddy molest you? Is that why you're a slut?"

Her nodding answer before slipping a thumb into her mouth. "I th-think so. In some ways."

Group claps. The loud throb of a recorded heartbeat. The numbing thump of a kettledrum.

Not once did Leah reemerge from backstage.

At long last, after the umpteenth rendition of *Thus Spake Zarathustra*, TD took a deep bow on the dais. "We'll be contacting you soon to make additional colloquia available so you can continue your growth. But for now I want to say *congratulations*. You're all on your way. I'm proud of you for having the strength to—"

"Get with The Program!"

After retrieving their cell phones and watches, the participants bustled to the exits, charged, exuberant, and babbling incessantly about how much they'd learned. Still competing for best in show.

A rush of light-headedness hit Tim, and he used an arm to lower himself back into his chair. He hadn't eaten or drunk anything since dinner two days before.

Stanley John strolled up and leaned over him, hands on his knees. "Hey, buddy. Great work today. I have some exciting news. TD wants to invite you into Prospace for a minute." Randall and Skate slid behind him, confirming for Tim that his cover had been blown. He was going to go the way of Danny Katanga, PI.

They slipped through the curtain. In the midst of a jamboree of toiling Pros, TD relaxed in an armchair, a white towel around his neck—Elvis after the second show at the Sands. To his right, Leah was breaking down the sound board; she took one look at Tim and turned her back. He was certain she'd given him up. He noted with some amusement that she'd loaded his duffel bag with cables.

"Tom, my friend, sit down." TD patted a flimsy folding chair opposite him, and Tim gratefully sank into it. Only now could he see that TD had freckles, pale and plentiful, dominating his youthful features. After performing for twenty-four hours, he burned with evangelistic zeal.

Skate circled behind Tim, and Tim kept an eye on his reflection in the side of a metal crate. He tensed, ready to fight or bolt with what strength he could muster. "It's a real pleasure to meet you, sir."

"Please, please. Call me Teacher." TD eased one leg over the other. "I find you very impressive."

Tim let out a shaky breath, which fortunately made it seem as if he were shocked and honored. His mouth had cottoned from dehydration.

"It takes real strength to enter the mind of your daughter's killer. I think you've made peace with the killer, and that's why you have nothing to say to him. I think you *haven't* made peace about something else. About how you dealt with your daughter's death . . . ?"

The painful secret, TD's hand whip of choice. Tim waited through the drawn-out silence, not wanting to commit Tom Altman to an unconsidered course of action. He resorted to understatement. "It was a difficult time."

TD's head dipped in a slight nod—the response seemed to be what he'd been looking for. "I'd like to advance you to the next step."

Leah wouldn't turn to meet Tim's eyes.

"Really? Like become a Pro?"

"We've only asked a few people—the Neos we see as *very* capable—to come to our ranch Monday for a special three-day retreat."

Leah froze, her shoulders and neck tensing.

"You see, this thing here today"—TD flared his hands—"this is only the beginning. A test model, no more. We're really optimizing—the Next Generation Colloquium we've been planning is new-platform software. Right now I'm interested in one thing and one thing only: selecting from the hundreds and hundreds of Neos the right few with the vision to take that next step with us. I'll be honest—we had closed the first platform, but we'd love to have you included."

Evidently Tom Altman's $90 million portfolio had checked out. The ingenious ploy—Inner Circle as bankroll for The Program's expansion—allowed TD to sidestep the encumbrances of attaining funding, repaying loans, or answering to a board. Even the process of weeding out the pikers he'd made profitable. Three hundred people at five hundred a pop—Tim's dad should have dreamed it up.

TD bent his head sympathetically. "What's wrong? I sense your hesitation. You can share it with me."

"I . . . well . . . I've just always believed in taking things slow," Tom Altman stammered.

Leah resumed wrapping a cable around her hand.

"That Societal Programming is precisely what stands in your way." TD's eyes, piercing and relentless, seemed fixed on a spot three inches behind Tim's head—a vintage technique for hypnotic induction. Tim relaxed his pupils, letting TD's face blur. "If you want to be free, you have to overwrite it."

Tom Altman mused on that, squirming a bit in his chair. "It's just a lot all at once, and I'm still a little hazy from my whole . . . experience. Can I give it some thought?"

"I'm sorry, Tom. It's a onetime opportunity. Things are moving really fast for us. And, hey, it's just three days. We're not asking you to sign over your house or anything."

Everyone laughed, and suddenly Tim was aware of their audience. Tom Altman joined in late and a touch eagerly. "There *is* more I want to find out"—Leah's cable wrapping grew furious—"about myself, I mean." Leah half turned, and Tim risked a glance at her profile.

TD nodded at Skate, who slipped out through the curtain, then he turned his intense focus back to Tim. "Today you were introduced to this new practice. This new reality. You have a responsibility to yourself now. But"—he slapped his knee and leaned forward—"maybe you're not ready after all."

Tom Altman steeled his neck a bit too dramatically. "I *am* ready."

TD rewarded him with a delighted grin. "Glad to have you on board."

"How do I get there?"

"Oh, we don't have people just *drive* to the ranch." TD's lip twitched at the vulgarity of the thought. "Randall will pick you up. Where do you live?"

"I've been knocking around between friends' guesthouses, actually." Tim added in a whisper, "*Divorce.*"

TD smiled understandingly. "Precipitated by your daughter's death?"

Tim affected more agitated body language. "Sort of. You could say so."

"Well, we'll have plenty of time to explore that later." TD bit his lip. "Randall can meet you here at the hotel Monday morning? Why don't we call it eight o'clock?"

Skate reappeared with Jason Struthers of Struthers Auto Mall, keeping him on deck near the curtain.

Still light-headed and weak, Tim stood.

TD shook his hand. "Welcome to the future."

Twenty-one

*D*riving home in the sunrise, Tim struggled to keep from nodding off. He felt blurry and dissociated, and his body couldn't comprehend that it was early morning. Unfortunately, his 5:00 A.M. wake-up call had made Will Henning no less animated. He'd gotten all blustery at the identification of Betters—at last a target. When Tim related his decision to abort the snatch, Will's voice hardened, giving Tim an idea of what kind of tyrant it took to push a $100 million film through production.

"How *dare* you flip the script on me. That wasn't your goddamn call to make. *I* am the client here."

"I'm a deputy U.S. marshal, sir. The Service doesn't have clients."

"You're back in the Service because of *me*. One call to Marco, you'll be driving a rent-a-cop cart at the Beverly Center."

"If you think that's the most promising way to meet your objectives, go for it."

"You think you can hardball me? I dealt with Marlon *fucking* Brando in the seventies." Tim laughed involuntarily. A gravelly exhale from Will. "You lying piece of shit."

"I promised I'd help Leah. Not kidnap her."

"We both know there's no difference right now."

"The only legal justification for taking Leah into custody against her will is if she's in imminent danger. She's not. She's in her right mind, there was no evidence of physical abuse—to be honest, I was impressed with her capabilities."

"You neglect to mention that her 'capabilities' landed her in a mind-control cult."

"And yours made you a Hollywood producer. I'm sure there are plenty of people who'd take issue with that choice."

"Don't fuck with us, Deputy. Emma's beside herself. We haven't slept in—"

"Sir, with all due respect, you are not the victims here."

"Now you're a shrink."

"No. It's just something I found helpful to remember in the wake of my daughter's murder." For once Will remained silent. Tim pulled into the garage and turned off the engine. His shoulders throbbed, sending pangs to the base of his skull. "Good-bye, Will." He snapped the phone shut and pulled himself from the Hummer.

Trudging through the kitchen, Tim swirled the punch cup he'd smuggled out of the Radisson, making the cherry beads of residue dance. He set the cup and an appropriated brownie on the table and moved to the living room, where Bear's slumbering form occupied the couch. Boston lay on the floor beside Bear, matching his heavy breathing, and Tim felt a stab of appreciation for their dutiful waiting.

In the bedroom Dray sat propped up on a wedge of pillows against the headboard, static-edged dialogue notched a few clicks too high on the TV. Dead asleep.

The face he caught looking back at him from the mounted mirror was as gray as the taste in his mouth. Acid no longer washed through his stomach—he'd gone past the point of hunger several hours ago. His heart jerked irregularly in his chest, still trying to recover its customary rhythm. Through bleary eyes, he watched his wife sleep, flooded with gratitude for the simple, familiar tableau.

Slowly he felt his body mellow into bone-deep exhaustion.

Dray's lids parted slowly. Her smile was so effortless and uncomplicated it moved right through him. She held out her arms and said in a sleep-cracked voice, "You're back."

She embraced him around the waist, and he ran his fingers deep through her hair, scratching, a sensation she loved when she felt tired or lazy. "Let me look at you." She pulled back. "Jesus Christ. You didn't look this bad when you held recon in a Bosnian tree fort for six days. What did they put you through?"

He managed to bumble out an incoherent summary. He was circling back through the Guy-Meds for maybe the third time when Dray nodded. "I get it."

"You waited up?"

"Tried. We thought you'd be home yesterday afternoon. I got stressed, and so I called Bear, and we sat up and pretended to watch a couple John Waynes."

"I couldn't call. There weren't phones."

She threw back the sheets. "Get in here." As he slid into bed, she leaned forward, swallowing hard. "I don't feel so hot. I trusted Bear with take-out sushi."

"Big mistake."

"Maybe my last." She watched him closely, brushing the hair off his forehead, the relief in her eyes palpable.

He lay back on his pillow, which felt inordinately lush. "It's a whole thing out there. A factory."

"I'm glad you decided to walk away. No matter what she's gotten herself into, she doesn't deserve getting duffeled to the curb and waking up daddy's little captive. We'll figure out the money. We always do." She kept smoothing his hair off his face. "Timothy, are you all right?"

"I don't want to leave her in there. I can't."

Dray's eyes flared a bit. She seemed to need a moment to tamp down her reaction. "She's lucky to have you. Leah."

"She doesn't have me. You have me."

Her voice kept its edge. "You know what I mean."

"There are dozens of people being *controlled*."

"Willingly."

"It's *not* willing, Dray."

"Calm down a bit. Let's talk this through. Going up to the ranch puts you in even greater danger."

"That's the job. We put ourselves on the line to protect people. That's what we do. Not just when it's convenient."

Dray pushed herself up so she was sitting cross-legged. "No, we put ourselves on the line to uphold the law."

He stared at the floor.

"There's no crime here," she said.

"I'll find one."

"Bill of Rights be damned." She softened her voice. "You went down this road before, Timothy. If you pursue this and there is no crime . . ."

Tim turned away from her.

". . . you'll end up on the outside again."

Now that he'd returned to a place where he could expect safety and sanity, his frustrations were welling up. "This guy's pulling in money hand over fist, and he's hell-bent on expansion. I'm not gonna let it happen."

"Are you sure that's what this is about?"

His eyeballs ached with fatigue. "Huh?"

Dray tilted her head at the hall, a gesture that had come to indicate Ginny and the loss of her. He flashed on his taking on Kindell's voice at the colloquium and a chill moved through his insides.

"Come on, Dray."

"You don't feel protective of Leah?"

"I do *now,* that's for sure. She covered for me and took some vicious punishment for it. That kind of thing is built in to a person. A kid like that deserves something better."

"Every kid deserves something better—but they don't receive it from the federal authorities. Thank God."

"She's *brainwashed,* Dray."

"Right. So she could betray you whenever—maybe she already has. You really want to put your life in this kid's hands? They could be waiting for you up there, tying the noose as we speak."

"She wouldn't."

"Oh, right. Because she has such good judgment? Either she's controlled, in which case you can't count on her, or she's not controlled, in which case she's there by fully exercised choice and you have to back off and leave her be."

Tim was tempted to acknowledge the sense of that statement. Instead he offered, "If she rolled on me now, she'd be punished even worse for not telling earlier."

"To this lay observer, she seems like a glutton for punishment." Dray bit the inside of her lip and rolled it between her teeth. "What's she look like? In person?"

"She's taller than I thought. Sort of a willowy build—"

"Willowy?" Dray's tone was a sure indication that he'd misstepped. "She's *willowy?*"

"Well, kind of slender, yeah."

Dray moved her book from her lap to the nightstand. The lamp rocked a bit on its base. "Okay, *willowy.* What else? Does she have flaxen hair, too?"

"Where the hell is all this coming from, Dray?"

"I don't know. Why don't you ask Leah and her *willowy build?*" The triangle of skin above the stretched collar of her T-shirt had flushed. "Why are you so impassioned about this case?"

"Seeing this event . . ." He looked down at his hands, which rested meekly on the turned-back sheets. He dozed off for an instant but caught his head as it dipped.

Dray's eyebrows lost themselves beneath her bangs; the heat had gone right out of her. After a moment she pushed two fingers into the ring of his fist, and he squeezed them. He took longer and longer blinks until he could no longer keep his eyes open. The last thing he sensed before drifting off was the caress of Dray's lips on his cheek.

A paw covered his entire shoulder, shaking him awake. Tim rolled over, sliding an arm across his eyes. "What time is it?"

Bear's voice—"High noon, podnah. The old man wants to see you."

Tim groaned and leaned forward, his joints aching. Evidently Will hadn't waited long to air his grievances to Tannino. "At home?"

"At the barn. He's been running the show through Saturdays for a while now. Taking advantage of availability pay. Some of us have already put in a half day."

Tim blinked into the light. Bear was contentedly munching a brownie.

"Where'd you get that?"

"Kitchen table. Why?"

"It's evidence, you dolt."

Bear stopped midchew and angled the brownie to reveal the near-perfect missing semicircle. "Hahng ohn." He scurried to the bathroom. Tim heard a plop, then the flush of the toilet. Bear reentered, using the inside of his shirt collar to wipe his mouth. "Okay," he said. "So no one ever has to know about that."

"Where's Dray?"

"I talked her into driving by the clinic on the way to the station. She was still feeling pretty nauseous from the sushi."

"Maybe she ate a bad brownie."

Bear did not return his smile.

Twenty-two

"**I** have an agenda. Senator Feinstein has an agenda. Will Henning has an agenda. You don't get to have an agenda." Tannino exhaled irritably, puffing up his white-dusted hair in the front. He cocked back in his chair, twirling the point of a silver letter opener against his thumb. "There's no room."

"This isn't an agenda. It's an obligation."

"Goddamnit, Rackley. I told you not to fuck around. I told you just to get the girl."

"Why? So he can do it to others? You can't save one person and leave the machinery functioning. What's the point?" Tim gestured at the framed confirmation photo behind Tannino. "You want your niece going off to college with—?"

"Don't personalize, Rackley. It's vulgar."

Tim sank back in the couch and did his best to ignore the fatigue headache that six hours of sleep hadn't quite vanquished. "You're right. I apologize. I just—"

"You just what?"

"I want to take the prick down."

Tannino's thick eyebrows rose. "You're more emotional these days, Rackley."

"I'm sorry."

"It's nothing to apologize for. Emotion. Just don't let it interfere with the job." Tannino tapped the letter opener on the edge of his knuckles. "I guess it'll sidestep the more sensitive issues involved with taking the girl into custody if you talk her out. You think you can?"

"I have a shot at it. Or I'll dig up evidence so we can disrupt the cult. If the cult disintegrates around her, she'll have to seek new options." Tim watched Tannino, but his narrow stare didn't give anything up. "Look, I'm not asking for something that benefits me here. I've got nothing to gain and less to lose."

"I'm not questioning your motives, Rackley. I'm saying you're a pain in the ass. And I *am* questioning your zeal. In view of last year's events, I'd be irresponsible not to."

"I promise you, Marshal, this is a threat we'd better pay attention to before it gets out of hand."

"I've got a loudmouth Hollywood producer crawling up my ass, calling you a diva." Tannino's lips twitched, and he looked away until the incipient grin no longer threatened. "You've dipped into the honey pot pretty good already, driving Hummers, wearing Cavaricci pants." Tim sensed Tannino's shift from pissed-off manager to long-suffering Italian paterfamilias. He was about to cave.

"Versace."

"Whatever. You have Thomas and Freed bloodhounding finances. Now you want more undercover at a secret location. This was not intended to be a balls-to-the-wall operation."

They stared at each other for a few moments, Tim letting the silence work on him. Finally Tannino snatched up the phone and dialed. He slid down the receiver and spoke over it. "Mention my niece again, I'll cut your eyes out." He snapped the phone back up. "Tannino for Winston Smith."

The hard-nosed assistant U.S. attorney was a vital ally to the Service. In the federal system, AUSAs make the world go round.

"I got a deputy going UC up on a ranch, scouting out a cult. I need to know if I can send him in with some transmitters. . . . No, we don't have enough for a wiretap warrant." Tannino's dark brown eyes fixed on Tim. "We don't have anything. . . . No charges brought." A sigh. "I know." He listened for a while, then said to Tim, "You were asked as a guest, correct?"

Tim nodded.

"What's that buy us? . . . Uh-huh. . . . Uh-huh. . . . Uh-huh. Thanks for nothing, Win." Tannino racked the phone.

"Okay, here it is: Since you were invited up, you can bring sound and image, but you have to keep it on your person."

"I can't wear a wire in. They could have me doing jumping jacks in the nude for all we know. Plus, these guys are too paranoid to do anything in front of me—a wire won't pick up what we need."

"Anything more, some defense attorney's gonna drop-kick out of court." Off Tim's expression Tannino said, "No one's gonna spank you for doing some extracurricular snooping, but running over a red flag from the AUSA"—he shrugged— "that could sink a case. You know this."

Tim's hands rose, clapped to his knees. "Looks like I'm going up naked."

"Looks that way."

*P*hone to his ear, Bear sat on Tim's desk, his feet in the bucket of the chair. The wood groaned as he jotted in the notepad pressed open on his knee. Holding engorged files, Thomas and Freed waited on him. All three turned as Tim approached.

Across the squad room, Denley and Palton rose from their chairs to steal a peek at him, Denley's lips moving as he supplied side-of-mouth commentary.

Tim Rackley, in-house novelty act.

Bear set down the phone and gathered up a scattering of printouts. "We'd better get upstairs."

Thomas and Freed didn't acknowledge Tim on the elevator ride up or as they passed through the bare offices vacated by the Secret Service. Thomas in particular gave off a smoldering resentment. Packing peanuts littered the floor like swollen confetti. Bear put a shoulder into the conference-room door to get it open, and they arranged themselves at one end of the oversize table.

Bear laid out his notepad, a variety of printed docs, and a

few sheets dark with scribbled writing. Across the table, Thomas and Freed exhibited an equally impressive array of paperwork. Stuck pressing flesh at a Head Feds dinner, Tannino had kept Tim waiting nearly an hour for their face-to-face. The deputies had spent the time well.

"I appreciate your jumping on this for us," Tim said.

"Let's get something straight right off the bat," Thomas said. "We'll work with you and we'll work well with you, but you can save your Boy Scout routine. Don't forget I pulled a fucking shotgun on you in an alley last March."

Bear held up his hands placatingly. "It's okay—"

"*Not with me.* I didn't like doing that. Not one bit. There was a moment where . . ." He stopped, his voice shaky, his jowly face flushed.

Thomas's distress caught Tim by surprise, undercutting his anger.

"We deal with enough shit on the job," Freed said in a more tempered voice. "You don't put a fellow deputy—let alone a friend—in a position where he might have to shoot you. It doesn't make for dreamless nights."

"You're right," Tim said as evenly as he could.

But Thomas wasn't done. "You don't think we all want to kick a little ass on the side sometimes? What you did, you embarrassed the Service. I was embarrassed to know you. I was embarrassed to have been your friend."

"His fucking daughter got *killed.*" Bear was on his feet, hands spread on the table. More intimately involved in Tim's trespasses, he'd already had the benefit of dealing with his anger and coming out the other side. He was no good at holding a grudge, and his loyalty, once renewed, had played revisionist historian with his own heated outlook during last year's tribulations. "He went through the wringer already, you smug fuck—court, media, jail. What gives you the right—"

"Bear. It's okay." Tim kept his eyes on Thomas. "I get it."

Thomas finally glanced away.

"Where should we start?" Tim said.

As Thomas continued to weather Bear's glare, Freed tapped his fingertips on the file before him. "As you likely surmised, Terrance Donald Betters is the principal of TDB Corp."

Bear slid a rap sheet from one of the stacks. "Born 'No Name Summers' to a teenage prostitute. Date of birth is different every time it pops up. We know he got hitched in '95. He deserted his wife, changed his name, and remarried. He would've gotten dinged for bigamy, but the first wife filed on grounds of desertion, inadvertently letting him off the hook. Divorced the second wife after five months. He has a certificate in biofeedback from a mail-order house, but he goes by 'Doctor' and tells people he's a Ph.D. His first cult, called 'Uroboris,' was composed of clients he stole from a psychologist he assisted in Oregon while using the name Fred Wick. The psychologist disappeared a few months after Betters started working there. Betters was never brought up on murder charges, but he got kicked out of the state for fraudulent activity. He came to California and started up a series of human-potential cults, each incarnation growing in size."

Freed's thin lips grew even thinner. "Ernie Tramine's substantial bank account was bilked—the money wired through a Cayman clearing account that was subsequently closed. Nothing concrete to link him to Betters. Nothing new on Reggie Rondell, but from what we've seen, his story checks out."

"You were right about the apartment where you had your first cult meet," Thomas said. "It's vacant. When I pressed the manager, he admitted that some college girl offered him a couple hundred to rent the pad for the day. She matches your description of Lorraine. I took a peek through the place—nothing. After the sign-up-fest, they cleared out."

Tim scanned over the numerous charges. *Theft by trick-*

*ery, 3-14-96—arrest only, DA reject. Embezzlement, 1-17-
99—acquitted after jury trial. Unauthorized access to computer data, 9-21-01—released, insufficient evidence.* "Busy
citizen."

"Busy enough to have learned his way around the law by
this point in the game," Freed said. "He's got no wants, no
warrants. He pays his taxes. We can't pry in with any wage-
and-hour laws since he pays his herd as dollar-a-year consul-
tants, and the Department of Labor won't be bothered
without a complainant. Betters picks extremely affluent people who sign their cash over to him—nothing illegal about
that."

"How about cooling-off-period laws?"

"It seems they all thaw out quite happily. No one's ever
come forward to protest."

Tim tapped Bear's elbow with a pen. "Reggie could open a
class action."

"Yeah," Bear said, "I'm sure he'll get right on that."

"Money trail?"

Freed said, "I called my hook at the IRS and spent the better part of ten hours rifling through Betters's filings, got dick
and more dick. The cash he protects in this elaborate offshore
scheme, that we had a tough time untangling, but it looks to
steer through all the right loopholes to stay legal. He con-
ducts business through a network of dummy corporations
and holding companies." Freed's clean-shaven face took on
the taint of a scowl, a rare show of emotion. "He's unscrupu-
lous as hell, but for the life of us, we can't find a single thing
he's doing that's illegal."

"How about the shrink who disappeared? And Katanga,
Will Henning's hired dick?"

"I tracked down the detectives for both cases," Thomas
said. "Nothing forensic, nothing circumstantial, nothing at
all. He's the king of Teflon this guy. Nothing sticks."

"What's he worth?"

"Upward of seventy million dollars," Freed said.

Bear let out a whistle.

"In 2000 he was living in a Silver Lake residence, long since sold. He's an Internet and P.O.-box junkie—your typical privacy freak. Different accounts under different names, the whole nine yards."

"How about the corporation?"

"It's been active. This year alone it bought land in . . ." Freed licked his thumb, turning back several stapled papers. "Here we go. Houston, Scottsdale, Spokane, Sylmar—right here in the North Valley, Fort Lauderdale, and Cambridge, Mass."

Bear shot Tim a knowing glance. Sylmar was a short drive from both Leah's former Van Nuys apartment and the San Fernando P.O. box.

"He's in escrow in Kushiro, Japan; Christchurch, New Zealand; and a village outside Hamburg. Seems to me your boy's looking to build an empire."

The thought brought a tingle across Tim's neck. "What kind of land?"

"Remote rural facilities. Former communes. Campgrounds. Retreats. Bankrupt rehabs. The place in Spokane's just fallow wheat fields."

"Tell me about Sylmar. Looks like that's where I'm headed."

"It's way up on the north peak of the Valley bordering Santa Clarita, smack in the middle of federal land—the Angeles National Forest. Colorful history to the place. Some Hollywood director built a ranch way back when, let it go to pot."

"Hollywood players and cult leaders, I'm learning, share a particular approach to the world. Doesn't surprise me they also share taste in real estate."

"For decades it was a home for fucked-up juveniles, but it went on the block about a year back. TDB Corp snapped it up. The Department of Defense got caught with their pants down—turns out they'd earmarked the area for a chemical-weapons incinerator facility. Talks were had, Betters wasn't selling. DOD sicced the IRS on him, got nowhere—not surprising."

Freed looked at his partner expectantly, and Thomas flipped through his notes, finger tracing down the sheets until it tapped twice. "June sixth last year, they sent in the FBI on some unsubstantiated fraud charges. They hit dead ends all around. To top it off, they got a bit aggressive. Things got ugly for a minute and a half. The ACLU cried religious freedom, though Betters's outfit insists it's not a religion. Betters, turns out, isn't afraid to get litigious. Next thing you know, the Feebs are facing a boatload of injunctions and criminal-action suits."

"Why didn't we hear about this?"

"It quieted down in a hurry. Betters hates press, and I'd guess the DOD wasn't eager for word to spread they were planning to put millions of rounds of decaying chemical weapons upwind of taxpayers."

Tim tugged on the collar of his shirt. "Christ."

"Special agent I talked to said Betters worked them like a Tijuana donkey."

"Impressive candor for the Feebs."

"He was a former Ranger."

"That explains it."

"Law enforcement won't go near the place now. It's a weird, scary group with an in-house staff of brainwashed lawyers. I think the cops and the agents figure, let sunning snakes lie. No one wants a civil suit up their ass."

Freed brought his hands to rest on the table. "Everything Betters does is just one inch legal."

"No layups," Tim mused.

"Not a one," Thomas said. "You want him, you're gonna have to go out and sniff the trail." He looked away sharply, disrupting the brief rapport they'd developed, and started shoving papers back into the files.

"Have you briefed the marshal on this?" Tim asked. "The stuff with the Feebs?"

Freed shook his head. "Your case, we'll let you spin it."

"He's gonna want no piece," Thomas said. "It's a hornet's nest."

Freed gave Tim a little nod before leaving, but Thomas ignored him. Bear and Tim sat for a while with their thoughts, crunching stray Styrofoam peanuts under their shoes.

Finally Tim said, "You send in the food samples?"

"Sheriff's crime lab."

"Aaronson still over there?"

Bear nodded. "Said he'd swing a twenty-four-hour turnaround. We get a good bounce, maybe you don't have to go undercover."

"What did you get on Skate Daniels?"

"Nothing. Name didn't put out."

"You try the moniker database? Odds are Mrs. Daniels didn't name her boy 'Skate.' "

"Right. No, I didn't." Bear held up his fists and squeezed—his big-shot way of cracking his knuckles. "Given all the pitfalls around Betters, how do we convince the old man to let you press forward?"

"I've already burned eight lives with him, so you'll have to suit up. Present it to him like an opportunity. Be excited—you're selling him on what great news this is. If we find the right leverage point and lean, there'll be a windfall of charges. Betters is Al Capone, and we're looking for income-tax evasion. Once we nail him, Tannino gets to scratch some back for the Department of Defense, get them that parcel of land, maybe even throw table meat to his buddies in the private sector. He goes into the next Puzzle Palace budget meeting wearing a red cape. Plus, it's his big chance to show up the Feebs, and we both know the thought of that makes his engine turn over cold mornings."

Bear tugged at his cheeks. "I don't know how you come up with this shit."

An image of himself at five years of age, working a mortuary parking lot in a snap-on leg cast, clutching to his chest a donation bucket his father had salted with a few creased twenties. Tim emerged from his thoughts to find Bear staring at him expectantly. "What?"

"I said the mutt sure as hell runs an airtight operation."

Tim curled his index finger into his thumb and held up his hand. Closing one eye, he sighted on Bear through the tiny O. "This big. We just need an opening this big."

Bear gathered his papers and rose. "What if he didn't leave one?"

*T*im grabbed a sandwich and holed up in the Cell Block comm center. The mood was grave. One of the on-shift detention enforcement officers sported a fresh shiner. Tim didn't ask.

He called Dray's cell and caught her on patrol with Mac. The foul yellowtail had finally finished paddling through her system; she spoke around mouthfuls of chili fries. The doctor had told her to take the day off and eat bland foods, directives that stood a stray dog's chance in Nam Dinh. She told Tim that the Asshole Car was cramping her Blazer in the garage, her implicit way of apologizing for her reaction to his ill-advised adjective last night. He informed her that a Hummer alone could accommodate his unwillowy build.

Logging a call to the sheriff's department, Tim asked the resource analyst to run Skate Daniels through the moniker database. For approximate age he guessed thirty-five, and he told the analyst to focus on L.A. County. Within ten minutes the identifiers and photo of the sole candidate checked into Tim's e-mail box. Skate's beauty-pageant features scowled out from the jpeg. Though in the mug shot he had a bit more tread on the tires, he looked dirtier and somehow unwound. Something, maybe The Program, had reined him in, given him focus. Tim played digit shuffle next, running Skate's SID, FBI, and Social Security numbers through an obstacle course of databases. As he clicked down the screen, his eyes locked on an entry, and he was hit with the minirush he got when a lead panned.

2-23-03. Daniels stopped for speeding violation at 6th and Hill in a red Mustang, license 9CYT683, passenger Randall Kane.

A few more keyboard gymnastics snared him Randall's identifiers, and, using county booking to round out both his and Skate's criminal histories, Tim printed and perused. His exhaustion made for blurry reading.

Both men proved to be habitual violent offenders who'd acquainted themselves with the edge of the penal system but never taken a big fall. Between them they'd caught some charges, everything from armed robbery to gross-misdemeanor sexual conduct to felony false imprisonment. They'd rolled through a few trials, copped a handful of pleas, and served a number of short stints. Seasoned in lawlessness but currently off parole, they were ideal knockdown men for Betters. Like the rest of his operation, they provided no legal pretext for further investigation.

A bang snapped Tim's head up from the monitor. Two feet from him, a felon howled, his mouth, cheek, and weak goatee smeared up against the bulletproof glass like a wet stain. Guerrera, forearm thick with tensed muscle, yanked the hefty prisoner back and threw him down the corridor, where three detention-enforcement officers subdued him handily.

Guerrera wiped a thin trickle of blood from his nose. "Try that shit with me again, *hijo de puta*, I'll use your nutsack for a speed bag." He stomped out of the cell block, muttering in Spanish.

Tim tied up a few loose ends online, then called Glen Bederman, apologizing for bothering him at home.

"How did you get this number? It's unlisted." A brief pause. "Okay, foolish question. What can I do for you?"

"Does the name Terrance Betters mean anything to you?"

"No. Why?"

Tim told him. Halfway through his account, he heard the creak of a chair absorbing Bederman's weight. When he finished, Bederman made a strangled little sound of disbelief. "I can't say I've ever heard of someone as ill prepared as you coming unmarked out of a twenty-four-hour induction session." He released a sigh. "Relieved as I am that you didn't throw the poor girl into a sack, I have to tell you—that was a reckless thing you did, going there."

"I'm about to do something worse. Monday I'm going undercover for a three-day retreat. I'd really like to see you before. Can I?"

"At this point I'd meet with you just out of curiosity. I have some appointments at my house tomorrow morning, but how about ten?" His tone took on an ironic edge. "I trust you'll be able to locate it on your own."

Tim thanked him and hung up, folding the papers into his pocket as he passed out through the security doors. Guerrera squatted in the hall, arms between his bowed legs, catching his breath. He gripped one hand with the other, turning it slightly. He looked up and shot Tim a wink. "Hey, Rack."

"Didn't you get the memo?"

Guerrera raised a single eyebrow with a slick proficiency that suggested practice, then the quarter dropped and he laughed. "Oh, about not talking to you. Actually, it was an informational video they circulated. How to snub you at the watercooler. Shit like that."

He shifted his arm and grimaced. His elbow was out of joint, the displaced bone leaving a pocket of skin at the tip. Tim crouched, and Guerrera relinquished his forearm to him hesitantly. Tim gripped it and tugged gently. The bone slid in its sheath and clicked home. Guerrera let his breath out through his teeth in a hiss, then laughed again. Sweat sparkled along his dense hairline. "Thanks, *socio.*"

Tim slapped him on the good shoulder and rose. He was walking away when Guerrera called after him. "They're mad the way people got mad at Pete Rose, you know. They feel betrayed because they believed in you."

Tim nodded, taking it in. "And you?"

Guerrera shrugged. "You were behind the trigger on the first shooting I was at." His accent turned "shooting" to "chuting." "The Martía Domez raid. You pulled some shit there the movies haven't thought up yet. I watched you after when my hands were shaking. You were as calm as a sleeping cat." He rotated his wrist slowly over, then back. "You taught me, *socio,* without teaching me. The way I see it, being mad don't buy me shit."

Guerrera turned his focus back to his arm. Tim watched him twist it gingerly for a few moments, then withdrew, heading to the elevators.

Twenty-three

Janie shook her awake. "Guess what? Guess what?"

Leah sat up in bed. A lifelong habit she'd yet to extinguish directed her torpid gaze to the clockless nightstand. Judging from the shade of gray muting the scraggly elm outside her window, it was around six. Even though he rarely attended, TD preferred breakfast to be served early. Between that and the stacks of GrowthWork the Pros had to complete every night, she didn't know how he expected them to get any sleep. She'd been so busy and exhausted she'd hardly had time to think, let alone reflect on her unsettling collision with Tom Altman or whoever he was.

"Well, guess! Oh, never mind. I'll tell you." Janie pressed her arms to her chest, fists shoved chinward, a cheerleader anticipating kickoff. "TD gave me the Scottsdale ambassadorship. I beat out Lorraine and Chad! Isn't that *great?*"

Leah felt a stab of envy. Her voice was still croaky. "Fantastic."

"I'll be the first ambassador—after Stanley John, of course, but he was a given. He's getting Cambridge. TD says Boston is almost as fertile a town as L.A. And guess what else?"

Leah swung her legs out of bed and blinked hard, fighting for alertness. She had to dig her nails into the dresser drawer to pull it open; both knobs had fallen off.

"Recruitment's on track to get a *thousand* Neos to the Next Generation Colloquium." Janie stood behind Leah, stroking her hair into place. "I'm moving out to take over Cottage Three. I gave you a high weekly report—I didn't even *mention* your rash hasn't improved."

"Listen, Janie, there was something I wanted to ask you about." Janie's unblinking stare made her uncomfortable, but she forged ahead. "Do you think some of the methods we use at the colloquiums are—I don't know—wrong? Like the ways we lead the Neos along?"

Janie laughed and ruffled Leah's hair. "Not at all, babe. You don't feed a newborn baby hunks of steak, do you? You feed them formula—something they can digest. The Neos are new to true growth. The last thing we want to do—for their *own* protection—is give them more than they can chew. Get it?"

"I guess." Janie's embrace felt warm and comforting. "Thanks, Janie."

"You should always come to me with your doubts. That's my job."

The doorknob squeaked as it turned, then Randall was inside. "TD wants you."

"Well, let me just throw on a sweater," Janie said.

"No, *you*."

Janie's smile hardened on her face. "I'll get her ready."

As Janie picked out her sweater, Leah palmed the spoon she'd hidden in the back of the drawer and slid it into her waistband. "I have to go to the bathroom."

"Hurry," Randall said.

She scurried down the hall. After brushing her teeth, she smoothed water into her hair but couldn't make her cowlick lie down. It wasn't until she sat shivering on the cold toilet with the stall door closed that she withdrew the spoon. She stared at her blurred, forbidden reflection in the curved metal, the first time she'd encountered it in weeks save for the fugitive peek she'd stolen from a mirrored wall at the Radisson. The poorness of the image helped her justify her right to it.

Her mind returned to Tom Altman. His handshake—cool and assured. What lies his attractiveness had concealed. His betrayal. Producer Henning at work behind the scenes.

But another thought loitered at the edge of her perception: That a man like Tom would come after her meant—possibly—that she'd done something to warrant concern. He seemed to have integrity. And yet how could he be so misguided about The Program as to want to kidnap her from it?

That she carried the secret of him through a place where even thoughts were prohibited felt like intimacy.

She jumped when the door banged open, and then Randall's wide boots appeared in the space beneath the stall. "What's taking so long?"

She set the spoon on the tile behind the pipes and flushed the toilet. "I'm ready."

Randall watched her closely when she exited, his eyes dropping to her nipples, visible beneath her thin cotton T-shirt. He pushed her sweater against her roughly. "Let's go."

"What about breakfast?"

"You're not eating breakfast today."

Outside, Cottage Circle sat dormant. A red-tailed hawk circled lazily overhead. As usual, Randall walked ahead of her down the trail. Flecks of lint from her sweater clung to his forearm hair.

TD was crouching near one of the wagon wheels lining his walk. He rose and stood motionless and alert, awaiting her, one hand turned inward as if cupping a drink. "My, you do like your sleep, don't you? Lorraine has been up for nearly two hours already. She cleaned the entire cottage."

Leah's rash felt dry and cracked in the cool air. "I'm sorry. I'm . . ."

"You're what? Tired?" He wore one of his hand-tailored oxfords, a midnight blue, the yellow stitching of his initials visible on a cuff. The unbuttoned shirt rippled in the breeze, revealing the slender plates of muscle that formed the oval of his stomach.

She nodded, face reddening. It occurred to her that she'd never seen TD so much as yawn.

The edge of something dark and shiny poked up above TD's hand, then withdrew. His eyes stayed on her. "You approach life from weakness, Leah. The Program can only do so much for you if you're not willing to work."

"I'm trying so hard. It seems like I go to bed late and get up early, but I'm not making headway. My body still feels weak."

Randall tapped a hand against his bald dome, and it made a faint slapping noise.

"This chronic-fatigue routine"—TD gestured with his cupped hand—"sounds like something you might have picked up in your Pepperdine days. Limitations you observed in others and took on unconsciously as your own." A scorpion scuttled into view, cresting the wall of his fingers. TD extended his hand as if presenting a ladybug, and Leah skipped back, startled.

TD's laughter assailed her. "The perceived world is just an illusion. Phenomena filtered through your five weak senses. The true world couldn't be perceived even if you had twenty senses. Or fifty. If you think you know how your body feels, if you think you know whether you're tired, if you think you know *anything,* that's just your ego succumbing to society's deceptions. You can't know anything. There's no such thing as anything. You are what you think. You fear what you decide to fear."

He twisted his hand sharply and clenched. His expression didn't alter. Not a trace of concern flickered through his eyes.

She finally averted her gaze. She struggled to make sense of what he'd been saying. "I guess I still don't have the control I want."

"This constant thinking about yourself, it must get exhausting. Maybe if you focused less on narcissistic you and more on your tasks, you'd find your Old Programming dissipating at a faster rate. It seems to work for other people."

Her face burned with shame. She'd been working protracted shifts every day for the Luddites in Expansion, troubleshooting the IBM relics that had been left behind in the adolescent facility's computer lab. She kept the network up and running so the team could continue cranking out business plans, white papers, valuation models. That she couldn't handle more was a sure sign of her glaring inadequacies.

"I'm going to give you an opportunity to help you out of your rut," TD continued. "Now that Chris is no longer with us, you'll take over the job of Webmaster. You'll work on my computer."

She almost couldn't believe it. "In the mod?"

"I expect the site to be ready to launch by the Next Generation Colloquium." She started to respond, but he held up his hand. "No excuses, just get it done. And remember, the mod is TD's own private space. You're a visitor there. Behave like a courteous one."

"Of course." But TD had already disappeared, the cottage door clanging behind him.

Randall and Leah crossed the small clearing. As they passed the shed, she heard the scrabbling of claws on wood, then Skate's voice soothing his dogs. The door, skewed on its hinges, swayed with the breeze, revealing a sliver of interior. Skate sat naked on a sagging cot, both dogs bellied down before him, their tongues working across the tops of his toes.

Randall busied himself with the myriad locks securing the modular. Finally he swung the door open, holding it for Leah. She entered the dusty room and let out a yelp. Wearing a sharp suit, TD stood inside, his arms crossed. She'd just realized that the figure was a life-size cardboard stand when the door closed swiftly behind her. She heard the scraping of keys as Randall locked her inside.

She surveyed her surroundings, noting the tiny kitchen and bathroom door. Six file cabinets lined the far wall, each housing five drawers and sporting shiny locks. A Post-it affixed to a knee-high stack of papers read *Randall, File by Monday*. Pushpins dotted a wall-mounted map.

A broad desk facing the window supported the computer system. A QuickCam was mounted atop the glowing monitor for video feed. Beside the mouse pad, files rose from a tray labeled *To Be Scanned and Shredded*. The unvented air smelled musky, like dried tea bags and standing water. A skylight brightened the room considerably.

Lidless boxes of paraphernalia and workshop materials littered the floor: *Get with The Program* guidebooks, *Living in the Now* pamphlets, colloquium registration forms, stencil-labeled binders proclaiming THE AMBASSADOR'S USER MANUAL. Some of the materials she'd seen being generated in rough form up in the computer lab, but she was stunned by how slick and professional they'd returned from the printer.

She sat in the desk chair. The entry password had already been typed, appearing as *****. She clicked "accept," and a note popped up on the screen, providing a list of the new features to be added. *Take photos of all materials to be offered for purchase. Import photos into online shop. Set up Web site*

*colloquium registration. Name database should include So-
cial Security numbers. Add hyperlinks for each new city.*

Leah found the desktop icon for the mock site—only when
it was finished would they put it online. At the top of the
screen, a clock ticked off the minutes, an added luxury. *6:23
A.M.* She hardly remembered the last time she'd been able to
ground herself in time.

Seized by an impulse, she jumped up and ran to the tiny
bathroom. Sure enough, a mirror. No window provided natural light; her shadowy outline stared back at her. Gathering
her courage, she reached for the light switch, feeling it brush
her fingertips. Finally she could get a real look at herself, not
just a blurred glimpse in the back of a spoon. She froze, her
corrective thinking clamping down fast and absolute. She
skulked back to the desk and buried herself in her work.

Though Chris had left the site in good order, there was a
tremendous amount to be done before the launch date. After
the first few minutes, Leah stopped glancing at the clock. She
furiously wrote code, nibbling her fingers as she used to in
college. That a combination of ones and zeros could engen-
der a digital world never ceased to amaze her. First there was
nothing, and then all of a sudden a berth existed in cyber-
space, a resting place for weary Web travelers, an om-
nipresent oasis. From chaos, order.

It wasn't until she stood and nearly fainted from light-
headedness that she realized it was past three o'clock.

She went to the locked door and banged on it. Only the
rush of wind and the scrape of a tree branch on the roof answered her. She banged harder, the thought of the mod's isolation just beginning to creep under her skin when a key slid
into the outside lock. Lorraine pulled the door open, adjusting
a robe over her bare body. She did not look pleased. "What?"

"I need to see TD."

Lorraine shot a sigh and headed across the clearing. Randall and Skate were nowhere in view, though one of the

Dobermans lay on the porch, piercing them with its blue-black eyes. They scooted past it into TD's cottage.

TD reclined on his bed, shirtless, his lips pursed around the base of a ripe strawberry. "Leah, dear. Have you eaten at *all* today?"

"No."

"You're such a strong worker. Been hacking away in the mod since morning. Amazing." Pausing to suck at the strawberry, he rolled his head on his plush pillow, directing a languid gaze at Lorraine. "Maybe if one of my other Lilies worked as hard as you, she would have been awarded the Scottsdale ambassadorship."

Lorraine lowered her eyes. He pointed at the floor, and she went to her knees.

"Now, Leah, what can I do for you?"

"I need to get online to download an add-in for some Flash animation."

He dropped a lazy hand off the bed and stroked Lorraine's hair. "Go locate Randall. He's re-marking the boundary lines on the north edge of the ranch."

Lorraine vanished in an angry swirl of robe.

TD slid off the bed. As he drew near, Leah dropped her gaze from his hypnotic eyes. Barefoot, he was about her height. She took in his scent, its hints of bark and iron. His head darted forward, mouth seizing her lower lip. She felt the gentle grind of his teeth, then the pluck of his lips as he pulled his face back off hers. He turned and headed to the kitchen.

Readying her lunch with his own two hands, he lavished her with attention. As she ate, he stood behind her and stroked her shoulders, her arms.

His hands ceased. "You made a special connection to one of the Neos at the colloquium. Tom Altman."

She felt her insides go slack. "I guess so."

"He asked you back to his group. And in the bus on the way home, you remarked to Winona that he seemed nice."

TD always knew everything.

"He's a very special new member of the Inner Circle. I'd like you to be his Gro-Par when he arrives." He paused, but she was too shocked to respond. "There's something upsetting in Tom's past that's holding him back, something about his daughter's death. You could be helpful to him as his Gro-Par by helping him name what that thing is. He'll share a room with you. See to his needs."

A great weight pressed down on her chest.

He studied her face knowingly. "You're upset that you're losing Janie."

Before she could respond, a gust of wind announced Lorraine and Randall's entrance. Bits of dead weed clung to Randall's overalls. He looked supremely displeased that his work had been interrupted.

"Leah needs a phone cord to log on to the Internet."

"I already put the phone cords to bed. The call sheets are done for today."

TD just looked at him.

Randall gestured for Leah to follow and led her to the shed. Two narrow cots crowded the floor. Randall gripped one by its metal frame and lifted it, stained sheets spilling over his arms. He set it atop the other, then got down on all fours in the cleared space and blew on the floor. Dust swirled up, revealing a safe embedded in the concrete. A single dot of metal where the cot leg ordinarily rested shone cleanly through the grime. Randall bent down, tongue poking into his upper lip, and worked the dial. He swung the lid open.

In the cavity lay a bundle of neatly wound phone cords.

Randall removed one tenderly. They headed back to the mod, and Leah plugged it in to the wall and the modem port on the computer.

Randall drew up a second chair. She logged on, found the appropriate site, and started the download. His elbow resting against hers, Randall kept his eyes trained unblinkingly on the screen.

Twenty-four

"**W**eapons of influence." Bederman settled into an outmoded armchair. "They've accompanied us into our most shameful hours. Witch-hunts. Blacklists. Death camps. Between the pages of suicide-terrorist training manuals. Up a con man's sleeve."

Tim set down his cup of now-cold tea, the cushioned wicker couch creaking with his movement. The country-decorated ranch house, located in the better section of Westwood just north of the university, could have been acquired from the producers of *Mister Ed*: checkerboard curtains, horsehair rugs, and a barn-red front door with white crosspieces. Save the bars on the windows, the lineup of dead bolts, and the occasional bleep of the security system, the place was old and homey and bizarre for a single man in his sixties. A cinnamon candle burned somewhere out of sight. Tim decided that Bederman was either a widower or he'd inherited his mother's house; if he were gay, he'd surely have better taste.

"Betters has added some clever, malicious riffs to an age-old song." Bederman polished his spectacles. "Vertical emotional dependence, directed deference to authority, a tightly controlled system of pseudologic, internal language walling up the insiders, dislocating newcomers. He's married two cult models, the psychotherapeutic cult and the self-improvement cult—think the Sullivanians meet Lifespring. Tell me the Program Source Code again?"

"Take sole responsibility for your life. Delete your Old Programming. Overwrite your Old Programming with your New Programming. Maximize your growth by minimizing your negativity. Negate Victimhood. Your behavior is for you. Exalt strength, not comfort. Strive for fulfillment, not happiness. Get with The Program." Tim could almost hear the chants in his head as he named them.

"And our dear friend Tom Altman wisely presented as a doer. I'm sure the Teacher sized you up as such—that's the biggest type of fish to fry for this kind of cult. Believers are automatically out, thinkers get tangled up in the logic, and feelers are too easy—no challenge for a showman like TD. Doers are men and women of action, which means they've almost certainly made mistakes in the past for which they hold some measure of remorse that can be turned against them. They also tend to have financial resources and they make great subleaders. I'm not surprised you made the cut from the LGAT—"

"LGAT?"

"Large-group awareness training. Now you're on to phase two—a Moonie-esque retreat. More Pros, fewer marks. All the better to crack you with, my dear."

"The Pros have this rosy-cheeked excitement about them. All the time."

"Nothing more than pinhead lesions from vitamin A deficiency, which—along with fatigue, disorientation, and vacillations in mental acuity—is one of the rewards of a carefully imbalanced diet." Bederman set down his cup hard enough that it rang against the saucer. "Take a detrimental or frightening state and reinterpret it as growth. That's the name of the game. That giddiness, that tingling, that high that you felt? Were you unlocking your true self? Experiencing the next stage of growth? No. It was the overbreathing, the chanting, the repetitive screaming, the arm thrusting, the standing and sitting—shortcuts to hyperventilation, no more. Did people faint?"

"Yes. Quite a few."

Bederman's voice kept a bitter edge. "All that heavy expelling of air produces a drop in the carbon dioxide level of the bloodstream—respiratory alkalosis, it's called. It causes dizziness, light-headedness, a loss of critical thought and judgment. Well known in the old-time religions. Add sleep deprivation and a few spiked refreshments to the mix, you can make recruits actively participate in their own debasement. Once that happens, they'll start believing they deserve it. Change someone's behavior and his beliefs will follow."

"It's like we're taught in Special Forces—if you're captured, only give up name, rank, and serial number. Anything more than that, they have a wedge to pry you open."

"With brainwashing at least you *know* you're in the hands of the enemy. Mind control—what Leah's up against—is more insidious." He took off his spectacles, rubbed his eyes, put them back on. "These situations—especially with a sole leader like TD bent on absolute control—only go in one direction."

They sat quietly for a few moments, and then Bederman said, "Remember the Heaven's Gate mass suicide down in San Diego? I was one of the first people through the house. Thirty-nine bodies, young and old. The smell . . . Jesus, the smell. You know that smell?"

Tim studied his hands. "Yes."

"As you well know, you can't get rid of them, those moments. I testified in a case early in my career where a six-year-old girl with Down's syndrome was flayed to death in a church. Johanna Yarbough. There were fifty adults present, including her mother. They took turns as the other children sat in the pews and watched. They were exorcising evil spirits from the girl. I always wondered what she was thinking, Johanna, when it was happening. Looking out at all those faces. That's what she knew of the world. That's what the world looked like to her."

"You hate them, don't you? The zealots?"

"Sometimes." Bederman's face looked weary; his jowls sagged. "But sometimes the oppressors are only victims who've advanced in the ranks. Sometimes you lose perspective, start hating them all."

Tim glanced around the room. The antique churn in the corner. Bows of raffia around porcelain candlesticks. A spray of dried flowers deadening the mantel. It was like something painstakingly replicated from a magazine photo or a childhood memory, a stab at some notion of archetypal domesticity.

"In the late seventies, I was a deprogrammer. There wasn't much literature about cult psychology yet and what there was was primitive. I had a 'patient' abducted and subjected to involuntary deprogramming in a locked hotel suite. I was young and enthusiastic and knew all the answers. On the third day, Joel slashed his wrists using glass from the bathroom mirror. They teach them that, you see, because it gets them to the hospital, where they can phone the cult leadership. The cult shows up with lawyers, frees the member, presses charges—you get the picture. But Joel was overzealous. After seventy-two hours, I can hardly blame him." A doleful grin. "He lost too much blood." His hands parted, then clapped faintly together. "I came apart afterward—spent a few years mired in self-loathing. My marriage didn't survive."

Tim glanced around—no pictures in sight.

"I'm a doer, you see. Just like Tom Altman." Bederman's tone regained its briskness. "My wife's remarried now, her high-school sweetheart. They're good enough to send a card every year at the holidays. And so it's just me and this little house. All these years I've been unable to change it. I keep wanting to do something to make it my own, but I suppose . . . I don't know. I put everything I have into my work, trying to get it right this time around, and the next, and the next." A melancholy chuckle. "I suppose I hope that'll redeem me."

"I know that hope."

They sat silent for a few moments.

Finally Tim said, "I want to save Leah, and I want to keep her intact."

Bederman's smile warmed his face. "She's not just a passive victim. She's a sensitive, intelligent person with feelings and doubts of her own. Encourage her to imagine other possibilities. Make it safe for her to express her doubts, to reconnect with her former life, with herself."

"How?"

He laughed. "How much time you got?"

"Until eight A.M. tomorrow."

He favored Tim with a little dip of his head. "You've got to play them as they play you, staying one step ahead of the game. A key strategy will be winning the confidence, even the trust, of the group. Leah has to know you're able to see it from her perspective. Once you know the Program doctrine, you'll be able to identify internal hypocrisies and inconsistencies. Stay focused on how cult members *behave*, not what they believe. You'll be interacting with her in a milieu where everything is carefully orchestrated to control her. See if you can establish enough trust to get her to agree to a consensual intervention, a meeting on neutral ground with family, friends, former cult members if you can find them, and a counselor."

"Maybe when I'm done doing all that, I could end world hunger."

"World hunger is passé. I'd recommend striving for peace on earth. Then if you perform well in the swimsuit competition, you can write your own ticket." With a professorial tilt of his head, he took note of the discouragement on Tim's face. "I'll help you."

Before Tim could express his gratitude, the doorbell rang.

"My eleven-o'clock."

Tim moved to rise, but Bederman gestured for him to stay put. He made his way to the adjoining foyer. On the doorstep waited a kid in his early twenties gripping a briefcase and wearing a black knit tie, a short-sleeved button-up, and dark slacks. The gold lettering on the bound book he clasped threw off a glint of the morning sun.

"Hi, Glen. Matthew Gallagher from the Brotherhood of the Kingdom. I came by Thursday evening . . . ?"

"Yes, of course. Come in." Bederman stepped back, letting

the kid enter. "I appreciate your agreeing to come back to see me on a Sunday."

"It's vital to spread the word, no matter the day or hour."

Bederman rested a hand on his back. "Impressive nonetheless. I'd bet you've always found outlets for that initiative."

Matthew moved stiffly, with little bend at the elbows. "I guess. But I'm here today to talk with you about the Kingdom of the Spirit."

"My friend here would like to join us. I trust that's all right with you?"　　　　　•

"The more the merrier." Matthew shook hands with Tim, sat on the opposing couch, and began to spread out pamphlets on the coffee table.

Settling back into his chair, Bederman folded his hands across the slight bulge of his belly and shot Tim a wink. "Well," he said, "we'd best get started."

Twenty-five

*G*reeting him at the Hennings' front door was a body-builder duo; it seemed at first glance that Rooch had been cloned in Tim's absence. Tim managed to distinguish Rooch from his thick-necked playmate an instant before the squeaky articulation removed all doubt. "Mr. Henning expecting you?"

"No."

Behind them the tile floors amplified a baby's cries. Rooch's twin chomped his gum. The bulge beneath his knockoff jacket was a pretty good indication that the death threats had rattled the Hennings more than they'd let on. His voice, accompanied by a waft of fruity breath, was better suited to his build. "You in the practice of just dropping in on people Sunday afternoons?" He offered a broad ledge of a grin, his dark hair pulled tight against his skull and taken up in a rabbit's foot of a ponytail. He was the kind of guy who'd had his ego rewarded enough that he'd arrived at the conclusion that his dickhead temperament constituted a kind of charm.

"Listen, princess, when you're teaching etiquette, I'll be sure to sign up. In the meantime, tell him I'm here."

"It's not that simple."

"Have it your way. Please inform Mr. Henning that I'm no longer available to speak with him. This was his window, and he missed it."

Tim started down the walk. He didn't get three steps before Rooch's hand clamped down over his shoulder, squeezing so tight he felt the bones grind. "Come on, hard-on. Don't let Doug scare you off."

"Doug just annoys me, Rooch. Does he scare you?"

Doug stood in the doorway. When Tim knocked shoulders with him on his way in, it felt like clipping a wall. Emma sat at the kitchen bar, bouncing the baby awkwardly in her lap, a pear-shaped Latina nanny looking on with concern. The baby's mouth was an almost perfect O; the volume issuing forth seemed an anatomical impossibility. A woman with wrenched-back hair to match her facial skin cupped a frothy cappuccino in both well-manicured hands, her smile like a slit in a sheet of Saran Wrap. Will and a young man in a pilled sweater were hunkered over something at the kitchen table.

Will and Emma noticed Tim at the same time. The baby's cries ceased the minute she was enfolded in the nanny's plump arms. Will brusquely rose and directed a dismissive nod in the direction of the table. The young man gathered a profusion of red-penned pages to his chest and scooted out.

Will rocked on his heels and said, "Word guy," by way of explanation.

Emma's friend gathered her purse. "Say hello to Leah. She's doing well at Pepperdine?"

Emma's eyes regarded Tim joylessly, even as she shoulder-clutched her friend and pressed cheeks. "Yes, wonderfully."

Rooch showed the friend out; it seemed Doug wasn't sufficiently housebroken to escort proper company.

"It's for Leah's own sake," Emma said with a ferocity Tim was surprised she could muster. She scurried beside Tim down the hall. "Janice's daughter, Leah's age, is going to be a *physician*."

"You don't say."

Once they'd descended into the oversize conversation pit of a living room, Will topped off a rocks glass. He'd yet to acknowledge Tim.

"You didn't have me fired," Tim said.

"You're still our best shot."

"I have some conditions."

"Why doesn't that surprise me? Next thing you'll show up with representation."

"Representation?"

"Never mind. What are your *conditions,* Mr. Rackley?"

"I'm going to try to convince Leah to come to an intervention."

Emma sank heavily to the couch. "This isn't some eating disorder."

Tim had Will's attention, so he forged ahead. "*If* I'm successful in getting her to a specified location, you're gonna play it at her comfort level. That means you don't so much as lock the door."

Rooch and Doug had taken up posts on either side of the living-room entrance. Tim cast a wary eye in their direction. They stood still and watchful, exuding intelligence.

"And you'll keep your help heeled."

"She climbed out a window last time," Will said. "It's for her benefit for us to be a bit more . . . forceful at the early stages."

"That'll only lead to more problems."

"I'm a producer. My job is to manage problems."

"Not this one."

"What about Betters?"

"Leave Betters to me."

Tim's tone seemed to conclude the matter satisfactorily for Will.

"What are we supposed to *do* at this intervention?"

Tim offered Bederman's card to Will, who held it by his waist and frowned down at it. "This is the leading guy in the area. He'll take your call."

"We don't need some counselor to teach us how to talk to our daughter."

"We need an expert to help us talk to someone indoctrinated by a cult."

"We know how to talk to Leah."

"Right. You can just slap her when she gets frustrating."

The glass froze against Will's lips. He lowered it slowly. "I was trying to reason with her. She'd shut herself off like a robot. Whenever I spoke, she murmured these self-help platitudes to herself, right over my voice."

"So you figured if you hit her, she might listen better?"

Blotches of red were starting to bloom on Will's cheeks and neck. "I never said I was a great parent. It doesn't happen to be one of my strengths. But the fault doesn't rest with me. There are a lot of parents who don't provide at all. Their kids don't join cults."

"I don't care about fault."

"What do you care about?"

"Your daughter."

Very slowly, Will set his glass down on the bar.

"I just here to get Leah out of this mess," Tim said. "The rest is up to you. I'm not a shrink—hell, I'm not even a parent. But I do know that if I was in your shoes, I'd want to give some thought to the things this cult offers her that you didn't."

Emma came up off the couch. "Who are you to talk to us that way?"

"Tomorrow night, at possible risk to my life, I'm infiltrating the ranch of a cult to try to help your daughter. That buys me the right to talk to you however I want." He turned to Will, who'd grown surprisingly quiet and thoughtful, his downbent head taking in Leah's graduation picture on the bar. "What's it gonna be?"

"Fine," Will said. "No power moves."

Tim offered his hand, and they shook.

*T*he weedy front lawn brushed Tim's calves. Boston stuck his muzzle through a rip in the screen door and tried to bark, but his constrained jaws managed only a muffled woof. Tim entered and crossed the stained carpet, junk mail and flyers crinkling underfoot, Boston threading his legs like a cat with a thyroid problem. He found Bear at the modest breakfast table placed injudiciously in the middle of the square of peeling linoleum that passed for the kitchen. Bear occupied the single chair accompanying the table; he'd removed the other three due to space considerations, a sensible decision but one that chipped away at Tim's heart every time he dropped by.

Bear was eating turkey chili out of the can and, judging from the smears on his chin, enjoying it greatly.

"Reggie Rondell called," Tim said. "He wants his housekeeper back."

Bear gestured around with a kidney bean–laden fork. "I keep telling Boston to clean up. Guess he's not trained." He retrieved a second chair from the garage and, gripping one leg, handed it to Tim over the table. They sat. Bear tilted the can toward Tim. "I think I got an extra fork around here somewhere."

Tim gestured a blackjack stay. "How'd it go with Tannino?"

"Your pitch made him scowl, but it also put a gleam in his eyes. He says you have one shot at it. Bring him back something concrete and we'll put Betters's dick in the dirt."

"I will. You insert a false death notice for Jenny Altman in the Hall of Records?"

"Yup. And injected Tommy Altman's name into academic records at Pepperdine. And left you a getaway car where we discussed. And took care of everything else."

"I got your message about Aaronson. He called with the breakdown on the food samples?"

"No pot or hash in the brownie, which was disappointing, but it had four times the normal amount of sugar." He frowned thoughtfully. "I thought it tasted too sweet."

"And the punch?"

"The punch was loaded up pretty good. Calms forte, kava kava, and valerian."

"They sound like Caribbean dances. Or venereal diseases."

"Those Caribbean venereal diseases are a bitch." Bear tapped a ba-dum-bum on the wood with two fingers. "They're roots. Kava kava and valerian are like nature's valium. They mellow out your nervous system, impair judgment, cause intense muscle relaxation—sort of like listening to Al Gore. Calms forte is a homeopathic remedy, does the same but more intensely."

"Can we move on it?"

"Nope. They're all legal over-the-counter substances. Aaronson said they've seen them used before by brainy little fucks looking to date-rape but not wanting a visit from DEA. He found melatonin in the mix, too, but again, manufactured hormones ain't illegal."

"How about intent? They're obviously trying to gain some advantage."

"That only matters if they're trying to gain advantage to do something illegal or coerce people into doing something they don't want to do. The stuff mellowed people out into an experience they elected to sign on for. Back to square one." Bear took note of Tim's expression. "Don't go off all half-cocked now."

"Meaning?"

"No offense, but your track record when the law doesn't conform with your expectations isn't exactly stellar."

"No. It's not. And as you've just pointed out, the law leaves a lot to be desired." Tim gestured for the turkey chili, and Bear stuck the fork in and passed it, looking at him pointedly. Tim took a bite. It wasn't half bad. "Don't worry. I'll do this one right." He stood and hefted the chair back over the table, setting it by the door to the garage. He paused on his way out. "Those poor bastards at the colloquium, you should see them."

"It's like those short people, Rack. At the convention. Being short, they'll find the short community. Your idiots who want to believe in stupid crap, they find other idiots who want to believe in stupid crap. It's hard these days to *believe* in anything. So they bond together and get handed the community doctrine—instant download, add faith and stir." Bear wiped his chin. His skin was sallow, sagging in folds beneath his eyes. "People like to fit in." He leaned forward in his solitary chair, the can of chili dotting the center of the round table like a candle. "I imagine it's easier."

Twenty-six

When Tim entered the house from the garage, smoke was seeping from the oven. Grabbing a pot holder from atop an empty Tombstone Pizza box, he yanked the charred Frisbee from the rack, doused it with the sink sprayer, and dumped it in the trash. He opened the window over the sink and waved the smoke away from the oblivious alarm. Then he slid open the glass doors in the living room to get a cross breeze.

Wiping his eyes, he returned to the kitchen. Black tendrils wisped up from the trash bin, so he poured in a few mugfuls of water until the sizzling stopped. A curled fax lay on the table beside a fan of junk mail—Dray's bloodwork from her visit to the clinic.

Smudges dappled the paper where she'd gripped it with hands moist from the freezer-burned pizza box.

Monospot: Neg

Hepatitis A Antibody: Neg

βhCG—Serum Pregnancy: Pos

His hand swiped for the chair back, finally found it. He leaned heavily and stared at the fax, his breath hot in his still-raw throat. When he finally looked up, the haze had cleared from the kitchen.

He walked over to the tiny desk near the door to the garage and rested a hand on the fax machine. Still warm.

He headed through the empty living room, down the empty hall.

Dray stood in the center of Ginny's old room, back to the door. The glow of the setting sun shone through the open blinds, silhouetting her stark form crisply—the bulge of the Beretta in her hip holster, the starched lines of her uniform, the laces of her boots.

Four walls, a rectangle of carpet marred only by the uniform stripes of the vacuum.

He tapped the open door with his knuckles, and she turned, looking at him over a shoulder. Her face was sheet white.

He moved to her and wrapped his arms around her waist, resting his chin on her shoulder. They both gazed out at the quiet street. The inextinguishable scent of Play-Doh materialized from the carpet like a ghost. One of the Hartleys' brood of grandchildren was trying with little success to get a Chinese kite airborne. Their cheeks brushing, they watched the colorful nylon dragon tumble across the neighboring lawn.

* * *

*T*hey dozed in a tangle of limbs and sheets, using sweaty proximity to fend off the pall of uncertainty that seemed to hover about the house. They didn't talk much, both sifting their individual thoughts first, as they'd learned to when stakes were high and vulnerabilities bared. Around three, knowing the morning promised him a reentry into sleep deprivation, Tim willed himself to unconsciousness, a capability he'd cultivated as a soldier.

The alarm pulled him from a placid sea of ink.

Lenient mattress, silky sheets, the morning smell of Dray's hair. He opened his eyes.

Legs tucked beneath her, Dray leaned forward on the points of her elbows. One hand propped up her chin, the other she held flat-palmed before his mouth. Her face was inches from his; he could sense the warmth coming off it.

A seam of light evading the curtain fell in a band across her cheeks, turning her eyes jade and translucent. Her mouth shifted, pulling slightly to one side.

"Be careful," she said.

Twenty-seven

"*Y*ou ever think about how our cells die, every minute of every hour? A skin cell lives only a couple of days. All our skin is dead on the outside. When you touch someone else, you're just pressing dead hide to dead hide." Randall's blocklike fists encased the top of the van's steering wheel.

Riding shotgun, Tim had the dubious honor of being the anointed beneficiary of Randall's morbid ruminations. Randall was considerably more social than Skate. He'd been social at the Radisson pickup, social up the 405, social along the 118 and the 210, and now social up Little Tujunga Road, the two-lane snake of asphalt that twisted through the fire-hazard hills of Sylmar. Tim found himself longing for Skate's sullen reticence.

In the back, four high-roller recruits sat crammed together, Shanna among them. Lorraine, the sole Pro, urged them into intimate conversation, gently rebuking them for missteps. Now that he'd endured the colloquium, Tim noted how un-cannily her affect and speech shared similarities with Janie's and Stanley John's—TD's personality downloaded through yet another generation. Firming her austerely fastened bun of auburn hair with acute plunges of bobby pins, she informed Jason Struthers of Struthers Auto Mall that he was being in his head, a censure he acknowledged once Shanna seconded it. Don and Wendy Stanford, who'd gone to the seminar to fulfill their tenth-wedding-anniversary resolution to experi-ence more growth in their marriage, wore sandals despite the chapping cold and matching fleeces sporting their machine-embroidered hedge-fund logo. They held hands until Lor-raine informed them their clinginess indicated that they were two people simultaneously hiding behind each other.

Heavy tint opaqued the back windows, keeping the others oblivious to where they were headed. Tim had wound up in the front only because he'd been the last picked up, a happy stroke of luck. Being Randall's reluctant travel companion bought Tim an unobstructed view of the route. Dressed wannabe in designer jeans and an overpriced forest green lamb's-wool pullover, Tim shifted uncomfortably, smooth-ing his now-brushy goatee with a damp hand. The Program-provided thermos of juice he rested on the rolled-down window's ledge, releasing its contents in increments to the wind whenever the van slowed at a curve.

Randall forged ahead in his lecture, lowering his voice to imply discretion. "Your face looks the same as it did ten years ago, but it's just been re-created over and over, old cells shedding, new ones filling in. We're formless, really, always changing, always dying."

Horses nosed out of sheds. Wind-blasted signs designating dirt offshoots announced shooting ranges, wildlife way stations, juvie probation camps. The hills billowed grandly, tinted russet by leafing scrub. Broken-down pickups languished in roadside aprons of dusty rock. Dead snakes sprawled on the baking pitch, smashed flat at axle-wide intervals. They passed a crew of youths clad in orange vests mechanically raking brush under the direction of a corrections officer accessorized with a steel whistle and failure-to-communicate mirror sunglasses.

As civilization receded, the others laughed, oblivious, and talked about perished siblings and deadening careers. Tim continued reviewing the world according to Tom Altman, a silent version of the Method actor's rehearsal he'd picked up as a kid watching his father try out new, affecting gambits in the bathroom mirror.

The sun beat down on the cracked dash, making Randall's arm hair gleam like black wire. "We've built our entire culture around sex. Orgasms, endurance, physique—the obsessions of modern man. But it's all a sham. Sex isn't anything." He turned off Tujunga onto an even more desolate road. The van hiccupped across the crude secondary asphalt, bouncing the passengers in their seats. Low branches of valley oaks screeched across the roof.

Confident from the recent spell of showers, a creek swept under them, bisecting the road. Chain-link fencing provided the van noisy traction across the mossy rocks, water assaulting the wheel wells. The others whooped and cheered.

They wound higher into the hills, bouncing in their seats a good twenty minutes until the van stopped. A waving Pro attended a metal gate bookended by pillars of river-rounded stones. He opened the immense padlock and waved them through. Randall eased the van up a crudely repaved drive.

Wild mustard enlivened the hillside in Day-Glo splashes. To the right a barbed-wire fence rose from dense mats of ice plant, pointlessly guarding a cliff face. They passed a cluster of cottages, arriving at a broad sprawling building that resembled a school—the former treatment wing, according to the decrepit signage.

The wildlife way station, two and a half miles back on the county road judging by the van's speedometer, was apparently society's nearest toehold. Tim checked his cell phone—no reception, no surprise. He turned it off to conserve the battery.

"We tingle and want and lust, but it's just a prelude for the encounter of gametes, a ploy designed for our hungering genes to forge a zygote. Sex is a loss leader, an excuse our genes export to our heads and loins so we'll smuggle them from warm body to warm body. Do you ever think about that?" Randall pulled into a parking space among a few other cars and two school buses and threw the steering-column gearshift north.

The others spilled out excitedly.

Tim offered Randall a numb smile. "Not until now."

S houldering the leather overnight bag monogrammed TA, Tim followed the trail of initiates into the building. The others gawked at the trees and barren hillsides, taking note of their surroundings for the first time. Lorraine hurried them inside. They passed a hospital-style check-in desk and several meeting rooms, antiseptic behind reinforced glass and rigid venetian blinds. Randall held open a door, and they shuffled in like pupils.

TD commanded a chair in the room's center. On the floor about fifteen girls encircled him, covenlike—the Lilies arrayed like hospitality girls. A single young man, a well-built Pro that Tim recognized from the Radisson, had been thrown in for good measure. Leah picked indolently at her shoelace, refusing to raise her eyes. Lorraine skipped a few steps and scooted into place among them, another perfect little daughter. Wearing the same sleeve-torn sweatshirt that showcased his shoulders, Skate stood with his back to the far wall.

"Where are we?" Wendy asked.

TD spoke. "You're in the here and now." One of the Lilies eyeballed Tim and whispered something to her neighbor. They giggled. TD looked at them, and they fell silent.

Randall started tugging the possessions from their hands.

TD said, "No books, no magazines, no Walkmans, no phones, no newspapers, no money—I follow these rules as assiduously as you will. This is a retreat, and retreat means a break from the distractions of the outside world. The more you sacrifice for yourself, the stronger and more fulfilled you'll become."

They relinquished their bags reluctantly. Randall and Skate searched them like airport security workers, sniffing perfume bottles, thumbing through makeup kits, and bunch-searching neatly folded clothes. Along with the items designated by TD, lighters, alarm clocks, vitamins, PalmPilots, and BlackBerries were placed in shoe boxes labeled by name. Don and Jason offered up their cell phones. Tim slipped off Will's Cartier and surrendered Tom Altman's keys and engorged money clip. The recruits' driver's licenses and credit cards would greatly aid TD in fleshing out their financial profiles.

The initiates were now pretty well trapped at the ranch—no cash for a cab, no cell phones to call for a pickup, not even loose change for a bus ride. Not that there was a bus within twenty miles.

Through all this the Lilies introduced themselves and offered testimonials.

"I used to eat to make my outer appearance match the way I felt about myself. I had an embedded need for others to see me as worthless and disgusting. I offloaded that need." Lorraine raised her tight sweater, revealing a pinched little waist. Wendy, who carried a bit extra in the thighs and rear, emitted a muffled exclamation.

In the corner Randall and Skate unzipped Tim's bag. A neatly folded polo underwent a good groping. His toothbrush holder was uncorked and eyeballed. The bag was turned inside out, a new pair of Nikes spilling to the floor. Tim prayed the false lining would hold.

"I used to be a real asshole," the male Pro, named Chad, was sheepishly conceding. "Just out for the buck. One of those idiots you'd see driving around Manhattan Beach, a USC B-school license-plate frame on my fully loaded Jag. I thought money gave me power." He made a derisive noise in his throat. "Now I have *strength*. Real strength."

Tim's book, *Learning to Forgive . . . Yourself*, was added to the growing heap of forbidden fruit, as was this morning's *Wall Street Journal*. The paperback he'd picked up yesterday and put through a few turns in the dryer to give it a well-thumbed appearance; the newspaper he'd crinkled industriously while awaiting pickup at the Radisson.

Fighting a twitchy smile into place, Leah related her rebirth into strength. "And I'd like to announce that I willed my rash away," she concluded. "It's gone."

Vigorous applause rewarded her. TD stroked her leg appreciatively. When he rose, she sat quickly. He gestured at the electronic organizers and reading materials. "Think of this as your Phoenix pyre." He pointed to the cover of Don's book, emblazoned with virile type guaranteeing a wealth of secrets and numerous habits of wildly successful briefcase toters. "This crap is precisely what you came here to delete." He snatched up Tim's book, reviewed it with a smirk. "This yours, Tom?"

Tom Altman smiled, in on the joke. "I'm beginning to think I might regret having brought that."

TD laughed, letting the paperback slip from his fingers to

the floor. "You five have been assigned Gro-Pars who will be with you for the duration of the retreat. They're here to guide you and to make sure you're taken care of."

Randall stuffed Tim's belongings back into his bag. Tim let out his breath evenly.

"Congratulations. You're the chosen few. Welcome to the family." TD embraced them like envoys with questionable agendas, clutching their shoulders and appraising them straight-armed before pulling them in, his doubts allayed.

A round of full-bodied hugs ensued. As Chad embraced Tim, his hands patted about his torso skillfully, a stealthy, impromptu frisk for a wire. When Lorraine hugged him, she felt the cell phone he'd stowed in his pocket and relieved him of it. As Tim joined the line to pick up his expurgated bag, Chad approached Wendy. "Hi there, Wen. Let's get to it." He led her away. Don, distracted in conversation with a solicitous redhead, hardly noticed. Lorraine and Shanna went off arm in arm.

The abrupt tap on Tim's shoulder was a marked departure from the ready affection flowing elsewhere in the room. Leah said flatly, "I'm your Gro-Par. Follow me."

Not sure what to make of their pairing, Tim moved swiftly to catch up to her. "Leah. *Leah.*"

She kept ahead of him, crossing a circle of soggy grass and entering one of the cottages. He followed her down a narrow hall past a few other bedrooms, into a room with splintery furniture painted a baffling shade of periwinkle. On the threadbare sheets, a spread of pamphlets awaited weary travelers in Gideon fashion: *Optimizing Program Software. The Six Keys to Offloading Dead Weight. Think Strong!*

Leah closed the door and whirled to face him. "You *lied* to me." Tim gestured for her to keep her voice down. She did but remained fierce. "Everyone lies to me. Tells me what to think. Well, I'm sick of it. I'm not some stupid girl who can't make her own decisions. You don't know a single thing about me, but you thought you'd just swoop in and rescue me, like some maiden in distress. Is that what you thought?"

"Yes."

"Well, some job you did." She was winding up into a panic, working her nails into her scalp at the hairline. "Who sent you? Will?"

"And your mother."

"Will's a dick."

"Yeah. He kind of is."

Her forehead crinkled. "So what are you doing here?"

She pointed at the first bed, and Tim unpacked a few shirts into the drawer beneath it. "I'm here because your situation is important to me and I want to find out more."

"And because my parents hired you to be here."

"No. I wasn't *hired*. I'm here as a favor to an old friend who knows them."

"You're wearing his *watch*." She yanked off her sweatshirt and tossed it. Purple bruises flowered along the backs of her arms, so dark Tim mistook them at first for tattoos.

"What happened there?"

She glanced down, covering her arms self-consciously. "None of your business." She retrieved her sweatshirt and pulled it back on, glaring at him.

He tugged a little too hard on the next drawer, and it came off its tracks. "I started this because of your parents. But it's become personal."

"Bullshit. You're a liar."

"I did lie to you, yes. I'm sorry. I won't do it again."

She took a step back and sank to the thin mattress of the opposing bed. He stuck his hand behind the discharged drawer and felt along the underside of the frame.

"I don't think I've had an adult apologize to me in my entire life." She remembered her indignation. "I love The Program. It's changed my life. This is where I belong. This is right for me."

"I'm not trying to take anything away from you."

"But you don't agree that this is right for me. You believe you know better. That you have the answers to what I need." She waited, arms crossed. "No lying, remember?"

"I don't think I have the answers. But no, I don't believe this is right for anyone. Except for TD."

"Stay here and I'll make you see it for yourself."

"That's a deal. You give me your perspective, I'll give you mine. We answer each other's questions. That's all I ask."

"We're not here to waste time on Off Program topics. If you cheat The Program, you're just cheating yourself."

"Then why didn't you turn me in? You've had plenty of opportunity. You could go tell TD now, in fact."

She seemed agitated and dismayed, at cross-purposes with herself, as if he'd just called a bluff she hadn't even known she'd made.

Someone banged on the door. A cheery female voice proclaimed, "Time for the Orae. Let's rock and roll to Growth Hall!"

"We don't want to be late. Put down your stuff and let's go. Not there—that's my nightstand."

"We're sleeping in the same room?"

From outside, "Move it, slowpokes!"

"We *have* to go."

"Not unless you agree on the deal. You proposed it." Tim extended his hand. Leah stared at it. "What's threatening about that? If I'm misguided, you should be able to set me straight. That's your job as my Gro-Par."

A manic thumping on the door made Leah jump. "Come *on,* guys!"

Leah seized Tim's hand, pumped it once, and threw it aside. "Now, let's go."

Outside, streams of Pros poured from the cottages. Tim and Leah joined the wake, climbing the hill. "Damn," Tim said. "I forgot my glasses."

"Forget it." Leah grabbed his arm, but he tugged free. "We don't have time."

"Keep walking." Tim turned, jogging backward. "I'll catch up to you."

She threw up her hands, exasperated.

He sprinted back to his room and ripped out his bag's lining, revealing a thin stack of papers. The padded tote strap encased five protein bars and a watch face, and beneath the Velcro hid a coiled-rod flashlight the diameter of a pencil. He yanked out the bed drawer and wedged the light, watch face, and four protein bars on the brief ledge beneath the frame. The papers he folded up and stuck into a Program pamphlet, which he left in plain view on the bed. He grabbed his glasses and zipped the bag back up, leaving the tab a finger's width from the stop. Wolfing down the protein bar, he banged into the bathroom, ripped up the wrapper and torn bag lining, and flushed the shreds down the toilet.

He raced back up the hill and caught Leah in line before the double doors to the Growth Hall. She looked nervous as they filed in.

Inside, everyone trod softly with mute reverence. Stanley John lethargically beat a kettledrum in the back. Using low-signature flashlights like movie ushers, Pros directed incomers to sit on the floor in neat rows. When Zarathustra inevitably spake, Tim felt a Pavlovian dampness beneath his arms—an unsettling response conditioned into him at the colloquium. The theme music's timpani reached a crescendo, a sheet of radiance rose from the footlights, and there was TD, a dark silhouette splitting the light.

"Here in this room, right now, we're part of the *awesome human experience* man has striven for since the Egyptians raised the pyramids." TD adjusted the head mike, bending it closer to his mouth. Stanley John's drum began to beat again, so soft as to seem a mere vibration. "Lie flat on your backs and close your eyes. You want to focus on your feet. . . ."

With a serene and deep-toned voice, he took the group under almost immediately.

Sensing the weight of his own face, which seemed to have a numb, post-Novocain droop, Tim comprehended for the first time how The Program applied layers of compliance. Even his guarded participation in the colloquium had implanted submissive behavior somewhere beneath his consciousness—now TD was presenting the cues to unlock it.

Bodies melted; heads lolled. Leah's breath hissed faintly when she inhaled; faint blue veins webbed through her fluttering lids. One row back, Lorraine whimpered and stuck a thumb in her mouth. The drum continued, heartbeat regular, a deep, soothing vibration that they'd known in their bones when they were still fetal-curled and breathing water. The room grew hot and damp—jungle weather, a climate of infinite possibilities. Tom Altman surely felt the allure; Tim himself was in danger of being pulled under.

"You're hovering above a new planet, in a distant solar system. Drift closer. See the red sands. The soft arcs of the dunes. You've never been to this planet before. No one has ever been to this planet before. It's *impossible* that *anyone* could ever get to this planet. See a single trail of footsteps leading over one of the dunes. Those are TD's footsteps."

Feeling encroaching drowsiness, Tim tuned out the drums and TD's voice. Biting his cheek, he let pain clear his head. Tom fell under the sway, letting his face and limbs go slack, but Tim remained vigilant inside him, calling forth an image of a locked safe and letting it expand until it blotted out sound and sensation. It was Tim's and Tim's alone, and no amount of prying at his senses would open it. He stayed with the safe for an hour, maybe two, aware of TD's voice only as a distant drone, the drums muffled like underwater reports. At one point, booted feet passed within inches of his face—Randall gliding through the dead-sprawled forms, a mortician taking roll. The feet paused—perhaps Tom's eyelids weren't flickering to code?—then finally moved on.

When at last Tim sensed the bodies around him pulling upward toward consciousness, he relinquished his hold on the safe and broke for the surface.

The drums faded, faded, stopped. Torsos rose. Arms stretched. Eyes blinked groggily. To Tim's left, Chad rubbed a knot out of Wendy's neck.

"In The Program, we defy inhibitions," TD said. "Inhibitions are lies implanted by society to hold you back. How many of you have ever been gripped with the urge to jump up on your school desk and scream? Or get up from your office chair and tell your boss to fuck off? Well, why haven't you done it? Worried what others will think? Worried about *consequences?* Denunciation? Ridicule? Shame? This retreat is your place free from all that. We are who we are, and we never apologize for it. The only thing we don't tolerate in The Program is *fakeness.* False behavior, intended to *gratify.* Intended to *please others.* To ingratiate."

"Who determines what's fake?" Wendy whispered to Chad.

"That's a great question. Hold on to it. It'll be answered soon." Eyes on the stage, Chad tapped his index finger against his lips.

"Take the hand of your Gro-Par," TD said. The Growth Hall rustled with torpid movement. Leah slipped her cool fingers into Tim's palm. "Release. Now kiss your Gro-Par. Feel the flesh of your Gro-Par beneath your lips. Feel how close you are."

Leah turned to him. The faintest traces of baby fat made her cheeks wide and firm, though her face was sculpted across the bridge of her nose, under her eyes, a band of womanly definition. Her hair shot in tufts around her neck, straight and layered. She closed her eyes lazily. Tim avoided the expectant lips and kissed her on the forehead—Tom Altman, man of scruples. Her eyes opened abruptly, more hurt than angry.

"Now turn to the person on your other side," TD said. "Kiss that person."

Tim and Wendy regarded each other awkwardly. They pressed cheeks like country-club matrons.

"Now with tongue," TD said.

The Pros engaged readily, as if returning to a well-loved game. Chad kissed the stubbled face beside him, his hands running through the other Pro's cropped hair.

"Deny your inhibitions. Repudiate your Old Programming. You're all consenting adults. You shake hands with people every day—hands touching hands. Who perpetrated the myth that touching tongues is somehow sacrosanct? Do you think you emerged out of the womb believing that? Come on."

Wendy shifted nervously, trying to locate her husband in the sea of undulating bodies, but the hall was too dim. She looked back at Tim, alarmed. Tom placed a hand on the back of her neck and drew her forward. He pressed his forehead to hers, which was slippery with sweat. Her damp skin brought out the floral scent of her perfume. Being this close to another woman made him feel peculiar and unsettled, which he imagined was precisely the point of the exercise. Clearly TD had a point about inhibitions.

"I don't want to do this," she whispered.

Tom nodded, relieved. They kept their faces pressed close.

A Pro in her thirties pressed her body up against a younger woman, her pelvis squirming on the woman's leg. Sounds of panting, deep-throated moans, rasping clothing.

"Stop," TD said. Activity instantly halted. Giggly and intoxicated, the Pros settled back into their places, the five flustered initiates following suit. Breathing hard, Jason Struthers cast an eye at his Gro-Par, whose attention was now devoted exclusively to TD.

A wave of levity radiated through the auditorium, the giddiness of relief.

"We're going to do an exercise called Stand Tall. It's played like this: Who likes the sunshine?"

The thunderous noise of sixty-eight Pros rising to their feet, Tim and Wendy following on a slight delay.

"Who likes the rain?" Stanley John called from the back.

About a third of the Pros sat. Wendy sat, but Tim and Leah stayed up. And so it progressed for about twenty minutes, TD, Stanley John, and Janie taking turns shouting out mindless questions as everyone tediously rose and sat like well-mannered camp kids.

Then Janie shouted, "Who's ever committed a crime?"

Tim stood, along with a good quarter of the room. All the ups and downs were making him light-headed. Heads swiveled as the Pros noted the movement of their peers. Stanley John, despite his projected mood of impulsiveness, scribbled notes on a pad.

"Who's had an abortion?" Janie cried out. "Come on—delete that shame."

Fifteen women stood, shifting uncomfortably on their feet. A few Pros nodded at them or yelled encouragement.

"Two abortions?"

All but six sat down.

"Three abortions?"

Only Wendy remained on her feet, her legs trembling. Janie was obviously working off previously acquired data, probably something dredged up in one of the colloquium's confessional drills. Rings of sweat stained Wendy's blouse at the armpits. Janie drew out the pause for maybe a full minute, leaving Wendy standing alone, enduring scrutiny from all sides. Finally Janie said, "Four abortions."

Wendy's hand flared out, searching for something, and Tim took it and helped ease her to the floor. "Don't let them judge you," he said. "Screw what they think." A surge of disquiet followed; he wasn't sure if the praise originated from Tom Altman or himself.

Stanley John again, standing proudly himself—"Who's masturbated in the shower?"

Rising. Sitting. Blushing. An anonymous giggle or two.

"Who's had an affair?" Janie yelled out.

Tim heard Wendy gasp. He followed her horrified stare

across the room to where Don had risen. He was being love-bombed from all sides—from those standing and sitting—for having the strength to own his behavior. Beside him the redhead smiled enigmatically.

"Who's ever thought about killing someone?"

Tim joined a handful of others on their feet.

"Who's gone ahead and done it?" Stanley John sounded exhilarated by the possibility.

Tim found himself alone on his feet when Enya burst through the speakers, cutting the game short. He sat, rattled by his autoresponse, ignoring Leah's inquiring stare.

People were hugging and squeezing and rocking as if they'd just discovered sensation and movement and some new club drug. Pros exchanged soothing phrases with their Gro-Pars like vows of love. Chad clasped Wendy to his chest; she'd broken down weeping.

Leah gazed at Tim through sweaty bangs. "What did you do, Tom Altman?"

Twenty-eight

*T*im moved with small groups or large contingents, but never alone. Leah stayed pasted to his side like an insecure date at a cocktail party. When he had to take a leak, a male Pro accompanied him to the bathroom door. When he got outside, he took a moment to breathe deeply and settle himself back into character. At a gathering under the dripping leaves of a pepper tree, Tom Altman eagerly denigrated his childhood, his parents, his lackluster marriage, his job, his riches, and everything else connected to his former life.

He, like the other initiates, was placed in his own group. After the Orae, Don had tried to maneuver his way over to his shell-shocked wife, but he'd been swept off by a tide of Pros. Tim hadn't seen the other recruits since. Any direction he looked, he saw three Pros beaming inanely at him. Isn't this fun? Ain't privacy deprivation grand? He let Tom get into the spirit of the game, reflecting the others' mock contentment until he felt it calcify into a perma-grin.

There were workshops and exercises and lectures and games and, through it all, a mind-numbing torrent of principles driven into his thinking by the Pros—drill sergeants made even more oppressive by their benevolent smiles. Taking advantage of the air of feigned openness, Tim cultivated an apprentice-like curiosity; he managed to survey more of the ranch's layout than was sanctioned. During a bout of atavistic roaring, he hyperventilated and started to keel over. He told someone that he was going faint with hunger and was informed it wasn't mealtime yet. His back was pounded affectionately, his hair ruffled, his cheeks kissed.

Eager to showcase Utopia, the Pros invited him to see the various departments beavering away. Tom Altman, doer and entrepreneur, embarked on the excursion as piously as a hard-hat-bedecked senator out to meet the ironworkers, his provocative queries a histrionic subterfuge for Tim Rackley's covert inquiry. *Good question, Tom—we escalate phase-one operational profit through the use of hidden—but lawful—costs.* The more masterful the legal contortion, the greater Tom Altman's admiration. Aside from Leah, who threw him furtive glares, the others were more than glad to flaunt their mastery of The Program's workings.

Tim was sure he'd be called upon soon enough to join the slave-labor force. There were trails to be cleared. Dishes to be washed. Septic tanks to be cleaned. Each task was ritualized beyond recognition, mechanical motions piled on top of mechanical motions until there was no space left for consideration. Tim wanted to ensure that Tom secured a useful position within The Program, one providing access to financial records; his eagerness seemed to play well for both his and Tom's agendas.

Regularly reapplied chalk lines delineated the ranch's borders, and the Pros abided the boundaries with religious attentiveness. Not a single sneaker tread scuffed the dirt beyond the white stripe. Tim observed one Pro shearing brush, bracing one hand with another so not even a stray knuckle would breach the invisible wall.

Slobbering Dobermans at his heels, Skate drifted by occasionally, always beyond the pale of interaction. Tim noted how even the dutiful tensed in his presence and cleaved all the more vigorously to guidelines. Randall appeared from time to time, issuing summonses for TD.

As far as Tim could glean, TD had built an impressive intel system—sixty-eight informants, sixty-eight willing confessors. Even negative thoughts had to be reported to Gro-Pars. And thoughts about having negative thoughts.

Throughout the day Tim played scout, mentally filing data on the maintenance sheds, the network of trails, the layout of the ranch and the land beyond its chalked perimeters. He searched for infractions of any kind—fire hazards, wetlands destruction, disposal of hazardous waste—but to no avail.

When mealtime did arrive—he guessed six o'clock by the sun's weary adherence to the western horizon—Leah informed him that retreatees were beneficiaries of a "purging diet." His questions as to what that entailed were met with customary vagueness.

A cafeteria abutted the Growth Hall. Under Leah's tyrannical direction, he helped wash the dishes left over from breakfast. The kitchen functioned with the monotony—but not the efficiency—of an assembly line. Tom's duty was to shake each wet plate exactly twice over the sink, then dry it with a clockwise rotation of the towel, starting in the center and spiraling outward. After drying the bottom in similar fashion, he was to wipe the rim all the way around in a single motion. After every five plates, he was to wash his hands and change towels. TD's monastic set of utensils was stored and washed separately by male Pros; the Teacher couldn't eat from anything touched by another's saliva. Or by a woman's hands.

Tim did a series of tests to see whether Leah and his fellow workers actually paid attention. Did they ever. He was admonished for drying counterclockwise, for interrupting his stroke around the plate rim, for neglecting to wash his hands. His errors were reported without fail, mealymouthed flunkies scurrying to Leah and deprecating him in Programspeak. It dawned on him that petty acts of defiance weren't going to win him Leah's—or the other Programmites'—trust. If he wanted to infiltrate, he'd better Get with The Program. He had a little chat with his alter personality, and Tom returned to plate drying with newfound vigor.

After places had been set, Tim sat with the others, hands in his lap, boiled cauliflower wadded on his plate. Fifteen minutes passed, sixty-eight Pros and five initiates waiting immobile and mute, eyes fixed on the food before them. Finally the clank of the door's push handle announced TD's arrival. He took his seat before a bowl of soup, bent his head to his first mouthful, and issued an almost satisfied tilt of the head.

TD's disciples began their meal.

Tim and Leah sat Indian style about two feet apart on his bed, facing each other. His bag rested bedside, zippered not as he'd left it, but snugly shut; he'd been right to remove the contraband.

The other Pros had scampered off to their jobs loading boxes, stuffing direct-mail envelopes—*Houston's Personality System Upgrade!*—keeping TD's empire running at full steam. Tim and Leah were alone in the cottage; Tom Altman and his $90 million in assets evidently required around-the-clock companionship. Tim had taken the opportunity to de-

mand question-and-answer time. The broom he'd leaned
against the inside of the front door would sound a crude
alarm in case of interruption.

Leah was vehemently defending her experience on Victim
Row. "I learned to accept my body. My rash went away,
didn't it?"

"How about the others who got yelled at? Did they all deserve it?"

"The Program is about *rejecting* pity. Everyone dreams
their own weaknesses into being. They need to be knocked
out of their complacency. The Teacher only yells at people
who let him yell at them."

"And Joanne? Remember everyone screaming at her?
Calling her an ugly pig? How did she *dream* her facial features into being?"

Leah bit her lip and glanced away—the first crack in her
assurance. "There's a reason the Teacher chose to confront
her on that. Maybe for her to learn something else."

"But you don't know what?"

"I don't need to know—Joanne does. It's her face, not
mine."

"You don't know the reason, but you're willing to dedicate
your entire life to the doctrine?"

She regarded him as a veterinarian might a stubborn mare
requiring worming. "Are you for real? How's that make me
different from any Catholic? I know the reasons TD gets me
to criticize myself. That's good enough for me." She started
to mumble some kind of dictum.

"What's that? What are you saying?"

"Your doubts are the last vestiges of your Old Programming. Your doubts—"

"TD must be pretty defensive about The Program if he
won't even let you think about it yourself."

She glared at him. "The Teacher's not scared of anything.
And I hold my own opinions."

"You say you hate being lied to. How about if I show you

that TD lied to you? Would that make you change your opinion?"

Leah's eyes darted hatefully around Tim's face.

"TD told you he's a doctor, right? That he has a Ph.D.?" Tim produced a document from its hiding place in a pamphlet and unfolded it.

"You agreed not to bring any outside stuff up here."

"Because TD doesn't want free information here. And you'll see why." He held up a copy of TD's mail-order certificate. She looked away, eyes on the dark window, her face sullen.

"*Look at it.* Answer me. That's our deal. We shook on it."

She studied the sheet for a moment. "So he has a certificate. They're just labels anyway."

"I don't give a shit if he took a first from the Canyon View Training Ranch for Dogs. I'm just asking why he lied to you."

"Maybe he got his Ph.D. after his certificate."

"This is what he did after his certificate." Tim held up TD's rap sheet.

She resisted looking for a moment, but her eyes were drawn to it. "No way. You doctored that."

"And I doctored the time stamp on the upper-right-hand corner? And the official seal from the U.S. Department of Justice?"

The broom handle clattered against the wood floor. Tim jammed the papers back into the pamphlet. Leah scrambled across the room, retrieved a stuffed binder labeled GROWTH-WORK from beneath her bed, and tossed it into Tim's lap just as the door opened and Randall leaned through the gap.

"It's gotta *all* be done by morning. You'll get more for tomorrow night, so make sure you complete it." Leah looked up and did a good job feigning surprise at Randall's presence—Tim was pleased to have enlisted her as an accomplice.

"What's with the broom?" Randall asked.

"We did some cleanup before GrowthWork," Leah said.

Randall's mouth compressed to a tight little seam in his

shiny face. The door creaked open farther, and he entered the room. He looked at Tim. "You're wanted in DevRoom A."

Leah glanced at Tim. "I need to do some work down in the mod. I'll be back with you later tonight."

"I look forward to it."

She covered her irritation nicely with a toothy smile.

Randall led the way up the hill. The treatment wing was unlit and empty. A swat of his hand brought up a river of fluorescents overhead, blinking on in sequence. No opportunity to theatricalize was missed. The halls intersecting the main corridor terminated in abrupt darkness.

Randall deposited Tim in one of the rooms. The triangular throw of light from the open door illuminated a plush recliner and a flimsy metal folding chair with its back to the door. On the floor in the corner was a phone with no cord. Randall said, "Sit."

As Tim approached the chairs, the door shut behind him, leaving him in total darkness. He'd taken note of the knob on his way in—a single-cylinder handle-turn, keyway on the outside. He felt his way over and gently jiggled it. Locked, as he'd suspected. Maybe he'd been discovered. He'd neglected to search his and Leah's room for a digital transmitter—TD could have listened in on their illicit exchange.

A single set of footsteps on the corridor tile. His executioner? Skate come to turn him into dog food?

Tim felt his way back and sat on the folding chair. He angled it slightly so he could see the door out of the corner of his eye without having to look over his shoulder. Key found lock with a metallic clink, then the door opened. TD's wiry frame cut a dark outline from the block of light against which Tim blinked.

TD clicked the light switch. "What are you doing sitting here in the dark?"

A crude test to gauge Tom Altman's compliance, as the chair-selection task had been. "Randall put me in here."

"I'm sure he didn't intend for you to wait in the dark." TD

sank into his recliner and studied Tim until he grew uncomfortable under the gaze. "You're pretty ripped for a CEO."

"A lot of tennis. The gym beats the boardroom. And until lately it beat home, too."

TD squinted at him, his freckle-flecked mouth tensing, the postage-stamp beard bobbing on the swell of his lower lip. He settled back, his hands smoothed flat on the recliner arms. Like Tim's father, he exhibited a despotic control over his hands, limbs, facial expressions—every movement seemed calculated and form-perfect. "Why do you think all the great human-potential movements start in California, Tom? What makes this glorious strip of coast and desert such fertile ground for personal growth?"

"An excess of sunshine and THC?"

TD laughed, but his smooth cheeks didn't crinkle. His eyes, an unlikely cobalt blue, were truly striking. "This is the frontier. The continent's edge. Manifest destiny still sings its siren song to pug-nosed blondes primping in Ohio mirrors and strong-backed boys stargazing in Maine. They come west like those before them, searching for they know not what. When they arrive at this brink of the world, there's nowhere left to explore, so they turn inward, explore themselves. And they find: the same old shit. I set out to create The Program partially in response to the crap being marketed as enlightenment."

His hands parted, then clasped. "I studied philosophers and priests, artists and scientists, and I discovered they were all selling more or less the same basic stuff, and it wasn't getting anyone anywhere. I questioned every idea I ever had, every belief that man ever held. The Program is a road map for others to do the same, to deconstruct society and history and rebuild themselves in this model. A model *not* of happiness. A model of *fulfillment*. A model of *strength*. Look at what I've done here at this ranch. Sixty-eight people. Sixty-eight masters of their fates. This will soon be a national movement. We have colloquia next month in Scottsdale and

Cambridge—already filled. Houston and Fort Lauderdale, still three months out, are almost half full. And that's on word of mouth and a few cheap flyers. No Web-site presence. *Yet*. No ambassadors on the ground. *Yet*. No books and audiotapes. *Yet*. No infomercials. *Yet*. It's all in the pipeline. They try to tear us down—"

"Who?"

"FBI, LAPD, IRS—pick a team sweatshirt. But they can't. We're *that* successful."

"Why are they trying to stop you?"

A quiet knock on the door presaged Randall's entrance. He removed a phone cord from within his jacket, plugged it in to the phone and the jack. An instant later the phone rang. TD picked it up and said, "Okay. Okay. What are the comps? So buy it, then." He hung up.

Randall removed the phone cord and left, and TD turned his focus back to Tim as if there'd been no interruption.

"Why are they trying to stop me? Why did they stone the martyrs? Serve up Christians to the lions? Ridicule Freud? Ply Socrates with hemlock? Sue Bill Gates? Force Galileo at threat of torture to recant his *Dialogo Dei Due Massimi Sistemi*? I'm saying the earth moves around the sun. I'm saying that we shouldn't bend to our weaknesses but make our weaknesses bend to us. It's that simple. And there's no denying it. I've had Pros lose weight, stop smoking, leave abusive relationships. I've had girls who could hardly make eye contact get up and shout in front of hundreds of people."

"Terror is a great and underutilized motivator."

TD bounced forward in his chair, excited. "Precisely. I put fear into people so they can face and eradicate it. Some find that radical—"

"No more radical than curing bacterial infections with mold. Or declaring the earth round. Or injecting children with polio to immunize them against it."

"Yes. Yes. *Yes*. History is punctuated by great, *radical*

ideas. The Program is the next step in mankind's evolution. Every Pro will beget ten more. It'll spread across the globe. Pity and shame will be obsolete. Guilt will be recognized for what it is—a vice." His piercing eyes blazed with messianic conviction. "Do you believe that's what guilt is, Tom? A vice?"

"The more I think about it, yes."

"I Googled you after the colloquium, but the search came up curiously empty for a big executive like you."

"My company did defense work. They like us to keep a low profile."

"Good at keeping secrets, are you?"

"Yes. I am."

"A lot of the sheep in the colloquia, they *want* to be controlled. They can't hand over control fast enough. But not you. You have an intuitive grasp of The Program's underlying principles. You're a man of action. Events don't happen to you—*you happen to them.*"

"I like to think so."

"And your divorce didn't just *happen* to you. Something led to it."

Tom Altman met TD's gaze head-on. "Yes."

"You alone cause *all* outcomes in your life. You alone."

Thunder rumbled through the floor, and Tim became aware that rain was beating down on the roof, that it had been doing so for some time now. A feeling of isolation descended. It was just him and the Teacher atop a hill, buried in the heart of a forsaken building, the windy night staved off only by graveyard-shift lighting and a feeble roof.

Emotion rose to Tom's face. He looked away, wiped his nose with a knuckle. "I found out who killed Jenny."

"You're a man of action. And resources."

Tom Altman stood abruptly.

"Sit down," TD said. "You can handle it."

"No. I want to stand."

TD rose from his armchair, confronting Tom face-to-face. "You solve your problems with money, Tom. Isn't that your Old Programming?"

"Yes."

TD's stare was sharp, unblinking. "You hired someone."

Tom Altman's eyes welled.

"Your wife couldn't handle the decision you made."

Tom choked out the words. "It wasn't just that." Tim felt lost under the spell—he'd completely slipped into character. He eased himself back down into the chair, TD mirroring his descent precisely, the eyes never leaving Tom's face. Tim caught up to what Tom was going to say just as the words came out. "He . . . he killed the wrong guy." The confession was another piece of Tom Altman's narrative, and yet it wasn't just fiction; it connected to the trail of bodies Tim had left in the wake of his rampage last year.

"I don't think so, Tom. He killed the right guy. You *identified* the wrong guy. Or your people did. But you were in a hurry, weren't you? And you had the money to make others hurry, too. Money killed the wrong guy. Right? Your money."

And so now, Tom Altman thought, you'll do me a favor and help me rid myself of that $90 million burden.

They sat together quietly, the storm raging outside, TD nodding as solemnly as a priest. He leaned forward, grasping Tim's knee with a surprisingly strong hand. "We're going to get you beyond this. You commit, and The Program will do the rest."

TD rose, and Tom, no after-the-fact wallower, followed his cue. The sterile corridor amplified the sound of TD's thick-heeled boots thunking tile. Outside stood Lorraine, cloaked in a charcoal slicker, the hood cinched tight so the trembling white drop of her face seemed to float in suspended misery. Her whitened fingers clasped a closed umbrella and a pair of galoshes, which she shakily offered to TD.

"Please go on ahead and prepare my bed. Then Tom will

be awaiting you at his cottage for his Night-Prep." She stood expectantly. "That'll be all."

She scampered off, reeling against the gusts of rain. TD ushered Tim back inside. The door scraped shut, reducing the din. TD leaned over to pluck at his laces, then tossed his shoes aside. "I'll send her back for these later. She's one of the good ones, Lorraine."

Tom Altman nodded.

"They're the most in need of being broken down and re-programmed. Women. For the most part, on the great gender assembly line, victimhood is installed with the uterus. Women are constructed to nurture. So what do they do with their pain? With their anger? They adopt it, devour it, dissolve it into their exalted ovoid wombs, pump it through their veins and arteries until their entire bodies are suffused with it, until they're sclerosed, rigor mortis–ed with victimhood. They need to be taken down to the studs and reconstructed. It's the only thing that works for them."

Thrusting his foot into a rubber boot, he flashed Tim an uncharacteristically rapacious grin—the wolf snout peeking from Grandma's bonnet.

"Ironically, women see men as gods because we destroy rather than create. And men have introduced virtually every groundbreaking idea that has advanced civilization. Only by razing do we reseed. Only by destroying can we innovate. Every great notion slays its predecessor. Video killed the radio star, my friend. Any bitch can whelp. The power to *destroy* is all that's ever bought a God respect. Yahweh was an Ugaritic figurine until he smote the Philistines, Allah a milquetoast before he sank Ubar into Arabian sand."

"How about Buddha?"

"Buddha has been consigned to taxi dashboards and faggot conversation pits." He patted Tim on the shoulder. "I'd lay your chips elsewhere."

TD pushed out into the rain, and they were both instantly

drenched. He pressed the umbrella to Tim's chest until Tim accepted it. TD winked, then strolled into the thunderstorm, arms swinging cheerfully, his pursed lips the sole evidence of a whistle.

Twenty-nine

Despite the downpour, Tim loitered outside his cottage, noting the wire-caged motion detectors that hung from the corners of the eaves like wasps' nests. Though they appeared functional, the encasing mesh had long rusted; the units were likely vestigial security precautions from adolescent-rehab days. Bricks embedded in the dirt on either side of the front step demarcated mini–garden plots, though nothing had grown in them in years.

Tim shoved on a brick with his heel, then pried at it until it rested loose in its muddy foundation, ready to be snatched and wielded in a jam.

He stood dripping in the doorway, battered umbrella at his side, enjoying the silence. The culties were still dispatched, tending to important matters of state like clockwise dish wiping.

The fire alarm was a low-grade blip-and-screech— cracked plastic patties in each room, red eyes blinking heedfully. D batteries—present. Wiring—senescent but still live. Even a few valiant sprinkler heads. No code violations there. He was grasping at straws; a faulty fire-alarm system would hardly strike Winston Smith as a pretext for a federal raid.

A closer examination revealed security mag strikes on the bedroom windows. He sourced the wiring to a pitiful alarm panel in the kitchenette. Its adapter plug could simply be pulled free from the outlet to disable the system. It reminded him of something he'd read once, that one could park a docile elephant by pushpinning its leash to the dirt.

He continued to snoop, cautious of Fräulein Lorraine's imminent arrival.

The pantry held cases of Red Bull and high-energy teas loaded with ginseng, ginkgo, and mahuang. An attic hatch gave roof access, but the opening had been barred, another boon from the ranch's previous incarnation. From film director's retreat to juvie home to cult residence—a consistently squalid tradition.

He chanced on a forbidden TV in one of the common room's cabinets, but a spin through the channels revealed static and more static. A sabotaged cable line and missing antenna explained the lack of reception. A cassette protruded from the video slit beneath the screen. Tim pushed it in.

TD standing on a mountain peak, one booted foot resting atop a boulder, an arm bent across his knee. At his back the sunset glowed theatrically, gold irradiating his fluffed-out hair and blurring his face. Tim found himself concentrating closely to bring TD's features into focus.

TD's voice came as a soporific monotone. "This is your crossroads. You can turn off the tape right now. Go ahead. Go back to your life. And, hey, if everything's perfect there, that might be a good idea. But if it's *not,* you'd better keep listening. This *very* moment can be the doorway to your potential."

Tim fast-forwarded a bit, watching TD's head waggle. When the camera pushed to close-up, Tim hit "play" and found himself in the midst of a kinder, gentler Guy-Med. The camera continued to drift and zoom, harmonizing with TD's murmurs. Tim studied the Guy-Med, noting his responses. Sharp, irregular pain seemed to prevent Tim from going under—biting his cheek was just as effective as digging his nail into his palm, and less easily detected. After another few minutes, he eased himself down to the ground and sat. He stifled a yawn. TD's hand drifted up into the screen, and Tim sensed his arm start to rise to match the motion, as if buoyed by rising water. He watched it drift toward the ceiling, unsure if it was detached from him or he from it.

The bang of the front door jarred him from his stupor. Lorraine plunged into the cottage, briskly sweeping water from her jacket sleeves. When she whisked off her hood, her bun came unfastened. She shook a finger at him. "You're supposed to be in your beddy-bye doing GrowthWork."

Tim stood, blinking hard, astounded. He turned off the tape. "Just trying to check the score of the game."

"There's no TV here. Only TD. I'm glad you saw the tape session, though. You liked it?"

"It's captivating."

She led him down the hall, chattering ahead of him. "What did you like best about the day?" He noticed a fallen bobby pin clinging to the hood of her slicker.

He answered truthfully, "My talk with TD."

"What was your favorite part?" She half turned, slowing, and he brushed against her, extracting the bobby pin from the wet lining of the hood. "How his mind works."

"Well, he must like how your mind works, too. You know, TD's never met alone with someone so early on." They reached Tim's bedroom. "And he's never done this so early either." Lorraine swung the door open. "Ta-*da!*" A thin blue polo awaited him, neatly folded, on the bed. He dragged off his wet pullover and put it on, figuring he might as well endure house arrest in comfort. Admiring his Pro-wear, he was surprised to find that his pleased expression wasn't entirely feigned. He recalled his impulsive desire for his mother's drafting table, masterfully implanted in him by his father.

"Look at this. You haven't even *started* your Growth-Work." She directed him onto the bed, then placed the hefty binder in his lap. "I'll go fix you a nice relaxing cup of tea."

When she disappeared, he cracked the binder, revealing a page importantly titled "Connecting with Your Inner Source." About two hundred pages, top to bottom with small print—2500 questions in all. Adding high-caffeine tea to the work burden would encourage sleep-defying diligence, leaving him exhausted and malleable in the morning. He retrieved his watch face and wedged it between his mattress and the wall.

Question 1: *As a child, I experienced my father as (a) controlling (b) manipulative (c) jealous.*

Question 8: *I was abandoned in childhood by (a) divorce (b) death of a parent (c) neglect.*

Lorraine came back with the tea and waited until Tim took a sip and feigned immense enjoyment. For about fifteen minutes, she sat on Leah's bed and watched him grow. Adjusting his glasses from time to time, he made a show of furrowing his brow, tapping the pen to his lips, studying the ceiling for inspiration—it was almost fun.

Through the window he saw Skate's squat outline pass at the edge of visibility, dogs padding beside him. On patrol. A silver key, pressed tight against the flesh of his throat, echoed the soft light of the moon.

Lorraine distracted herself by stretching her swanlike arms over her head, remembrance of ballet lessons past. Tim stole a glance at the watch face—9:48. He flipped to Question 2148 and underlined it, then went back to circling answers indiscriminately.

The rain had finally slowed, though the breeze threw an erratic splatter against the pane. The air of the poorly insulated room seemed dense, aspiring to ice. Finally the others began trickling back to the cottage. Doors opened and closed up the hall.

"Okay, Tom," Lorraine said, "just keep on working like you are—you're doing great. Stay in your room and focus. It's really important you devote this time to yourself." She rose. "Mind if I borrow your sweatshirt? It's in the thirties out there."

"No problem."

Directing a grateful grin at him, she departed. He poured his tea through a crack in the floorboards at the back of the closet, then ate a protein bar and waited for Skate's next loop around Cottage Circle—10:25. Tim underlined Question 2225, then sneaked to the door. The minute he opened it, a bucktoothed Pro popped up from a recline on the facing common-room couch down the hall. "Hey, Tom. Can I help you with something?"

"No. I just have to go to the bathroom."

"Well, hurry up. If you cheat your GrowthWork time, you're—"

"Cheating myself. So right." Tim brushed his teeth before a mirrorless rise of wall and returned to his cell.

Randall took a spin past the cottage at 10:47—Tim underlined Question 2247—and Skate reappeared on question 2313. The timing of the patrols seemed arbitrary, driven by the whims of the Protectors, and so a log probably wouldn't serve Tim well. Skate paused outside on the gone-to-mud path rimming the circular lawn and stared through the window at Tim, probably assuming that the interior light prevented him from seeing out. The Dobermans heeled, plumes of hot breath issuing from jagged mouths, and Tim was struck anew by the Pros' capacity for selective blindness. How could they not take note of a prison patrol on their jolly ranch? Tim's father and TD were right about one thing: The human willingness to surrender critical thought was staggering.

When Tim glanced back up, Skate and the dogs had evaporated in the rain-slatted darkness. He dug for his sweatshirt in his bag before realizing he'd loaned it to Lorraine. Yet another shrewd ploy; borrowing it would permit the cold to intrude on his sleepiness and discourage unsupervised wandering in the night. He wound himself in the thin sheet, keeping an eye on the window. For an hour he watched the spattering puddles, but there was no sign of the Protectors.

For the first time since he arrived, he allowed his thoughts to pull to Dray. She was lying in their bed right now, her hand resting on her belly, monitoring the life within. She was probably reading something moronically escapist to ward off Ginny's ghost and her apprehension about Tim. Leah's photo, nestled lovingly in Will's billfold, came to mind. Tim reflected on the agony of relinquishing a child to the world and watching it batter her. And then, as he'd been taught during a bone-crushing week in the Fort Bragg barracks, he buried all that was personal.

He redirected his attention on his strategy. He was out of his element; he was dealing not with criminals per se but exceptional manipulators. Bankrolling Tom Altman to the tune of $90 million might have been a mistake—it was increasingly clear that he'd garnered more of the group's focus than Tim had intended—but it also offered him unique access to TD. Tom's parsing out of his woeful tale had set the stage for even more interface. It was essentially a flirtation; TD's attentions would persist if Tom Altman proved malleable but not easy. Tim had his own share of remorse to add to Tom's fictional reserve over the botched murder-for-hire, a benefit when confronting TD's uncanny aptitude for scenting susceptibility. But he'd sensed already TD's ability to reach through Tom Altman and rattle the emotions caged in Tim's own chest. Tom was no longer merely a cash cow; his was the head TD wanted on his wall. As TD continued to leverage Tom's points of vulnerability, Tim would find TD's.

Tim curled up to maintain body heat and imagined he was standing ankle deep in a sizzling pool. He let the water climb, warmth claiming his calves, his knees. He was asleep before it hit his waist.

* * *

Tim felt a tug at his belt, then a cool hand slide beneath the band of his boxers. For an instant he was certain he was still dreaming, but then he caught Leah's slender wrist, yanked her arm away, and sat up. She reached for him, and again he repelled her.

"Leah. What are you doing?"

"What's wrong?"

"Hang on. Just stop."

"Look, I'm only trying to help you past the divorce. TD thinks you're a little hung up."

She kept moving toward him, so he gripped her forearms. "I don't want this kind of help."

"Then you'll probably need some time in the Growth Room."

"That's fine."

"Well, not with me. I'll get sent there, too."

"So say we had sex. Tell him whatever you need to."

"He'll know."

"Then tell him I couldn't get it up."

At last she stopped, stunned. "Really?" In the refracted light of the moon, she looked about fifteen years old. She was shivering violently. "He'll take you apart for that. Humiliate you."

"If it were true, it might upset me."

She drew a deep, shaky breath. "What's wrong with me? I'm too ugly?" She was trying to goad him into it first with insults, then by appealing to pity. Right on Program.

"No. I don't have sex with whoever TD tells me to. That's my own choice."

"Fine. You'll deserve what you get, then. It's not my problem."

"I never said it was."

Some of the anger left her face. "*Did* you just get divorced?"

"No." Tim pulled his sheet across her shoulders, then retrieved the one from her bed and wrapped it around her as well. He rubbed her arms through the thin fabric. "What's the Growth Room?"

She described it, trembling with the memory and the cold, her hands instinctively sliding over to cradle the backs of her arms.

Tim said, "And you think that's intended to help you grow?"

"TD doesn't like putting me in there any more than I like being in there. But he's strong enough to do it anyways. You break down muscle to rebuild it, right? Like the Source Code says—exalt strength, not comfort."

"The Source Code is bullshit, Leah. It's decorative."

"Decorative? It's the whole basis of The Program."

"The basis of The Program is implanting self-loathing and anxiety."

She laughed sharply. "Yeah. Sure. I'd love to see The Program you're talking about."

"Then I'll show it to you."

His pledge seemed to intimidate her. "You can't grow without suffering."

"Maybe not. But that doesn't mean that all suffering leads to growth."

"But this *does*. It puts me in control."

"Nothing can *put* you in control. You have to put yourself in control."

"Oh, sure. Like *you* want to do that. TD warned us about people like you. You probably want to turn me Catholic again, like my mom."

"I don't care what you think, as long as you think for yourself."

Moonlight cut her face down the center, leaving it half in shadow. "And how will you know I'm doing that?"

"When other ideas no longer threaten you."

One of her hands curled in the other, a nesting fist. "I wasn't supposed to see my parents that time. I took a huge risk in going. When Janie found out I went, I got put on Victim Row for a week straight, every day." She sank back against the wall. "And for what? To get yelled at by Will and my mom? Slapped? Told how worthless and stupid I am? If I *did* have any doubts about moving up here . . . well, they pretty much vanished that night."

"Sounds shitty."

"Shitty, but nothing new. They've never cared about me. Will made me skip my junior prom just so he could pull me up onstage with him when he won Producer of the Year, then he left the stupid Beverly Hills Hotel after in his limo and forgot me. They make me go to Uncle Mike's every Thanksgiving, and I end up getting a rash because I'm allergic to cats."

As she continued reciting the injustices she'd suffered over the years, Tim recalled his own upbringing with dark amusement. When he was ten, his father had shaved his head and taken photos of him to submit with doctored medical reports to children's charities.

"Could be worse," he said when Leah paused between bullet points. "No matter how you've been made to feel about it, getting left behind at the Beverly Hills Hotel hardly constitutes abuse. Not by my standards *or* The Program's."

"So if I complain, then I'm under mind control, and if I say I'm fulfilled, then I'm under mind control. Neat little trick you came up with."

She hopped off the bed, flung his sheet back at him, and retreated to her mattress.

Tim heard her teeth chattering. "You want my sheet?"

"*No.*" More shivering. Then she added, "Thank you." Rain tapped gently on the window; if the room weren't so frigid, it might have been soothing. Just as Tim recaptured drowsiness, Leah asked in a tiny voice, "What was Jenny like?" Then, a moment later, "I've answered your questions. You said you'd answer mine."

The crisp air made the back of his throat tingle. "Her name wasn't Jenny."

Leah made a gentle noise in her throat—his risk noted. "What was your daughter like?"

"She was the kind of kid you loved so much that you didn't want her to change. But you wanted her to grow up, too, because you couldn't wait to see who she'd become."

"Your answer's all about *you*. Jesus, do all parents think the world revolves around them? What was she *like?*"

"Remembering's not easy, Leah." His mouth cottoned, and he ran his tongue across his dry lips. "Her death made me afraid to go to sleep because I couldn't stand remembering when I woke up. Those first few seconds in the morning, when you think everything's like it should be . . ." He watched a raindrop streak down the black sheet of the pane. "Sometimes I still forget."

"You can't answer the question, can you? You can't answer without talking about you and your suffering. I mean, your little girl *died*. . . ."

Leah's breathing became barely audible. She was crying as silently as she could. He wondered whether the tears were for herself, whether she knew the difference.

Ginny Rackley, Our Lady of Projection.

"Maybe you're right," Tim said. "In which case you might want to recast your tragic interactions with Uncle Mike's cats."

"First honest thing you've said tonight." Her voice was bitter. "I guess we're both victims."

More rain, more quiet.

"What happened to her? Your daughter."

"What I said at the colloquium."

She shifted in bed; he could sense her eyes trying to penetrate the darkness. "I'm sorry," she whispered.

Tim lay for a while, listening for her breathing to steady. Then he crossed the cold floor and draped his sheet over her thin frame.

Thirty

Along with the light-headedness, his exhaustion helped lower Tim's inhibitions. Last night he and Leah had been awakened every hour by a different Pro clanking around outside their window in a professed effort to repair a faulty water pipe. The early-morning battery of workshops made the colloquium seem like a week at Club Med. Weirdly, even though he knew his success depended on his participation in Program activities, an instinctive resistance—his Old Programming?—was hard to shake.

As Tim played possum among the cadaverous Pros, TD's speaker-enhanced voice began its narcotic susurration—Guy-Med, round one.

The Pros bent over their knees, foreheads pressed to the cool floorboards, yoga on Quaaludes. He peeked at Leah; she hadn't gone under yet.

Skate walked the aisles like a whip-wielding boss man. Tim waited for his footsteps to recede, then reached over and dug his thumb into Leah's Achilles tendon. She yelped and jerked. Skate pivoted, but Tim had withdrawn his hand. Skate walked back toward them, his footsteps vibrating the floor beneath Tim's forehead. Tim watched Skate's frozen shadow, the hump of Leah's body. He could see her eyes blink, confusion giving way to anger. He'd stopped breathing.

She rustled but stayed in position. Finally Skate moved on. Leah waited until it was safe, then shot Tim a glare. He winked at her, seeking to infuriate her further. Flustered, she turned her face back to the floor, but he could tell he'd successfully distracted her from the Guy-Med.

TD's voice stayed mellifluous and soothing even as the words began to take on menace. "You're *afraid* of the person next to you. To them, *you don't exist.* Think of the person on your other side. They *terrify* you. If you were *bleeding to death,* you'd be too *afraid* to call out. And even if you did, they wouldn't stop to spit on you." His breath whistled across the mike. "Everyone around you *hates* you. Everyone in this room *scares* you. You are completely *alone.* You are completely *isolated.*" He intoned the words like a bedtime story.

From the back of the room rose a plaintive keening. Almost inaudible, but others picked it up. Some Pros writhed; others froze on their sides, hands clasped over their ears. Shrieks echoed around the bare auditorium, thrown back from the corners.

"There is *no one* here with you." TD was almost consoling. "There is *no one* in the entire world that you aren't afraid of. You are *completely alone* in the world."

Leah's downturned, sentient face had gone a sickly hue.

"**I**'ve realized that you were always an awful brother to me." Shanna sat spotlit onstage, clutching to her ear the cordless phone Randall had presented in the Growth Hall like a parchment bearing a royal decree. Somewhere hidden away was the base unit. The Pros sat in perfect silence, attending Shanna's every word. "I no longer have any use for you."

Tim sat with the other initiates in the row of folding chairs. At his feet lay the shoe box filled with his confiscated belongings. At TD's behest he'd donned the Cartier. TD looked on encouragingly from the shadows.

"I never want to see you again." Shanna's voice warbled slightly. "Good-bye."

When she hung up, there was a moment of breath-held silence, during which her tortured swallow was audible to the first few rows. Then TD edged into the light beside her and raised his hands, striking them together once, the lights eased up over the audience, and thunderous applause burst forth.

A smile twitched on Shanna's face. She rose and gave a joking curtsy.

TD strode before the others. The clapping ceased immediately at his voice. "You're unfulfilled because you're mired in the past. Innovators look *forward*. They break free of convention. Drop your baggage—whatever's weighing you down."

The lights faded until only a new glowing circle remained, this time encasing Jason.

He peered down at the shoe box before him. The crowd seethed with mute anticipation. He reached in hesitantly and withdrew his wallet, the jangle of his shifting keys amplified in the silence. He pulled out a wad of twenties, ripped them up, and threw the pieces. They dispersed in a green cloud.

The audience, hidden in darkness, went nuts.

He pulled a family picture from the wallet and held it up. "This is my wife, Courtney, and my two kids, Sage and Dana. I love them very much." No reaction from the crowd. "But guess what? Sometimes I get claustrophobic. Soccer practice and nannies and the baby's got another sore throat—sometimes I lose sight of myself in all of it. Sometimes I wonder how the hell I wound up here, where, between work and home, I don't have a single minute in my day that's my own." He shook his head, lips rolled over his teeth, lank ponytail swaying. "Well, at this retreat I'm here for *me*." He ripped the photo in half, and the room erupted. School photos of Sage and Dana followed, scraps flung from the stage glittering in the beam of light.

Lights up. Cue applause. Thunderous affirmation. People were jumping and screaming euphorically. Jason continued to shout avowals, a widemouthed exorcism.

The rapture was cut short with a stern flash of TD's hand. "Good progress, Jason." He prowled the stage now, dispensing hard-won wisdom. "A partial commitment to The Program gets you nowhere. You're either with The Program or you're Off Program. There is no in-between. That's being halfway cured of cancer or climbing halfway up Mount Everest. The Program requires *dedication*. Dedication is absolute. The Program is paramount above everything in your life. Paramount above children, parents, spouses, work, money, fame, ego. And why shouldn't it be? It's your *life*. It's your *future*. What's anything else worth when you don't have control of that?"

The faces remained unlined and inscrutable, a sea of catatonia.

TD moved toward Tim, and the spotlight came up on them. Tim could feel the heat coming off TD, mingling with the burn of the stage lights. A hand dropped onto his shoulder, gave it a little squeeze. "Tom, are you committed to The Program?"

At once nothing existed but the beam of light, lowered over him like a cage. Even the pressure of TD's hand had vanished. Tim squinted and sweated. Dust drifted like white sand swirled underwater; a moth made jagged upward progress toward the lighting grid. "Yes."

"I'd think a businessman like you would be tied to material possessions. To stuff. You're not gonna try to drag a yacht through the eye of the needle, are you, Tom?"

Tom Altman emitted a sharp little laugh. "No."

"Are you sure? A guy like you has got some options. Why search for strength when you can go buy a Humvee? A Humvee could make you feel like a real man. Don't you think?" TD drifted back into view, his eyes blazing into Tim's. "In fact, why face your problems at all when you can *pay* someone else to deal with them for you?"

The silence was overpowering. Tim could see only darkness beyond the tight scope of his spotlight. "I have everything I could want," he said. "But it doesn't mean much to me. Numbers in an account, that's all. The Fed raises interest rates, your assets drop. The Fed lowers rates, your assets rise. I've gotten so far away from what I set out to do. From what I thought I wanted." Tim felt himself getting surprisingly worked up over the burdens of imaginary affluence. He took a rattling breath, which reverberated around the Growth Hall. For all he knew, the Pros had cleared out, leaving him sitting on a stage in an empty auditorium. "I've been arrogant. I've assumed power I shouldn't have had. I've made some mistakes I wasn't entitled to make. And, even worse, I've gotten away with them. Living my life tied to that . . . it's no way to be."

TD stepped into the shaft of light, joining Tim. "Why don't you do something to liberate yourself from it? Break away."

"I'm ready to."

TD continued staring, lips tensed, waiting to dispense approval.

"What?" Tim's voice cracked with genuine emotion. "What can I do?"

"Only you can answer that. It has to be what's right for you." TD's eyes flicked to the eighteen-karat watch on Tim's wrist, resplendent in the glare.

Tim removed the thirty-thousand-dollar timepiece and let it dangle from a finger. TD held his hand out, and Tim leaned forward, dropped the watch into TD's cupped hand.

The lights came up, and Tom Altman was back in the world, his spirit one Cartier wristwatch lighter.

Exhausted and drained, the Pros milled around the Growth Hall, group leaders directing them to various workstations. No mention was made of breakfast.

The calling out of assignments impressed upon Tim the daunting scope of the organization. Nathan—Literature, Dev-Room C. *Spectacular job on the glossy four-color trifold.* Shelly, Andrea, Dahlia—Accounting, LabSpace 1. *Let's finish those second-quarter estimates!* Ted—Expansion, Dev-Room B. *The Maui proposal is lagging, and the Houston projections slipped 3 percent.*

And on it went, a never-ending situating of spokes in

wheels. The manpower-to-cost ratio was staggering—sixty-eight affluent, educated people working themselves to exhaustion for a dollar a year.

"Tom." TD had glided up behind him. He placed an arm across Tim's shoulders, drawing him away from the others. "After seeing how well you fit in here, I might be so confident as to say that an ambassadorship has your name on it. Pick a city, and we'll go in." His hand shot up from his pocket, the Cartier hanging from the wall of his four fingers. He extended his arm.

Tim feigned astonishment. "That was my Renunciate. It's not mine anymore."

TD ran his tongue along the inside of his lip, making his patch of beard undulate. "It's a gimmick, a set of psychological training wheels for the rest of them." He nodded at the Pros, still clamoring around the group leaders. "You and I know they require it and you don't. You and I, we know what's *underneath*."

TD reached to hand Tim the Cartier, and Tim stepped back, feeling a stab of agitation. "I don't want the fucking watch, all right?"

TD watched him, pleased. "That's commendable. But don't kid yourself. You killed a man *not responsible* for your daughter's death, and you think you're atoning by driving around in your Hummer and *feeling bad?* How do you think that person's family feels?" He examined Tim's face, his eyes. "Giving up a watch isn't renouncing your former self. It's renouncing an *accessory* of your former self. And you and I both know what you have to give up is a *lot* deeper than that."

He tilted his hand, letting the watch slide off into Tim's hands, and walked off.

s Tim and Leah passed along the rear of the cafeteria, she averted her eyes from the side of the walk-in freezer so as not to catch a prohibited glimpse of her reflection. She forged ahead of Tim, cresting the north rise of the ranch, her feet plopping through a stretch of weedy field steeped in rainwater. Indistinct clouds, the color of dirty ice, smudged the sky.

TD had lowered a digital camera on a lanyard around her neck—her task was to capture some inspiring shots of the ranch for the nascent Web site. She'd barely spoken to Tim since he'd harassed her during the Guy-Med, but Gro-Par convention meant they were stuck together. The Program required constant companionship, a weakness Tim hoped to spin to his advantage when it came time to extract her.

Leah traced the perimeter of the ranch, keeping dutifully south of the chalk line. She snapped a picture of the mist settling into the distant hills. "It's always better to upload digitals. The guy running the site before insisted on scanning prints, but that gives lower resolution."

Tim took up the proffered conversation. "You must be glad to be running it now."

"I am." A trace of girlish pride found its way into her smile. "I guarantee you I love programming more than anyone else up here."

"What about it do you love?"

"Its simplicity. There's an elegance to a good program. A finite number of keystrokes in a particular order yields a predictable result. When there's a malfunction, the code can be tested, diagnosed, repaired. It all works the same ways, abides by the same laws." She scowled. "Programs beat people that way."

"We have more glitches."

She looked at him sideways, wearing a half smile. "That's right."

Though Tim had only a vague idea what time it was, the gray sky suggested dusk was encroaching. They walked for a while in silence. "What you said last night. About my daughter. I think you're right. I spend too much time talking about her murder, her absence, and not enough time talking about her. I think when I get back to talking about her, I'll remember what it was like to be a parent, not just a victim-by-proxy." A thought of Dray stole through his defenses. "I need to do that."

A turkey vulture lazed in circles over the distant water tower, drawing Tim's attention. Leah inhaled sharply. One hand covered her mouth, the other pointed at his feet. Expecting a rattlesnake, he looked down. His foot had strayed over the chalked boundary.

"You crossed the boundary." Her tone wasn't scolding; it was shocked.

He stood still, one leg on either side of the divide. "What did you think would happen if someone stepped over?"

"I don't . . . I don't know." She drew near, studying his foot. "I never thought about it, I guess." Her voice hardened. "We don't leave the ranch. Not even a footstep."

"Do you think it'll damage you to step over?" He offered his hand to her.

She studied his face, then the chalked line, then his face again. The heel of her sneaker rose, but the toe stayed planted. She stared at his hand for a long time. Her cheeks were splotched from the wind.

She reached out, her fingers hesitant, and took his hand. She waited for him to pull her. When he didn't, she put one foot across. Her other hand came up to his chest, as if she were breaking a stumble, and they faced each other. Despite the cold, the tips of her hair had darkened with sweat.

Before her mood could turn, Tim stepped back across. She was shaking as they made their way back.

*T*D twisted the mike free from his headset and handed it to Shanna.

Assembled in the Growth Hall in an immense circle around them, the Pros stretched their limbs, blinking the grogginess from their eyes. Tim watched by Leah's side.

Shanna stared at the little black bulb of the mike, opened her mouth, then hesitated.

Stanley John began to stomp his foot on the floorboards, slowly, rhythmically. A few Pros joined in, then a handful more. Within seconds the auditorium thrummed with the beat. Tim watched the skin of Leah's face smooth until it was devoid of expression, cadaverous. Her cheeks vibrated as she slammed her foot down, paused, slammed again.

Shanna was breathing hard, hand resting on her chest. TD hovered with a placid grin. She whispered something to him. He spread his arms. The pounding ceased.

She leaned awkwardly over the mike rather than raising it to her mouth. "I've decided to break my ties with my old self."

The flare of noise startled her, her eyes widening as the Pros charged her. Ecstatic embraces. Sports-arena whistles. Julie and Lorraine held hands around her, leaping for joy. Confused at first, she joined in. Soon she wore a similar face-splitting smile.

Tim caught himself clapping like an idiot. He searched for the other initiates in the crowd—Jason was joining in, babbling about catharsis. Don wore a vicarious smile. Wendy alone looked troubled, standing at the fringe of the festivities. Chad found her immediately, pulling her into a spontaneous hug, the embrace of two fans brought together by the winning touchdown.

From the rear, Stanley John pressed forward, bearing a stack of legal-size documents.

*T*im sat on the toilet and devoured a protein bar—his second to last. He licked the inside of the foil wrapper before ripping it up and flushing it. Shaving without a mirror proved a challenge, but he managed as he had on deployments. He used his free hand to help guide the razor around his goatee.

He knocked the blade against the lip of the sink and walked down the hall, his shoulders slumped with fatigue. The floor felt glacial through his socks. He pushed open the door to find Leah on her bed, facing the wall, her spine a pronounced stroke on the arc of her bare back. Bathed in the throw of light from the room's sole lamp, her shoulders heaved once, then stilled.

To Tim's surprise she didn't whip the sheet across herself or reach for her shirt, which lay puddled by her pillow. Instead she rolled over, revealing the profile of a modest breast and an angry red inflammation on her chest. Her face was slick with tears.

She sat up, collected her shirt, and stared at the rash. "It's your fault it hasn't gone away." Her voice was little more than a hoarse whisper. "Please don't tell them."

Before he could respond, she reached over and clicked off the light.

Thirty-one

Arms crossed over his knees, Lorraine's bobby pin pinched between his pale lips, Tim sat up in bed, waiting for Skate and the dogs to make their next pass around Cottage Circle. He wore two T-shirts beneath the sweater he'd pinched from Leah's drawer and an extra pair of socks. Trash bags, procured from the bathroom, encased his legs to the knees; he'd used shoelaces from his hipster Skechers to cinch them in place. Minutes before, he'd crept down the hall and unplugged the alarm's adapter, laying it beneath the outlet on the kitchenette counter.

Across in the dark, Leah was breathing raggedly, having cried herself to sleep. She'd refused to talk to him, a backslide in rapport.

The leaves of the elm said the wind was blowing east at a good clip, a Santa Ana riptide mountain-funneled back across the plateau. Tim would have to stalk Skate downslope to avoid the Dobermans' scent cone. He stared at the desolate ring of grass until Skate appeared, shuffling heavily by, the dogs' paws plunking in puddles.

Tim pushed open the window, eased himself out, and crouched at the base of the wall, mindful of the motion detector dangling from the roof's northwest corner. About forty yards away, one of the Dobies turned, ears perked, and looked directly at Tim. Forest green fleece pulled *bandido* style up over his mouth, Tim didn't move, didn't blink. The wind livened, whooshing in his ears. The dog stayed on point.

Skate snapped his fingers, and the Doberman reluctantly turned to trot beside his companion.

Tim pursued them, moving from cottage wall to tree trunk, not wanting to lose them in the darkness. Through the plastic bags, his feet left smudged, scentless indentations. When Skate banked around the lawn's far curve, Tim struck out swiftly for the trail leading down to TD's cottage. His jeans whistling at the inseam, his sheathed sneakers sliding on loose rock, he sprinted down the slope.

He reached the forbidden clearing and paused at a leaky pine, taking in the half-submerged wagon wheels, the grand porch, the candle flicker visible through the side window. Opera blared from TD's cottage. Across the way, Skate and Randall's shed nestled within a mass of brush. Orange light shimmered through the seams of the slatted wooden door. A silhouette crouched inside—Randall. Black smoke fumed from the pipe chimney, diffused by the rain cap. A blaze of fiery ash hiccupped out, then Tim heard the clank of an iron door. Judging from the gaps between the warped boards, the shed's frigidity outnumbered even that of the cottages; they probably kept the fire going all night.

Tim circled the clearing, ducking through bushes and rake-like branches. He passed behind the shed, close enough to peer through a rift in the wood. Randall relaxed shirtless on a cot, his flesh sleek with perspiration and jaundiced from the flames. He was reading a letter and chuckling maliciously.

The door to the mod confronted Tim with a rise of locks and a padlock dangling from a hasp staple. He plucked the meager bobby pin from his lips and twirled it between two fingers. Cold bit into him at the wrists and neck.

He humped his way up a nearby oak, bark scraping his cheek, then swung out along the branch. He absorbed the three-foot drop to the roof with a deep-knee bend, making barely a sound. Four screws secured the skylight pane in its housing, so he rebent the bobby pin to form a flat length and worked it until his fingers cramped. Once the top screws were loosened, he slid the pane out of its housing. He removed the trash bags and stuffed them in a pocket. Gripping the edge, he swung down into the mod, landing softly on his clean Nikes.

He pulled the flexible-rod flashlight from his back pocket and uncurled it. The confined tactical signature illuminated TD standing in the room, arms crossed confidently. Tim started at the cardboard display. A few moments' pause helped him level his breathing and stop smiling at himself. Then he moved systematically through the modular, searching through boxes and crates. He turned up a staggering array of propaganda and a locked Pelican case he presumed held ordnance; a barrel key in the bottom desk drawer fit the case, which opened to reveal a cache of fifteen handguns. Not wanting to pause to write down the registration numbers, he resecured the case, making a note to return to it if he had time. He couldn't risk a spin through the computer—his tech skills weren't good enough to justify the risk of a glowing monitor—but the bank of file cabinets beckoned.

Torturing the bobby pin further, he got through the crappy locks. He sat on the floor with the flashlight goosenecked between his teeth, flipping through file after file. All five drawers of the first cabinet housed prospective land purchases for TDB Corp. Various business models and proposals filled the next cabinet, many of them too complicated for Tim to assess.

The bottom drawers held social-science research. *Table 1-9: Increasing Immediacy in Obedience-Inducing Force. Chart 4: Compliance as a Function of Demographic Group. Generating Socially Undesirable Behavior: A Reward-Cost Analysis.*

TD had compiled his own database to underpin The Program.

Moving quickly, Tim evened documents' edges, realigned paper clips in their grooves, replaced folders in their hanging files. At the snap of a twig or the rattle of the wind, he'd click off the light and take a position of cover beneath the desk; the vigorous weather proved an impediment to swift progress.

He came upon lists of all sorts. A list of Decrees for TD's higher-ups—*Do* not *make spontaneous eye contact with the Teacher;* a list of Glitches—*Touching the Teacher's skin when you are menstruating;* a list of System Errors—*Taking any action without your Gro-Par;* even a list of Invisible Viruses—*Having negative thoughts about The Program.*

One file was stuffed with letters from TD bearing his signature stamp. Tim fanned the stack, eyeballing one in the middle—*The Teacher forgives you for having an unflattering dream image of him last night.* The adjacent file explained the mass-produced absolutions—letters to him from the Pros, begging forgiveness for everything from unauthorized masturbation to clandestine snacks.

The final two cabinets accommodated the most disturbing materials, dossiers on every Pro and initiate. Glancing through them recalled the eeriness Tim had felt perusing his own file in the midst of last year's mess.

The meticulous logging was mind-boggling. Sleep schedules. Weekly Gro-Par reports—*Winona complained twice yesterday of missing her twins*. Self-report forms—*Name your complaints about The Program you least want to say out loud*. Medical reports from the ranch physician, one Dr. Henderson, who seemed to double as a shrink—*Chad complained of perianal itching; he believes it's stress-related. He's not yet fully sublimated into GrowthWork; he recalled weight-lifting fondly*. A peek inside Dr. Henderson's file revealed him to be a podiatrist who'd had his license revoked for selling OxyContin, a juicy nugget rooted out by an outside PI, one Phil McCanley. TD had created a time-tested system for psychological leverage—trickle-down snitchonomics.

Tim found Leah's file and spent more time on it than was judicious. *Primary trauma—father's death. Primary phobia—cancer. Primary victimization—enabling others in their victimhood. Point of leverage: stepdad.* Below this the wrongdoings Will had ostensibly perpetrated upon Leah— the precise list she had regurgitated to Tim last night. Having scrutinized similar lists in countless other files helped put Will's allegedly abusive parenting in perspective. Dr. Henderson had much to report on Leah's rash. A pink bow fastened a bundle of love letters Leah had written to her new self. A note jotted on TD's letterhead made Tim's stomach churn: *Latent feelings of unwantedness and minor instances of neglect serve as tenable areas of exploration. Guide Leah to recall physical and sexual abuse.*

Tom Altman's file held exhaustive financial information regarding his phony portfolio. Not surprisingly, *murdered daughter* was Tom's key point of leverage; Tim felt another wave of shame at having exploited the trauma so cheaply. The file was updated to include TD's suspicion, then confirmation, of the murder-for-hire, as well as the fictional hit man's blunder. Tom's bout of impotence had already appeared, as well as his extensive dish-wiping miscues from yesterday's lunch. His divorce was noted as well. All in all, the file declared him an exceptional candidate.

A gray file in the back of the drawer caught his attention. The tab read *Dead Link,* and as Tim flipped through it, he realized it was different from the others he'd seen. No photo, just a name—*Wayne Topping*—a computer folder designation—*c:/TD/docs/deadlink4/*—and a status entry—*Missing.* Tim went back through the other drawers and came upon several more Dead Link files hidden among the others. Each seemed to correspond to a person who'd left or been removed from The Program. Ernie Tramine's status at the Neuropsychiatric Institute was noted. A girl had killed herself at the Le Brea Tar Pits—Tim recalled the newspaper story from several weeks ago—and more suicides were reported, neatly closing out three more files. According to his folder, Reggie Rondell was checked into a psychiatric ward in Santa Barbara. Another girl's status was listed as *Active.*

Before Tim had time to contemplate the chilling ramifications of the Dead Link files, a faint shout froze him up. Replacing the papers neatly in the file, he eased the drawer closed. A twist of the bobby pin, which he'd left protruding from the lock, sealed the cabinet. Sensing the ground vibration of someone approaching, he scampered to the skylight and pulled himself to the roof. Lying flat, he secured the pane. Another yell, distorted in the wind but nearer, reached him.

He peeked over the mod's edge in time to see the twin black streaks of the Dobermans beelining into the clearing.

*L*orraine's head bobbed industriously in TD's lap. His arms, spread wide, clutched a silk pillow on either side. A fat, three-wick candle cast a tranquilizing glow. He regarded the pistoning seal of her mouth for a moment before turning his attention back to a spot on the duvet cover, which he worked at futilely with a thumbnail.

Jessye Norman wailed to a close, the CD rasping quietly as it spun down.

A fierce snarling outside shattered the room's calm. He was on his feet, silk robe settling over him like a cape, his momentum knocking Lorraine off the bed. He shoved through the doors and out onto the freezing porch, standing barefoot with a jagged triangle of chest revealed.

The dogs had fallen on someone. They snarled and shoved back with their legs, heads shaking to tear flesh.

The shed door flew open, and Randall emerged just as Skate burst from the trail into the clearing, whistling around his fingers. The Dobermans dropped their prey, trotted to Skate's side, and sat whimpering lustfully, tongues working their wet muzzles. Bawling, the figure found her feet.

Nancy wore the same denim dress she'd had on when she'd been taken away, but it was tattered—torn at the collar, streaked with grime, missing half its buttons. She'd withstood the dogs' brief assault—aside from a missing shoe and a nasty bite on her right calf, she was surprisingly intact. Her hair, sweat-pasted and knotted, stuck out at all angles, the light roots prominent. Snot smeared her upper lip. She stooped in the thickening rain, favoring her right leg. "Please, TD," she said. "Please take me back. They left me. They dumped me by the tar pits."

TD's face held utter delight. "You got here *yourself?* How?"

The sole of her remaining shoe was almost entirely worn away. "Hiked. Walked. Hitched."

His eyes went to her muddy knees. "Crawled."

"That, too."

A pleased smile touched his lips. He nodded at the dogs. "Glad to see you got a warm welcome from Sturm und Drang."

A tiny voice called from behind him. "TD?"

He didn't turn his head. "*Get back inside.*"

Lorraine scurried off.

"Please take me back," Nancy said.

TD's lips curved into a grin. "No. Never."

She cringed. "I can help. I'm indispensable." Blood ran down her ankle, leached up by a ragged sock. Her appearance spoke of endless miles, wrong turns, the groping hands of truckers. She braced herself and took a last-ditch shot. "I know *everything* about The Program. You'd rather have me here than somewhere else."

Skate's mouth parted at the poorly veiled threat. The dogs revved at his side, the mingled scents of blood and fear driving them wild. TD broke the standoff with laughter. In a moment Nancy joined him with a relieved smile, nervous eyes darting.

The aftermath of amusement lingering on his face, TD turned back to the door. "Get her out of here. Correctly this time."

From his flattened perch on the mod's roof, Tim watched the scene unfolding in the clearing about thirty yards away. Renewed gusts of rain rattled the leaves on the oak overhead. A lightning flash strobe-lit the woods.

Randall disappeared back into his shed and emerged clutching a shovel and a flashlight. Skate snapped his dogs into a sit-stay and headed for the trees, prodding the shell-shocked woman before him. She tripped, and Randall hauled her up and pushed the shovel into her hands. His mouth moved, and then Tim heard the faint sound of Skate's chuckle.

There is a starkness to watching someone about to be killed. Ruthless executioners—whether common murderers or soldiers—comprehend the deadness of their victims even before they're dispatched. They handle them like ambulatory meat. And most victims seem to grasp their deadness as well. They can walk on their own, draw breath, even clutch the shovel that's to dig their grave, and though a glazed cognizance may take hold around the eyes, they can't catch up to their fate, can't seem to bend their minds around the fact that the thought they're endeavoring to think is going to be their last. Most unsettling is the inescapable fact that there's no romance in death, no grand horror even, just the final footsteps, a muffled pop, a body wilting to the ground. Despite his time spent dug into trenches and kicking down slum doors, Tim had never quite adjusted to it. Not that he wanted to.

He slid off the roof and jogged through the clearing toward the woods, mind racing to generate a plausible plan of attack. The Dobermans snapped and yowled but stayed put in their sit-stay as Tim had gambled they would. Despite their racket, there was no movement at TD's cottage.

Saliva flew from the dogs' jaws, great foamy drops that mingled with the downpour. Tim disappeared into the woods, skidding down a bank of mud and almost tumbling over. The air was thick with rain and wet-bark scent. Tim pressed on in the direction of Nancy's death march, shouldering through brush, his breath clouding humidly about his head.

A gunshot.

The storm swallowed the reverberation. Turning a desperate 360, Tim saw only trunks and leaves, no hint of light or human movement.

A piercing whistle split the air, a two-note blast. When Tim heard the dogs galloping through the clearing, he realized that the sound was Skate's release command. He scrambled down a slope, ducking behind a brace of rock. Snarling, the dogs approached. Claws scrabbled on rock, then two black streaks flew overhead, hit ground, sprinted toward their master.

Tim bent over, sucking air. A few seconds passed. A few more.

Then, carried to him from all sides in the trick wind, came a heightened roar, the teeth-sunk growl of dogs on flesh.

Tim watched the rain pool around his shoes.

After a moment he pulled the trash bags from his pocket and slipped them over his feet. He headed after the dogs, switching direction after a few minutes. He searched the terrain, always navigating with crisp 90-degree turns to keep his bearings. The sound of voices drew near. Randall and Skate passed about twenty yards away, the dogs scampering ahead, muzzles dark and sopped. Randall clutched a mud-caked shovel.

When they crested a hump of granite and dropped out of sight, one of the dogs howled, probably picking up Tim's scent back by the rock. Then, over a growl of thunder, he heard Skate laughing, "Go git it."

Listening for the dogs, Tim moved in expanding circles, trying to locate the grave. The windswept ground was blanketed with leaves and fallen branches. It was useless. After about a half hour, he headed back, reminding himself he had only to get through tomorrow and the retreat was over.

Now he had plenty to bring back to Tannino.

He avoided the part of the woods he'd entered, emerging on the far side of TD's cottage. When the wind shifted, he could hear the dogs snorting along his old trail deep in the woods.

TD's cottage was dark, but the shed glowed with stove light.

Tim made his way cautiously up the trail, through Cottage Circle. He arrived back outside his room. Ducking, he reached up and tugged at the window.

It had been locked.

Thighs burning, he eased himself up to peer over the sill. Leah's pale face, inches from the pane, caused him to jerk back. The muscles of her jaw were corded with tension. He gestured for her to open the window, but she met him with a glare.

Her expression changed when she glanced behind him. As she yanked open the pane and helped him inside, he glanced over his shoulder. A far-off flashlight bounced up the trail from the clearing. He was careful to keep the muddy trash bags off the bedspread. He tugged them inside out as he removed them, then pulled off his shoes.

They sat quietly by the window. Skate and the dogs materialized from the rain, shadowy apparitions. The dogs were hyped up, their stick legs blurring, snouts swiveling. Their heads dipped to the ground, vacuuming scent, but then something caught their attention ahead. They burst past the cottage, barking, Skate jogging after them.

Tim and Leah exhaled simultaneously. She backhanded his shoulder. "What the hell are you thinking? Do you have any idea what he'll do to us?"

"Skate and Randall killed a girl. In the woods."

"What? Does TD know?"

"He told them to."

"You saw them murder a girl?"

"I didn't actually see it." His wet socks ice-crackled as he crept to the door. "I have to wash off these shoes in the bathroom."

They worked their way slowly over the creaking floor, slipped into the bathroom, and huddled in a toilet stall. Tearing the plastic bags into pieces and tossing them in the toilet, Tim explained to her what he'd seen.

"I'm sure there's an explanation. You didn't find a grave." Though they were whispering, her voice was high-pitched, desperate, and he had to hush her.

"She was just another loose end tied up. TD keeps track of everyone in The Program and everyone who's left The Program."

"He doesn't care about people who leave."

"I saw the files he keeps on them. Listen to me carefully, Leah: Nobody gets out of The Program. Not without winding up dead, missing, or in a nuthouse."

"No way."

"That's what the Protectors *do,* Leah. That's what they're here for. They're dangerous men."

Her face tensed with uncertainty, but then she dropped her eyes. "Of course they're dangerous—they're like cops." She put a particular emphasis on that last word.

Tim looked at her skeptically.

Another flicker of emotion crossed her face. Still, she

wouldn't raise her eyes from the patches of plastic floating in the toilet. Then the affect vanished. She regarded him with perfect calm. "Why should I even talk to you? You're trying to persecute the Teacher."

"I'm here to protect you *and* to try to stop him from doing this to others."

"What are you, in the CIA or something? You're a spy, aren't you?"

"No. I'm not. You don't like spying?" Again she averted her eyes, an infuriating trick she practiced every time he threatened to pick up ground. "The Program is *built* on spying. You should see the file TD keeps on *you*. All your finances"—she pushed her hands over her ears, so he raised his voice to an angry whisper—"dating back months before you even became a Pro." She closed her eyes; her lips were moving. He grabbed her wrists and yanked her hands off her ears. Startled, she opened her eyes. "He's created an instruction manual for how to handle you. You know what it says to do if you try to leave? Tell you that outside The Program you'll get cancer."

She was weeping silently now. "Don't grab me."

He pulled his hands back. She started rocking and hugging herself. He flushed the toilet twice and rinsed his Nikes off in the sink. She followed him silently back down the hall, fell into bed, and lay with her back to the room. He sat beside her, resisting the parental urge to pet her back.

"I'm sorry I grabbed you."

"You don't have any right to handle me that way."

"Of course not. No one does."

"There *are* no files. I don't believe you."

"I held them in my hands, Leah. Yours and the Dead Link files for people who have left. Or tried to leave."

She sat up, back against the wall, studying him. "What do you want? From me?"

"When I leave tomorrow night, I'd like you to come with me to meet with your parents the way you tried to before. But this time I'll make sure it goes better."

She laughed quietly. "You're going through all this shit just to try to get me to do *that* again?"

"You'll have a chance to explain to them why this is right for you."

"Are you paying attention to anything that's going on? I have no need or obligation to explain myself to my parents. So they can kidnap me."

"I won't let that happen. You have my word that you can come back if you want to."

"Like I trust you. And besides, there's no way TD would let me go."

"So you *don't* believe TD when he says everyone is here by choice?"

"It's more complicated than that. There are reasons. He won't let me just *go*."

"Leave that up to me."

"It'll never work." She fisted her bangs hard. "You can't just leave the ranch."

"What do you mean? I'm not a Pro yet. And the retreat ends tomorrow."

Her eyes darted away. "TD wants you here. He wants all the initiates here, but you're special to him. He treats you differently, bends the rules for you." Her eyes flicked to the Cartier. "I've never seen him do that before."

"Then what's to say I can't get him to bend the rules again?"

"Even if he did let you leave, there's no way *I* could go."

"Pretend I could arrange it."

Leah stared at him, her mouth drawn tight.

"I told you, Leah, The Program is a one-way trip. And I know, now, that this is a dangerous place—and not just psychologically. This might be your only shot to get out. If I can arrange it, will you go with me?"

She lowered her hands and glared at him. "No. I won't." She stared at the rain-flecked window. "I started this, I'm going to finish it. I'm fulfilled here."

A movement drew their attention to the window. Skate and the dogs, patrolling the far edge of Cottage Circle. Leah shivered inadvertently.

Tim studied her reaction. "Really?"

She made no response.

"Leah, has anyone *ever* left the ranch?"

Thirty-two

*L*eah had been too agitated to sleep. She'd risen with the sun and waited shivering outside Cottage Three. Finally the door banged open, and Stanley John exited briskly, adjusting his shirt, not even noting Leah's presence to the side of the front step. A few moments later Janie emerged, using her fingers to comb her hair back into place. "Hi, babe." She kissed Leah on the forehead. "Why up so early?"

"There's something I wanted to ask you."

"Sure thing."

Leah picked at one of the empty belt loops on her pants. "Has TD ever had any . . . problems with the law or anything?"

"All great leaders have been persecuted. Especially when they set forth a new doctrine. Think of Martin Luther King, Gandhi. Heck, think of Jesus."

"So that's a yes?" Leah had tried to keep her frustration out of her voice, but Janie's expression indicated she'd failed.

"Did your parents fill your head with this nonsense that time you went home? *You* were persecuted that night, remember? And now you're gonna buy into the lies your persecutors hurled at you." Janie shook her head. "Really, Leah, I thought you were beyond this."

A familiar sensation overtook her—that she was shrinking

away, not in size but distance. She felt perspective-small, a dot on a horizon.

Janie combed her fingers through her tangled hair. "I'd just hate to think . . ."

"What?"

"Well, thoughts like that are really malignant. I'd focus on the Source Code before your negative energy manifests physiologically and turns carcinogenic."

Leah felt anxiety clench her stomach—Janie's response seemed straight from the secret file Tom had claimed to have found. But it also seemed right. The thoughts Tom had put into her head *were* diseased.

"Okay, Janie." Leah's voice was quiet, deadened. "I will."

The Pros sat in monklike silence, lined in neat rows before bowls of oatmeal. Tim cast a curious sideways glance at Leah, who'd been turning in her chair to look at the other tables.

She finished appraising the far corner of the cafeteria and leaned toward Tim. "Everyone's accounted for," she whispered, face flushed with relief and vindication. "There's no missing girl."

Stomachs grumbling, they awaited TD's arrival.

"And here we have Tom Altman. . . ." TD paced the lip of the stage, emceeing the festivities. "A big shot. Handsome, rich, successful."

To commemorate the retreat's last day, each initiate had to undergo a turn on Victim Row. Tim's stomach churned—he was up to bat. His legs cramped from hours of sitting. Sweat pasted his T-shirt to the chair back. If he heard *2001* one more time, he thought he might start beating his own head like Rain Man. Shanna waited calmly in the chair to his right; to his left, Wendy sat trembling.

Skate looked on from the door, his hands resting on the erect heads of the attendant dogs. Tim raised his eyes to Randall in the back and thought about both men in the rain, body heat wisping from their shoulders, prodding the doomed girl before them. The way she'd clutched the shovel. The joke Randall had cracked just before they'd vanished into the trees.

TD placed his hands on Tim's shoulders. The lights dimmed, and the drum resumed its slow rumble.

A winning smile directed at Tim from up close. "But it seems you have a little problem *performing*." A scattering of giggles. "A little performance anxiety, Tom? Afraid you can't *measure up* to expectations?"

Leah's face, blanched and upset, stood out from the crowd. Tim wished he could convey to her that his chagrin was feigned.

"I think it's more than that," TD continued. "I think you felt impotent when your little Jenny was taken and *killed*."

Tim felt a distinct rise in his temperature.

"You neglected her. Where were you that day when she was walking home from school? Seeing to *business?* Counting your *money?* Socking away more in the bank account so you and the missus could maintain your lifestyle? What killed her? A psychopath? Or her parents' hideously yuppie self-involvement? You *made* her a victim, just like yourself, didn't you? If you'd done something differently that day, that week, you could have saved her life. She could still be your daughter. She could be waiting for you at home *right now*."

Having unearthed Croatian mass graves, having beheld through 8×50 binocs the public stoning of a raped Afghan twelve-year-old, having used both hands and a knee to hold together the shrapnel-shredded skull of a platoonmate, Tim noted with alarm his rising discomfort. The one benefit of his distress was that the surfeit of emotion was easy to channel into his performance. His face burned; sweat ran into his eyes. Though he willed himself to sit, in his mind he leapt from the chair, palmed TD's skull and his beckoning chin, and twisted through the crackling resistance. He bombarded himself with violent fantasies, mostly to fight off the image of Ginny. But the heat, hunger, and fatigue loosened his control, and his daughter's face drifted into focus. The haze of freckles across her nose. Her awkward, second-grade grin. The gap between her front teeth. The wisp of hair he'd freed from the corner of her mouth as she lay cold and inert on the coroner's slab.

He held his eyes on Leah. A tear beaded on his lower lid; a blink pushed it into a downward trickle. Leah matched it. And his next.

"Once she was dead, you thought money would get you past it. Money turned into *power.* You took *action.* You decided the rules *didn't apply* to you. You decided you were *above the law.* And now you're *afraid* of your power. So afraid you've gone *soft* with fear. What did you use your power for that has you so cowed?"

The four murderous weeks of last February came back to Tim in a rush of faces—Jedediah Lane, Buzani Debuffier, Robert, Mitchell, Rayner.

Tim had completely left his body—he saw TD's mouth moving soundlessly, the spread of faces before him, gleeful and vehement.

When he refocused, TD was saying, "The only way to eliminate that fear is to face it again. Are you ready to face it?"

"Yes." Tim's voice held a note of pleading he didn't recognize. "Yes."

"You need to use your power again and use it *right.*"

"How?"

"Someone's family has been prying into our business. There's a danger that threatens us all, living right here among us." TD halted before Tim, eyes picking over him. "We won't risk betrayal. We won't stand for impostors."

The shift to menace, in the midst of Tim's disorientation, froze him in a perfect, breathless moment of panic.

His gaze steady on Tim, TD snapped his fingers and held out his hand, a doctor awaiting a scalpel. Skate crossed to the stage and lifted his shirt, revealing a handgun pressed into the sweaty flesh of his gut.

Tim snapped into absolute clarity. His breathing evened out; his heartbeat pulsed at his temples clear and steady like a metronome.

Skate plucked the weapon free and slapped it into TD's hand. Holding the gun limply before him, TD turned and walked back to Tim, his footsteps clacking in the silent auditorium. A Sig Sauer P245. With its compact frame and big caliber, it was a street-smart relative of the Spec Ops–issue P226 in Tim's gun safe.

Had he really put his life in the hands of a nineteen-year-old? Tim risked a glance at Leah; she looked horrified. He'd worry later about whether she'd sold him out; for now his concern was seizing the gun from TD. Six rounds in the mag, one in the pipe meant he could take TD and both Protectors and still have three bullets left to fend off the mob. If the dogs attacked, he'd shoot upward into their open mouths or offer them a shirt-wrapped forearm to gnash, getting in tight enough to press muzzle to fur so the gun would discharge noxious gases into them along with the lead.

TD reached out. Tim tensed, ready to strike him at the wrist and elbow. He could picture the arm bending, the gun driving up, the muzzle snugging beneath TD's chin for the discharge.

But the barrel was facing away.

Tim slid the proffered weapon from TD's hand.

"Shanna's folks, you see, are pretty influential people. They're sending investigators after her, calling police departments. We can't afford that. And we certainly can't afford to let her leave here knowing all our secrets."

Shanna's mouth hung open, her lower jaw edged forward.

"Tom, prove that your devotion to The Program is absolute." He grasped Shanna by both shoulders and gazed down at her paternally. "Let's see if you can do a job *yourself* instead of paying someone else to do it for you."

A hush settled over the crowd.

The kettledrum started up, slowly matched by stomping feet.

TD wouldn't commit so flagrant a crime after all his subtle machinations to avoid illegality. Tim gauged the weapon in his hand. It felt light, as if the magazine were empty, though he wouldn't bet Shanna's life on it.

Shanna was wheezing. She fell off her chair onto her knees.

Tim debated running a press-check, pulling back the slide to expose the bullet, but it required both hands and would surely give away his facility with weapons. He cast his mind back to sticky-eyed gunplay near Jelalabad, where his platoon had forged through a wind-induced brownout into dark tunnels. They'd learned to check if their Sigs were fire-ready by fingering the extractor. The sliver-wide leaf spring, which pulled spent cartridges out of the barrel, protruded ever so slightly when there was a round in the chamber. Walking over to Shanna, Tim moved his trigger finger up and ran it along the chamber portion of the barrel, past the ejection port. The extractor sat flush.

Shanna cowered before him, pale-faced.

The room rocked and thumped and hummed.

Burning with delight, TD awaited Tom Altman's next move. Tim raised the gun, aimed directly at TD's forehead, and pulled the trigger. The hammer fell with a faint click.

A shocked silence.

Tim blew imaginary smoke from the barrel and tossed the gun. It clattered on the stage. Tom Altman's exercise complete.

TD watched him, frozen in a moment of amazed respect. He began to clap, and the Pros erupted in applause.

Shanna collapsed on the floor.

"Brilliant," TD murmured, his voice barely audible over the roar of the audience. "Fucking *brilliant*."

The Pros stormed the stage, swept Tim up, and jumped with him. The scene resembled the cascading-confetti finale of a political convention. A path parted before TD. He snatched Tim into an embrace, his whisper cutting through the ruckus. "You're ready now, Tom. No more games."

As the celebration lingered, Tim and Leah headed out the Growth Hall's rear exit.

"The gun," she said. "How did you know?"

"I knew."

They passed behind the cafeteria, and Leah again instinctively turned away from her reflection in the walk-in freezer. Tim caught her, turning her toward the side of the freezer. She froze, her head tilted to the ground. He kept his hands on her shoulders, gentle but firm.

For nearly a full minute, they stayed perfectly still, Tim waiting patiently, Leah stubbornly avoiding her reflection.

Finally she lifted her eyes. Tentatively she raised her trembling fingertips, pressed them into her cheek. Tim stepped back, leaving her alone with her mirrored image.

She smiled. She fussed with her hair. She made a snarly face at herself.

A one-note gasp of a laugh seemed to catch her by surprise, a cautious peal of delight.

Honing his clockwise wiping technique, Tim worked beside Leah. Lorraine and Shanna were elbow deep in suds. Chad stacked the plates.

Stanley John burst through the swinging doors and said, "Chad, the Teacher wants to see you. *Now.*"

Chad stopped, plates clutched between his hands. He set

them down on the counter and walked from the room.

"What's going on?" Shanna asked.

"Wendy's not getting with The Program," Stanley John said. "TD wants to switch him out, put Janie on her."

Lorraine dried her hands, then cupped Shanna's cheeks. "I never have to worry about *you* being Off Program. You're the perfect Gro-Par."

Shanna blushed and covered her grin with a soapy hand.

"If you stay on track, you might even get asked to be one of TD's Lilies."

Shanna's grin faded. She bit her cheek and glanced away.

"Speaking of Lilies," Stanley John said quietly to Lorraine, "you'll never guess who showed up in the middle of the night. Nancy Kramer."

Leah stiffened.

Tim recognized the name from TD's file cabinets—the Active Link. She'd been successfully converted to a Dead Link last night.

Shanna and Lorraine stacked the final wet dishes before Tim and Leah and then left. Stanley John followed them out, drawing close to Lorraine, his voice barely audible. "Guess she passed the Darwin test at the tar pits."

Tim and Leah dried in silence for a while, Leah fighting back tears. "You don't have to gloat."

"She's dead, Leah. I don't want you to end up with her."

They worked in silence for a while. Leah finally reached TD's plate, sitting by itself on the counter. She produced two brand-new towels, using them like pot holders so her flesh wouldn't come in contact with it. She paused, staring at the blank white plate, tears running down her cheeks.

"Yes," she said. "I'll go with you."

She spit on the plate, polished it, and continued her work.

Thirty-three

*W*endy confronted the stack of legal documents before her. "I don't think I'm ready to do this."

She sat beside her husband and Tim on the Growth Hall floor, surrounded by Pros. An orb of light encapsulated the group, a perimeter of darkness hemming them in. Jason Struthers, like Shanna, had already elected to stay on and enjoy Pro status. The devout attention he'd enjoyed since signing on the dotted lines had left him in near rapture.

And then there were three.

The inner core of encircling Pros included all the heavyweights—Lorraine, Winona, Janie, Stanley John, and, of course, TD. A clamp-jawed man in his early thirties, a Program attorney named Sean, sat up front as well, next to a trim, bearded fellow of the same age—the good Dr. Henderson, complete with a yachtsman's physique and John Lennon spectacles. Winona clutched a notary stamp, signature log, and a mini–ink pad for fingerprint confirmation. The voluptuous redhead had parked herself behind Don, touching his hips with the points of her spread knees, stroking his back lazily. She slid a Montblanc up over his shoulder and down the front of his chest.

There was no Enya, no *2001*, no kettledrum, just an excruciating silence.

Tim flipped through the carefully prepared documents before him. A general power of attorney. A durable power of attorney. A power of attorney for each of Tom Altman's banks and brokerage firms. Transfer of assets. Deed of gift.

In consideration of goodwill and other good and valuable consideration, receipt of which is hereby acknowledged, I hereby grant and convey the following to TDB Corp . . .

I, the undersigned, hereby make, constitute, and appoint TDB Corp my true and lawful Attorney for me and in my name, place, and stead and for my use and benefit. . . .

. . . designate TDB Corp with broad powers to ask, demand, manage, sue for, recover, collect, and receive each and every sum of money, debt, account, legacy, bequest, interest, dividend, annuity, and demand . . .

There was even a postal form for Tom Altman to forward his mail to The Program's P.O. box, a surefire way to certify that not a single investment statement slipped through the cracks. TD would keep them under his thumb until he'd bilked every cent from every account, leaving them rattling husks like Ernie Tramine and Reggie.

The comprehensiveness of the paperwork was astonishing. In fact, The Program's team knew more about Tom Altman's portfolio than Tim did. He mused on Tannino's masterful ways of building fraudulent paper empires.

Wendy squirmed under the panorama of staring eyes. Beside her, Don broke the standoff, grabbing the pen. Leaning over, he began to sign the forms furiously. The crinkle of turning pages was drowned out by a respectful ripple of applause, a golf clap punctuated by doting exclamations—tentative still, as Don's work was not yet complete.

The redhead squeezed Don excitedly from behind. Wendy watched the well-manicured hands kneading her husband's lateral muscles. Her voice was shaky. "Don? Honey? I think we should talk about this."

Continuing to flip pages, Don kept his head down, focused athletically on the task.

"C'mon, Wen, what's to talk about?" Stanley John said.

"I think . . . I think we should talk to Josh. He *is* our CFO."

"Here we care about the future." Sean folded his hands contentedly. "Not the past."

"Why isn't Josh here, too?" Winona said. "When you and your husband chose growth, he chose to lag behind."

Janie said, "You can figure out later if Josh is part of your future. For the time being, why don't you Live in the Now? Let all that other crap go."

TD reclined on elbow-locked arms, taking in everything with a creator's pride.

Don finished, slapped the last form facedown on the floor, and looked up with shiny eyes. "I'm staying on. I'm going forward. I'm not dragging all this with me."

A cry of joy was raised, the rush of euphoria so disorienting that for a moment Tim joined in the thrill. Between hugs and pats, Don signed the notary log Winona presented. Standing still amid the swirls of movement, Wendy looked shaken. Her imploring eyes met Tim's. He forced himself to look away.

TD stood, and everyone quieted, settling back on the floor. Now, magically, only Tim and Wendy remained in the center. Don had been whisked out by the busty redhead, no doubt to collect his due rewards. With a flourish, TD produced the Montblanc and extended it to Wendy. She stared at it a few moments, gulping air, then took it.

The squeak of a sneaker on the floorboards. The rush of wind across the roof. Someone unzipped a jacket in the back.

"I'm sorry," Wendy said. "There are too many people this would affect."

An instant, horrifying transformation of faces. Disapproving head shakes. Heartbroken frowns. Pros could no longer bear to make eye contact with her.

"That's a shame, Wen," Stanley John finally said. "You're getting pretty Off Program. This is about *you*, not others. But we'll sort it out in Workshop tomorrow."

"Tomorrow?" She stared from blank face to blank face. "I've got a full day of meetings tomorrow. I'm already behind from—"

A clamor of protest. "Don't go backward, Wen."

"Tomorrow's the most important day. It's gonna be so much fun."

"This is a critical time for you," Stanley John explained. "You're between two stages, in limbo. You can't regress now.

Who from your old life would understand you now? After everything you've accomplished? After everything we've shared? The abortions. Your time with Chad. You've done things, Wendy. We're the only ones who understand you now."

Wendy's predicament seemed to jar Shanna. For the first time since they'd arrived, she resembled the awkward college kid Tim had met outside the college counseling center.

An edge of fear undercut Wendy's evident anger. "This is a three-day retreat. I'm ready to leave."

"You're free to go. But there's no van going back to the city tonight."

"I want to make a phone call."

Dr. Henderson made a tsking noise. "You don't want to bother friends and family now. At this hour? It's a long ride."

Tim thought of the zero-bars cell-phone signal, the severed cords in the bank of phone booths, Wendy's oblivious bantering on the drive up as the landscape flew by unheeded outside the van's blacked-out windows.

"Fuck this." Wendy's voice quivered with fear. She stood and exited abruptly, walking away from the group to the unlit reaches of the auditorium. Shanna looked shaken by Wendy's departure—her first glimpse over the walls of pluralistic ignorance. Allowing any initiate to witness another's hesitation was, as Tim saw it, TD's first strategic error.

Several Pros were on their feet, but TD waved a hand calmly, and they sat. Tim squinted to make out Skate guarding the door. Wendy hesitated for an instant, but Skate obligingly snapped the dogs into a sit-stay, and she stormed past. A gust of wind announced Wendy's exit, and then the door's creaking return restored the calm.

Good old Tom Altman remained, alone in the glowing center of a ring of expectant faces. From all sides glassy eyes peered at him.

"How do you feel about your time here?" TD said.

"It's been amazing," Tim answered truthfully.

"But you need something else, don't you? What else do you need?"

"Well, The Program opened up all this psychological . . . *material.* And I realize now the ways I've chosen weakness, the mistakes I've made. But I don't know how to . . ."

"Atone?"

"Yes," Tom said softly. "Atone."

"We're helping guide you to that atonement." TD nodded at the paperwork before him. "What allowed you to hire someone else? To order the killing of another man? The *wrong* man?"

Tim let the epiphany burst across Tom Altman's face. "My money."

"The money that led you to think you could get away with it. The money that *let* you get away with it. Start fresh, Tom. Rebuild. You've got no wife, no daughter, no house. All you have is yourself."

His voice sounded tiny, lost in the expanse of the silent hall. "And my guilt."

"Of course your guilt. Your guilt is your past. If you want to get rid of it, you'll have to get rid of the one thing that binds you to the past."

Tom Altman wiped his eyes. "My portfolio."

The Pros started to murmur, then call out their support. It seemed the entire world was aimed at him and him alone. A few strokes of his pen could unleash untold elation.

Tim held up his arms. The sound ceased. The rush of power he felt at the crowd's instant reaction provided a tiny window into TD's life.

Tom Altman's voice was choked. "I don't want it. I want to be free from it. Who cares if I default on the deal? I don't want *any* of it." He leaned forward, pressing the pen to the top sheet of paper.

"*Wait,*" TD said.

Tim's father would have been proud.

"What do you mean, 'default on the deal'?"

Tom wrinkled his face. "Well, I can't just pull out of my legal obligations to the shareholders and the board. There are limitations on divesting. It's a public company. I could turn over my corporate position and assign my assets to The Program, but that would take some hammering out."

"How long?"

"I have meetings stacked all day tomorrow and Friday with my legal team. I can't imagine it would take longer than that to figure out how to go about it. But you know what? What do I care anymore, right? I'm leaving it behind to Get with The Program."

"Maybe you should get all that ironed out, then make a clean break. Outstanding business, so to speak, can sometimes distract from growth."

"I don't really want to go back," Tim said. "I have much more to learn here." A church murmuring of amen equivalents. "I'm in a reflective space right now, and I feel rebuilt. I don't want to be around people who might not be receptive."

TD's face tightened—the first sign of discomfort Tim had witnessed in him. "Your Gro-Par should go with you."

Tom Altman waved off the suggestion. "No, I don't want to take Leah away from—"

TD's eyes bored through Tim. "It'll be much better for you if she goes."

"Well, I guess if you feel that strongly . . ."

A paternal smile quickly smoothed TD's face. "I think it's best."

A burst of cold air heralded Wendy's entrance. Bent arthritically at the waist, she clutched her windbreaker closed at the throat. The door swung shut behind her.

Already a cluster of Pros was moving to encircle her, bearing blankets and steaming cups of coffee that had appeared as magically as the corridor of soft-glowing light leading inward from the door. They bundled her up, whispering greetings, bearing her lovingly back into the fold.

* * *

*L*eah bounced as the van pulled out from its slot behind
the Growth Hall. Tim rode shotgun, his overnight bag
and reclaimed shoe box of goods at his feet. His thoughts
turned to the briefing he'd owe Tannino, how he'd present the
case to come back for TD.

Randall drove by the treatment wing, humming to himself—the "Ode to Joy." The Pros were out about Cottage Circle, attending to their tasks and activities robotically.

Not a single gray face rose to note the van as it glided past.

Thirty-four

*E*ntering from the garage, Tim found Dray at the kitchen
table, playing solitaire, silhouetted against the drawn
blinds like a fortune-teller who knew something about dumb-
bells. The last time he'd seen her playing cards was when
he'd gotten home from a post-WTC deployment to Uzbek-
istan that had gone overtime; now, as then, she'd looked pale
and exhausted, worn down by concern. He paused silently in
the doorway and stopped, forearm across the jamb, just
watching. She looked up and started, sending three clubs and
a spade airborne, and then she was up and in his arms.

She nuzzled her forehead into his neck, tight-squeezing
his waist. Then, as was their ritual, she felt his arms, his
chest, his back, searching out injuries. She pulled off his fake
glasses and tossed them disdainfully on the table, then ran
her hand over his goatee. "Can you shave this?"

"Not quite yet."

The smile lines around her eyes faded. "You're going back?"

"Maybe. If we can't flip Leah, I have to accompany her back Saturday so I don't blow her cover."

Dray bit her lip. He rested his palm on her stomach, which bulged ever so slightly below the toned muscle. She read his eyes, flattened her hands over his.

He felt her tense up.

Pulling back, he followed her stare over his shoulder. Leah stood in the doorway. With a sleeve-covered hand, she brushed her shaggy hair out of her eyes. "Sorry. I know you said to wait, but the dark and the quiet . . . I guess I'm not used to being alone."

Seeing Leah in this context, Tim was struck by how gaunt she was. She pulled off her sweater, her undershirt's V neck dipping to reveal the rash on her chest and the overpronounced strokes of her clavicles. The artificial light lent her arms' bruises and the smudges beneath her eyes a seaweedy tint.

Leah extended a gangly arm. "Hi. I'm Leah."

Taking her hand, Dray looked at Tim, and Tim tilted his chin in a faint nod.

"Andrea Altman," she said.

"I need to . . . uh, call the ranch and leave a voice mail. Every three hours."

Tim had been given the same phone number; if he needed to speak with TD, he was to call and leave a voice mail requesting a phone appointment. He'd receive a return call within three hours from one of the Pros, giving him the time at which he should call back.

Tim drew his cell phone from his pocket. "Use this. Don't place any landline calls from here, okay?"

"Okay." She started to dial, but her legs gave out.

Tim caught her, and Dray pulled over a chair. Leah bent her head into her hands. "Sorry. I'm sorry." She took a few deep breaths.

Dray filled a pot with water and put it on the stove. "Let's get some food into you."

"I don't want to be any more trouble."

Dray flashed her patented no-nonsense stare—eyebrows up, forehead wrinkled. "I wasn't asking."

*W*hen the shower ran in the little bathroom across the hall from Ginny's room, the pipes in the adjacent master wall hummed. Sitting on the bed, giving Dray the CliffsNotes rundown of the retreat, Tim realized that those pipes had been silent for the last year.

After waiting until Leah disposed of a full plate of pasta and two chicken-patty sandwiches, Dray had dragged the air mattress from the garage rafters and inflated it in Ginny's room. Unlike most tough women, she had patience for fragility, though now that she wasn't in Leah's pitiable presence, her magnanimity was wearing thin.

"I need your help," Tim said.

"We're not running an orphanage here."

"She got sucked into something over her head. She just needs a little space to—"

"She made those choices. *She* did. Like kids choose to shoot up or knock off 7-Elevens. We don't provide turndown service for them." Her sigh puffed up her bangs. "And now she knows where we live. And she's planning to return to the enemy camp."

"I'm hoping we can talk her out of it."

"That's another thing. After you risked your *life*, she's down here to . . . what? Test the waters?"

"We'll do the intervention first thing tomorrow morning. Let's hope she goes home with her parents from there."

"And if she doesn't, then you escort her back to the ranch? That's crazy-making."

"It's how the law works. We can't just hold her against her

will—you're the one who was so adamant about that earlier. Why do you have a problem with her now?"

"She *did* try to fuck you."

"She was under the impression that I was single."

"Oh," Dray said. "Well, then."

The pipes ceased their murmuring, and Dray left to make up the bed.

Tim called Bear and debriefed him quickly so he could start in on the Dead Link leads. Then he removed his badge and .357 from the gun safe. He clipped the holster at his right hip, then sat on the bed, holding the five-point star in his lap, running his thumb across the silver-plated brass. TD's words worked on him still, even through the second skin of his assumed identity. Tim *had* been arrogant. He *had* assumed power that should not have been his. He *had* killed the wrong people, not those responsible for his daughter's murder.

Though it was barely after ten, Leah fell out in minutes, snuggled blissfully beneath an abundance of winter blankets in Ginny's otherwise bare room. Zipping up his jacket, Tim paused in the doorway, peering in. A chocolate bar lay half eaten on the floor within arm's reach of the pillow. To ward off loneliness, Leah had asked for a radio; from Tim's paint-splattered boom box, James Taylor wearily bemoaned flying machines in pieces on the ground.

In Tim's boxers and a stretched T-shirt, Dray padded up the hall from the kitchen, turning off the lights along the way. The shushing of her footsteps ceased.

Breathing quietly side by side in the darkness, they watched Leah's sleeping form.

"**N**ot at your house. It's important we meet on neutral ground." The finality in Tim's voice elicited a glance from Bear in the driver's seat.

The Dodge wasn't the most soundproof of vehicles; Tim

had to stick a finger in his ear so he could hear Emma's faint response on the cell phone. "How about at my brother Michael's, then? He lives in Westwood."

"She's allergic to cats," Tim said.

"So?"

"Uncle Mike has cats."

If the bemused noise escaping Bear's throat was any indication, Emma's silence connoted shock. "I suppose he does," she finally managed.

A rustle as the phone was handed off, then Will's gruff voice cut in. "What's this? Where are we meeting?"

"I'm working on that. Keep your schedule clear in the morning."

Tim heard Emma murmuring in the background, then Will said, "Not too early. We want to be our best for this. The baby's given us quite a week."

"Leah's had quite a week, too." Tim snapped his phone shut.

The Dodge rocked as they pulled into the motel parking lot, the vacancy sign crackling like a bug zapper overhead. Bear angled into a space. "You want me to wait here, right?"

"Yeah. I'm sorry." Tim got out and headed for the brightly lit front office.

Reggie's head snapped up at the chiming bells. "Oh, c'mon, what now?"

"I got her out. But only for two days."

"Man, you are incorrigible."

"I took your advice. I'm leaving it up to her whether she wants to go back."

"Good for you. Thanks for dropping by."

"I need somewhere to hold an intervention in the morning."

It took a moment for realization to dawn, and then Reggie leaned back. "No way. I want no part of this. I've done what I can for you."

"You're not doing this for me," Tim said. "I've got a girl contemplating leaving The Program, leaving TD." Reggie shriveled at the names. "Well, here's your chance."

"*My* chance?"

"To stand up. To help someone else walk out. You said you're stuck because you never got to choose. Well, now you get to choose."

Reggie coughed out something unintelligible. "Good manipulation. You learned well from TD." He returned Tim's stare. "There are hundreds of seedy motels around here. Pick one of them."

"I don't want one of them."

"What if they find out I helped?"

"They think you're still in the bin up in SB. If they even knew you were here, you wouldn't be here. As you said, you're the sole survivor. They won't get it wrong forever. We have to crack The Program open. I need your help to do it. This is the first step."

Reggie bit his bottom lip so it bunched out as if he were dipping tobacco. He bobbed his head, mulling it over. "So you want a room."

"And I'd like you to be there. To help talk to her."

Reggie laughed sharply. "Yeah, right. Like her parents will let me anywhere near her."

"Her parents aren't running this. The girl needs you."

Hopefulness brightened Reggie's face, then vanished, replaced by his accustomed affect, that of someone treading water with sapping strength. His forehead knitted. "I don't have . . . I don't have anything to offer."

"You're gonna use that for the rest of your life?"

He shifted his weight from one foot to the other, then back again. "Sorry." He shook his head. "I've faced my demons already."

"Yeah? And who won that staredown?"

Reggie squirmed under Tim's look and finally broke eye contact. His pale arms rose and fell limply to his sides, a gesture of defeat. "I'm a coward, don't you know?"

Only the perpetual gurgle of the new fish tank broke the silence.

"So that's the bottom line?" Tim said. "All the bullshit you told me about never getting to decide for yourself—just an excuse you mutter to let yourself off the hook?"

Reggie bobbed his head, blinking hard. "Maybe so."

The bells jangled loudly as Tim exited. He climbed into Bear's rig. Bear read his expression, surmised he wasn't in a sharing mood, and reversed out of the space. He tugged the gearshift down and hit the gas. The seat belt locked suddenly across Tim's chest.

Reggie stood feet from the front grille, hands thrust into his pockets.

Tim shouldered open the door and set one foot down on asphalt, regarding him over the outbent hinge of the panel. Wisps of steam seeped from the rattling hood.

Reggie withdrew one hand, something gleaming in his fist. He tossed it at Tim who caught it single-handed. A key. Room 3.

Tim glanced back up, but already the office door was swinging closed, muffling the complaint of the bells.

A discordant banging, like the clap of a loose screen door, snapped Dray awake. She rolled onto her stomach, hand digging through her kicked-off uniform on the floor and emerging with her gun. Since Ginny's death, she left the Beretta lying around rather than committing it to the gun safe at night, a foolish compensatory extravagance.

Grabbing the cordless, she shuffle-stepped across the room and let her muzzle lead her pivot around the jamb. The radio in Leah's room was audible from the hall, playing something undulating and beatific. Dray peered around the corner. Sitting Indian style on the mattress, Leah rocked forward, beating her forehead against the wall and whimpering.

The song, an amalgam of electric keyboard, Illiean pipes, and plaintive exhortations to sail away, seemed the perfect score to the disturbing scene.

Dray called out to Leah three times, drew no response, and tugged her back from the wall. Blood matted her bangs, streaked the bridge of her nose. Leah shrieked and jerked away, hurling herself back at the wall.

Dray fought her down, pinning her with a knee across the chest, and fumbled the phone to her ear. She reached to turn off the boom box with her foot, but it was too far a stretch. Tim picked up on the first ring.

"She's in some kind of trance, banging her head, and she won't stop—"

"I can barely hear you."

Leah bucked and screeched.

"She's crying out, and the music—"

"Is that Enya? On the radio. That's one of her triggers. Turn it off."

Dray rolled off Leah and slapped the power button. Leah's thrashing quieted. Dray snapped her fingers in front of Leah's closed eyes, a Hollywood technique of dubious efficacy. "Now what the hell am I supposed to do?"

"Talk to her. Tell her to come to."

Dray smoothed Leah's hair off her face; the abrasions, despite their yield, appeared to be minor. "Leah, wake up now. It's time to wake up."

"Tell her to *come to*. Use that phrase."

When Dray repeated the command, Leah's eyes fluttered open, showing a lot of white. The pupils slowly pulled down into view. Leah lurched forward violently. An instinctive "ssshh" emerged from Dray's tensed lips. Leah's eyes darted around until she seemed to recognize her surroundings, then she released a shuddering sigh and burst into tears.

"What's happening?" Tim asked.

Leah curled into a ball, clasping Dray about her waist, pressing her face into her side. After a moment Dray reached down and stroked her head. "We're okay now."

Thirty-five

Freed's Porsche dripped oil in Tannino's driveway, parked beside the marshal's Bronco and his Sunday car, a classic Olds—champagne with velveteen interior. Further diminishing the repute of vanity plates, Freed's license read FRNSHME, a tip of the hat to the family biz.

Freed and Thomas awaited Tim and Bear inside, along with Tannino and Winston Smith, the federal prosecutor, who gripped the brim of his trademark felt hat with both hands like a farmer awaiting a bank loan. They sat ensconced in a devouring sectional sofa while Tannino's wife and sister bustled clamorously, brandishing espressos and dishes of confetti candy. Various sloe-eyed antecedents peered out from garish frames on the piano.

Tannino's wife cupped a hand on Tim's cheek. "Tim, sweetie, I haven't seen you since all that . . ." A wave of her manicured hand finished the sentiment. "Let me bring you some figs. George, I have the perfect thing." Aside from judges, she was the only one to call Bear by his given name. "Zucchini flowers I made for dinner. You sit."

Tim and Bear's bumbling demurrals went largely ignored.

Tannino's niece practically skipped out from her bedroom, all done up and date ready. The men smiled and did their best not to observe her—she was stunning, and Tannino was vigilant. She and Tannino kissed, a quick peck on the mouth that somehow wasn't creepy.

"This kid she's dating"—Tannino pointed at the door through which his niece had just departed—"got picked up for shoplifting—"

"Marco," his wife snapped, handing Bear a plate. "He was *eleven*."

Bear took advantage of her distraction, enfolding a greasy zucchini flower in a napkin and pocketing it.

Tannino's sister paused from collecting doily coasters and crossed her arms. "Winston, drink your sambuca."

"Thanks, but I'm—"

At her cocked eyebrow, Winston complied. She kept an eye trained on him until the coffee bean clicked against his grimace.

To great relief, Tannino announced, "We're going back to the study."

"Marco," his wife protested, "your guests are hungry."

He spread his hands and patted the air, and that was that. Like a troop of Cub Scouts, they trailed him down the dimly lit hall, the walls offering grisly renderings of saints undergoing sundry ordeals. The study doors rolled shut, and they were safe.

Tannino snapped his fingers. Bear handed him the engorged napkin, and the marshal slid open his window, whistled over one of his retrievers, and shook out the contents.

The men took a moment to reinflate themselves.

The marshal steered Tim into a distressed leather sofa and examined him, brown eyes shiny with paternal relief, maybe pride. "I'm glad you're safe."

Winston and Freed echoed the sentiment. Thomas nodded.

Tim removed an unmarked VHS tape from his jacket and tossed it on the couch. "Take a look at this when you get a chance. It's a video indoctrination. The next phase of The Program lets Betters condition people without even having to be there."

"The girl," Tannino said. "What about the girl?"

"We're meeting with her parents in the A.M."

Winston's mouth was watering from remembered sambuca. "What'd you dig up on Betters?"

Tim debriefed them. He recalled every detail he could, not shying away from the times he'd started to go under during Program drills. Thomas seemed to have softened by the time

Tim finished recounting his humiliations; indignity endured for the cause could dull even the sharpest of resentments.

Leaning against the big-screen TV, Bear hummed with energy. "Get us a search warrant, and let's go tune the mutts up."

The AUSA, an unreluctant bearer of bad news, announced with a defensive edge, "I need a better supporting affidavit." Winston held up his hand, fending off an all-sides protest. "You're asking me to process a search warrant that's going to cause a major escalation in a volatile situation. This is a cult on remote terrain with armed members. It'll take a regiment to serve a warrant—we can't exactly send two deputies up there to ring the doorbell and have a look-see."

Tannino pressed his thumb and index finger to his eyes, letting them slide with the skin of the lids. Not a good sign.

Winston said, "You'll recall, Rackley, that the FBI already went this route and wound up with nothing but a mouthful of lawsuits they're still choking on."

"A girl was murdered. I'm an eyewitness declarant."

"You actually *saw* her get shot?"

"I heard a gunshot."

"In a lightning storm."

"The dogs came out of the trees with glistening muzzles."

Winston folded his hands across his knee. "So they were healthy dogs."

"Three people went into the woods. Two came out."

"We find the defendants guilty, Your Honor."

Annoyed, Tim turned his attention to the marshal. "We need to get up there with cadaver dogs."

"After the rains, in wild terrain, we'd need a lot of time." Tannino's voice was softer than Winston's, more regretful. "We can't just march in and set up camp for a few days. Not without a solid foothold."

"Look, Rackley," Winston said. "Of course we all know that the girl was probably killed. But that doesn't matter. What matters is sufficient grounds or concrete evidence to justify what would be tantamount to a federal raid. You haven't established probable cause. We need *grounds*."

"Leah told me that Nancy was repeatedly sexually coerced."

"Hearsay."

Bear said, "How about the Dead Link files? Everyone who's left The Program either committed suicide, disappeared, or wound up in the loony bin."

"It's systematic," Tim added. "No one who can expose The Program gets out intact. TD won't risk it. Not at this stage."

"Again, nothing to take to the bank," Winston said. "You can look into those names further—"

"I did," Bear chimed in. "Except for Reggie Rondell and"—he flipped open his notepad—"Wayne Topping, who Freed's still working on, we verified TD's intel. It's correct on all the other Dead Links."

"Keeping folders on expunged members is not a crime. And it's not news that these people are missing. They've been missing ever since they joined this cult. If we could *legitimately* determine the nature of the Dead Link computer files, perhaps we could make a case, but just name and status on a sheet of paper? Uh-uh."

"Can we get him on assault?" Tim said. "The Growth Room is a ritualized form of torture. As is severe sleep deprivation."

"You're asking for a full ART deployment because someone got pinched and skipped a nap?"

"Don't be dismissive. There are valid grounds for assault charges here."

"On whose behalf? To have the victims *themselves* be hostile witnesses? Well, just read *Helter Skelter* for what a breeze that'll be."

"Bugliosi got convictions for Manson and his cohorts."

"After a nine-and-a-half-month trial that cost nine-point-one million dollars—in 1971 dollars. And here we've got no dead Sharon Tate with whom to incite the masses."

"Betters, unlike Manson, has broad appeal. He'll be operating in six states by the end of next month."

"And by all legally visible indications, he'll be doing it lawfully." Winston leaned back on the sofa, letting his hands rest on his knees. "We can't use anything you uncovered in the modular office. Betters has a reasonable expectation of privacy in that space."

"Come on, Win," Tannino said. "We all know how the game is played. I told Rackley myself he should—"

"I don't want to know that." Winston feigned being dazed, tapping his ears. "I seem to be having some problems with my hearing."

Tim said, "You can't make a case off *anything* I brought you?"

"It's fine investigative work, but if we ever threw it into the ring, it would do nothing but elicit a volley of suppression motions. Any search warrant would be quashed, the evidence thrown out as fruit of a poisonous tree." Winston smiled wearily and said, only half jokingly, "Our old nemesis, the Fourth Amendment."

Tim felt his confidence sapping. He was grateful to Freed for stepping in.

"We have evidence of Betters fraudulently acquiring tens of millions of dollars."

"What fraud? From what I've heard, Betters uses no scheme or device. They sign over their assets because he asks them to. That's their right."

"You could argue diminished capacity."

"Being a brainwashed idiot doesn't fall under any legal definition of diminished capacity. And even if it did—again, who's pressing charges? Certainly none of Betters's myrmidons. It's Stockholm syndrome times sixty up there. Plus, where's the federal hook? So far we're talking state charges, and believe me, an overburdened DA isn't gonna want to take it up the line any more than I do."

"Stockpiling weapons?" Thomas asked.

"Rackley found no claymores, no grenades, nothing illegal. Betters can amass handguns galore as long as they're not clearly linked to criminal intent."

"I'm sure they're all registered," Thomas muttered.

"We can't take a chance of that magnitude on the hope they aren't."

Tim's mouth tasted bitter. "So you wouldn't grant me a surveillance warrant to gather evidence, and now you won't move forward because I don't have enough evidence."

"Well, yeah." Winston was silent, as if this tautology were a self-evident truth. "There are laws, Rackley. They're not perfect, but they're what we have. And if the marshal and the U.S. Attorney are gonna bend them on a case, you're not exactly the deputy—" He caught himself. "Look, you did a fine job here. I'm equally frustrated that we can't do more. And I know I'm the bad guy, getting called in here to say what's gonna fly and what isn't, but we're dealing with a lot of scrutiny these days. Constitutional protections have eroded substantially under Ashcroft and the Patriot Act, and I'm not gonna be the poster boy for the backlash. We're all on the same team—we need to protect the DOJ *and* the Service. One misstep on a thing like this is all it takes. We'll have international press coverage, TD's zealots foaming at the mouth, civil libertarians invoking the holy trinity of goat-fucks—Ruby Ridge, Wounded Knee, Waco."

Tim looked at Bear, who had the benefit of a night-school J.D. under his belt. He cursed softly and swiped a palm across his thick neck—not the clarity Tim was looking for.

"Listen," Tannino said. "Terrance Betters is a thorn in the side of the federal government. The IRS has a crush on him, DOD wants his number, FBI, too. I'd love nothing more than to light his ass up, but I can't risk going in there and coming out with my dick in my hands."

"When guys are as clever as Betters, sometimes the resources it takes to nail them aren't worth it." Winston rose and pointedly dusted his hat with two swift slaps. "My advice: Keep the girl out and forget it. Don't hand Betters a cause for action—hand him plenty of rope and then wait." He nodded at Tannino. "Please thank your wife for the libations." He considerately closed the doors shut behind him.

A foul mood lingered in the room.

"I'm sorry, son." The grooves around Tannino's mouth and eyes were deeply pronounced; playing the bureaucrat never failed to age him. "I think this one's run its course."

Tim nodded once and rose.

"Rackley. I need the . . ."

"Right." Tim withdrew his marshal's star, mounted on its leather tag. "I appreciate the work."

Freed studied the carpet; even Thomas coughed uncomfortably.

Tim handed the badge to Tannino, who unhappily took it. Tim unholstered his .357, set it on the desk, shook hands all around, and left.

Dray sat propped up on the mattress, Leah asleep beside her, one arm thrown across Dray's stomach. A bloodied washcloth lay balled on the floor beside a microcassette recorder.

When Dray saw Tim in the doorway, she eased out gingerly from beneath Leah's arm. Sweat glazing her face, Leah groaned and nestled into the stack of sheets.

"Why don't you pull the covers off her?" Tim whispered.

"She likes being hot." Dray clicked the "rewind" button on the tape recorder. "You get the meeting set?"

"Nine o'clock at Reggie's motel. What's that?"

"I convinced Leah to record her seven A.M. check-in message to TD so she could sleep in. I'll be up—I'll just call the number for her and play it." When they stepped into the hall, she took note of his expression. "What's wrong?"

He gestured for her to follow him into the bathroom. As he

took a steaming shower, she sat on the toilet so he could finish filling her in. She didn't say much; there wasn't much to say.

He dried off, brushed his teeth, and got into bed. Beside him, Dray had her nose buried in a book, her prerequisite to sleeping. Continuing to read, she reached over and took his hand. He stared at the gun safe, the ceiling, the dark leaves tapping softly at the window.

Without lifting her eyes from the paperback, Dray said, "She is rather willowy."

Thirty-six

Walking down the hall, Tim could hear the murmur of Dray's voice. Morning light suffused the kitchen, a pale stillness that bleached the polished counters.

Leah's mouth hovered over a bowl of Lucky Charms, her pistoning arm providing elevator service for yellow moons and blue diamonds. Despite nearly twelve hours of unrestricted access to the kitchen, still she ate like a war orphan. Between her and Dray, Tim was beginning to feel anorexic.

Leah wore Dray's favorite academy sweatshirt; when she caught the milk dribbling down her chin with a swipe of the sleeve, Dray didn't even object. Leah's skin was a healthy, well-scrubbed pink, her hair shiny and nicely combed, bangs covering the abrasions at the hairline.

"Morning," Leah and Dray said simultaneously.

Tim forced a smile. An emptiness had replaced his stomach since he'd surrendered his badge last night. "Ready?"

Leah released a shuddering sigh.

Dray popped her vitamins, then tapped a few extras from

the jar and pushed them across the table at Leah. "Grab some juice and take these."

Leah got up and perused the inside of the refrigerator. "Orange juice or apple?"

"Whatever you want."

Leah stared at Tim as if he'd spoken another language. Tim stared back. Leah glanced inside the refrigerator, then at Tim and Dray—a momentary crisis. "Just tell me."

"Go on and choose for yourself, Leah."

Leah reached tentatively for one carton, then the other. She shook her head, and tears streaked down her cheeks.

Dray got up, pulled out the OJ, and poured her a glass.

"**I**f we attack the cult directly, she'll either shut off or drown us in dogma," Bederman said. "Focusing on the cult's controlling aspects will get us further. But she's got to make the connections herself."

Tim sat beside him on the sagging twin bed they'd pushed against the wall to make room for a ring of chairs. Reggie had moved the plastic wastebasket so he could settle on the floor with his back to the corner and the brown paper bag in his lap. After a cursory examination of the motel room's furnishings, Emma had elected to stand, remaining cautiously erect in the center of the thinning carpet. When she'd met Reggie, she'd taken his hand with a thumb and two fingers, as if grasping a soiled diaper.

Will faced the gauzy window curtains, his hands clasped behind him. Outside, a garbage truck impaled a Dumpster and hoisted it overhead, curling like a great clanking scorpion. The Dumpster discharged its contents and began its noisy descent.

"Perhaps you could turn around?" Bederman said.

Will pivoted, thumbs bent over the rim of his plastic cup. On the sill rested two empty minibar Absoluts, caps discarded among the dead flies. Though he'd forgone a tie, he looked ridiculously formal in a suit.

Through wire-frame spectacles, Bederman regarded him evenly. "We've got to help her envision a happy future outside the cult."

Lank hair down in his eyes, Reggie spread his arms. "Ta-da!"

"We want to give her as much of a sense of control as possible. Reggie's got the right idea, sitting on the floor so we don't seem threatening."

"I'd prefer not to sit on the floor," Emma said.

"Perhaps you could consider a chair." Bederman gestured at Will, who'd moved to lean importantly against the bureau. "And you, too."

Emma brushed off the seat with her hand and sat at the edge. "I feel like I don't know who she is anymore. If she does come home, it'll be like having a stranger—"

"You'll need to go to therapy," Bederman said. "All of you."

Will remained standing. "What is it with this town and shrinks? For people here it's like going to the barber." He drained his cup and dropped it into the wastebasket. "I haven't gone to a shrink in fifty-eight years—"

"Big surprise, that," Reggie said.

"—and I certainly don't need to start because my step-daughter got herself turned around."

"It was my understanding that Leah is your daughter," Bederman said. "By adoption."

Tim said, "To salvage your family, is it such a sacrifice to sit in an air-conditioned office for an hour a week and talk about your mother?"

Emma's face took on a sudden sternness. "Sometimes I think we'd all be better off if we just let her go ahead into whatever life she wanted."

Will went rigid. "*Emma.*"

A knock sounded at the door, and then Dray stuck her head in. "Ready?"

Bederman nodded. Dray held the door open, her attention directed patiently just around the jamb. Maybe a full minute passed. Finally Leah trudged into the room. Dray withdrew silently, closing the door.

Leah swept her fingers over an ear, hooking back her stray hair, and risked a glance up at her parents. "Hi."

Emma gasped. Tim wondered what her reaction would have been to seeing Leah before she'd cleaned herself up. Will had gone back to assessing the garbage truck's progress. In Leah's gaze at her stepfather's back, Tim felt the burn of her desired approval.

"Hi, Will."

"Turn around and face your daughter," Bederman said.

Bent slightly at the waist, Will raised a hand to his face and held it there a moment. When he finally turned, his eyes were moist but his expression impenetrable. "Leah."

They studied each other. It was as if they were alone in the room.

"I'm Glen, and this is Reggie. We're here with your parents because we want to find out more about you—"

"Why are my parents here?"

Emma remained frozen in the chair, her face drawn and bloodless. Will's hands fussed as if desirous of a rocks glass.

"Well," Bederman finally said, "because they love you and they're concerned about you."

Leah kept her eyes on Will. "Really?"

"Yes, really," Will said. "Christ, Leah. This has been awful for us, your mother—"

"I'm sorry to have made your life difficult."

"—you running off half-cocked—"

"Mr. Henning." Bederman's voice had the sharp anger of a disobeyed parent, and as much authority. Amazingly, Will was silenced; he appeared shocked at his own obedience.

Bederman removed his spectacles and polished them on his shirt, first one lens, then the other. "Would you like to come in and sit down, Leah?" With an open hand, he indicated one of the chairs. She sat, and the others joined her, except Reggie, who stayed in the corner, looking as if he might barf.

"I love The Program," Leah said. "It's the most important thing that's ever happened to—"

"That's just what you think *now*," Will said.

Bederman silenced him again with a terse gesture and said to Leah, "I understand that. And we want to talk more about that. But at some point we'd also like to hear a few of the things you *don't* like about The Program."

Leah's cheeks colored. "There's nothing I don't like."

A grimace tightened Will's face. "She's brainwashed. Completely—"

"I am *not*."

Bederman directed a stern look Will's way before turning back to Leah. "Nothing on earth is perfect, right?"

Leah thought this one over for a few moments. "I don't know. I haven't experienced most of what there is on earth."

"Is The Program perfect? I mean *flawless?*" Bederman pressed on gently when she didn't answer. "Everything has flaws, right?"

Leah shifted her jaw to one side, then back. "So I'm told."

Bederman asked Leah to enumerate some of The Program's positive aspects. Will and Emma squirmed during this but didn't interject. After spending some time talking about what Leah liked about the group, Bederman resumed his earlier line of questioning. "What are some of The Program's flaws?"

"I guess . . . I guess it's not growing fast enough."

Will made a perturbed sound through his teeth.

"Okay," Bederman said. "That's a fair answer."

Leah scratched her rash, hard, through Dray's sweatshirt. "And maybe . . . maybe I wish it was a little more forgiving." A flash of panic in her eyes. "But that's just my weakness—"

"No," Bederman said. "That's a fine answer, too." His hand rasped across his well-trimmed beard. "Is there *any-thing* that would make you consider leaving The Program?"

An immediate answer—"No."

"Nothing at all? Use your imagination—it doesn't have to be real. Say you found out they were planning a mass suicide or running a child-pornography ring."

"Or the extermination of the indigenous people of Guatemala? It's not possible. TD's no more capable of that than we are."

Will made an exasperated sound against his teeth, but Bederman just smiled at her. "Okay. Okay." He nodded a few times thoughtfully. "If you'd never met TD—if TD and The Program didn't even *exist*—and you could do exactly what you wanted to do with your life, what would that be?"

Chewing her lip, she thought for a few minutes, shifting in her chair so she sat nearly sideways on her hip. Tears welled in her eyes, and then she said in a cracked whisper, "I don't think I want to answer that right now."

Will said, "We're all *here* for you to answer—"

"*We* invited *her*. She came at *our* invitation, as much to ask us questions as to answer ours." Bederman's voice stayed soft, but it had taken on an edge. Will's testiness might have met its match.

Leah's eyes had gone cold. "You don't know anything about TD. He *knows* what works for people. You're just too weak to want to see it."

In the corner Reggie's head snapped up. He'd been so silent, Tim had almost forgotten about him. "I thought that, too," Reggie said. "I really did."

Leah twisted in her chair to stare at him. Her mouth moved, but no words came out.

Reggie leaned back, compressing his shoulders as if trying to melt into the wall. "That's right—I'm the one lucky bastard who made it out. So I'll put it to you: If *you* were the enlightened one, would you act how he does? Break people down? Take their money? Have virgins rouse him in the morning with hand jobs?"

Emma sagged back in her chair. Will tensed. "Is that true?

While we were desperately looking for you, you were off at a ranch jerking off some false messiah?" Emma moaned, and Will laid a protective hand on her shoulder. Leah looked away. "Jesus," he continued, "did you even *think* about how worried we—"

"No, I didn't think about you. Either of you. I thought about myself and what *I* wanted for once." Leah looked squarely at her mother. "I don't have to take on your weaknesses."

"Take on our weaknesses?" Will was apoplectic. "You sound like a machine. What you're doing up there, Leah, has got nothing to do with being *strong*. It's laziness. You're too lazy to face the real world."

"Hey, Pops," Reggie said, "when's the last time you hauled your ass up at six and worked a twenty-hour day?"

"You evidently know very little about film production. I've done it plenty. And it's a bit more stressful than watching the fish tank at a roadside fuckshack. What goes on at that 'ranch' is not work. It's immaturity."

"Don't attack *him*," Leah said.

Bederman started to object as well, but Emma cut him off, all gentle reason and apologetic eyes. "You've *always* had poor judgment, Leah."

Leah blew out a shaky breath. "It's just like he warned me."

Will's face was twisted with disgust. "What does that mean? What did *the Teacher* tell you?"

Leah bent her slender neck, studying the carpet. "That you'd insult me and my practices. That you'd rant, not listen."

Will sputtered for a moment before finding words. "You leave us no choice. You spout recorded nonsense that *can't* be listened to. There's no reasoning with you."

"Well, how about you, Will? You have your head in a bottle half the day and the other half it's up Colin Farrell's agent's ass—is that living in the *real world* like a *mature* person?" Leah turned to Emma, who was drawn back in her chair, hand clasped to the silk scarf knotted at her throat. "And *you're* gonna teach me about judgment? St. Ursula has noth-

ing on you in the martyr department. People don't even exist
to you—they're just walking potentials for inconvenience."

Will withdrew a cell phone from his pocket and punched
one button at length. His sweaty face was trembling. "I'm not
going to sit here and be judged. It wasn't easy being your parent. You can pick at us all you want, but *you're* the one who
made a foolish, dangerous decision. What you're doing is
stupid, Leah. Everyone in this room knows I'm right. We just
have to pretend to indulge you so—"

"Don't you *dare* presume to state my position," Bederman said.

Tim rose toward the door, eyes on Will, the cell phone in
his lap. "What was that?"

The knob jiggled, and Rooch and Doug shouldered in. Tim
swept Leah behind him. Bederman and Will were yelling at
each other. Emma leaked tears, kneading her slender white
forearm against her belly with a freckled hand. Shoving himself back into the corner, Reggie bent his arms over his head
like a kid in a duck-and-cover drill.

"Enough of this nonsense, Leah," Will said. "The car's
waiting."

Leah clung to Tim's back. "You swore. You swore you
wouldn't let them."

Dray arrived, winded from the brief sprint across the parking lot, but Rooch put an arm across the doorway, blocking
her entry. Doug tugged up his shirt like a dealer punk, showing off the handle of the big-dick .44 Magnum at his waist—
no respect for the weapon. Neither Tim nor Dray was armed.

"Hey, now," Will said nervously. He raised a placating
hand to Doug. "Hey, now."

Bederman backed away until he bumped against a wall.
Through his shirt Tim felt the heat of Leah's face pressed to
his shoulder blade.

"*Will,*" Emma said in a hoarse, outraged whisper. "We
never—"

"You don't want to do this," Tim said. "You're committing an armed kidnapping and assaulting a sheriff's deputy and a federal officer."

"You're not a federal officer," Will said, "since last night." He gestured at Doug to lower his shirt and looked at his daughter. "We're trying to do what's best for you. We're trying to protect you."

"You'll go down for this," Dray said.

"You call your contacts, Mrs. Rackley, I'll call mine." Will turned back to Leah. "We're not wasting any more time. You've made your point. We can work it out at home. Let's go."

Leah stayed put.

Reggie stood up. "Look at me. *Look at me.*" Will finally acknowledged him. Reggie knocked his chest with his fingers. "You want *her* to end up watching the fish tank at a roadside fuckshack? Just keep it up."

Will's tough façade wavered. "We can't have her go back to that place." He pivoted back to Doug. "Take her, and let's go."

Doug worked his gum nervously. Though, like Rooch, he outweighed Tim by at least fifty pounds, he was no longer exuding confidence.

"Let me make something clear," Tim said. "If you make so much as a move toward her, I'll break your arm."

Rooch held his ground at the door. Doug pulled the revolver from his waistband, keeping it angled limply at the carpet.

Emma let out a strangled little gasp.

"Doug," Will said. "No need to—"

Tim's voice remained calm, his hands spread slightly before his chest, ready. "Never draw a weapon unless you're prepared to use it."

Doug's wide jaw bounced as he clicked his teeth. "What makes you think—"

Tim darted across the tight circle of chairs. The edge of his right hand struck the top of the rising barrel, fingers curling near the base of the hammer and locking the cylinder. He twisted down and away, his other hand striking Doug's hyperextended elbow, which broke with a single sharp pop.

Doug yowled, his torso diving to the floor. Tim stepped over the distorted arm before Doug hit carpet, straining the now-limp limb at the socket, the grotesque bend of the forearm permitting Tim to aim the double-clutched revolver directly at Rooch's head.

Doug's shoulder, smashed across his face, muffled his groans.

Rooch's forehead had compressed into a mass of wrinkles.

"Release," Tim said.

Doug writhed on the carpet. "I . . . can't."

Tim eased the arm back a few degrees, and the fingers popped open on their own. He snapped the gun wheel free and thumbed it into a spin, letting the bullets drop one by one into his palm. He pocketed the empty gun and said, without removing his eyes from Rooch's, "Dray, come on in."

Rooch moved out of her way, and she stepped through the door and over Doug's body.

"Leah, you're going to step back and sit on the bed now," Tim said. "Go on."

Wiping her nose, Leah moved over and sat.

Tim grasped Doug beneath the arms and hoisted him to his feet. "Rooch is going to drive you to the Brotman Medical Center to have your arm set."

Doug swayed a bit. "O-okay."

Tim gave him a little shove toward Rooch, who tucked his bull neck beneath Doug's functional arm and helped him out. Tim closed the door and stood for a moment, holding the knob. Finally he advanced on Will, who shrank back against the wall. Tim brought his face within inches of Will's and said, "I would advise strongly against your considering another stunt like that."

Bederman glared at Will, clearly too disgusted to speak.

Her makeup staining her bleak face, Emma headed out. Will cast a defeated, heartbroken glance at Leah. "That's fine. You want to ruin the rest of your life, you have my blessing. Go ahead."

He paused at the door. A slight movement turned his profile so it pointed at Leah, even if his eyes did not.

"I'm sorry, sweetheart," he said, and then he walked out.

Reggie lingered alone in the parking lot as the others left, scratching his neck and walking in tight circles. Tim paused pulling out of his parking space, watching Reggie through the window. He killed the engine, glanced at Dray and Leah. "Hold on a sec."

He headed over to Reggie, but Bederman stepped out of his car and got there first. Tim lingered back a few steps.

"May I walk you to your room?" Bederman asked.

Reggie exhaled deeply, then nodded like a little kid.

They walked down the corridor together, Bederman tapping Reggie on the shoulder when he walked past his own door.

Reggie turned the key and shoved.

Blinking curiously, Bederman beheld the impressive condition of the room. "Okay, okay." He made a ticking noise with his tongue. "Are you happy living here?"

"Yeah. Thrilled."

They stood side by side, regarding the room like a swamp they were considering plunging into. Tim watched quietly, not wanting to interfere.

Reggie kicked the toe of his shoe into the ground. "It's like everything else. Just so fucking *daunting*." They stood outside the threshold, looking in. "I can't do it anymore. I can't go in there."

"Maybe fifteen minutes," Bederman said. "Maybe fifteen minutes cleaning up a day isn't daunting."

Reggie chewed his lip, mulling it over.

Bederman waited. And waited.

Finally Reggie said, "Maybe it's not."

Resting a hand on Reggie's back, Bederman strode with him into the mess.

Thirty-seven

Leah left another check-in message for TD and went straight back to Ginny's room. Tim walked around in the cold of the backyard, finally settling on top of the Costco picnic table.

He replayed the cell-phone message he'd received that morning: "I've been thinking about the drafting table, Timmy. I think your mother would want you to have it. Come on over tomorrow night—I'll be up late."

He saved the message, stuffed the phone into his pocket. Contemplating the palm fronds scattered at the base of the back fence, he realized he'd grown less meticulous in keeping up the house. Until last year he'd been just as uptight as his father, and though no one would now accuse him of slackness, he would occasionally let dirty dishes languish overnight. Maybe he'd recognized the futility of feigning control. Or maybe he was just worn out.

What would Monday hold? Once again keeping the world safe for sheet metal? TD's empire would continue to metastasize, and Leah could very well resume being a cog in it.

He heard the sliding door thunk closed and then the crunching-leaf sound of Dray's approach. Her boots struck the far bench, the tabletop, then she slid down behind him, legs outside his, gloved hands cinching around his waist. She set her chin on his shoulder.

"Growing up with my dad, I was never taught the moves. So I tried to . . . I guess fake it. I felt like the other parents really knew what they were doing. Part of me was always waiting for Ginny to catch on."

"You were a great father to Ginny."

"Maybe that's why I stay in touch with him. My dad. To remember what I never want to be."

"You still need that?"

When she was inclined, Dray could serve up a hell of a rhetorical. They watched a dead frond try to windsurf up the back fence. Determined bastard.

Dray said, "Will just called."

"He wants to swim by and bump the prey again? Forget it."

"We're not her parents, Timothy. At some point you've got to let her go."

"It's not that simple."

"Nothing's simple," she said.

The frond rattled against the wood like a dying manta ray. "I'm all over the map," he said. "I want to protect her, and I want her to protect herself. I want her to trust me, and I want to prove her trust right."

"None of it's gonna get us Ginny back."

He bent his head. Dray brushed his hair back from his forehead. Rainwater ran across his lips, some of it salty.

*W*ill answered the door himself, the cavernous house behind him emanating the sound-swallowing hum of emptiness. He wore eyeglasses in thin gold frames, the arms pinching his graying hair at the temples and making it bow out in wisps.

"Thank you for coming."

Tim followed him across the tile, their footsteps echoing off the high wooden ceiling beams. They turned right and headed down a broad hall, passing a set of yellow-and-blue paintings composed of blown-up benday dots. Entering a vast office, Will crossed the hardwood floor and collapsed into a mesh chair behind a glass-topped desk the size of two doors laid end to end. A director's chair embroidered with WILL HENNING, EXECUTIVE PRODUCER sagged under a heap of scripts. Three sets of French doors spilled out onto the back lawn and a Bahamian-blue slab of an infinity pool.

Interspersed with movie posters, framed photos of Leah dotted the walls. Leah on the awkward brink of her teens, spouting water in a swimming pool. Leah blowing out ten candles mired in a daunting restaurant dessert, Wolfgang Puck beaming at her shoulder. Leah wearing a life buoy like a sash, perched on the arm of a kid encumbered with an ill-fitting sailor's cap and an oversize Adam's apple, the anchor-bedizened streamer overhead proclaiming, CALABASAS HIGH JUNIOR PROM—SET SAIL FOR ROMANCE!

Striking a contrast with the sleek furnishings, a lopsided ashtray sat on Will's desk, glossy from some classroom kiln. LH was etched in the side. Tim had never seen Will smoke and, from the sweatsuits, algae juice, and exercise room, guessed he did not.

Will wore a smirk, but his eyes were gentle. "How old does a woman have to be to no longer decamp to her mother's?"

Tim, who felt as disconnected from sitcom marital humor as from jokey golf maxims, managed a sympathetic shrug.

"She's exhausted, which is her version of pissed off. Long Beach for the weekend—I'd rather take bamboo shoots under the fingernails, but Emma finds it a haven. I sent Rooch and the nanny to look after her and the baby." Will's lips pursed. "Doug elected to take a few days off."

Aside from a plaque declaiming, THE SLEEPER CELL, $367,923,000 DOMESTIC GROSS, the wall behind Will was dedicated to photos of him and Leah together—picnicking at the Hollywood Bowl, posing courtside with Shaquille O'Neal, riding in a limo with Will hoisting up an award like a title belt.

"The phone rang more then." Will pointed to an impressive desktop telephone. "That quiet—it's a kind of death knell for a producer. It used to be you needed a head of gray hair to run a studio. Now they're fresh out of braces, telling you to cast a rap star, hire some MTV epileptic to direct." The lighting accented his crow's-feet. "I used to have it figured out, but they went and changed the rules on me. Now kids in Zegna suits tell me I'm their inspiration, I get lifetime-achievement awards. It's all so . . . *posthumous.*" He studied the quiet phone. "There's a reason all our heroes die young. The older we get, the less we have figured out."

Still standing, Tim slid his hands into his jacket pockets. "She kicked your ass in there pretty good. Leah."

Will nodded solemnly. "I've had better meetings." He turned to the glass doors, watching the yellow husks of leaves cartwheel into the pool. "Leah's father was a contractor. Simple guy. He died slow and hard. When I met Emma, she needed to be taken care of. She'd had Leah young, missed out on the part of her life that was supposed to be easy. And she was intoxicated by this whole world, the glamour." A wave of his hand encompassed the room with its myriad Hollywood trinkets. "She wanted this new life, and I wanted to give it to her. That can be intoxicating in its own way, playing Richard Gere."

"And Leah?"

His smile was soft, almost shy. "It's different when you take someone else's child into your life. There's no genetic imperative. You either fall in love with them or you don't. With Leah it took me about five minutes."

"When's the last time you told her that?"

Will fidgeted in his overpriced chair. "You get into these patterns with a kid. You give so much to them, so goddamn much. Now this cult leader wins her over so . . . *cheaply.*" His face darkened—anger shifting to grief and back again.

"She's still your daughter."

Will pulled open a desk drawer and hefted a sheaf of photocopies onto the desk. He fanned it with a thumb, showing off page after page of handwriting. "I've sent her a letter every week since she's been gone. She hasn't responded to one of them. Not one. Holding out hope takes its toll. It eats at you from the inside. How long am I supposed to keep at it?"

"All I can tell you is, we're meeting again tomorrow, same place, same time."

Will made a muffled, pensive noise and swiveled in his chair, watching the wind work the eucalyptus. He didn't seem to notice when Tim lifted two photos off their hooks.

"I'd like to show these to Leah."

Will responded with a vague flick of his hand that Tim took to be affirmative. As Tim left, Will's back stayed to the door.

T im tapped the door with a single knuckle, the same knock he'd used on Ginny the night a car-bomb threat had called him away from father-daughter night at Warren Elementary. Jacket folded over his arm to hide the framed photos, he eased open the door to find Leah lying on the mattress, facing the wall. Sluggishly, she propped herself up and sat cross-legged, facing him.

"Listen, I appreciate what you've tried to do for me here, but these are my decisions. And they may not look perfect from the outside—or even the inside—but they're all I have. I think I'm ready to go back to the ranch. It may be dangerous for some people, but it's the only place I belong anymore."

"Give it one more shot, Ginny." He caught himself a second too late, his face burning.

"Who's . . . ?" A strangled little noise of recognition terminated Leah's question. When he could finally look her in the eye, she returned his gaze evenly. "Look, I know you're worried about me, but you're trying to save your daughter here. And you can't. Where does that put you? Or me?"

It took him a moment to answer. "You're right. I'll try to stop."

She rubbed at her rash through her sweatshirt.

"I'd like to have another meeting tomorrow," he said. "With Dr. Bederman and Reggie."

"How about Will and my mom?"

"Your mom went to Long Beach—"

"Of course. With the baby."

"I'm sorry."

"And what about Will?"

Tim flared his hands to show he didn't know. Leah looked crestfallen. "What's the point of doing this, then? *I* certainly don't want to. Who cares?"

"I do."

"Great. After nineteen years of life, that's what I've got left outside The Program." She looked away. "No offense."

He pulled the first photo out from under his jacket—Will grinning beside her in the limo, the award raised over his head. The etching on the brass plate clearly read PRODUCER OF THE YEAR.

"Will didn't leave you behind at the Beverly Hills Hotel that night."

Her eyes darted over the picture. "That must have been taken on the way there."

"The award's right in his hands, Leah." He drew out the second photo—buoy-ensconced Leah setting sail for romance. "Will also didn't make you miss your prom."

Her voice took on a hint of desperation. "The pictures must be fakes."

He set the photos down beside her. She stared at them, disbelieving. Her shoulders sagged, and her body seemed to go limp. With shame, Tim realized that some petty part of him shared her disappointment. He'd unwittingly staked himself on the notion of Will as the evil father, on a fantasy bond between himself and Leah, orphans of neglect. He'd done on his own what TD had prompted Leah to do—indulged his own childhood pains, licked his wounds, carved out a part of his identity around his victimization. The underpinnings to TD's gibberish revealed their precious-metal gleam: The truth is fluid; reality is interpretation; belief drives perception.

Watching Leah collapse onto the mattress, Tim felt world-weary and old; he'd long learned that exhaustion is the price of dispensing with simplistic answers. Relinquishing clarity didn't feel noble; it felt like a surrender to disillusionment.

"It's not possible." Leah averted her gaze from the photos. She was drowning. "I remember . . . I swear I remember. . . ."

"I'm not denying Will screwed up sometimes," Tim said, "but you can't lay everything at his feet." He paused, and when he continued, his voice was gentler, more humble. "Trust me—you don't want to spend your adult life harping on the things he did wrong."

She found a foothold in anger. "So you're on his side."

"There are no sides, Leah."

"It's my memory." She dug her hands into her hair, making it stick out between her fingers in brown tufts. "It's what's in my head. It can't be wrong. It *can't*. Will never cared. He never wanted me around."

"What about all the letters he's sent you?"

A blank stare. "What letters?"

"He's sent you a letter every week for the last three months." She blinked at him, nonplussed.

"I saw copies."

"I never got any letters," she said quietly.

"Don't you think it's a bit odd?" Tim bolted off the mattress, startling Leah. "You never got *any*?"

"We don't need distractions from our work in The Program. TD and the Protectors deal with our mail for us." She took in his expression.

" 'Deal' with it? What mail *do* you get?" He was already walking backward toward the door, pulling on his jacket, digging the cell phone from his pocket.

Three faint lines appeared in her forehead. "None."

Thirty-eight

For a rail-thin postal inspector, Owen B. Rutherford was surprisingly intimidating. He wore a perpetual half scowl, half squint, as if braced for an imminent fight. The federal-issue Beretta 92D strapped to his hip provided backup for a stubborn jaw and determined eyes. Comb marks had fossilized in his fine, dark brown hair, which he kept in a knife-edge left part. His skin, pasty and speckled with moles, was flushed to an inhuman shade of magenta in twinning ovals on his cheekbones. His irritation at being roused from bed had dissipated immediately when he'd been apprised of the situation.

Tim and Winston Smith sat on either side of him. Tannino looked on from behind his imperious desk, waiting for Rutherford's livid silence to give way to words. Bear had taken up his usual post, leaning against the wall by the door, blending into the wainscoting.

"What we have then"—Rutherford spoke quietly, restraining his rage—"is willful, systematic obstruction of the mails. What you're telling me is that at least sixty-eight individuals forward their mail to a P.O. box and this man has it picked up and somehow disposed of, day after day, week after week?"

"Yes. None of it gets through." Tim realized he was employing the mollifying voice he usually reserved for interviewing family members of victims.

Rutherford fanned his flushed face with his open notepad.

Tannino spread his hands, then folded them. "What's that give us?"

"What's that give *you?*" Rutherford shot a glance at Winston, who nodded him on severely. "Most obviously a Title

18, Section 1708—theft or receipt of stolen mail matter, generally. But between theft, obstruction, and destruction, we could have over two hundred federal, criminal, and civil statutes."

Bear chuckled, a low rumble. "There's your probable cause."

"We still have the hostile-witness problem," Winston said.

Rutherford's tone was sharp, annoyed. "What hostile-witness problem?"

"They're cult members. Maybe they don't mind not getting their mail. Maybe they'll say they gave Betters permission to destroy it or whatever he does."

Rutherford regarded Winston like something he'd picked out of his teeth. "This is not a crime committed against the address*ees*, Mr. Smith. Do you know what a thirty-seven-cent stamp buys you?"

A wrinkled V appeared between Winston's eyebrows. "I, uh . . ."

Not only was Tim glad to be out of the line of fire, but seeing Winston Smith off his game was not without its own satisfaction.

"Not just delivery service. Oh, no. The thirty-seven cents buys you a fiduciary relationship with the United States Postal Service. We are custodians of private property. Namely: the mail. That private property belongs to the *sender* until it comes into the hands of the intended recipient. These jelly-spined bliss ninnies can't grant the right for their leader to destroy incoming mail before it comes into their actual possession—it isn't their mail to relinquish. First-class mail must be delivered, forwarded, returned to sender, or sent to the mail-recovery center." Rutherford ticked off the points on his fingers. "Any other act is a violation of the rights of the *sender*. A violation further of the sanctity of the mail and— make no mistake—it is as such a felony in its own right."

"What does Betters *do* with the mail?" Tannino asked.

Tim said, "Let's get a warrant and find out."

"We trust this kid?" Winston asked. "Maybe she's teeing us up for Betters."

"I trust her."

"It's a big ranch," Tannino said. "I don't want to play Hans Blix."

"Then send me back in," Tim said. "I'll come back with on-the-ground intel. We have the Arrest Response Team serve the warrant, I'll steer them to evidence like a guided missile"—a nod to Winston—"ensure you can make a case even if the Dead Links don't yield."

Tannino frowned thoughtfully but didn't respond. Winston rose and whispered in Tannino's ear like a defense attorney. He returned to his place on the couch and repositioned his hat on his knee.

"Hey," Tannino said in a self-mocking monotone. "I just had a great idea. Maybe we could send out a mailing to various cult members from my office—phony flyers for a seized-car auction or something—documented and sent first class."

"I think that's a fine notion," Winston said.

Bear grinned at Tannino. "Feel like being a complainant?"

"He violates that mail, the federal government is the complainant," Winston said. "Then we'll see about indicting him under RICO, getting him more time on the charges."

Rutherford referred to his oversize digital watch. "Tomorrow's Friday. If you get the flyers to me by nine A.M., I can arrange same-day delivery."

"That works out fine," Tim said. "Betters is expecting me back Saturday."

"I don't know about this," Tannino said. "Your cover's getting thin. You go back up, you'll have to sign the financial docs. These guys don't sit on their hands—they'll want to start digging into the financials first thing Monday. Even with my hooks in place, no way we can stall them out without them realizing Tom Altman's all smoke and mirrors. They'll make you within forty-eight hours."

"Then give me forty-eight hours."

Thirty-nine

*T*he dusty motel room seemed emptier without the Hennings. Dray sat in with Tim, Reggie, and Bederman. Leah had entered the room sped by anticipation, but the energy seemed to go right out of her when she saw that Will wasn't there. After a while Tim removed the vacant chair, but still she glanced at the door every few minutes. In the absence of her parents, her mood mellowed quickly from defensiveness.

"Go back to the first time you ever heard of The Program," Bederman said. "Did you think you'd dedicate your life to it?"

Leah pressed a sweatshirt-covered hand to her nose, obscuring her eyes. "No."

"What did you think of it?"

"I guess I thought it sounded a little weird. A little . . ." Leah gave another glance at the door.

"Yes?"

"Controlling, maybe."

"What do you think you would've said if I told you that six months later you'd be living up on a ranch with no telephones?"

"And that I'd lose touch with all my friends and family?" She tugged at a lock of hair. "I probably . . . wouldn't have believed it."

The soft knocking sent her stiff in her chair. The door creaked open, and Will stepped inside, casual in khakis and an untucked polo, his cheeks dusted with stubble. His eyelids and upper cheeks were heavy from sleeplessness, his hair loosed from its usual neatness. He scratched at the back of his collar, one elbow sticking up in a triangle. "Am I still . . . uh, welcome?"

Bederman glanced at Leah.

"If you behave yourself," she said.

His shuffle betrayed an uncharacteristic lack of confidence. Pulling over the chair, he eased himself down, leaned forward, and squeezed Leah's forearm once, gently.

"I was just about to ask Leah what convinced her to join," Bederman said.

Leah's neck tensed; Will's presence had put her back on alert. "At the first meeting, I felt this amazing connectedness. I guess that's what I've always secretly wanted—to feel like I belong. Everything's so cynical these days, yet here were all these people together for a common goal. Growth."

Her eyes never left Will. Tim prayed he'd keep his mouth shut; wisely, he did.

With a pinch of the frames, Bederman adjusted his spectacles. "I feel that way sometimes when I lecture."

"Really?"

"Absolutely."

Tim's mind wandered back to the night last February when Franklin Dumone had mysteriously shown up at his door, rainwater dripping across his solemn face, claiming to hold the answer to Tim's anguish over his lost daughter and the legal system that had set her killer free.

Tim rarely spoke about the Commission to anyone besides Dray; he had trouble getting the words out. "I know what it's like to get seduced by a group. It's like they're speaking your most private desires right at the moment you've almost given up on them. I fell in with a group like that after my daughter died, but they were working their own agenda behind my back the whole time."

Leah was rocking herself in her chair. "Sometimes I don't want to do what The Program says. . . ."

Will made a soft noise in his throat. Tears were running down Reggie's face, though he remained perfectly still.

". . . but TD says it's for my fulfillment," she continued.

With a cocked wrist, Reggie smeared tears off one cheek. "If it was for our own fulfillment, he wouldn't deprive us of sleep and food to control us. He wouldn't turn us against one another. He wouldn't . . ." His bitterness evaporated; his breathing turned shallow.

"Wouldn't what?" Leah said.

Reggie fought out the words. "Discard people like trash."

The sudden display of emotion caught even Bederman off guard. Leah alone responded without missing a beat, leaning over and rubbing Reggie's shoulder.

Reggie did not raise his head. "He made me feel like I was so feeble. Like without him I was just some useless piece of shit who didn't deserve to hold down a spot on the planet."

Leah stopped. She scrunched her eyes shut and started murmuring to herself.

Dray reached for her, but Bederman shook his head. The room's stuffiness grew oppressive. Tim fanned the front of his T-shirt, waiting for Leah to raise her head. It was a long wait. When at last she looked up, red streaks stained her face. Her nails worked her rash through her sweater in fussy, nervous strokes.

"If this is wrong," she said, "if I see this is wrong, then I have to admit everything else was wrong."

"The Program is set up to make you feel that way," Bederman said. "So you see a lack of options. So you feel trapped."

"But I turned my back on *everything*. I struggled so hard to be a Pro." Blood dotted her sweater beneath her collar where she continued her frantic scratching. "I've given everything up, burned every bridge, cut every tie."

"Not every tie," Will said.

Her frozen stare at first registered only alarm, but then her eyes moistened and her forehead started a downward crinkle into a sob.

Bederman said, "Where do you want to be five years from now, Leah? Ten years?"

Her short hair whipped her cheeks when she shook her head.

Tim started to say something, but Bederman cut him off with a sharp, excited gesture.

"I'd be a Webmaster, I guess. Maybe even a software designer." A wistful smile grew on her face. "I always wanted to live in San Francisco."

"You can still do those things," Bederman said. "All of them."

Her mouth narrowed. "But I'm naked without The Program."

"Honey," Dray said, "it won't feel that way forever."

"If I leave, I won't have anything left to give." She was really crying now. "I'll be broken. Damaged goods. Let's be honest—no one will ever want to date me, be my friend. It's not like they were lining up before, and now I'll be some cult freak."

"Thanks." Wearing a wry smile, Reggie waved to an imaginary audience. "I'll be here all week."

She laughed through her tears. "You know what I'm saying. I mean, Beverly Cantrell's gonna be a fucking pediatrician. What am I?"

Will said, "Beverly Cantrell is a cryogenic Victorian priss who needs her adenoids removed."

Leah wiped her mouth on her sleeve like a little girl. "I always thought you liked Beverly."

"I hide in my office when Janice exhibits her at our house."

"I wish I knew. I would have hidden with you."

"I wish you had."

The sparkle in Leah's eyes dwindled. "What am I supposed to do, Will?"

"Come home, to start."

Leah's face crumpled again. She rose abruptly, pulling off her sweater. "I need some air."

Tim stood, a little too quickly. "I'll take you for a drive."

"I want to be alone." She charged out so quickly she left the door open behind her, letting in a revitalizing breeze.

"What if she calls the ranch?" Will asked just as Tim said, "What if she heads back?"

Bederman said, "Let her go."

Will ground one hand into the other. "Maybe we should follow her."

"You can't follow her for the rest of her life," Dray said. "You'd do better not to start."

Tim's phone rang, and he flipped it open. "Hello?"

Freed said, "Your last Dead Link's a ghost."

"Wayne Topping?"

"Yeah. Doesn't exist. Nothing came back. Just wanted to let you know."

When Tim hung up, Will was staring at him. "You did say 'Wayne Topping'?"

"The name ring a bell?"

"Yes. That's the alias that Danny Katanga used. Our PI who went missing."

Tim blew out a breath. "TD's got a file on him. The kind of file that means he's probably dead. I'm sorry."

"So am I."

The stagnant heat leaked from the room, the door swaying with the April breeze. The patch of sunlight thrown through the window stretched and turned gold against the worn carpet. Reggie laced his hands and stretched. At the hour mark, Will took to pacing. Only Dray was calm.

Tim had finally come to grips with Leah's being lost when a faint cough announced her presence. She stood like a waif in the doorway.

"I accept it. I accept they used mind control on me."

Will let out a muffled noise of relief.

"But I have to go back. They'll make hell for Tom if he goes up without me."

"How do you know I'm going back up?"

"I saw how excited you got about the mail thing. I'm not an idiot. Trust me, if you go back alone, they'll know something's wrong."

"I'll say your parents kidnapped you."

"They'll suspect you. And they'll find out."

"You can't be reexposed to that environment," Bederman said. "There are too many triggers there. You're fragile."

"I'll risk it."

"I think you've taken enough risks," Tim said.

"So have you."

Will rose and walked to the door. When Leah didn't move, he waited by her side. Tim could see that it was killing him to act patient, but he did.

Finally Leah said, "Maybe you're right." She crossed and hugged Reggie. "Thank you."

Reggie held her for an extra beat, his eyes shut.

She moved to embrace Bederman, but he leaned back and took her hands instead, squeezing them warmly. She hugged Dray next, then stopped in the center of the circle, facing Tim. "I . . . um, I don't know what to say."

"Me neither."

They looked at each other a moment longer, and then she followed Will out.

Party

Pants loosed around her hips, Dray lay sprawled on the bed, arms stretched to the headboard, shoulders propped on a bank of pillows. Tim's face pressed into the warmth of her bare stomach, her C-section scar a smooth ridge against his cheek. He closed his eyes, and he listened.

"I was thinking we should turn the study into a nursery," Dray said.

The skin of her belly was impossibly soft.

"When you get back this time, maybe we really settle. I mean, no more life and death, no more secret missions and undercover ops. We'll be a nice, dull-as-hell family in Moorpark with a nursery painted blue and yellow. And we'll talk about diapers and how we wish we were rich enough to afford a nanny, and we'll shut it out, the whole world. It'll just be us three, and everything will be safe. A made-for-TV life."

He kissed her stomach, then laid his cheek on it again.

He thought he heard a heartbeat. Was it possible to hear a heartbeat already? It must have been Dray's. Or his own.

She took a deep breath. "Sometimes I wonder if I've got enough left to make another run at a blue-and-yellow nursery."

"You do."

"Oh," she said. "Are you still here?"

He knew she could feel his smile against her skin—he felt her stomach tense on the verge of laughter. "Don't," he said.

That sent her over the edge, her laughter bouncing his head. He made pained groans and objections, as if the abdominal tumult were inflicting great abuse on him. Finally she quieted, sniffling a few times.

Dray was never big on tissues.

She watched him curiously as he stood and pulled on his shoes, but she didn't ask where he was going. He paused by the door. "Ginny's bottom lip disappeared when she smiled."

Dray made a soft hum, a noise of pleasure and longing mixed together.

He said, "Remember her laugh when she really got going?"

"The hiccupping one?"

"And when she colored the bottoms of her feet with Magic Marker and ran around on the new carpet? That expression she'd get when we'd ground her—the slanted eyebrows? Furrowed brow?"

"The demon-spawn scowl."

They looked at each other, smiling.

"Yeah," Dray said. "I remember."

*T*im's hands sweated, as they always did when he approached the front walk. The bordering lawn, uniformly green, rose to the precise level of the concrete. Like Tim's lawn used to. He stood in the night chill, the parked Blazer at his back, and gathered his courage.

After hitting a snarl of traffic—L.A.'s eternal antidote to sanity—he'd found himself in Pasadena, then at the house.

It struck him that The Program's regression drills didn't depend on implanted memories alone. Most people had pain that could be accessed and exploited, exposed nerves to pluck like harp strings. TD sniffed out the hollows in which trauma was buried; he cracked people wide, and they welcomed him like a conquering god.

Tim stepped up on the porch and rang the doorbell. A snowball plant rose from a terra-cotta pot, the perfect bulb of the crown picked clean of dead foliage. A single brown leaf lay on the soil.

The even cadence of footsteps. A darkness at the peephole, then his father opened the door, blocking the narrow gap with his body. "Timmy." His eyes flicked over Tim's shoulder at Dray's Blazer. "You brought the truck for your mother's desk?"

Tim had been steeling himself, but he felt a sudden calm. "Why do you always want to bring me down a peg?"

Easing out on the porch, his father plucked up the solitary dead leaf and folded it into a handkerchief he produced from his pocket. He returned to his post at the door. "It's nothing personal. I make it my business to oppose self-righteousness."

"So you started on me when I was five."

"That's right."

"That's bullshit. It was personal. Why me?"

His father looked away, and in that instant Tim saw him

with detachment—a man in his fifties standing in the doorway of another suburban house. His father kept his eyes on the street, his face pale. "Because you thought you were better than me."

A car turned onto the street, its headlights bleaching the house.

He cleared his throat, fixed his gaze on Tim. "Why don't we haul that desk out for you so you can get on your way?"

"I don't want the desk."

If he was disappointed, he didn't show it. He nodded definitively, a single dip of the chin. "Where's your music, Timmy?" He crossed his arms, a union-boss show of opposition. "This is your big scene, isn't it? You sat at home, dreamed it up, dreamed up how you could take a big stand against your old man, and here you are, your moment in the sun. You deserve a musical score, don't you think?"

A beep sounded—an annoying rendition of some classical motif. Tim followed his father's gaze down to the electronic monitoring bracelet at his ankle.

The parole officer's beckon.

Tim's father glanced back up, a ripple of chagrin disrupting the inscrutable mask.

The halting melody followed Tim back down the walk.

As Tim folded clothes neatly into his overnight bag, Dray watched him morosely over the top of the paperback she was pretending to read. He'd already touched up his disguise, trimming his goatee, plucking his false hairline, giving his hair a touch-up rinse.

He finished packing and joined Dray beneath the sheets.

In less than eight hours, he'd be sitting in the passenger seat of Randall's van. He rehearsed his story in his head, trying to make Leah's desertion plausible.

They made love deliberately, taking nothing for granted.

Each touch seemed heightened—she shivered when he kissed the edge of her wrist, the inside of her elbow, the point of her jaw.

They fell asleep in a warm tangle.

Forty-one

*T*he phone rang at six-thirty, jerking Tim from a deep sleep. He'd no sooner pressed the receiver to his ear than the marshal let loose with a string of Mediterranean expletives. After a few disoriented seconds, Tim caught up with his stream of discourse.

"This morning I find my niece—God bless her—zoned out on the couch, phone bleating in her hand and Betters's video in the VCR. She called in and signed up for the Next Fucking Generation Colloquium—put two grand on *my wife's goddamn Visa*."

Tim sank his teeth painfully into his lower lip; a chortle here could prove fatal. Beside him Dray shifted and groaned unhappily.

Tannino didn't pause long enough for Tim to respond. "Bring me something back, Rackley, however small, to get us on that fucking ranch. Once we're there, we're gonna go full bore on his ass."

*L*ooking crisp and mean in her uniform, Dray stood in the driveway as Tim backed the Hummer out of the garage. The steam from her coffee mixed with her clouding breath to shroud her face. A furious knocking on the passenger window made him punch down on the brakes. Leah gestured emphatically at him, running around to the driver's side.

When Tim rolled down his window, she said, "I want to go. The mail goes into TD's cottage, and only Lilies, Protectors, and Stanley John are allowed in there. You can't get your hands on that stuff. You need me."

"It's not safe for you up there."

"You don't get to decide that for me. You said it was my choice. I trusted you."

"Leah—"

"No, wait a minute. Since I've been off the ranch, I've been mostly upset and scared. But you know what? I'm sick of it. And the more I think about it—him, everything—the more pissed off I get. Now I want to go back there. And you can't stop me."

In the rearview, Tim noted her taxi pulling away from the curb. "No," he said. "I can't."

"What about Will?" Dray asked.

"I left him and Mom a note explaining."

"A note," Dray said. "Swell."

The Hummer idled and shot exhaust. Leah appealed to him with earnest eyes.

"Get in," Tim said.

*L*eah fidgeted in her seat, her foot twisting around the back of her calf as if scratching an inextinguishable itch. They passed a long school bus filled with chanting students waving pennants—just another away game in paradise. Leah watched it recede into traffic. "Do you know what it's like? To leave something that means everything to you?"

His back pocket still felt empty without his badge. It had been presented to him on a Georgian dais at FLETC graduation, and he'd silently pledged to hold and honor it until it was sunk in Lucite and holding down the stubs of his pension checks.

The clouds broke furiously, unleashing torrents of rain. They fought through clots of traffic and minilagoons, moving from one freeway to another until they finally exited. Leah's silent discomfort grew more pronounced as they neared the Radisson.

She let out a terse little laugh, then stared bitterly at the dash. "When they make you smile all the time, you know what? You start to believe it."

Wet gusts buffeted the windshield. Tim turned right into the circular driveway. Up ahead, a familiar, disproportionate form cut a block from the gray downpour. As the Hummer crept near, ducked valets scurrying alongside it, Randall appeared—the large head, the swollen arms, the jagged mouth with spaced, glinting teeth, so much like a child's sketch.

He raised an arm in silent greeting, and they stepped out into the deluge.

Party-two

Through the welcoming fanfare, through the full-body hugs and Skate's rooting in their pockets and bags, through the ceaseless kettledrum, the age regressions to abysmal childhoods, the group breathing, the weepy confessionals, Tim and Leah kept close, their shoulders brushing when they stood, their heads pressed together during floor-squirming exercises, Leah panting and sweating and pressing her nails into the soft underskin of her arm, Tim's voice staying slow and steady beneath the wails and shrieks and the low-resolution rumbling of the storm outside. In fine form, TD strode the stage, his voice a teasing build of outrage that roused the crowd to spurts of chanting, until all at once the spotlight plucked Tom Altman from the profusion of bodies writhing and twisting in orgiastic frenzy. Sean, Esq., bore the documents to him, overlapped on a silver tray like a spread of hardwood-smoked delicacies, and as Tim bent to press the tip of the fountain pen to paper, the crowd climaxed into riotous applause.

When the sweaty burden of continual embrace at last lifted and the fluorescents flickered on, Tim stood stunned and blinking, his clothes gripping him like a cowl of seaweed, Leah going pale at his side as if she were barely holding on.

She laced her hands behind his neck, doing a drunken girl's slump into his arms so he bore most of her weight. Her mouth found his ear, whispering between pants, though he couldn't make out all the words.

". . . couldn't . . . without you . . . don't know . . . hold out long . . ."

At once Janie was by her side, prying her off, sliding her neck beneath her arm. "You two are mighty close now—great Gro-Par bond. *Someone* taught you well."

Tim met Janie's silent-comedy wink with a weak smile. When he turned, he nearly collided with Randall's chest. Skate slid around to his other side.

"TD wants you in DevRoom A," Randall said.

Leah looked panicked at the prospect of his leaving, but he tore his eyes away and followed the Protectors.

Neither touched him, but they trapped him in the space between their bodies as they escorted him from the auditorium. They threaded through several paired Pros exuberantly rehearsing their recruitment tactics for the Next Generation Colloquium.

"I bet you never got anywhere by turning down new opportunities!" an East Asian girl implored her role-playing opposite.

At the far wall, Stanley John berated a muster of Pros for being brainwashed idiots—desensitization training to make them impervious to future persecution.

Skate led them down the hall. When he pulled the door open, Tim stepped inside, unsure what to expect now that Tom Altman had ostensibly signed away control of his holdings. TD awaited him, his armchair pulled in to a card table, a deck in his hands.

Always a shtick.

The door eased shut behind him. The Protectors had gone.

"Please." TD shuffled the deck, cut it one-handed, then shuffled again. "Sit." His hands blurred, and the first two floors of a house of cards appeared. "You're now a true member of the Inner Circle. A founding father."

Tim did his best to plaster a pleased smile across his face.

"Let me tell you what you have here." Even as he turned his gaze to Tim, his hands moved swiftly, confidently—within seconds eight more cards held firm in a tilted lean. "Endless possibility. Zero boundaries. Success—you know as well as I do—is a house of cards." As TD spoke, he pointed to each level in turn. "Belief is on the bottom. Then actions. Then emotions. Then thought. And finally . . . the result. But"—his finger snapped upright—"the minute you have a doubt . . ." His eyes staying on Tim, he flicked a bottom card, and the impressive structure tumbled. TD's pupils were like obsidian—compressed darkness, sleek and impenetrable. Tim felt them probing his brain, and he broke eye contact, though the heat of TD's glare didn't subside.

"That will happen to The Program if we flinch. It would have happened to your company if you showed weakness. It could have happened at any point during your negotiations to sell, right?" He looked to Tom for an answer but continued talking. "The Program is reaching critical mass. It can grow five times, ten times faster if you and I run the business aspect of it together."

He directed his attention back to the cards, which drew themselves into his hands like metal shavings before a magnet. "Give it some thought."

Forty-three

*T*hough the storm had quieted, the sky stayed murky, like churned-up water. Leah followed Randall down the curving trail, her adrenaline quickening.

Every step brought her closer to TD's bed.

Her mind was clear, but her body had shown itself willing to betray her. In the Growth Hall, her breath had moved through her as if directed by another entity. She'd grown sweaty and languorous, desirous of dissolution. Swept off by the rising trumpets, she'd almost surrendered to the thunderous chants, the lulling monotone. The stronger she'd fought, the more painful it had felt, like flailing offshore with a cramped leg.

After dinner she'd managed only a few minutes alone with Tom in their room before Randall's summoning knock.

Walking down the corridor of brush, she willed herself under control.

The Teacher's cottage drew into view. Across the clearing, the usual smoke twisted up from the stovepipe of the shed. Through the open door, she saw the soles of Skate's feet, bare and stained, pointing up from the cot. The dogs arose with ferocious snarling, startling Skate back to life. Leah froze, but Randall's hand grasped the back of her neck, squeezing gently as he steered her forward. Wearing a stretched pair of underwear, Skate hunched over the dogs in the shed, ordering them into submission. They yelped and snatched at each other.

Randall delivered her to the front room of the cottage and left her with trembling legs. She heard TD's raised voice above the deafening blast of the four-nozzle shower, dictating orders to Stanley John. Lorraine was probably in there

with them, either extracting hair from the soap between lath-
erings or on her knees beneath the spray, prepping him for
Leah.

In its place beside the door sat the white plastic bucket,
U.S. POSTAL SERVICE emblazoned on it sides. She raised the
top envelope from the stack, reading the return address: *Office of the U.S. Marshal. 312 N. Spring St., G-23.* The envelope was a Day-Glo, yellow—hard to miss.

She ran to the door and called for Skate across the clearing, not too loudly. Putting the dogs on a sit-stay, he came
grudgingly, buttoning a pair of tattered jeans on his way. The
Dobermans snarled at her, rising on their haunches. Skate
paused before the porch, his face blank.

"The mail's here." She held out the tub, praying the next
step would be self-evident.

Skate tugged his underwear out of his ass. "I know. I just
brought it."

Whatever response she'd been expecting, it wasn't that.
"Uh, TD just told me to tell you."

"He done sorting it?"

Behind her she heard the shower go off, and her stomach
turned to ice. "Yes."

With a grunt he lifted the crate from her hands and headed
back across the clearing.

Her heart racing, she watched to see where he was going.
She recalled that the mod had a paper shredder.

A hand closed on her shoulder, and she yelped. Dripping
and naked, TD smiled down at her, his erect penis brushing
her stomach. "I missed you."

TD had only to raise his eyes and he'd see Skate with the
postal bucket.

By the bathroom door, Stanley John scribbled down a few
more notes and Lorraine wiped her mouth and glared at her,
TD's towel folded over an arm.

The sight of TD up close unsettled Leah further.

She forced herself to look into the hypnotic eyes. Across

the clearing she heard a door close, but she couldn't tell if it was the shed's or the mod's. She moved away from the door, smiling mechanically. "I missed you, too, TD."

Lorraine presented Leah with the towel. Her stomach roiling, she dried TD off as he stretched and yawned, seemingly impervious to the icy breeze seeping through the screen door.

He strode to the bedroom, Leah still toweling his legs as he moved, sorting through the jumble of her thoughts. He closed the door behind them. Leah continued to dry his back, hoping to buy a few more minutes, but TD pulled the towel away from her and dropped it on the floor. He placed his hands gently on her shoulders and walked her back until the bed pressed against her legs, until she fell on the mattress. He ran a hand up the inseam of her jeans, splaying his fingers near her crotch to part her legs.

"You never yielded to me," he said. "Sexually. Don't you think it's time?"

"No."

His eyebrows twitched upward, the slightest show of surprise. "What did you say?"

"I don't feel ready."

"You don't want to say that to me." He made a tsking noise with his tongue, his muscular hands gripping her forearms, steadily moving them down to either side of her. "Don't you want to give up your need to stand out? Don't you want to fit in and be part of a family for once in your life?"

He crouched over her, his smooth-skinned face looking impossibly youthful, the unlined visage of a Renaissance angel.

She felt revulsion pressing at the back of her throat like vomit. "No."

"Yes." A smile lit his face, showing off the perfect line of his teeth. "Yes, yes, yes."

She resisted, but he was sufficiently overpowering to make clear she had no options. He manipulated her body with a calm forcefulness, guiding her through the motions of undressing, navigating her arms from the shirt as if changing a doll with stiff limbs. Then he pushed down on her knees, forcing one leg straight, then the other, and pulled off her jeans.

Wearing a soft, paternal smile, he kept his eyes on hers. "There you go. Let me show you."

He sank on top of her, his right knee pinning her left leg down, the kneecap boring into the soft flesh of her inner thigh. She was trapped—she couldn't react violently without giving away her greater deception. TD secured her arms, vise-gripping her wrists in one hand. Through her panic Leah felt his left knee dig between her clenched legs, forcing them open. It rolled up the curve of her right leg, trapping it, too. His practiced dexterity was all the more sickening.

"You're all alike. You think your virginity is so cosmically important, as if God and mankind have nothing better to do than worry about girls keeping their cherries intact. As if your body is some holy shrine. As if it matters at all when you let a man inside you. It doesn't. You'll see. This will be so good for your growth, Leah. You'll learn so much."

His face had darkened with blood, accenting the chestnut square on his chin, the whites of his eyes. He twisted a finger in the side of her panties.

For a moment she thought she'd started screaming out loud, but then an idea sailed into her head, cutting through the imagined noise. "You're right, TD. But that's not why I don't want to be with you. It's because . . . well, when I changed this morning, I noticed . . . uh, some midcycle spotting and—"

He stiffened. Panic touched his eyes, and he scrambled off her. "Out now. Off my sheets." He stumbled backward across the room. "You should never come into my cottage this way."

Leah's thighs and wrists throbbed. TD's face burned with rage; Leah's rash seethed. As she tried to dress quickly, he shooed her out, carrying half her clothes.

"Leave. *Now*."

Over the din of the crickets and the bang of the screen door, she heard him crying out for Lorraine, his voice holding a jarring note of distress.

Forty-four

Stretched shivering beneath two sheets, Leah lay on Tim's bed, breath pluming from her mouth at intervals. Tim sat beside her, plastic bags wrapping his shoes, bobby pin set between his teeth, one hand resting on her forehead.

Waiting.

Amid all the activities, dinner had conveniently been forgotten. Tim's stomach growled despite the enormous breakfast he'd eaten in preparation. He pulled a protein bar from its hiding place, broke it in two, and gave Leah half.

They chewed in sullen silence.

Watching the rain bounce off the puddles outside, Tim grew increasingly tense. Still no Skate, no Dobermans.

The best time for Tim and Leah to escape would be tomorrow during the predinner Orae. That left him roughly fifteen hours to gather whatever evidence he needed. Tonight provided his last chance to recon under cover of darkness, but if Skate had reported on Leah's meddling with the mail, he'd likely be walking into a trap.

He waited a few more minutes, then opened the window and dropped outside. Leah shut it behind him, and her face drifted down out of view.

Tim made his way from cabin to cabin, pausing at the edge of Cottage Circle. He forged through the brush to the north of the trail, taking a more direct route to the shed, one that provided him better cover. Brambles and branches tore at him, forcing him to move more or less parallel to the trail. His plastic-sheathed feet found sloppy purchase in the mud.

He heard the whine of dogs around the bend of the trail, followed by Skate's two-note whistle, releasing them to seek.

He crouched in the dense foliage, biting on the bobby pin,

shifting slightly to improve his obstructed view of the trail ten yards south. The dogs swept past, Skate lumbering to catch them.

One of the dogs circled back and sat, nose twitching, glaring downslope. Tim hoped the rain provided sufficient scent cover, that the winds wouldn't shift, that the spindly branches around him wouldn't crackle.

Skate stopped by the dog, his broad boots pushing mounds into the mud. "Whatcha smell?" He scratched the dog's scruff.

Tim held his breath. Skate squatted, bringing his face inches from the dog's saliva-wet snarl to mimic its sight line down the trail.

Inadvertently overlaying Tim's scent with his own.

The dog backed up, shaking its head, sneezed twice, and trotted after its companion. Skate remained on his haunches, head pivoting. Just before he turned to face Tim, Tim drew the bobby pin into his mouth and closed his eyes to hide the white glint.

A plop of a footstep. Then another. He opened his eyes and made out Skate's receding back. He exhaled and pulled himself free, branches scraping him through his clothes. Wet wind whipped his face as he jogged to the clearing.

As always, the shed glowed orange. Passing behind it on his way to the mod, Tim discerned Randall's stooped, bulky form and heard the complaint of the stove door's stubborn hinges. The chimney coughed out a burst of ginger flecks, and Tim halted, realization striking.

So brilliant—hiding in plain sight.

He inched forward, minding his foot placement, trying to get a look through the rift in the planks of the wall, but he couldn't make out more than a slice of Randall's empty cot.

Randall came into view, one ash-covered finger tracing down a computer printout nailed to the wall. His nail tapped twice, leaving smudges. He flipped his cot over, fussed with the dial on the hidden floor safe, and removed a phone cord.

He snatched a mechanical clock from its perch on a crude shelf, took note of the time, and scurried across the clearing.

Before the screen door of TD's cottage swung shut, Tim was inside the shed, negotiating the cramped space around the overturned cot. The postal bucket sat empty on the floor before the open loading door of the potbellied stove. Inside, a scattering of paper curled in a leaping yellow flame. A few of the marshal's letters remained partially buried in the cinders—Tim noted the writing on the unopened envelopes before fire consumed them. Plenty of legible scraps peppered the mounds of cooled ash to the sides.

He turned to go, his hand pressing on the wall as he high-stepped over the cot. Something poked through the skin of his palm, and he jerked his weight off, almost falling. The nail impaling the computer printout.

TD's Phone Sheet, April 24. Callers' names, precise times of incoming calls, and topics were listed neatly in three columns. *Ross Hanger, Merrill Lynch. 4:10 P.M. Re: JS's preferred securities.* TD had wasted little time digging into Jason Struthers's financials. Tim was turning to go when another entry caught his eye. *Phil McCanley, Lowdown Investigations. 11:00 P.M. Re: TA update.*

A tingle ran across the small of Tim's back. TD's extensive extracurricular investigation was closing in on Tom Altman. Tim could play a cover game in the interrogation that would surely follow the call, but there was no way Leah could stand up to equal scrutiny.

His eyes found Skate's clock: 10:59 clicked to 11:00.

Across the clearing in TD's cottage, the telephone rang.

Tim leapt over the cot through the door and hit a full sprint up the trail. He skidded out onto Cottage Circle. Sheets of rain cut visibility to less than ten yards; he couldn't make out Skate or the dogs. To his right, past the line of cottages, stretched the woods, the creek, and, miles beyond, a beater of a pickup Bear had left for him roadside at Little Tujunga, the keys hooked behind the rear license plate.

Tim had all the evidence he needed. With ten strides he could vanish past the cypresses and be gone.

Instead he streaked toward his cottage, head lowered to cut the rain. He closed the front door silently behind him, leaned the broom handle against it, and eased down the hall.

Leah shot up in bed when he entered. "What? What's wrong?"

"We have to go. *Now*."

She scrambled into a sweatshirt. Tim kept watch at the window but took in only darkness and a blurry stretch of driving rain. A flash of lightning illuminated the empty trailhead.

"Which shoes should I . . . ?" She shook off the question and pulled on her sneakers.

Tim slid the window open and swung one leg out. Leah faced him at the sill, her teeth clicking. "I'm scared."

"Good."

The broomstick clattered.

She bit down on her lip and followed him out. They ran for the woods downslope, stumbling and falling on the way. Shouts from Cottage Circle urged them onward. They reached firmer ground beneath the trees, but still Leah couldn't keep up.

Twinning howls split the air.

The plastic bags around Tim's shoes had grown tattered, but they were better than nothing. He swept Leah up in his arms and ran with her for about twenty yards to disrupt her scent trail, but the terrain was rough and they made poor time.

Leah's words were muffled against his neck. "I can run. I can do it."

He set her down. They tripped over rocks, mud caking their shoes. They crested a rise and saw the engorged creek sweeping past below. Tim turned, trying to sight flashlight beams, but there was just streaking rain, rumbling thunder, the ever-closer barks of the dogs leading the party onward.

"We have to wade upriver to lose the dogs."

Leah regarded the angry caps, the rock-dashed currents. "It'll sweep me away."

"Stay near the bank."

He took her hand, and they skidded down the embankment. Icy water claimed their legs to the calves, and they slogged upstream, ducking fallen trees. A howl broke through the sounds of sloshing, maybe a half mile back.

A sudden wash swept Leah off her feet. Tim went down on a knee but kept her slippery hand. Water battered his chest. He yanked her toward a calmer patch and drew her near; she locked her legs and arms around him. She was quivering violently, her cheek as cold as porcelain against his neck.

He stumbled forward, bearing her weight. A rock turned underfoot, and he fell, shoved himself up with an arm, kept going. Her sweatshirt rode up beneath his grasp; he regripped and was shocked at the rigor mortis–ed feel of her flesh.

The erratic splashing behind them grew steadily louder. He paused, panting, bracing one leg against a boulder.

Leah's head rolled back. Her lips were faded blue, her breath cold against his face. Her voice was little more than a whisper. "I don't even know your name."

"Tim."

A faint smile. "Tim."

Waist-high water swept through them. Her frail frame clenched around him. He felt the knot of her wrist-clamped hands at the back of his neck. Strands of hair lay stiffly on the bleached skin of her face; beads of water dotted her cheeks.

"It's so far." She blinked weakly. "It's okay. You go."

Her chilled forehead found the hollow of his eye. Her lips brushed his cheek, the edge of his mouth. He held her, inhaling her. A few shouts, just around the bend, matched by a chorus of barks.

He waded to shore and set her on her feet. Her knees buckled, but she stayed upright. They could hear distinct footsteps now, the scrabbling of paws across stone.

She stared at him without comprehension, arms clamped over her torso, hands clutching the balls of her shoulders.

Three shadowy figures emerged from the downpour, the Protectors looming on either side of TD. Skate had leashed the dogs; they bobbed in the water, straining like hooked fish. The men shouted and closed on them.

Tim lowered one shoulder, his face twisting with rage. "*Stop chasing me!*"

He backhanded her so hard she left her feet, her rain-heavy hair whipping across her face. She twisted and hit mud. Tim broke for the creek, and Randall slammed into him and spun him roughly, hands working the frisk.

Randall snapped Tim's head forward in a full nelson; Skate pressed a knife to his belly.

Disoriented, Leah fought herself up to her elbows. TD leaned over her. She began to cry, and Tim was certain she was going to reveal everything.

Leah lay skinny and wet in the mud, her tangled hair draped across a swelling cheek. She choked out the words. "I w-woke up when I heard him close the window behind him. I ran after him. He's *my* Gro-Par. I didn't want to get in trouble."

Tim felt a rush of affection for her. Afraid of what his face might show, he turned his head and spit.

TD shushed her, stroking her hair. "No, no, no. You did brilliantly. We just found out he's a fraud."

"A fraud?"

"Don't worry. We'll move you back in with Janie. She'll take care of you, my sweet." TD kissed her head and stood. "You laid a hand on one of my Lilies." He seemed amused, almost pleased. "Who are you?"

Tim glared at him. Skate ripped the plastic bags from his feet and threw them to the wind.

TD pulled off his jacket and wrapped it around Leah. Her teeth chattered fiercely.

"So I won't get p-punished?"

"No." TD turned his enigmatic grin toward Tim. "Let's save that for our friend Tom."

A lot had changed in the five or so hours since Tim had last been in DevRoom A, none of it for the better. Skate overflowed the folding chair beside Tim, stinking of canine, flicking the dirt from beneath his nails with the tip of his hunting knife. Randall stood behind Tim, arms crossed, Mr. Clean gone sour. One elbow resting on the card table, TD leaned back in his armchair, the picture of leisure.

"Let me guess," Tim said. "You want me to pick a card."

TD offered a smile. The rain had cut the poofiness from his hair; he looked even slighter than usual, a wet rat.

"The license plates on your Hummer are registered to Tom Altman. Nice touch. But you see, we're more thorough than that. So I sent my investigator down to the Radisson to peek through the windshield and run the VIN number. It seems the vehicle traces to a Theodore Caverez of La Jolla. Theodore was indicted on drug charges two months ago, his vehicle seized by the federal government. And I can't believe our friend Tom Altman bought his Hummer at a police auction—doesn't match his carefully constructed profile, does it?"

Tim tried not to shiver, not wanting to broadcast weakness.

"You came here for a purpose, Tom."

"Doesn't everyone, Teacher?"

"A *seditious* purpose." His grin growing strained, TD tugged at a freckled ear, his first sign of impatience. "Do you think you're the first virus to try to infect our organization? You're all after something, someone. I may have been fooled by your façade, but I know what you run on underneath. I can read you— I always could. You were heading back to home base. Clearly you got whatever it was you were looking for. What was it?"

"Fulfillment."

TD leaned forward, training his eyes on Tim's. "You think you've got something on me."

"I'm just a guy who decided to Get with The Program."

TD's smile showed off the muscles of his cheeks, his neck. He nodded at Randall, who stepped back and opened the door. Skate remained immersed in his grooming.

Tim regarded the open door skeptically. "That's it. I can just walk out of here?"

"Of course. What do you take us for? Criminals?"

Tim rose and moved sideways to the door, keeping all three men in his field of vision.

"Best of luck, Mr. Altman."

Cautiously, Tim brushed past Randall. He jogged down the hall, glancing over his shoulder, and burst through the double doors. The rain had stopped finally, but the air felt wet and heavy. The paved drive sparkled, the asphalt slick beneath his rubber soles.

Skate had carried Leah back, delivering her into Janie's arms. She was surrounded by doting attendants in Cottage Three and in no shape to run, even if she did want to risk blowing cover.

He would come back for her.

At the front gate, Chad paused in his patrol and squinted from beneath a yellow southwester. As Tim neared, he turned silently and shoved the gate open.

Watching him warily, Tim slipped through. He continued jogging on the dirt road, still unconvinced of his easy freedom.

The mud-sloppy road slowed him. Each step pressed hard denim edges into his thighs. It seemed he was walking forever, but each turn only revealed another stretch of road. When at last he reached the swollen creek, he had to stop and rest, hands on his knees, gathering his courage before another plunge. He grimaced and waded in.

The flat-laid chain-link fence intersecting the creek bed aided his crossing, but during a few weightless steps in the middle, the current threatened to sweep him away. He managed to slog forward, a spray of water slapping him in the face. Sputtering, he crawled out and staggered to his feet.

His elbows and knees ached. Dirt gave way to asphalt. Finally he stepped out onto Little Tujunga. The road was quiet this time of night. He jogged south a quarter mile in surreal silence, stepping over felled branches. The dilapidated pickup drew into view, nestled in the overfall of a weary pepper tree. He located the key beneath the rear plate. Just as he slid it into the door, he heard the rattling approach of a vehicle.

He turned as the van braked sideways, tires chirping. The rear door slid open, and Stanley John, Chad, and Winona climbed out, followed by Dr. Henderson. Randall kicked open the driver's door with a grin, his size-fourteens shattering a glass-still puddle.

Tim stood slightly stooped, panting, as they unhurriedly fanned out around him. Randall's shirt bulged at the belt buckle. Stanley John and Henderson wore Sig Sauers in right-side hip holsters, Winona a .32 cal and a salacious grin.

"Funny," Stanley John said without a smile, "we were just leaving the ranch, too."

"And we happened upon you," Randall said.

Slowly, deliberately, they drew near, a lasso contracting— they wanted to take him alive.

Randall all but blotted out the gaping door of the van. He tugged a Dirty Harry .44 Magnum from his belt—the same gun Doug had pulled on Tim the day before yesterday. They were almost within reach. Tim put his back to Winona, the weakest threat and least likely first assailant, keeping Randall directly in front of him.

Chad's lack of weapon betrayed him as the takedown lead; he shifted his weight from leg to leg, then dropped one foot back in a boxer's stance. Tim's head swiveled to keep the four men in view. Randall clutched his gun at waist level, pointed at Tim's feet. His compact frame rippling with energy, Stanley John held his hands loose in a chopping style that announced martial-arts training.

Tim willed time to slow, and it obeyed him. In his peripheral, he picked up the flutter of Stanley John's nostrils, the silver button of the holster snap just under the hammer. He sensed Winona step back, Henderson sidle to the rear position. Chad tensed through the shoulders and bladed left to protect his vitals, the final move before a charge. Randall's neck flexed, his mouth creaked open to issue the go command.

Tim snapped his head back, cracking Henderson's cheek, his arms already moving to snatch the Sig from Stanley John's hip. His left hand popped the holster snap as the right found the grip. He fired the instant the gun cleared leather, the shot blowing through Stanley John's right hip, the recoil momentum propelling Tim's cocked elbow back into Chad's throat as Stanley John's disbelieving howl wavered high and thin. Since Chad had lost the drop, Randall wisely skipped back out of reach, gun rising to level as Tim swung the barrel, seeking the expansive target of his chest. A kick to Tim's knee from behind wobbled him—the reverse head-butt had not connected with Henderson as brutally as Tim had hoped—and the Sig drifted wide, the sights floating across a drift of asphalt and rocky roadside banks. Randall's fingers tightened on the Magnum, his face a malicious smear that Tim barely had time to register before his vision detonated into a white blaze that diminished swiftly to black.

*H*alfway up the hill, Leah sensed the throb of the kettledrum, badly played by someone other than Stanley John. It found resonance in the pit of her stomach, the soles of her feet, the pulse at her nape. Janie and a huddle of Pros attended her like handmaidens, crowding her line of sight, stealing her oxygen, seeming to note her every expression.

A seam of yellow showed between two clouds, a wink of the just-risen sun. Leah's mouth remained cottoned, though her splitting headache had subsided; her concern for Tim had allowed her only fitful sleep. From the buzz around the ranch, she'd gleaned that TD had let Tim walk away, but she knew better than to trust anything.

When she entered the Growth Hall, she returned TD's cryptic grin from the stage, then broke free from the others, standing to the side, steeled with some inner conviction.

Her teeth stayed clenched, her neck firm.

The drum continued with cardiac regularity. The lights dimmed. TD began his Orae.

Her arms crossed, Leah watched him pace as one hour dragged into the next. A band of sweat glittered across her brow. She swayed once, twice, then sank down to the floor.

Her shoulders slumped.

Her eyes glazed.

Porty-five

Sunday passed in slow motion. Since Dray didn't have a shift to take her mind off the clock, she tried to keep busy, plodding out a five-mile run in the morning, painting the garage door, logging some trigger time at the range, even going to McLane's with Mac and Fowler and pretending not to be bored as they ranked the asses of the Dixie Chicks between gulps of Rolling Rock. When pressed, she cast the tiebreaker for Martie.

At night she couldn't even manage to recline; she sat in bed cross-legged, paperback bent open on her knee, watching the stubborn goddamn clock make like a snail on bennies. By dawn she could have powered the house's major appliances with the hum running through her body.

She called Bear for the umpteenth time. He picked up on a half ring.

"Anything new on the pickup?"

"Denley and Palton just did another drive-by. It's still bedded down." His voice sounded troubled. "The key was sticking out of the lock, like someone beat a hasty retreat. And Palton, uh . . ."

Her hand tightened around the phone. *"What?"*

"Palton spotted some blood on the ground. Near the car. Look, I shouldn't have even told you—"

Heat rushed into her face. "The fuck you shouldn't have."

"Could be raccoon meets fender, all we know."

"The raccoon put the key in the lock, too?"

"They called in CSI. It's still showering up there. The blood washed away before the van got up the hill. The criminalists lifted a thumb spread off the key, though—the oils on the underside held through the moisture. They'll scan it as soon as they get back to the lab."

Dray reached for the Beretta, her hand closing on the comforting grip. "Let's go in."

"We've been here before, Dray. And you're always the one to say the procedures don't apply selectively. Even if we could prove it *was* his blood, it was on public property. And if it wasn't his, it doesn't establish probable cause with respect to the ranch—"

"God*damn*it." She took a few deep breaths.

"We're covering every angle. Tannino's working the DA and the bench, Denley and Palton are sweeping the area, Thomas and Freed are here with me combing the files. Guerrera was ready to go Rambo—Tannino threw him up in an observation post just to get him to shut up. He's got eyes on the ranch's front gate—business as usual. It goes without saying, everyone's taking it personally." Bear kept his voice light, but his shaky sigh betrayed his apprehension. "I'm sure Tim's gonna pop up somewhere safe and sound and laugh at this circus."

She didn't want to ask, but the words came out anyway. "How much blood was there?"

The painful pause reminded her of the condolence calls they'd received in the wake of Ginny's death.

"A lot," Bear said.

* * *

They beat him to awaken him. They beat him to move him. They beat him with fists and rubber hoses. When they briefly left him, they propped a speaker against the wall to blare discordant sounds at irregular intervals—deafening hisses like static, screeches like rakes on chalkboards. They kept on in shifts at first. Randall asked the questions, maintaining a low, calm voice even as he mopped crimson from his knuckles with a crusty throw rag. At this point they were careful not to break anything—this would be a marathon, not a sprint.

They needed to leave plenty of room for escalation.

The butt of Randall's gun had left Tim's right eye swollen shut. His clothes were torn, Will's watch smashed but still clinging to his wrist. Tim withdrew into himself as he'd been taught during SERE training—three summer months slapping mosquitoes in North Carolina heat, his instructor's West Point–ring–fortified knuckles pounding into him the four dire arts: Survive, Evade, Resist, Escape.

He started by reconstructing his and Dray's house, room by room, drawer by drawer. Itemizing the detachable heads to the spiral screwdriver in the second tray of his toolbox, he heard himself grunt and moan and yell, but he was pleased to note that he did not unmask Leah.

Randall was by far the most skilled, though Henderson surprised Tim, applying pressure to the tracheal cartilage, the brachial plexus, the hypoglossal nerve, all the while preserving a detached, scientific focus that Tim was impressed a failed podiatrist could muster. Chad had little stomach for violence; he rarely put his weight behind his punches and winced at impact. The only true break Tim got was when Winona took point on the action; he'd laughed the first time she hit him. Randall had stepped in to provide tutelage, demonstrating for her on Tim's ribs, and that had stopped his laughter pretty quickly.

When Tim's visitors drifted through the thick metal door,

he caught a glimpse of the hall outside, Stanley John lying against a stack of empty wooden pallets, hands pressed to his shattered pelvis. The door's sucking back to the jamb severed Stanley John's howls abruptly. Someone, presumably the good doctor, had dressed his wounds, but he was sure to bleed out soon enough. At one point, when Tim feigned passing out, he was party to a hushed conversation between Randall and Henderson weighing the risks of a hospital trip. Whatever they decided, Stanley John's bandages grew soggy and his screams continued, growing ragged until Randall began urging him to be a man.

From what Tim could glean, he was in a janitor's room in the back of a commercial building. Like the walls, the floor was concrete, so cold he thought his bare skin would stick to it when he moved.

When they left him long enough for the blood streaming from his forehead to clot, he began groping on the floor, pressing his fingers along the dark seams of the room. He found a broken segment of the Cartier's case and began scratching at the wall with the protruding lug. His fingers ached. An inch-high pyramid of concrete dust formed on the ground near his elbow, though he barely made an indentation.

Randall entered, crossed his arms, and laughed darkly. "That wall's a foot thick and reinforced with steel. Keep scraping."

Tim felt Randall's hands close around his ankles. He was dragged away from the wall, laid out for Henderson, who watched from behind round spectacles, rubbing his soft hands.

When Chad pushed in through the door, Stanley John's hysteria rose to crescendo. He was pleading to be taken to an emergency room.

Exasperation showed in Randall's scowl. "Can't you get him to shut up?"

"He's in a lot of pain," Chad said.

Winona ruffled Tim's hair, her long nails scratching scalp.

"Our boy Tommy here's in a lot of pain, you don't hear *him* impersonating a howler monkey."

Randall wrapped a rag around his bruised knuckles and stepped forward. "Give it time."

As Henderson calmly worked Tim's vital points, Randall interspersed questions with the pain.

"You came for Shanna, didn't you? You knew each other before? Is Leah involved with you? You were looking for financial records?"

When Tim emerged from the unlit tunnel of his thoughts, his eyes found Randall's, and he slurred through a swollen lip, "I'm going to kill you."

Something in Tim's voice made Randall blanch. He wiped the sweat from his forehead—it hadn't been there a moment ago—and continued.

At first Tim's captors had snickered and joked, but as the hours passed, they grew exhausted. The break times between sessions grew longer, leaving Tim more time to work at the wall with the ground-down watch lug, wincing through the sporadic blasts of noise.

Randall returned and appraised Tim's meager headway, amused. "How's the progress?"

When Tim didn't respond, he bound Tim's ankles and propped him in a chair. Chad bent back Tim's arms, pressing his wrists together so Winona could straddle his lap as she worked. She spent some time on his face, a stone-heavy costume ring augmenting her punches. Her eyes gleamed; her red mouth glittered. She was enjoying herself.

Randall began a soft repetition of the same questions. "Who are you?" His teeth clicked as they waited through the silence. "LAPD? FBI? What were you after?" A flash of anger stiffened his body, and he shouldered Winona aside, wanting at Tim—"Open your fucking hole and *speak*."

Tim barely had time to dip his head so Randall's fist would connect with his hard crown. Randall stormed out, Chad and Henderson trailing, Winona wearing a healthy flush and panting from the exertion. As he shoved out through the door, Randall grimaced at Stanley John's shrieking. Tim saw him reach for the .44 on the table. The door swung shut, and a crack echoed off the concrete walls, cutting short Stanley John's last whimper.

Some raised voices—Randall and Henderson having it out. Tim strained, making out little more than mumbles.

Randall's voice briefly rose into audibility. ". . . getting out of hand. I say we cut our losses. You two get the body in the van . . ."

Tim tilted forward, falling from the chair. He pressed his ear to the floor. Henderson's and Winona's voices faded into the distance. A few seconds later, Tim thought he sensed the rumble of the van's engine turning over. He fought the rope from around his ankles, dragged himself to the wall, and continued his tedious etching with the watch lug, freeing a scattering of dust and a few thumbnail-size chips.

Finally he rested, the floor a slab of ice beneath his cheek. He worked off his shoe, rolled off his sock. He prepared, and he waited. When the speaker screeched again, Tim yanked the wire from the back panel, cutting the sound short.

A few seconds later, Randall's enormous frame blotted out the rectangular throw of light from the doorway.

The door creaked shut. Randall took a few steps and squatted, spinning the frayed end of the stereo wire between a blunt finger and thumb. His eyes shifted to Tim. He rose.

Tim shrank from his advance. As Randall drew near, a slash of a grin bulging his underbite, Tim sprang up, grip tightening around the end of his blood-soaked sock, the fist of powdered concrete pulling hard and dense in the toe. He twisted hard like a fastballer, pain screaming through his hips, his torso, his arm, aiming for the fragile part of the skull at the temple. Randall jerked a half step back, a surge of fright seizing his features like a hiccup.

The makeshift sap missed Randall's blind-flailing arm and struck the side of his head with a dull pop, caving it in.

Randall's bowels released with a gurgle. His knees gave, and he toppled over, the sock wedged inside the neat oval of missing skull.

Tim frisked him but found no weapon. He staggered to the door and peered through the tiny square of glass at the top. His face a fishy gray, Chad mopped Stanley John's juices around on the slick floor, making little headway.

Tim gently tried the knob. Locked.

To buy some time, he let out a few groans, as if he were still being tortured.

A scouring of Randall's pockets turned up a driver's license. Lightheaded, Tim made his way back to the door and started working the lock, but the license was too wide for Tim to get a good angle.

Chad looked up and let out a garbled cry.

Tim began bending Randall's license back and forth lengthwise. "Let me out."

Chad was quivering. "Where's Randall?"

His tongue felt like an anvil. "Turn on the light and see."

Resting the heel of his hand on his pistol, Chad inched forward. His fingers found the switch and flicked it on. Tim stepped aside to provide a good view, and Chad let out a gasp.

His voice rose to a desperate whine. "You're gonna be in deep shit when Dr. Henderson gets back."

Tim managed to rip the license in half along the seam. "I won't lay a finger on you. I'll just walk out of here. You can say it was Randall's fault. That he came in and left the door unlocked. He certainly won't mind."

"You're out of your mind. Like I'd let you out now."

"If I stay here, you'll regret it."

"Yeah, right. *Sure.*" Chad's chest shook with a few sobs that he hid under a nervous stutter of a laugh. "What are you gonna do?"

Tim turned his head slowly, eyebrows raised, indicating Randall's body.

Chad's face convulsed as if he'd bitten into something sour.

Tim slid the halved license beneath the latch bolt and shoved the door open.

Chad yelped and drew back against the wall, the Sig pointing at Tim's head though Tim was a good ten feet away and could barely stay on his feet.

No exterior doors in view. The only window had been blacked out.

Tim heard Winona's voice before he saw her. "Chad, Dr. Henderson says if there's gonna be *two* bodies, we should prepare them inside before—"

She rounded the corner, nearly colliding with Tim. Her eyes barely had time to flutter wide with alarm when Tim struck her above the ear with the side of his closed fist.

She glided weightlessly a few feet before collapsing to the floor.

Tim faced Chad across her body. The gun shook in Chad's hand.

Winona stirred and coughed up a mouthful of vomit on Chad's shoes. Broken blood vessels squirmed through her right cheek like crimson maggots.

"If you call out," Tim said, "I'll come back and kill you."

He left Chad frozen and hobbled down the hall, his bare foot slapping linoleum. A window looked out on Randall's van, still parked tight to the building beside a sporty Lexus—Tim's ears had betrayed him. Displeased and slightly panicked, Henderson was aborting Plan A, tugging Stanley John's stiff body back out of the van. It landed on the asphalt with a thump.

Searching for an exit, Tim slid past the window and banged through two swinging doors, leaving bloody handprints on the metal plates. The sound boomed back from the distant reaches of a massive warehouse.

He wiped the run of blood from his eyes and halted, shocked. Rising vertiginously from a bedrock of pallets were colossal pillars of videotapes, DVDs, and CD-ROMs, all sporting TD's close-up and a jagged advertisement bubble proclaiming, *Your Free Program Software!*

A virtual army of tape sessions awaiting deployment.

Tim took a few shaky steps into the product labyrinth, disoriented by the surrounding sameness. He registered a flutter of footsteps at the doors, then a shout. More voices answered; all three were on the prowl now.

Tim dashed between two forklifts and down a lane of DVDs, trying to source the voices. He followed a forced turn and came up against a wall of videotapes, TD's portrait leering at him in mosaic from beneath endless cellophane wrappers.

An engine revved sharply, then tires chirped against concrete. Truck forks punched through the rise of VHS cassettes, bringing them raining down on Tim.

He was buried instantly.

Forty-six

At 7:12 P.M. Dray snatched the phone off the hook the instant it chirped, knocking over an untouched glass of vodka she'd poured and sat staring at since Bear phoned an hour ago to let her know the print from the car key was a seven-point match.

Bear said, "We didn't find him—"

Her breath pushed through her teeth like steam.

"—but Metro Division just got a hit on Leah's car."

"I could give a shit about Leah's car right now."

"They pulled a guy over off Florence downtown, pretty far afield from the ranch. Denley and Palton took over custody, picked him up from Parker Center. We've got him upstairs. Name of Leo Henderson." Bear cleared his throat, then cleared it again. "The thing is . . ."

"Yeah?"

"The thing is, we found some supplies in the trunk."

"Like what? Bear? Like what?"

"Heavy-duty garbage bags. Bleach. Lye. And a hatchet."

Dray let out a noise she didn't recognize.

"Thomas and Freed are working him."

She snapped into focus. "On *what?* They'd better not be mentioning Tom Altman or if Tim *is* still—"

"They're just questioning him on the car and the supplies. But he's not putting out. He sits there wearing this complacent smile. He's got the thousand-yard stare and everything. And his knuckles are bruised."

"He was coming from Tim." She drew a deep breath. "Or going back to him."

"Maybe he hasn't done it yet."

"I can't hear 'maybe' right now, Bear."

They both let the silence draw out and out until Dray almost forgot they were on the phone. Finally Bear grumbled under his breath, a litany of seething fricatives.

"Say I tell Thomas and Freed to take a coffee break. Say I go in there and me and him work some shit out."

Dray pressed a hand to the bridge of her nose. "No, no violence like that. The rules apply when it's our family on the line, too. If they don't, the rules don't mean shit. And *we* don't mean shit." She realized she was standing, and she eased herself down into a chair. A stampede of anxiety overtook her; she waited for the dust to settle. She couldn't survive another funeral. She couldn't endure identifying Tim's body, seeing the cold face beneath the Tom Altman–dyed hair and fake goatee. An idea sailed through her grief, setting her back in the chair.

"Bear?" Her voice was shaky, excited. "Bear, where's Leah's car?"

"Police impound lot. They towed it to the one on Aliso off Alameda. Why?"

"We gotta make a phone call."

* * *

Wearing dark slacks, twice-cuffed shirtsleeves, four-inch lifts, and a contentious scowl, Pete Krindon approached the heavyset city worker at the impound lot. The guy manned a station resembling a Hertz rental booth near the front gate. Behind the high-rising fences capped with barbed wire, Ferraris and Pintos commingled, an egalitarian paradise for the appropriated.

The worker tugged at his jowls and suspiciously regarded the biohazard-orange zippered bag swinging at Pete's side.

Pete's hand moved to his hip; a badge glinted, then disappeared. "Derek Cliffstone, Department of Homeland Security. I'm looking for a stolen Lexus IS 300, license plate four-xray-union-Paul-zero-two-two, impounded this A.M. from a Middle Eastern male, alias Leo Henderson."

"Leo Henderson?"

"Persian. They make 'em light-skinned, too, there, chief." Pete leaned forward in his oxblood loafers, the heel of his hand resting on his holstered Glock. He ran his tongue along the inside of his lower lip and spit on the curb. "Sometime today might be nice."

Pete set the orange bag on the counter as the worker drummed reluctantly on a computer keyboard.

"You want a look, you're gonna have to produce a warrant—wait, wait, *wait!*" The guy scrambled back off his seat. "The fuck is that?"

Pete finished tightening the rubber strap on his gas mask. He dug through a selection of filters, mumbling under his breath, "Anthrax, smallpox, sarin nerve gas—a*ha*, VX." He screwed the filter into place beneath the nose cup. "Sir, we have reason to believe the trunk of that vehicle might contain some hazardous material." His voice sounded metallic and alien. "Parking-space number, please."

Ashen, the guy stared at him.

"Parking-space number, *please.*"

His hands sprang forward onto the keyboard, knocking over a cup of coffee. "Three eighty-five. In the northeast corner."

"Thank you. Please do not move from this spot, sir." Pete presented him with a business card, the Homeland Security seal glimmering in gold. "This is my supervisor's telephone number. Should you hear an explosion, please contact him immediately."

Before disappearing behind the first row of cars, Pete offered a salute that the baffled worker returned. Then he tugged off his mask and smoothed his fire-red locks back into place.

He found Leah's car quickly. Wriggling beneath, he affixed a transmitter to the undercarriage. He whistled as he strolled back, a classical piece he'd picked up from watching Bugs Bunny.

The worker was standing precisely where Pete had left him, frozen like a timorous four-year-old regarding a jack-in-the-box. His hefty frame settled with relief at Pete's reappearance.

"Wrong vehicle, chief. My apologies." Pete took his sweat-slick hand, nodded curtly, and headed for the street. "Your country thanks you."

*W*hen Bear kicked open the interrogation door, Henderson bolted upright in his chair. On the opposite side of the scarred wooden table, Thomas and Freed stood.

"Leave us."

Bear remained stone still in the doorway as the deputies exited.

Henderson started breathing hard. "I *said* I want to call my lawyer."

Bear laced his fingers and cracked his knuckles.

"You can't just hold me here."

Bear snapped forward, flipping over the table with a swipe of his hand. It struck the wall upside down about five feet up.

He seized Henderson's shoulders, shoving him back in the chair so the rear legs creaked under the weight.

Henderson finally opened his eyes. Bear's face was two inches from his.

"You're free to go."

Henderson swallowed hard. "What?"

Bear released him, and the chair thunked down on all four legs. Bear strode to the glass, squaring off with his reflection. "The Hennings are not pressing charges. They've written their daughter off. And her car. It's your lucky day, scum-suck. Get the fuck out of here." He tapped his foot twice, then whirled around. "You waiting on an apology?"

Henderson scrambled off the chair and out the door.

*B*y eleven-thirty, desperation had cast its shadow across Dray, leaving her scared and agitated. She'd put on her uniform in an attempt to feel tougher. A stroke of sage paint marked the back of her hand from painting the garage door yesterday morning. It seemed like months ago.

"What the hell's taking so long?"

Bear leaned back on his couch, readjusting the pump-action shotgun across his thighs. He'd already donned his black cotton gloves and steel-plate boots; his ballistic helmet, goggles, and tactical vest were piled on the floor at his feet. He'd informed Tannino that a confidential informant was phoning in a related tip, and the marshal had put the ART squad on high alert.

Bear said, "It probably took Henderson a while to get the Lexus processed out."

"I thought you called and took care of that."

"I did. They had a shake-up earlier, though, a bogus terrorist threat or something, got them a bit scrambled on paperwork."

"How do we even know we can trust this guy? I mean, what's our guarantee he knows what he's doing?"

"Pete Krindon," Bear said, "knows what he's doing."

The phone rang, causing Boston to startle up from his nap near the dog bowl.

Dray snapped it up.

"McKinley and Seventy-sixth," a voice said, and then the line went dead.

*B*ear knew better than to ask Dray to wait at home, but he told her she'd have to stay in his truck during the tactical strike. They drove over in silence.

A throw of storage warehouses were packed within a so-called industrial park that was neither industrial nor a park. Lots of parking lots and barbed wire. Bear cut the lights, and they drifted silently down the paved drive.

Aside from the van and the Lexus parked next to the primary warehouse, the area was deserted.

A great place to kill someone.

They left the truck behind the loading dock around back, then did some preliminary reconnaissance, taking note of voices and vibrations.

Within minutes the Beast rolled up to the staging point and disgorged the geared-up ART squad members, who mustered between the old retrofitted ambulance and Bear's rig. The deputies greeted Dray as if she were one of their own.

Brian Miller squat-leaned against the black-painted side of the Beast, POLICE U.S. MARSHALS rising over his head in white letters. At his side, Precious was locked on—no panting, no tail wagging, no growling—her wolf-yellow eyes standing out against her black Labrador coat. An Alpo-fueled early-warning system for rigged doors and booby traps, she was the top bitch on the Explosive Detection Canine Team. A Thomas Harris devotee, Miller had named her after Jame Gumb's poodle.

Maybeck reacquainted himself with his battering ram with a flurry of superstitious taps and squeezes, a ballplayer's on-deck bat ritual. He'd brought the damn thing with him from the St. Louis district; at Miller's promotion party, Maybeck's wife had joked that she'd caught him dressing it up in their daughter's Barbie outfits.

Thomas and Freed produced dueling pairs of night-vision goggles and eased around the corner, wind snapping at their block-lettered nylon raid jackets. The others circled up, the muzzles of their MP5s angled to the asphalt. Bear alone used a shotgun. Charged with double-aught buck, the cut-down twelve-gauge was fitted with a fourteen-inch barrel and a pistol-grip stock. The sight of Bear wielding it in full gallop was apocalyptic.

Miller unfurled a fax of a blueprint on the ground, pinning it open with a rock and his boot. Bear's gear rustled as he lowered himself over it. Speaking quietly despite the high wind and the hundred-yard distance to the target location, he conveyed where he and Dray had picked up activity within the building.

Miller nodded and took over. "We have a meat wagon on standby just outside the park in case of injuries. Metro's been alerted, but we don't have time to wait for them to set up a secondary perimeter outside the gates . . . ?" He regarded Bear and Dray with raised eyebrows, and they shook their heads in concert. "We're gonna go in heavy, a ten-man no-knock." As he ran through the entry plan, he tapped the blueprint with a chewed nail, indicating the coverage areas for each two-man cell.

Thomas and Freed scurried back around the corner. Thomas's mouth was drawn tight, spreading his mustache, the cracks around his eyes pronounced in his weathered face. He handed off his night-vision goggles and gestured. Miller took a peek, grimaced, and handed off the NVGs down the line. Dray noted the way each deputy's face changed, and she pulled the goggles from Bear's hand and looked into the green-cast world.

A handsome, well-built kid was pacing outside an open

door to the warehouse near where she and Bear had heard voices. Fuzzy streaks stained his hands to the forearms; blurry smudges marked his T-shirt, his jeans.

Red always came out hazy through night-vision optics.

The kid bent over and put his hands on his knees, as if fighting nausea. He retrieved a bottle of bleach from the trunk of the Lexus, steeled himself at the door, then reentered.

The next thing Dray knew, Guerrera's hands were under her arms and he was helping ease her the rest of the way to the ground.

"We don't know nothing," Guerrera whispered. "Not yet."

A flash of embarrassment cut through the agony grinding at her. She stood up but swayed on her feet, Palton and Denley stepping to her side.

"I can't go in with you, right?"

Miller's face said there would be no discussion.

"I'd better get the hell out of your guys' way then."

She pulled herself into the passenger seat of Bear's truck, leaving the door open.

They stacked up along the loading dock in their two-man cells, MP5s low-ready across their chests, waiting for Miller's go command.

The battering ram swung at Palton's side. Precious idled tight at Miller's legs.

Monsters with goggle eyes and Kevlar helmets, they seethed and bridled, body armor rustling.

Miller's raised fingers vanished one by one into his fist, and they were off.

*W*inona was squatting above the toilet, careful not to touch ass to seat, when she heard the faint shuffle outside. She jerked up her pants and hopped onto the sink, bringing her face to the window in time to see what looked like a geared-up SWAT team sweep past, quiet and lethal. She muffled a yelp with her hands.

She listened for maybe thirty seconds, then shoved open the window. Squirming out was easy, but the six-foot fall scraped her palms and jarred her wrists and knees. She ran down the length of the warehouse toward the front gates of the park.

She was just coming up on the loading dock when a dark form melted from the shadows and a female voice said, "I don't think so."

Winona swung blindly. A series of blows buffeted her—a forearm knocking away her punch, an open-hand strike to the side of her head that set her ears ringing. A boot clipped her knee, two hands locked behind her neck, and then she was ridden down to the asphalt with such force that all eight of her fingernails snapped on impact.

She whimpered into the ground as a knee dug into her back, and then her arm was wound behind her like a clock hand. Metal pinched her at the wrists, then the ankles.

Behind them, at the warehouse entrance, the world seemed to explode.

*M*iller yanked Precious clear. Maybeck took down the frame with the door, the battering-ram-propelled dead bolt blazing through the shoddy carpentry. He pivoted out of the way as Bear swept past in the number-one spot, holding the action back on the pump handle, Thomas and Freed at his elbows. Denley hummed a long-drawn-out hum as he always did on entry, though it was barely audible above the tramping of boots.

MP5 pressed to his cheek, Guerrera squared off with the darkness to their right, his weapon-mounted flashlight illuminating push doors and the warehouse proper that Bear and Dray had deemed empty.

The others swept toward the throw of light at the end of the hall. They flung around the corner as if propelled, immediately breaking toward the threats.

"U.S.Marshalsgetthefuckdown!"

Bear's mind raced to catch up with the gruesome tableau. Seven garbage bags tidily knotted. Crimson-tinged runoff spiraling down a drain. An ominous black doctor's bag. A soaked mop propping up the handsome kid from outside. Henderson backpedaling to a table bearing an array of pistols, one yellow dishwashing glove spinning to the floor, the other still encasing his left hand.

Bear's shotgun coughed out a *shuck-shuck* as his wide frame floated forward, his boots barely touching the blood-and bleach-slick concrete. To his side, Thomas and Freed hammered the kid, proning him out.

The discarded glove slapped the floor.

Stumbling to a knee, Henderson reached the table, his free hand grasping the nearest gun. The Magnum discharged into the far wall just as Bear's shotgun rammed into his face, the muzzle finding the hole of his mouth, splintering teeth and pinning his head to the floor. Bear's foot smashed down on his wrist, snapping it, and the .44 bounced free.

Bear felt the bore of his Remington grind against the soft flesh at the back of Henderson's throat, and he thought about seven well-knotted garbage bags, his finger tightening on the trigger.

Henderson's eyes bulged until his lids disappeared, blood drooling from his split lips.

Bear stood poised over him, sweat hammering through his pores. His left ear rang—the ricochet had screamed right past his head.

Somewhere Precious was yelping.

He withdrew the shotgun from Henderson's mouth.

Palton flipped Henderson like a pancake, cinching flex-cuffs around his wrists.

The other deputies were fanning out, kicking doors, two cells peeling back to help Guerrera sweep the warehouse. A shard of the blacked-out window had fallen away beneath the bullet hole. Outside, Precious lay bowed on her side, hind legs scrabbling on asphalt; she'd taken the ricochet. Miller crouched over her, his eyes wet.

From a dark doorway, Thomas cried out, "Bear. *Bear!*"

Head buzzing, Bear trudged over. It was like walking through syrup.

He braced himself, forearm against the jamb.

In the center of the maintenance closet, a bloody face intercepted the dim plane of light from the open door.

His lower lip had come loose; a flap lay across his cradling palm like a cut of meat. He peered out from a black eye swollen to the size of an orange and rasped in a halting, just-audible voice, "Master Sergeant Tim Rackley, date of birth 10/4/69, service number five-four-eight-seven-nine-zero-five-three-three."

Forty-seven

*T*he sterile light felt like pins sticking in his eyes. He squeezed his lids shut and tried to roll over, but his body did not respond.

The clatter of gurney wheels, the sickly-sweet smell of antiseptic, the throb of a needle in his arm—he was in a hospital. He heard some commotion at his bedside; his brain fought to make sense of it.

The bed creaked as someone leaned over him, and he inhaled her blissful scent—jasmine, lotion, gunpowder.

"County was closed to trauma, so we medevacked you to UCLA Med Center. It's Thursday, April twenty-ninth. Five thirty-two P.M."

Thursday night. Jesus, he'd lost two days.

"You're going to be okay. Henderson shot you full of

Versed. The ART squad pulled you out of that warehouse. Do you remember?"

He shook his head. His memory held nothing between killing Randall and waking up drugged in his cold concrete box, squinting against the round shimmer of Dr. Henderson's lenses. Henderson had proceeded to beat him senseless.

"We've got to get Leah out." His voice, hoarse with dehydration, was unrecognizable. He managed a few sentences to fill her in, the effort leaving him exhausted.

He heard a scratching of pen on paper; God love her, she was taking notes. "Were there more than five kidnappers?"

Eyes still closed, Tim counted sluggishly, then shook his head.

"We found seven garbage bags sharing what was left of Randall Kane and Stanley John Mitchell." Her voice wavered; Tim could tell she was overcome, sticking to shop talk to hold herself together. "We hooked and booked the other three."

A cranky female voice—"Officer, you'll need to ask him questions later."

"I'm his wife."

"Oh."

When Tim smiled, something poked into his lower lip. He heard her make a soft noise—she was grinning back—then he felt her cool hand on his forehead, and she said shakily, "Boy, oh, boy."

He reached for her, and she took his hand and pressed it to her chest. After a moment he moved his palm down. She unbuttoned her uniform, and he slid his hand through, resting it on her stomach.

Some forty-five minutes later, a harried doctor blew through the room, eyes glued to a chart. He addressed Tim as Mrs. Gonzalez and told him his baby was safe in the nursery and his hysterectomy had gone smoothly. Only Tim's pained chuckle had made the doc glance up, then he'd checked Tim's vitals, mumbling about idiot nurses, and scurried out.

Dray went to raise hell.

Soon after she got back, two physicians sounded the doctor-patented knock-and-open at the door. "Mr. Rackley?"

"Uh-huh."

"We worked on you Tuesday night. Your wife said Dr. L. didn't discuss your condition with you?"

"He said I can resume breast-feeding immediately, as soon as I'm off Percocet."

"If you can find someone to breast-feed you, have at it."

The other doctor with him, an attractive blonde with faint but pervasive facial scarring, laughed. She passed him a clipboard, and he squeezed her wrist to thank her. Tim's eyes went to their matching platinum wedding bands.

"You sustained multiple rib contusions and a hairline fracture on the right sixth. Not much you can do about the break, but be careful. I reset your nose. No septal hematoma, so you'll just have to tough it out for a while." His fingers fluttered gently around Tim's right eye. "No orbital fracture, no internal injuries, but you're beat up all over. Your right knee is probably in the worst shape—you have multiple torn ligaments and extensive bruising and swelling. We had to shave part of your goatee—"

"No problem," Dray said.

"—so we could get that lip stitched up. I had plastics come down, and they did a fine job, nearly twenty-five sutures. We don't want to disappoint the paparazzi, right?"

He extended a hand, and they shook, Tim's IV tube pulling tight. Tim recognized him and started to say something, but the doctors' pagers went off simultaneously. Like mirror images, they tilted the units, scanning the text screens. They filed out before Tim could thank them.

Just before the door closed, Tim heard the male doctor's voice once more, directed at his wife. "Nice to meet a fellow tabloid star."

*T*he ICU attending finally cleared Tim to a private room with a phone. He was dialing before the nurse withdrew. He reached the marshal at home and recounted his experience, beginning to end. The fading buzz of his painkillers and Tannino's palpable relief had made the conversation take a few demonstrative turns, but they'd both steered back to the case each time. Dray sat bedside, holding his hand.

"Leah's being held under duress," Tim said. "And I'd say my face removes all doubt as to what TD's henchmen are capable of. We need to move."

"Let me get on it right away," Tannino said. "I'll touch base first thing."

Tim received a flood of visitors for the rest of the night. Bear dropped in first, but he kept getting misty-eyed and stepping out into the hall to make calls on his cell. Palton, married fifteen years, brought flowers for Dray. For the first time Tim could remember, Denley didn't crack any jokes. Smelling of aftershave, Freed left his date in the lobby so he could run up. Guerrera gave Tim the St. Michael medallion from around his own neck and said Tim could wear it even though he wasn't Catholic.

Tim took it, figuring he needed all the help he could get.

Before leaving, Guerrera hooked Tim's head with his wrist and tugged him in for a brief, awkward hug that hurt Tim's ribs.

By eight o'clock most of the ART members had called or stopped by. Nothing like saving someone's life to make you feel indebted to him. Tim's mind moved again to Leah clinging to him in the icy current, teeth chattering.

Once Bear reappeared with a pizza and a six-pack, Dray left to get Tim some clothes and toiletries. Tim couldn't drink because of the Percocet, but Bear didn't need much help with the six-pack. Or with the pizza, for that matter.

Tim asked after Precious; the ricochet had shattered her femur, and Denley had mentioned she was going to be put down. Like grounded spy planes, tactically trained dogs have too much intel embedded in them to be released from government control.

Bear wiped red sauce from his chin. "Actually, I'm gonna

take her. I figure Boston needs a friend." He mistook Tim's distracted silence for amused disapproval, and his tone gained a slightly defensive edge. "You know Miller calculated she's saved seventeen lives. The boys are gonna pitch in for her surgery."

"Count me in. I owe her for that shotgun-rigged garage door in Tarzana."

Bear finished up and crammed the pizza box diagonally in the tiny trash can. He bent his head as if lost in thought, wrinkles gathering beneath his chin, his eyes going a little shiny. He cleared his throat as if he were going to say something, but he just squeezed Tim's arm and left.

Tim used the control on the nightstand to click off the lights. The blinds were still open, the city casting a pale blue glow across the blankets. He elevated the mattress so it pushed him into a sitting position, then stared blank-eyed at the empty room for a while.

Being alone made him uncomfortable.

He realized that was because he was trying so hard not to think about what had just happened to him. It was only in the quiet that emotion reattached itself to what he'd endured. He'd been trying to hold off sensation since he'd first come to in the concrete room, but now the details came floating back in a dirty tangle, like a drain-dredged snarl of hair.

His breathing grew ragged. In seconds he was drenched with sweat, his heart double-thumping—a problem he'd encountered now and again since Croatia.

He stared at the call button but couldn't bring himself to push it.

When the doorknob turned, he tried to call out Dray's name, but his throat felt like a tightening fist.

Thomas stepped through the doorway, squinting at Tim's shadow. "Hey, Rack, you up?"

Tim managed a nod.

"Look, I just wanted to say"—Thomas studied the floor, shifting his weight uncomfortably—"all that shit . . . between us before . . ." He took note of Tim's expression for the first time. "You all right?"

Tim nodded, his chest hammering up and down.

"You want me to call a nurse?"

Tim shook his head.

Thomas stood staring at him for a bit. Then he walked forward cautiously and sat beside Tim on the mattress. Tim's breathing evened out, the faint, asthmatic rasp slowly fading from his inhalations.

Thomas sat at his side for about an hour in perfect silence, hand resting on his shoulder as he breathed away a panic attack. Eventually the walls ceased pressing in on him, and Tim drifted off into exhaustion. When he awakened a few fitful hours later, Thomas was gone and Dray was back sleeping in her chair.

*T*he marshal came by first thing the next morning, wielding an oversize basket of muffins and looking none too pleased about it.

He set the muffins on the floor and said, "The wife."

"She bake them herself?"

"I'm afraid so." He approached Tim and stood with his hands clasped behind his back, yellow cuffs peeking out of a brown sport coat. "You look like the friggin' bride of Frankenstein, Rackley."

"You look like Erik Estrada's ginzo uncle."

Tannino laughed, and then his smile faded back into his game face. "We couldn't get Squeaky Fromme or the other two mutts in custody to flip on Betters. They said the kidnapping was their idea. Inspiration struck when they saw you on the road."

"Of course. Betters works like that. Whatever you do, it's always your idea."

"Now they're lawyered up, want to plead guilty, jump on the grenade for Betters." Tannino ran a hand through his resilient salt-and-pepper bouffant. "You're sure you never overheard them mention reporting to Betters?"

"Never even spoke his name."

"The perfect cutout crew. They land in shit, Betters has total deniability. He doesn't give a damn about cutting them loose, and they're happy to brave the clink for him."

"Is Winston worried about making his case?"

"Stanley John's murder we can't really hang on anyone, since Randall Kane was the trigger man, and he's currently tied up in Hefty bags. But the three kidnappers we've got by the nuts. You'll need to testify, of course. But for Betters the kidnapping's pretty thin."

"We can get him on the mail charges, right? Marshal?"

"I'm sorry, son, but Win says we can't use the burned mail for a warrant."

"What?" Tim shoved himself up in bed, the sharp pain in his ribs making him groan.

Tannino was at his side, easing him back down. "You couldn't identify the mail from outside the shed. You had to open the door to make a positive ID, and that mires us in 'reasonable expectation of privacy' again." Tannino raised a hand before Tim could protest. "However. Win *is* supporting a warrant based on your kidnapping. Conspiracy charges should grant us the right to search the ranch for communications from Betters, maybe an evidence trail for the bleach, lye, hatchet, and garbage bags. Once we're up there, we accidentally stumble on additional evidence and move from there. Thomas and Freed get their mitts in those filing cabinets, who knows what they'll turn up."

"We've got to get the girl out."

"We will."

"What kind of time frame are we talking?"

"I can't make any promises, but soon. Listen, Rackley, you've done your job, now let us take it from here."

"What am I supposed to do?"

"Have a muffin and relax." Tannino shot Tim a conspiratorial look, picked up the basket, and dumped it in the trash on his way out.

D ray came back after her shift and made Tim walk a bit. Unsteady on his feet, he had to lean on her heavily. His knee was pretty torn up; he walked in short, wincing steps.

"She probably thinks I abandoned her. Leah."

"She probably thinks you're dead or you're doing what you *are* doing—trying to figure out a way to get to her."

They passed a cheery bald woman pulling an IV pole.

"Was she aware that you found any evidence on the mails?"

"No. I just grabbed her and ran."

"Then she probably still thinks you don't have enough to justify a raid."

"You know they already grilled her about the time she spent with me off the ranch. If she survives that, they're watching her every move. If TD sees a ghost of a suggestion she's in on anything, she'll get her own Dead Link folder." He set down too hard on his right foot and stifled a grunt. "Will was right. She would have been better off in his custody."

Dray's mouth firmed. She shot him a disappointed look but didn't elaborate.

Finally he said, "What?"

"Valiant of you to beat yourself up further, but you know damn well that wasn't your call to make. It was Leah's. Kids become adults, Timothy. That's what happens."

The aching intensified beneath Tim's ribs. "I guess that's something we never had to deal with."

Dray's neck tensed beneath his arm. "Yet."

They limped along at his pathetic pace. His legs wobbled, and Dray tightened her grip across his back.

"Come on. If you make it to the gift shop, I'll buy you a Mars Bar."

It hurt like hell, but it felt liberating to be vertical. His gown was drenched by the time they arrived. Waiting in line, Dray spun the rack, then plucked a greeting card from its perch. "Remember this one? *'A sad, sad day has come, e'er full of many mourners, But your beloved keeps the watch, in heaven's fairest corner.'* Ca-*rist*."

The woman ahead of them shot Dray a glare and scurried off, purchases clutched to her chest.

Walking back took nearly twice as long. Tim had to pause three times to rest.

They sat together watching the blind-split sun creep in wavering lines across the floor. The attending finally dropped in and cleared Tim to go. As Dray helped Tim switch out his knee immobilizer for the brace, the door creaked open.

When Tim saw Winston Smith at Tannino's side, he knew something was wrong.

Winston's face was pale. "The judge didn't find sufficient evidence for a warrant."

"You've got to be kidding me. What the hell do I have to bring you? Video footage of Betters sawing off someone's head?"

"It's a tough situation—"

Tim gestured at his battered body. "No shit."

Dray shifted angrily in her chair, but she restrained herself from saying anything.

Winston eased forward. "I'm with you on this one, Rackley, but the magistrate judge didn't see a nexus between the kidnapping and the ranch. We found a receipt for the bleach, lye, bags, and hatchet in the trunk of the Lexus—they bought all the stuff *after* they left home base. We've got three suspects and three matching confessions. All the evidence was at the scene. There's nothing we need up at the ranch to make the case. We've got zip to tie Betters in, and, given the politics, no judge is gonna be eager to climb out on a limb."

Dray calmly asked, "You wouldn't call that warehouse full of Betters propaganda a *nexus?* It's a twenty-five-fucking-thousand-square-foot nexus."

"It's rented storage space. Stanley John's the one who

picked out the site, signed the agreement, oversaw the operation. It was his gig."

"Thomas and Freed are looking into it further," Tannino said. "The good news is, we froze the warehouse as a crime scene. Which means the video sessions don't ship."

"Peachy." The back of Tim's throat was bitter from the meds. "Maybe you could ding Betters with some late fees at the library, too."

"It's something, Rackley."

"He'll make more tapes."

Tannino scowled, no doubt recalling his niece's credit-card transaction. "It buys us a few days, at least."

"A few days for what?"

Tannino averted his eyes.

Leah was at risk of being reindoctrinated or just killed. TD was roaming his grounds with immunity. Stanley John's absence would put a bump in Program operations for about five minutes before a horde of eager Pros scrabbled forward to compete for the position, and the cottages were full of human fodder to replace Chad, Winona, and Henderson. TD doubtless had hired muscle to replace Randall already.

The Next Generation Colloquium was in seven days. The foundation under TD's rising empire.

Tim batted a bowl of Jell-O off his nightstand. It hit the far wall, spraying green chunks, then hula-ed loudly on the floor. By the time the clatter ceased, his rage had dissipated, leaving him embarrassed and tired. He couldn't remember the last time he'd lost his temper, and putting the hurt on a bowl of lime Jell-O wasn't exactly worth the relapse.

Tannino's hands were raised in surprise.

Tim pinched his eyes, trying to salvage something, anything. The tang of iodine lingered in the room. His ribs gave off a dull throb each time he inhaled.

Tannino and Winston retreated, the door clicking timidly behind them.

Forty-eight

While Dray showered, Tim hobbled around the living
room, focusing on straightening out his right leg to
diminish the limp. His crutches he left leaning against the
coatrack. Gauging by the news briefs cutting in on KCOM's
shock-and-awe Friday-night programming—*Monster Truck
Mash* followed by *Prison Fights Caught on Tape*—press coverage of the kidnapping seemed light, especially compared
to what Tim's past travails had elicited. Tannino had made
sure not to disclose Tim's name, though it was only a matter
of time before it leaked.

Toweling her hair, Dray found him musing over his 18
USC statute book at the kitchen table. The points of her jaw
flexed out. "Stop acting like you have no resources without
the Arrest Response Team standing behind you. Think about
Leah. You can help her without a semiauto in your hands."

"How?"

"Maybe I talk to the sheriff and see if there's any move *he*
can support. Maybe you lean on Chad, make clear that he'll
never regain nirvana now that TD's cut him loose. Maybe
Bear shakes up Phil McCanley, TD's dick at Lowdown,
again. Maybe we let leak to TD that Winona's singing in her
jail cell—he distrusts women to begin with, and it could fuck
with him pretty good if he thinks she's using Program secrets
to barter with the prosecutor." The doorbell rang, and she
moved to answer it, shaking her head. "TD's a creative guy.
We need to come up with creative solutions, not sit here mop-
ing and banging our heads against the same wall."

Using the chair back, Tim pushed himself to his feet and
followed her.

Will waited on the porch, ensconced in a tube of dry air afforded by a black umbrella. He held a briefcase. Emma huddled behind his shoulder.

Tim wasn't sure what to expect until Will's face softened. He said, "Christ," and extended his fingers halfway to Tim as though reaching for something.

The Hennings followed him and Dray in and sat.

Will took in the patches of stained gauze on the floor, the line of prescription bottles on the coffee table. He ran a hand over his face, tugging at the bags beneath his eyes.

"This thing didn't go down like we wanted it to."

"No," Tim said. "It didn't."

"We received a troubling e-mail purporting to be from Leah."

Will removed his laptop from the briefcase, set it on the coffee table, and booted it up. Dray plugged in the modem cord to a phone jack, and he logged on.

Emma kept her face lowered, hands twisting in her lap.

An e-mail popped up from customercare@getwiththe program.com.

> Mom and Dad. Please leave me to make my own decisions. I am fulfilled. If you send another kidnapper after me, I will press charges. Leah.

Tim sat quietly, poking at his interior lip sutures with his tongue.

Will's face contorted, just for an instant, and then he coughed into his fist, regaining control. He looked at Tim, still struggling with his grief. "You gave her a lot. No matter what's happening up there, I have to believe that's doing her some good."

Emma gathered the lapels of her raincoat and said in a distant, almost pensive voice, "Well, she's lost now."

"Don't underestimate our daughter." Will's ready conviction seemed to surprise everyone in the room, including himself. "That e-mail doesn't mean anything. For all we know, TD was breathing over her shoulder when she wrote it."

"You're right." Tim grabbed the laptop and pulled it in front of him, knocking over some prescription bottles. He studied the screen, then clicked through the routing information, the jumble of words and numbers at the bottom of the e-mail. A hyperlink stood out in blue.

Tim caught Dray's eye, excited, and clicked it.

Another screen popped up.

if Tim's alive tell him not to come up here for me. many more protectors. skate's on me almost all the time. i'm working on the website in the mod, have snatches of time alone when skate takes a leak or delivers TD his phone cord. what do you need to get a full force up here? do NOT write back here—send to my hotmail address.

Tim stood up too quickly, sending a jolt of pain through his knee. "We've got to forward this to Tannino and Winston, have the Electronic Surveillance Unit take a spin through it to see if we missed anything. We'll send her a list of the evidence we need."

"How will she get it to you?" Will asked. "It's not like she can fax it out. The phone cords are guarded, and it sounds like she's only alone for minutes at a time."

"And from what you've said, there's no way she'd be left alone even for a minute when the modem's plugged in," Dray said. "If she was, she could easily have sent a private e-mail and erased its trail. The fact that she encoded a hyperlink probably means she prepped it when she was offline, then piggy-backed it in when Skate or someone provided the phone cord."

"And sat watching over her," Will added.

"Then how will she get our response?" Tim asked.

"You can set a computer to autodownload your mail whenever you log on," Dray said. "I do it at the barn sometimes. She could have it saved to a hidden file and read it when she's alone and offline."

"Maybe we e-mail her back, have her hide the evidence somewhere we can pick it up," Tim said.

"They're on her twenty-four/seven," Dray said. "Plus, even under normal circumstances, no one leaves the ranch."

"Say you arranged a rendezvous when everyone's sleeping," Will said. "You could sneak back on the ranch for a hand-off, then come back with a warrant and get her at that point."

"A meet would put her at too much risk." Tim pointed at the screen. "She's clear that I shouldn't go up there."

"Maybe you don't have to." Dray's brow was knitted, the idea still dawning. "Maybe we don't go to her. Maybe we wait for TD to bring her to us."

Tim, Will, and Emma looked at her blankly. Dray was smiling now, excited. "Come on, guys. Get with The Program."

*W*ithin thirty minutes of Tim's call, Winston Smith and Tannino had come up with their wish list. In addition to evidence supporting the host of mail charges—the one sure thing—they wanted any information on the Dead Link files, which now certainly included Tom Altman. Thomas and Freed added numerous financial records they hoped would give them a toehold, and the return e-mail was sent out from Will's computer and phone line by Roger Frisk, one of the ESU deputies. The e-mail included instructions for Dray's plan—where they'd retrieve Leah, what signal she should wait for—as well as suggestions as to how she might smuggle the evidence off the ranch when she left.

When asked to help, Bederman agreed immediately, a devious gleam taking hold in his eyes as Tim and Dray relayed the details.

Tim decided to drop in on Reggie alone. His room was hardly sparkling, but the furniture had emerged and the trash had been cleared out. Clothes remained strewn across the floor, but the carpet was visible in patches and the bed was made. Reggie followed Tim's incredulous stare around the room, trying to restrain a proud grin.

Tim's limp and scars didn't seem to register with Reggie until Tim recounted what had gone down. Reggie's face grew gray and tired; Tim was sad to see his levity depart. When Tim asked him to participate, Reggie nodded morosely, and Tim had to ask him again to make sure he understood the request. Only after Tim left did he realize that Reggie's brown paper bag of drugs hadn't been readily apparent.

Aside from a physical-therapy session each morning—an interminable hour in the clutches of a springy gum-smacker named Cindi who persisted in treating him like an osteoporotic centenarian—Tim spent his time with Dray, Reggie, and Bederman, organizing their game plan, and on the phone with the marshal and Winston Smith, running through various contingencies.

Tannino had transferred Tim to disability, a clever move to keep his deputization active. The external stitches came out of Tim's lip on Tuesday, leaving an angry snake of a scab along his chin. He eventually conceded that Cindi's perky instruction was effective; he was getting more ambulatory, though he wouldn't be swing dancing anytime soon.

Still they hadn't heard back from Leah, though Tim had Will checking his e-mail every hour.

Wednesday after his physical therapy, Tim went into Ginny's bare room to stretch. As he sat on the carpet, leaning forward over his purple knee to bring a burn to his hamstring, it struck him that he was tired of holding the room in fearful reverence.

The yellow-and-pink wallpaper was sun-faded, the top corner of one strip lifted away from the wall. He walked over, reached up, and smoothed the thumb-size tab back into place. Stubbornly, it sagged away again. It would need regluing.

An urge overtook him, and he grasped it and ripped. The band of paper swooped from his hand to the wall like the train of a dress. He stared at the messy diagonal tear, expecting to be overcome by remorse or sorrow, but he felt only a bizarre giddiness.

He hobbled around, snatching away great strips, watching the painted flowers puddle at his feet. Popping a handful of Advil to appease the ache in his knee and sides, he retrieved his wide-blade scraper and a platform ladder and stripped the gummy residual down to the drywall.

When he was done, he washed out the fake highlights in his hair, shaved the remnants of his goatee, put on Levi's and a white T-shirt, and studied himself in the mirror. His colored contacts he'd left behind at the hospital. His eyebrows and part had grown back. The scab on his chin had resolved, leaving behind a glossy seam.

Aside from the swelling that broadened his nose, he looked less like Tom Altman, more like himself.

He was waiting outside, listening to the wind through the white oak, when Dray came to pick him up for the ultrasound.

L eah's response came in that night. Will reached Tim at Bederman's to report that another e-mail within an e-mail had arrived. It contained three words:

See you there.

Forty-nine

T he service elevator dinged open, and Tim and Reggie stepped forth. A bulky Protector guarded the waitstaff door, barrel chest stretching the seams of his blue polo.

"Hey, pal, you're not allowed back here."

Having removed the old disguise elements and—with Pete Krindon's help—added a few new ones, Tim wasn't immediately recognizable as Tom Altman. His recut hair, clean shave, and green-tinted contacts lent him a different appearance from afar—and his facial swelling helped, too—but he was still glad to be confronting a new hire. He snapped his fingers, halting the Protector's approach. "You'd better step to and Get with The Program, my friend, unless you want to reserve a spot for yourself on Victim Row. Now, where's Skate Daniels? I thought this was his post."

"I . . . uh . . . the Teacher wanted him up at the ranch to keep an eye out after all the . . . uh, mix-ups this week." He bobbed his head uncertainly, his tone hesitant but respectful. "Um, who are you again?"

Tim placed a hand on the guy's chest, steering him aside. "I'm the head of East Coast Expansion, and this is my assistant. You question me again, I'll have you fired. Got it?"

An openmouthed nod.

"Step aside."

Reggie at his back, Tim shoved through the doors into the ballroom proper, the sudden heat making his lips stick to his teeth. Reggie kept his head ducked so none of the venerable Pros would recognize him.

They'd sent Dray and Bederman through the official channels, since they ran no risk of being identified. They'd made false reservations in advance; Will had gladly paid their $2,000 entry fees.

The partition between Hearspace and Actspace had been removed to accommodate the wider horseshoe, composed of close to a thousand chairs. Bear had brought them word of this after managing his way in last night posing as a building inspector. The altered floor plan was to their advantage—it would be easier to create diversions during Actspace drills, and now they could do so with Prospace in sight.

Neos grazed on punch and cookies at the back, eyes bleary and manic at once, like those of depleted gamblers hanging on for a last good hand. The blue-shirts moved through them, offering refills and pawing affectionately at arms as the rumbly, incomprehensible sound of chanting monks spilled from hidden speakers.

Two more knockdown men guarded the black curtain leading to Prospace—as Tim had anticipated, there'd be no sneaking backstage to Leah during Guy-Med. Three more Protectors prowled through the audience. They wore blue shirts to blend in, but they were scruffier and bulkier than the other Pros, easy to pick out. One of them would likely move to Randall's old post at the main exit once the festivities commenced, and Tim guessed the others would take up positions on either side of the stage.

Tim spotted Bederman and Dray as they walked through the entrance from the landing. He and Dray made eye contact, exchanged an across-the-room nod.

Reggie exhaled in a hiss as the drum started its build, and the Pros whipped the Neos into a frenzy, everyone scrambling for the horseshoe.

Dray and Tim arrived at one side of the U at the same time, securing two seats side by side. They did not acknowledge each other. Bederman and Reggie did the same across the way. Dray mopped at her forehead, her hair already darkening at the edges with sweat. The woman beside her slumped over, already spent from the heat and the spiked punch, and Dray shouldered her back upright like an irritable economy-classer on a commuter flight.

Tim tried to locate the rest of his incoming class—Don Stanford and Jason Struthers were on the far side of the horseshoe, proudly displaying blue polos. Wendy slouched in her chair, working a thumbnail between her teeth. He did not see Shanna.

Janie took the stage alone—no Stanley John to play Sonny to her Cher—and began recounting the rules. Her voice trembled slightly at first, but she gained confidence as soon as she started rattling off the conditions.

Dray made sounds of annoyance as she listened, eliciting a few stares.

"Everyone strong enough to pledge not to leave *no matter what,* stand up," Janie said chirpily.

A grand rustling as almost everyone rose, including Dray, Bederman, and Reggie.

Tim remained seated. The lights dimmed, and the spotlight, clumsier than Tim remembered, sought one dissenter after another. Janie harassed them until they either rose or exited. At last she turned her focus on Tim, his new look holding up from the distance. "And how about you? What excuse making are you going to use to justify undercutting your growth here today?"

He'd almost forgotten the hardwired embarrassment of sitting while everyone else stood, the shame of being on the receiving end of hundreds of glares.

Even shouted, his answer sounded meager in comparison to her miked preemptive strike. "From what I've seen, I'm not sure if I like The Program yet. If I decide that I don't like what's going on here, I'm leaving. Thank you for having me here today."

Janie sneered, her lipsticked mouth parting to issue a prepackaged reply.

Tim stood up abruptly and began clapping. Across the horseshoe, Reggie and Bederman joined in, and then the other Neos, confused, were clapping, drowning Janie out.

When the applause died down, Tim was standing in conformity with everyone else, short-circuiting Janie's usual recourse. She reddened and continued with the next rule. "Okay, if you came here with someone else, please change your seat now."

The Pros paid close attention, double-checking some of the Neos to make sure they hadn't cheated. Tim and Dray waited through the seat shuffling, as did Reggie and Bederman.

Janie regained her confidence swiftly, finished her introduction, and had them do some hand-holding and group breathing. Then a few Pros jogged around the edge of the chairs and counted them out into groups. Dray gave Tim's hand a squeeze and broke off with Janie, her leader.

The Program's lantern-jawed attorney, Sean, a thirty-something bundle of grating vigor, ran Tim's group. He'd been particularly insidious at the retreat, a sly elicitor of signatures on dotted lines.

"Now, everyone needs to circle up and—"

"Excuse me," Tim said.

"Yes?"

"I'd heard some rumors that you guys practice deceitful methods—"

"That's ridiculous. *Ridiculous*. This is an honest, forthcoming organization."

"—and that you could be pretty abusive on some of the Neos."

"I don't know who you've been talking to, but they're obviously pretty weakness-oriented."

A few of the others in Tim's group bristled nervously. A Neo with a supplemented hairline chimed in, "Sounds like he's already taking a victim posture, Sean."

"That's absolutely right. Now, are you done wasting everyone's time on your personal issues?"

"Just wanted to make sure."

They coughed up their cell phones and watches. Sean produced a stack of forms and led them through writing their individual Programs.

When it came Tim's turn, he announced, "My Program is: I participate in activities that give me self-esteem, and I have the courage to decline to participate in those activities that do not."

Bederman had come up with the wording in the Blazer on the way over, eliciting a high five from Reggie.

Sean grimaced. "That's not a good Program. I think we should change it to: I experience self-esteem as I participate in the activities here today."

"No thanks."

"I *really* think—"

"Hey," a quiet, older man in a button-up said, "it's his Program. Let him write what he wants. That's the whole point of this thing, isn't it?"

After a hushed consultation with two roaming Pros and growing dissent in the ranks, Sean grudgingly moved on. They finished the recitation of their Programs, and Sean took them through a few sharing exercises before announcing with great reverence that they were ready for their first game: Lifeboat.

Within minutes Tim and his group members were gathered on the carpet, arguing their right to one of five spaces on a lifeboat as their imaginary ship went down. Sean alone commanded a chair. He perched above them, countenancing their pleading with a stately air.

All through Actspace, Neos from other groups groveled on the floor, the seated Pros rising above them.

An obese black woman in Tim's group was pleading, "My two baby boys already lost a father. If I'm gone, they'd have no one to take care of them."

"Sorry," Sean said. "I don't buy it. You sound like you want to be around for your kids, but you said nothing about *you*. Why should *you* live? Why should *you* get a space over these twenty people?"

Across the ballroom stirred a minor commotion as Bederman addressed his group with great animation. In the far corner, Reggie was arguing vehemently with his leader, those on the carpet around him growing visibly unnerved. Neither of them was able to draw a Protector from his post; no doubt TD had instructed his new muscle to leave the psychological maneuvering to the Pros.

"You're not even sitting up straight," one of Tim's group members added. "It doesn't seem like you really *want* it."

The black woman started to cry. A roaming Pro rested a hand on Sean's shoulder and puffed out his cheeks to imitate her fatness, drawing scattered laughter.

"What's this one crying about?"

"There's no one to take care of my boys," the woman wailed, sweat and tears moistening her dark face. She was shivering against the blasts of air-conditioning.

"You can't even think of a single reason why you should live. I bet you only *had* kids to give meaning to your pathetic life."

"You're a selfish parent!" someone cried out. "What do you have to offer your kids anyway?"

"Get your own life," a wild-haired woman in a fluttery blouse hissed. "Quit sucking your kids dry."

Sean said to the black woman, "You just committed suicide with that answer, Charlena. Lie down on the floor. *Down on the floor.* Be still. You're drowned. Next."

And so it went.

When the group's focus turned to Tim, he said, "This is stupid. If the boat's going down, we're not gonna have all this time to argue about a lifeboat."

"Afraid to answer the question, Tim?"

"No. I just think this game is idiotic. Why don't you pick something that makes sense instead of berating everyone?"

Sean directed an imploring look at one of the roaming Pros, who started toward them but got tied up in another dispute, not surprisingly, in Dray's group.

Sean glared at Tim, stalling for time. He adopted a singsong voice. "Our friend is making his usual excuses here, guys. Is he On Program? Guys?"

"Yes." Charlena propped herself up on her elbows. "He is, actually. He said he wouldn't do any activities bad for his self-esteem. I wish I'd written *that* damn Program."

"*You lie down.* You're *drowned,* Charlena. Do I have to remind you that you committed suicide?"

"What you're trying to get us to say is that we'd step on *anybody* to get a space on that lifeboat," Tim said. "That there's just us, and we decide our reality, and our reality should be power. So here's my reality: How about I kick you in the fucking head, *Sean,* to get on that lifeboat?" When he stood up, he drew the attention of both Protectors guarding the Prospace entrance, but neither started toward him as he'd hoped. "Who the hell are you to tell everyone that caring about anyone is committing suicide? How about I pull you off your throne and I decide *you* committed suicide by being such an asshole? Then the rest of us can take our turns treading water around the lifeboat so no one gets too tired, and we're all nice and safe when the rescue boat comes. How about that, Sean?"

"I vote him," Charlena called out. She covered her mouth comically when she remembered she was supposed to be drowned, but the others were already chorusing their approval.

"He's a strong leader. He tells it like it is."

"I want *him* on the lifeboat."

A plastic smile spread itself across Sean's face, but it did not touch his eyes. "Very good, Tim. You made it aboard."

Tim eased himself back down to the carpet, favoring his right leg. The others pounded his back and congratulated him.

The roaming Pro whom Sean had signaled finally extricated himself from Dray's group and ran over, huffy and red-faced. "Group Five needs an extra person. I need to switch you—"

"No thanks," Tim said. "I experience this group as growth-oriented, so I'm staying here."

Sean cleared his throat. "I think maybe you could benefit from—"

"Please, Sean. No negativity." Tim smiled inanely. "We're all happy with me staying, right guys?"

Rousing applause overpowered Sean's objections. He finally nodded curtly at the other Pro, who shrugged and moved on.

The chanting monks blared, and they all scrambled for their seats in the darkness. Dray was breathing hard, exhilarated. "I'm taking that blond bitch *apart.*"

The trumpets sang, and then TD glowed into sight onstage like a Vegas performer.

"My name is Terrance Donald Betters, and I'm here to talk to you about your *life.*"

The Pros shouted, "*Hi, TD!*"

"Our world, our society, is filled with *victims*. This is America. Nothing bad's supposed to happen to us. Someone else is always responsible. Someone *else*. Granny dies of old age? Sue the hospital. Twist your ankle in a pothole? Sue the city. Get hurt fucking off on the job? Worker's Comp. Economy tanking? Go to war. Get pregnant? Have an abortion. Decide to carry it to term? Give it up for adoption or, hey, just go on welfare. Last year a burglar fell through a skylight on a building that wasn't to code, sued the company he was robbing, and *won!*"

Neos began picking up the Pros' cues, nodding and shouting agreement.

"Unemployed? Blame affirmative action. Poor and black? The man's holding you down. We can't possibly handle *our own messes*. We can't possibly forge *our own solutions*. People have no accountability, and it's sickening."

"*Excuse me!*" Reggie was standing on his chair, waving his arms.

TD stopped, jaw sagging.

"Why are you changing the temperature in the room?"

TD's eyes burned with a cold rage. He signaled for the lights to come up. "Okay. You've just stopped the entire colloquium." He folded his arms. "Are you happy with yourself? You agreed to no interruptions."

"Can you answer my question, please?"

"Hey, everybody, does it sound like this guy is Off Program? How do you feel about his ruining your—"

"*Answer the fucking question!*" Dray shouted.

TD's head pulled back. "Of course we're not altering the temperature."

"I brought a thermometer!" Reggie shouted, withdrawing it from his jacket pocket. "The temperature in this room has gone from seventy-four degrees to ninety-one degrees to—"

TD shaded his eyes, glaring at Reggie. "I know you. You're one of The Program's few rejects." One of the Protectors by the stage caught TD's eye. TD gave a tiny head shake and turned back to the crowd. "Now and then, people can't Get with The Program. They come apart the minute they're held accountable for—"

"I'd like to point out that rapidly altering the temperature is an unethical mind-control tactic!" Reggie shouted.

"He's a loser!" one of the Pros shouted.

And another—"Sit down and shut up! We want to get back to Growth."

"I think you've heard your answer, my disgruntled friend," TD said. "People are here to grow, not to complain. Keep your negativity to yourself so we can move on. What do you say, folks? What do you say?"

The Pros picked up TD's clapping, and some Neos joined in.

The lights faded again. TD adjusted his head mike, walking across the front of the dais, his profile cut from the rising footlights. "You think in the old days people had Claritin for *allergies,* antibiotics for *infections,* Band-Aids for *scrapes?* Hell no. In the old days, you got an infected tooth, you knocked it out with a rock. We've medicated ourselves into fragility."

Tim shouted out, "Why don't you disclose to everyone that you've had three felony convictions?"

Pros from all around the horseshoe shushed Tim severely. TD paused, glaring out at the darkness, then chose to continue. It took him a few moments to find his cadence again. "You are all extremely privileged to be attending the *original* Next Generation Colloquium. Today is the template for The Program's future, the launching pad for the biggest movement society has ever seen. From here we reach out to other states, to thousands of new people. And you should all be proud that you're part of this. You *stepped up to the plate.* You decided to *seize control of your reality.*"

"So why are you altering our reality by putting relaxation supplements and manufactured hormones in the punch and cookies?" Dray yelled.

About twenty blue-shirts screamed at her to shut up.

Near the back someone shouted out, "What'd you put in our food?"

TD's face had taken on a bit of a shine in the lights. A single bead of sweat emerged from one of his sideburns. "Listen"—a pronounced swallow—"you can follow The Program and *maximize* . . . or you can stay mired in your Old Programming and be *victimized*." He strolled to stage right, his step resuming its bounce. "I can see that this group is all *knotted up* with *control*. You've got to *let go* if you want to *grow*. Now I'd like everybody to lie on the floor. That's it." On cue the heat began to blow. "We're going to do a guided meditation that will help us visualize our—"

Bederman rose abruptly. "Are you licensed to administer hypnosis in the state of California?"

Bederman's group leader crawled over and tugged at his pants to get him to lie down, but he slapped away her hand.

TD's jaw flexed. "We're not practicing hypnosis here. We're simply meditating."

Bederman cupped his hands around his mouth, projecting his voice. "Guided meditation is a form of hypnosis. Everyone in this room should know that."

TD's mike-enhanced voice overpowered Bederman's protests. "Your scare tactics aren't working on anyone here. All these people came for a reason. They've chosen *growth*. They can make their own decisions without your interference." The applause was scarcer this time around. "Now we're going to focus on our breathing and take a visit to our childhood."

"I've already been to my childhood!" the old guy in Tim's group shouted out, and a handful of people laughed.

TD's voice grew strained. "Clear your mind. This is your time."

"I'm not comfortable doing this," Tim shouted. "I'd like to refrain from this portion of The Program. Anyone who's not comfortable should know—"

"Lights up!" TD screamed. *"Him.* Out. He's obstructing all progress."

The muscle-bound thug whom Tim had brushed aside by the service elevator appeared at Tim's side. He gripped Tim's arms and hoisted him up, but Tim yanked himself free. The Protector who'd shot TD the inquisitive look earlier jogged over from the stage.

The others in Tim's group clamored around them. "Leave him alone."

The guy grabbed Tim again, and a group mobbed around them, moving with a sluggish, rhythmic energy.

"Get that victim out of here, Deano!" Sean yelled.

The air was damp and palpable, tinged with the smell of sweat and activated deodorant. Others were shouting from all around the horseshoe.

"This is bullshit! He's the only one telling the truth around here."

"He's Off Program. He's interrupting my process!"

TD's voice boomed through the speakers. "Sorry, my friend, but this is a victim-free zone. You'll have to take your negativity elsewhere."

Deano seized Tim, and Tim struck him once, hard, a right cross on the jaw. Deano staggered back and sat down on the floor.

Silence fell across Hearspace. The other Protector shook Dray's hands off his arm. Deano rubbed his jaw in disbelief.

Tim turned around to face TD across the crowd. "Rule Number Two: No leaving. No matter what."

TD seemed to weigh the costs of a physical display, his eyes taking note of the Protectors at their various posts. He fluttered a hand, and the lights went out. A brilliant flare lit him angelically onstage; a second, smaller spotlight fell over Tim. The lighting seemed more mechanical—Leah had plenty of reasons to be distracted right now.

"Since it's *so important* that your *needs* and *fears* are addressed, even to the *detriment* of *all these people,* I'm gonna give you the attention you crave." TD snapped his fingers, and, after a brief delay, a fall of light illuminated the row of empty chairs on the dais behind him. "I have a seat reserved for you right here on Victim Row. And guess what, Mr. Negativity? You get to be the *only one* up here. You can have *all my attention* so these people can see what a *victim* is truly made of, and then *maybe,* just *maybe,* we can move ahead with The Program. How does that sound? What's the matter? More objections?"

Tim squinted from his cylinder of light, absorbing the glowing chairs onstage, the silent rage emanating from dozens of unseen lackeys, the breath-held anticipation of the crowd.

"Do yourself a favor and sit back down." TD snickered and turned away. "Let's get on with The Program."

Tim's footsteps echoed off the ceiling. The spotlight followed him to the dais. The air breezing around him grew so cold his breath misted.

TD swiveled, watching Tim's approach over a shoulder.

Tim took the dais, his spotlight dissolving in the brightness, and sat in the middle chair. TD circled him appraisingly, mouth brushing the mike, not yet taking in Tim's face.

"Okay, so here's the guy who has it *all figured out.* Let's hear why you don't want to change."

"I'm not comfortable with—"

"You're not *comfortable,* huh? No one ever grew by being *comfortable.* The aim of The Program isn't to make you feel *comfortable.* It's to make you *grow.* It's to make you—" TD touched his fingertips to his ear.

"Get with The Program." It seemed mostly the Pros responded.

"What's he got to do?"

A more hearty chorus this time. "*Get with The Program.*"

"Can I finish speaking, please?"

"No one's stopping you, champ, despite your *whining* and *complaining* that you're being interrupted." Still facing the crowd, TD exaggerated a pout, his lower lip pushing out, curling the soul patch. "Maybe it's hard for you to speak because *everyone around you* is tired of your having all the answers. Maybe you need to shut up and learn something for once instead of *complaining.* Instead of *having things your way.*"

"I'm not comfortable with how you're treating everyone in this room. We've been lied to, we've been abused—"

Again the mike overpowered Tim's voice. "If you don't want to *change,* go back to your miserable life. We made that clear to everyone at the outset. We were right up front with it. No small type. If you think you have *everything figured out,* obviously you've got *nothing left to learn.* The Program works for those who commit to it. Go on. If your life is perfect, walk on out of here."

"So I have to be perfect to object to how I'm being treated?" Tim's voice was growing hoarse competing with the mike.

"No. You just have to keep your word. Sean, where's his Program? I'd like to see his Program."

In the shadows Sean was waving his arms before his chest, trying to warn TD off.

"What do you say, folks?" TD boomed. "Should we find out what kind of *know-it-all* we have here on Victim Row?"

Sean's objections were lost in the roar of the crowd.

"I said bring me his Program. *Now.*"

Sean trudged forward, bearing the form. TD hurried to the edge of the dais and snatched it from Sean's reluctant hand. "So"—a glance to the sheet—"*Tim.* Is this how you live your life? Making promises and *breaking them?* Going *back on your word?* No wonder you're *unhappy.* It says right here . . ."

TD raised the paper, tapping it knowingly with a bent finger. The Pros clamored happily. He read, " 'My Program is: I participate in activities that give me . . .' "

His lips moved soundlessly as he scanned ahead, his face reddening.

His eyes flicked up, cold with fury.

Reggie's voice from the darkness. "What's it say?"

Then Dray's—*"Read it!"*

Discordant shouts broke from the audience, voices Tim didn't recognize. The crowd was divided, threatening to slip entirely from TD's grasp.

TD seemed to cast about for his next aphorism, and then a smile slid across his face, covering the uncertainty. "You have a problem with authority. Especially when it's right."

"No, you have a problem with authority because you're abusing yours."

"I bet people *hate* being around you." TD drew near to Tim, looking him squarely in the face for the first time, noting the bruises. "You look beat up. I bet you piss people off. I bet the people in your world get so frustrated with you that they have to resort to physical—"

TD's pupils contracted, sharp with sudden recognition. A gasp jerked his chest.

Tim rose and twisted the mike from TD's head. TD was too stunned to react.

The Protectors bridled uncomfortably, waiting for a signal from TD.

Tim held the black bud before his mouth. "I'm here because I believe that this is a dangerous, unethical group that utilizes methods of mind control. I was told by my group leader that The Program was honest, forthcoming, and nonabusive. Well, they went Off Program with me, so I'm going Off Program with them and walking away."

A few people shouted out, then a few more, the noise growing rapidly until the ballroom seemed to vibrate with protests.

"What'd they put in our food?"

"Will someone please tell me why we have to be here for twenty-three hours?"

"Turn the lights on! Turn the goddamned lights on right now!"

Tim's voice boomed through the mike. "Turn on the lights, please."

Neos and Pros alike squinted in the sudden brightness like cavemen emerging into daylight. Most of the Pros looked rattled, even worse than the Neos.

All hell had broken loose in the auditorium.

"I want my money back."

"It's fucking hot in here!"

"What the hell kind of scam is this anyway?"

Tim dropped the mike at TD's feet.

TD gathered his arrogance about him like armor. "You think you've won something here?" He gestured at the pandemonium below. "A hiccup. I can replenish my human resources with two weeks and a soapbox. And when I do, you'll be sorry you *ever* tangled with me."

Tim leaned in until he could see the light freckles scattered across TD's face. "We're not done yet."

The audience had swept away the thugs guarding the exits. The Protectors by the stage were engaged in crowd control, but two at the Prospace entrance stood firm, though they looked eager to join the fray.

Tim rode a rush of people away from the stage. Dray and Janie were up in each other's faces, yelling like a baseball coach and an umpire squaring off over a bad call. Dray spotted Tim coming and peeled out toward Prospace.

She reached the Protectors before Tim, feigning panic. "A big fight just broke out on the landing!" she shouted over the din.

Both guys looked for TD, but he'd vanished into a mob of blue-shirts at the foot of the stage.

Bederman arrived, winded. "The Pros at the check-in desk sent me to get help. A brawl just broke out."

The Protectors forged off through the scattering crowd.

Tim shoved through the curtain into Prospace. Six blue-shirts were furiously packing up. Facing away, Leah was bent over the sound board, desperately working the dials, her hand covering her earpiece to try to hear what was going on. Tim called out once, his voice lost in the commotion, then he grabbed her shoulder and spun her, her hair flying and settling around the wrong face.

Shanna.

"Where's—" He caught himself in time, then peered around. No sign of Leah—that explained the bad lighting during the theatrics. Had she been caught searching for evidence? Was she dead? Had she changed her mind?

Shanna looked at him, squinting to see through the disguise. "Tom?"

Dray and Reggie fanned out, shoving off approaching Pros and checking behind the crates and wardrobes. Bederman shot out the emergency exit but came back shaking his head.

Dray said loudly, "TD's not back here."

Tim picked up the protective charade. "We'll get him in the lobby."

They stormed out. Sweat trickled down Tim's sides as they crossed the ballroom, stepping out onto the landing. Demanding their money back, furious participants mobbed the five frazzled blue-shirts working the cash boxes.

Janie was dressing down one of the Protectors for manhandling a Neo. "We can't afford that kind of behavior, *especially* now."

Lorraine and a cluster of group leaders sat shocked by the elevators, weeping as if someone had pulled into their hamlet on a Harley and told them God was dead.

"It's not possible," she murmured. "It's not possible."

Tim and Dray spilled down the stairs with the stream of deserters. Outside, Pros milled around, lost but seeking contact, the bizarre scene like the parking-lot prelude to an AA meeting. Blue polos rained down like graduation caps. Wendy tugged hers off and flung it, hopping up and down in her undershirt with a few other Pros.

Bederman and Reggie caught up to Tim and Dray, and they circled to the rear lot and climbed into the Blazer. Janie, Sean, and a few diehards were shouting for the Pros to get ready to leave, but the two Program buses remained largely empty.

Tim fumbled Dray's phone out of the glove box—she'd wisely left it behind—and dialed Will's number.

"Where the hell have you been?" Will greeted him. "I left you twenty fucking messages."

"They made me surrender my phone like last time," Tim said. "We didn't get her. She wasn't there."

"I *know*. I got an e-mail from her. She's in trouble."

As Dray pulled out, TD emerged from the fire exit, shirt untucked. His perfect posture had eroded; he stood stooped, shoulders wilted.

Reggie rolled down the window as they passed and extended his middle finger.

"Marco's en route," Will said. "Get here as fast as you can."

TD's eyes found Tim in the passenger seat. The Blazer veered around a celebratory huddle of liberated Pros. TD smoothed his shirttails back into his pants, his shoulders pulling square, and watched with a cool, dead stare until they turned the corner.

Fifty

*T*he Blazer pulled through the Hidden Hills gate right behind Tannino's Bronco, the two vehicles caravanning to the house. High noon blazed off the hood of the Blazer, the temperature climbing toward ninety. L.A. summers came on fast and hard, sometimes overnight.

Tannino shook his head as Tim and Dray approached him on the walk—he didn't know anything yet. He looked past them at Bederman and Reggie and said, "Wait out here, please, until we know what's going on."

Rooch opened the door before they could knock and led

them in. A cast encasing his arm to the biceps, Doug offered Tim a peacemaking head flick of a greeting. From deep in the house, the muffled sound of Emma's crying overlapped with the baby's screams.

Will sat cocked back in his mesh chair, working his cheek with the cap of a pen. His eyes stayed on the computer monitor as they entered.

They circled behind him. His e-mail account was up on the screen, three messages from customercare@getwiththe-program.com occupying the in-box. They'd each come with an attachment, judging from the already-downloaded icons on the desktop—two jpeg photos and an mpeg video clip.

Tim's head buzzed, an ache cramping the temples. Judging from the look on Will's face, he did not want to know what the e-mails held.

Will double-clicked on the first jpeg. A photo appeared, resolving slowly in several waves. The potbellied stove in Randall and Skate's shed, the loading door open to reveal burned fragments of mail amid mounds of ash. Fluorescent yellow scraps from Tannino's mailing stood out against the soot. Tannino tapped the screen eagerly, indicating them. "This establishes time frame."

The second jpeg showed the shed from outside, TD's cottage in the backdrop.

Tim's hands were shaking with excitement.

Tannino flipped open his phone.

"Wait." Will still did not look up at them.

He clicked the mpeg. The little clock icon seemed to blink interminably as the segment loaded. The image popped up, Leah hunched in front of the computer in the mod, staring into the QuickCam mounted atop the monitor. The glow from the screen lit the room a pale blue. One of the file drawers to her right sat open. Over her shoulder the ceiling was barely visible and the dark, offset pane of the skylight.

The time stamp on the e-mail said 4:41 A.M.

Just before the colloquium had begun, when TD and the

other Pros were heading down to the Radisson. Tim wondered how in hell she'd managed to get her hands on a telephone cord to send out the e-mails.

She spoke with hushed urgency. "I couldn't get enough time alone to get done what I needed to, so I screwed up the Web site launch to make TD ground me from the colloquium. I'm sorry I couldn't get word to you, but I figured it was worth the risk to get more time up here with most everyone gone. Will, you should have downloaded two digital photos by now." She glanced nervously behind her, though the mod was empty. "And show Tim this, too." She held up a piece of paper.

Tannino said, "Pause that."

Will froze and enlarged the image. TD's letterheaded memo became clear.

1. *Mail is to be picked up at the P.O. box every two days.*
2. *Mail should be delivered to the Teacher's cottage and set inside the front door to the right.*
3. *When the Teacher is done sorting through it, he will place it to the left of the door.*
4. *Mail is to be picked up and disposed of in the stove in the shed.*
5. *Mail should never be opened by anyone other than the Teacher.*

The list continued, thirteen points in all, punctuated by TD's flowery signature.

"Holy Mary." Tannino flipped open his phone and started punching numbers. "There's our hook. They'll be renting his ass in Men's Central by the end of the week."

Dray kept her eyes on Will. "What's the problem?"

Will's hand slid over and clicked the mouse again, unfreezing the mpeg.

Leah hopped up and returned the memo to its place, sliding the file drawer quietly closed. She came back over and leaned in front of the QuickCam. "I found"—she swallowed hard—

"I found a letter you wrote me, Will, scanned into the computer." Her eyes moistened. "I wanted you to know I read it. TD stole it just to pervert the personal parts, use them against me." Her tone hardened. "I have more information for Tim, but nothing I could send out fast, so I figured I'd get you what was concrete and fill you in on the rest when you get here. Now, don't worry. I erased the digital photos and the e-mails I sent. I even programmed this one to delete as soon as it's sent."

Dray gasped, which she rarely did. Tim turned to her in surprise, but she pointed at the screen.

In the background the faint reflected light on the doorknob behind Leah began to shift. The door eased open, and a dark, bulky figure slid into the room. Leah remained leaning forward, oblivious.

The shadow inched toward her, a fall of light unmasking an edge of Skate's leering face. He took another silent step forward as Leah smiled into the mini camera.

"I'm perfectly safe."

She reached for where the mouse would be, and the video went to black.

Fifty-one

While Tim went out of his mind with impatience, Winston reviewed and reworded the affidavits that Tim had drafted while bouncing in the passenger seat of Tannino's Bronco on the way over. They caught the magistrate judge, a white-haired fixture of the court named Judith Seitel, on the bench; she considered Tannino's mad gesticulations in the back of the gallery with mild amusement before signaling them to wait for her outside chambers until she could break away.

Tim, Dray, Tannino, and Winston Smith sat like school-children, lined on a wooden bench in the courthouse corridor. Their cell phones chirped every few seconds like angry insects. To ensure that the operation would be locked and loaded by the time they arrived at the pre-step-off point with search and arrest warrants in hand, Tannino alternated calls between Miller, who'd activated the ART squad, and the station captain at La Crescenta, whose sheriff's deputies serviced Sylmar.

It was already after three o'clock—every minute passed with kidney-stone agony. Tim tried to keep his mind off what was being done to Leah right now as they waited in the air-conditioned hallway. If she was still alive.

Winston flipped through the search-warrant affidavit, reviewing it a final time. "You'll only be authorized to search the shed, Betters's cottage, and the modular office where the memo was stored and the mail scanned—the areas relevant to mail destruction and theft."

"We've got to be able to look for Leah, too," Tim said.

Winston nodded sagely. "Given this is an armed camp, known members of which we've already charged with kidnapping a federal officer, you can take extra precautions to assure your safety. It might be prudent and reasonable to move cottage to cottage to neutralize potential threats."

"Can we seize the computer in the mod?"

"We have to find something incriminating on it first. The warrant should clear you to click around, look for mail-related evidence, like the scanned stolen letter Leah mentioned. Get in, get something concrete, then you can take it into evidence and spend more time with it in the lab." He winked. "Then we can get into the Dead Link files we don't yet know are stored on the hard drive. Let's hope they put out for us."

Tannino nodded at Tim. "We'll bring Frisk from ESU in case he has to do some hacking."

Tim checked his watch again.

"I hate to be the one to say it," Dray said, "but what if she's already dead? I mean, Betters wasn't coming back to the ranch in the best mood after we clusterfucked his colloquium. She might be six feet under in the woods."

Tannino paused from his call, tucking the receiver to his neck. "We need cadaver dogs."

"You can't bring cadaver dogs to investigate destruction of the mails," Winston said. "It doesn't fall under the warrant's scope."

"The mail charges buy us dick at sentencing. I want a body."

"Then you'd better hope you trip over one."

Tim tilted his face into his spread hands, working the angles like a Chinese puzzle box. He pictured Skate and Randall marching Nancy into the woods, her pale hand clutching the shovel that was to bury her corpse. His head snapped up. "We're short a dog."

Tannino said, "Hold on," into the phone and shot Tim an inquisitive stare.

"Precious is injured," Tim continued. "We're short a dog. We ask the sheriff's department to supply one of their own since they're backing us up on the entry."

"Cover your ears, Win," Tannino said.

The AUSA shook his head and trekked down the hall. Tannino nodded for Tim to continue.

"We make sure they supply a patrol dog that's *also* a cadaver dog. Then we make sure it does its scent work in the process of securing the camp."

"Are there double-duty dogs?" Tannino asked. "And handlers who are deputies?"

Dray was already dialing. "They're mostly weekend warriors, but Mac's got a deputy buddy over at Walnut who works Canine, too."

"It's an armed camp," Tannino said. "We *had* to sweep the woods with dogs for our own safety, Your Honor. One of them just happened upon the dead body."

Tim said, "Precisely."

"I always said you should've been a lawyer, Rackley."

"Looks like I'll have plenty of time for a career change."

"This thing goes smooth, you might not have to worry about a career change." Tannino met Tim's puzzled gaze. "We pop Betters, there's gonna be a lot of tail wagging up the chain. Maybe I get my way."

"Let's not get ahead of ourselves. Let's just get Leah."

Trailing her black robes, Judge Seitel turned the corner. She raised a wary eyebrow at Winston as he scrambled to present her the affidavits.

"Let's hope you brought me something I can put my name on this time around, gentlemen. Even an old girl wants to say yes now and again."

Fifty-two

*T*he marshal screeched over on the side of Little Tujunga near the dirt road that twisted up the hills to the ranch. Tim leapt out before the Bronco stopped. Two Expeditions, a rusty Pathfinder, Freed's Porsche, Bear's Ram, and six black-and-whites from the La Crescenta Sheriff's Station crammed the dirt turnoff. More vehicles stretched up the roadside, including the Service's armored personnel carrier, a military peacekeeper they'd dubbed the Pacemaker for all its hours in the shop. Painted black right down to the bulletproof turret, the APC looked like a Humvee on steroids. Tim had requested it over the Beast in case the flooded creek a mile up the road still proved treacherous.

Miller stood with one foot on the running board of the APC, the deputies and geared-up ART members circled around him. Chomper poked at Bear with his snout until he lowered a hand to scratch behind his ears.

Denley was emerging from his wife's teal Saturn and taking a good ribbing for it.

Tim ran over, warrants triumphantly raised over his head, flapping in the wind. Miller snatched them from his hand, squinting to read them in the dusk.

The station captain, a box-headed ex-Marine who went by Duke, glanced over Miller's shoulder. "What's the fire? We could've served these tomorrow."

"Leah Henning moled out the evidence for the warrants." Tim held up Leah's graduation photo, the one from Will's wallet, and the men handed it around the circle. "She got caught."

Duke took note of his expression, snapped his chin down in a nod. "Right."

"You see this girl, you bring her to me. Got it?"

Bear tossed Tim a vest, and he zipped it over his T-shirt as he introduced himself to the sheriff's deputies. Owen B. Rutherford nodded at him severely from the back. Though Tim had alerted him largely as a courtesy and he'd have to wait back at the staging point with Dray and Tannino, Rutherford was fully decked out—raid jacket, shotgun, shoulder-slung MP5, Beretta, gold-and-blue postal inspector badge dangling from a chain around his neck. Mail defilers beware.

Tannino jogged over, Dray at his heels, then assessed the crew.

Miller glanced at his watch. "Thomas is en route."

Duke said, "The secondary is up, but we can't get airtight around the rear boundary given the terrain. We'd like to get a few more units positioned—"

"We don't have time," Tim said.

Duke looked at Miller, and Miller shrugged.

The Lincoln Navigator skidded up, and Will, Rooch, and Doug hopped out. Tannino snapped his fingers for them to stay put away from the briefing area.

Miller jerked his head at the Navigator. "Who bought the senator's boyfriend front-row tickets?"

"He did," Tannino said. "Don't worry—I'll babysit him at the staging point."

Tim's lip tingled along the scar, an itch too deep to scratch. "Where's the dog?"

A soft-voiced deputy with a droopy mustache pointed to a leonine German shepherd gazing forlornly from the passenger window of a Volvo. "That there's Cosmo. She's L.A. Sheriff's and OES cadaver-certified."

Miller tossed the deputy a Racal portable. "Channel forty-eight. Make sure you don't break in if she alerts over a dead squirrel."

The deputy bobbed his head. His name tag announced him as Danner. "Don't you worry 'bout no dead squirrels. Cosmo's like that squinty little bastard from *The Sixth Sense*. She howls, there's a corpse talkin' to her."

A few of the deputies chuckled.

"How many people are up there?" Denley asked.

"Could be seventy, probably less," Tim said. "We busted up their last meeting, so I hope we knocked loose the fence-sitters."

"So what's left are hard-line zealots eager to die for Allah."

"Remember, we're just serving a warrant here. It's our job to make sure this doesn't spin up."

"Tell that to the David Koresh motherfucker," one of the deputies said.

Tannino stuck his head into the circle. "This thing goes Ruby Ridge, I will personally chew off your ass."

The deputy's grin faded.

Miller had ordered some of the deputies to carry less-lethal. Bear handed around the Remington 870s, the clear rounds showing off the stuffed beanbags inside. Maybeck shouldered the big-bore launcher and dug in the APC for pepper-spray canisters.

A county fire ambulance pulled up, red light strobing through the darkening air. Miller gestured at them, and the driver nodded, cutting the lights and idling at the curb. Law-enforcement and emergency-response vehicles crowded Little Tujunga. Drivers were starting to rubberneck.

Duke and his deputies peeled out to shore up the secondary perimeter, leaving behind four units to join the caravan of vehicles to the front gate.

Thomas jogged up the road, ballistic helmet under one arm, waving what looked like a rolled blueprint. "Sorry. I stopped off at the barn to grab the topograph for the ranch."

Miller stretched out the blueprint and squatted over it.

The ART members were heating up, checking shotgun slides, testing the portables, changing out flashlight batteries.

For a moment Tim took it all in—the vehicles jammed along the road, Denley snugging his goggles into place, the grind of steel-plated boots into dirt, the smell of gun oil, the big-barreled shotgun breach-broken over Maybeck's arm, Guerrera tugging on thin black gloves, the splotches of dried sweat staining the tactical vests, Bear thumbing round after round into his magazine.

Tim came out of his reverie, and everyone was staring at him, stacked back three deep, curved in a fat arc around the front of the APC.

He realized that the circle had re-formed around him, that he was standing in the center.

Miller nodded at the unfurled topograph. "Your show, Rack."

*M*aybeck firmed two tempered steel hooks around the bars of the gate, and the APC lurched back. The cable groaned, and then the gate popped free, skidding in the mud. The abandoned guard station seemed a pretty good indication that The Program's ranks had been thinned by the unsuccessful colloquium, but Tim wasn't going to count on it.

The sheriff's deputies lined out across the gap, guarding the staging point, Dray and Tannino holding back with them.

Bearing his various weapons like a downsized Rambo, Rutherford paced ravenously, pausing to flash the ART squad a flight-deck officer's thumbs-up. Waiting between Rooch and Doug far from the deputies' vanguard, Will caught Tim's eye and gave him a serious nod.

Tim and Bear were the first over the fallen gate, the others drawn behind them, stacked in two-man cells with their shoulder weapons low-ready, sweeping up the hill like a force of nature. Tim's badge bounced on his belt. His head buzzed with adrenaline. The five thrusts of cypress, the jagged ice plant like shag carpeting along the drive, the sharp tree-bark taste of the breeze—it was all disorienting yet familiar, a place he'd visited in the hazy grasp of a dream. They pierced Cottage Circle, the full authority of the federal government blazing its way through forbidden land. The Pros on the circular lawn gaped at the rapid approach. Tim noted bodies in the windows—he'd guessed right, catching them in their cottages before the nighttime Orae.

"U.S. Marshals, we're here to serve a search warrant," Tim shouted.

Miller forged forward, Chomper straining on his lead. Denley and Palton peeled off to run a recon loop around the treatment wing and Growth Hall. The others began knocking and moving through the buildings, two cells per cottage. The first rule of any operation—clear and contain before progressing.

Tim and Bear took Cottage Three, Leah's last-known, Thomas and Freed covering their rear. Most of the rooms were empty. In the kitchen Lorraine was bouncing up and down, rubbing her arm as if trying to erase a stain. She looked aged beyond her years.

"Where's Leah?"

She kept scrubbing, her voice a panicked whine. "Everything's falling apart."

Tim left Bear to frisk her and headed down the hall. He let his muzzle lead as he shoved through doors. The first two rooms were empty.

In the next, Don Stanford and Julie huddled together on an

unmade bed. Tim lowered the MP5 and shuffle-stepped toward them, patting them down.

Julie started to cry. "The Teacher said people were coming to kidnap us."

"We're not here to harm you."

Freed stepped in and asked them to move outside.

Heart pounding, Tim headed to the final bedroom. Aside from a few raised voices, torn away in the wind, it was quiet outside. No gunshots.

He saw two feet shadowed beneath the door gap, so he stood to the side of the jamb and shouted, "U.S. Marshals. Open up."

No response.

"Open the door *now*."

He pivoted and kicked, the in-swinging door striking flesh and eliciting a pained grunt. Janie spilled on her ass, gripping a swollen wrist, a kitchen knife on the rug beside her. "*Asshole*."

He kicked away the knife, and she scrambled for him, nails tearing against his bulletproof vest.

Slinging the MP5, he flipped her, cinched flex-cuffs around her wrists and ankles, and frisked her. Beside one of the beds, a spray of wildflowers leaned from a cone of cardboard.

"Where is she?"

Janie tossed her head to the side, laughing. "She got hers."

Tim hauled her outside and handed her off to Haines. She was still struggling against the flex-cuffs, so he had to put her on her chest.

About thirty Pros milled around on the lawn under Miller's watchful eye, looking dazed but compliant. Even Deano, the burly bouncer who'd tangled with Tim at the Radisson, was deferential in the face of the ART squad's authority. Weapons lowered, ART members were moving the last Pros and Protectors—save for Skate—from the cottages to the lawn. No struggles, no flex-cuffed suspects except Janie, no white tear-gas smoke seeping from doorways.

The area was now cleared, the population safely contained. His dread growing, Tim moved among the scattered Pros, spinning a few of the girls around to peer at their faces.

Palton cut in on the primary channel to declare the treatment wing and Growth Hall empty—that meant Leah was downslope in Skate's shed, TD's bedroom, or the woods. The thought drove Tim toward the trailhead. Bear met him at its brush-funneled entrance, Thomas and Freed falling in behind them. Guerrera, Maybeck, and Zimmer joined their wake from one side, Palton and Denley sweeping in from the other. Danner jogged to catch up, leaving slack in Cosmo's lead, and Roger Frisk from ESU brought up the rear.

Elephant grass and chaparral crowded them at the shoulders. Tim tapped his belt to reacquaint himself with his can of pepper spray; they were entering Doberman country. The wind whipped upslope, carrying the reverberating wail of an opera singer.

They broke into the clearing, which sat still and peaceful, bathed in an orchestral swell from TD's stereo. Save the smoke splitting the rain cap of the shed's chimney like languid steam, there were no signs of life. Denley started his preentry hum.

"Seek, girl, seek." Danner unsnapped Cosmo's lead, and the German shepherd bounded off into the woods. Raising the shotgun across his chest, he lumbered after her.

A blast of Italian reverberated off the trees. ". . . *in Ispagna son gia mille e tre!*"

Tim and Bear stormed the shack first, kicking in the door.

No Skate, no dogs, just the potbellied stove spewing sparks, the mail tub sitting empty before the open loading door.

Bear keyed the portable to the primary channel. "Be advised assault dogs are unaccounted for."

Maybeck shouldered his tear-gas shotgun, trading it for a crowbar he kept hooked in his belt. Moving swiftly toward the mod, he hand-signaled Denley, Palton, and Frisk, though the music would have drowned out a shouted command.

Already Tim was moving across the clearing toward TD's porch. MP5s raised, Guerrera and Zimmer were spread on either side of the door. Freed held open the screen.

A swift peek ascertained that the front room was empty. The stereo volume was cranked so high that, even through the closed bedroom door, the crackle of interlyric static sounded like bubble wrap being crushed.

Tim sidled in, Bear at his shoulder, Thomas and Freed riding their tail.

Tim paused before the closed door and drew in a deep breath. Jamming the stock of the MP5 to his shoulder, he raised a steel-plated boot and kicked right beside the handle. The door splintered inward as they exploded into the room.

TD jerked upright in his bed, bare chest slipping into view beneath a silk robe. A naked girl—maybe Leah—was on her knees on the floor before him, sobbing and covering her face.

"Hands up! Hands up!"

TD spun away from them, his hand sliding between the dark sheets. Tim crossed the room like a projectile, seizing him with two fistfuls of robe and hurling him. He hit the wall-mounted stereo at eye level, the sound cutting off in time to accent his crash to the floor.

He'd come out of his robe, his bruised, naked body rendering a frisk unnecessary, but Tim kept the MP5 trained on him, his finger firm against the trigger.

With a forearm, TD swiped blood from his split nose. Bear flipped back the sheets, revealing the stereo remote TD had been reaching for.

The crying girl looked up at them. It took a moment for Tim to register her face as Shanna's. Freed picked her discarded T-shirt off the floor and handed it to her. Quivering, she pulled it on.

TD was blinking hard, sucking air, his face warring between disbelief and burgeoning outrage. For months he hadn't so much as been bumped into, and now he lay sucking floor dust like a bitch-slapped socialite.

"Get up." Tim tugged the arrest warrant from his pocket. "You're under arrest for destruction of the United States mails."

Betters rolled to a sitting position, making no effort to cover himself. "Is that all?"

"Where's Leah?"

"Leah, Leah, Leah." TD shook his head. "Can't quite place the name."

"If you hurt her . . ."

"Well, I'm certain of one thing. If she *was* hurt, it certainly wouldn't have been me who did it." His eyes flicked from Tim's face to the MP5 pointed at his head. "Tempted to shoot me?"

Tim's boots knocked twice against the wooden floor. TD looked up at him with something like amusement. Tim drove the blade edge of his hand into TD's upper lip, the pressure making him shriek and rise to his feet. Tim straight-armed him into the wall, freeing the metal handcuffs from his belt. They were loose on TD's girlish wrists, so Tim interlocked them to pick up the slack.

"Tempted?" Tim said. "Not for a second. Not with where you're going."

Bear threw the silk robe over TD's shoulders. "Maybe we book you in like this, see how they dig your Prince getup in the tank."

"Actually, I hear mail offenders are greatly feared on the inside."

Frisk's voice sputtered from the primary channel—"*Fucking computer in here's got more levels of security than I've ever seen.*"

TD grinned. "Good luck there, Neos."

A howl sounded from deep in the woods.

The first hint of unease crossed TD's face as he took in their expressions. "What? *What?*"

Their portables all sputtered at the same time, and Danner's voice crackled through. "Cosmo just alerted on a fresh female cadaver. Looks like the rain washed away part of the grave. I've got visual on an exposed head and upper torso."

A deep red bloomed beneath TD's cheeks, making his freckles disappear.

"Does the name Nancy Kramer ring a bell?" Tim said.

"Never heard it. We get trespassers—I order them removed. I don't keep track of the Protectors' recreational activities. They could be dumping nuclear waste out there for all I know. You'll have to do better than that." TD cocked his head, studying Tim. "I'd never kill someone. I don't *have* to. You think I seek control from people? Not nearly as much as people want to *give up* control to me. That's why you'll never get me. I've never done anything to anyone they didn't want done to them." His eyes locked on Tim's. "Including you."

Danner's voice cut in. *"Hang on. We've got another body here."*

Tim felt his stomach drop out of his body. He thought of Will down at the staging point, no doubt privy to the same radio transmission. He thought of Ginny on the coroner's table, cold and firm, the wisp of hair in her mouth.

Bear said, "Go make the ID. I got him."

Tim shot past Guerrera and Zimmer at the door, shouting into the radio for Danner to give him his bearings.

"—northeast about a half mile, just past a low run of granite."

Tim crossed the clearing at a dead sprint, crashing into the woods.

The Racal coughed out the updates as the rest of the operation wrapped up.

Denley in the mod—*"We can't access the corresponding Dead Link computer files. The folders are useless on their own—"*

Tannino shouting, *"Can you make a positive ID on the body as Leah Henning?"*

"—the face is messy with mud—"

His right leg throbbing, Tim stumbled between trees, over

rises. Behind him he heard Bear, Thomas, and Freed spreading out in the woods, shouting to one another.

A gunshot came at him in surround sound—echoing through the trees and amplified on the portable—and then a flurry of barks and snarls.

Bear's voice issued from the portable. *"We're on the way."*

Tim accelerated, trying to ignore the screeching pain through his leg, radio pressed to his lips. "Danner. Danner. *Danner.*"

He'd just hit the granite hump when he heard the double whistle—Skate's release command. Before he could raise the MP5, a Doberman flew through the brush at him. He got an arm up in the jaws before he went down, and he rolled to a stop at a broad pair of boots, looking up past the slobbering jaws at the bore of a Sig Sauer and Skate's face.

Skate's fingers snapped, and the dog released Tim's arm and sat. At the sloped root of an oak, Cosmo squared off over Danner's body, snarling at the other Doberman. Danner's hand, gripping his shoulder near the base of his neck, was slick with blood. He was breathing but weakly.

Part of the hillside had slid away under the weight of the rain. Just past the oak, a half-exhumed corpse thrust up from the earth like a vomited secret. The female form was sticky with sheets of mud, like a tar-mired seagull. Ten feet to its left, a gnarled hand reached from the earth like a B-movie effect.

The image of Leah carrying her own shovel to this spot made Tim cringe with grief. He flashed on a crime-scene photo of Ginny, the snow-angel imprint her torso had left in the muddy creek bank where it had been found.

Skate stripped him of his weapons and said, "Git up."

Tim found his feet. The sounds of the other deputies grew fainter—deputy marshals in the woods was like the start of a bad joke.

Skate nodded at Cosmo. "A person, sure, but I couldn't shoot no dog."

One of the Dobermans lunged for Danner, but Cosmo repelled him. Skate put his dogs on a sit-stay, his index finger pointing to the mud. They froze, black-marble eyes on Cosmo, licking their chops, the scent of Danner's blood driving them wild.

Skate's cheeks were heavy, almost mournful. "You had to come poking around in paradise, didn'tcha?"

Tim held his hands up, loose, a feigned "keep cool" posture that kept them ready. The semiauto was double-action; Skate would want to cock it for a smoother pull.

Skate took a step forward, a tear beading on the brink of his eyelid. The gun bucked slightly in his hand when he thumbed the hammer. Tim lunged for him, catching the barrel in the rising fork of his right thumb and index finger, his left hand chopping Skate's elbow, bending the arm. The gun snapped up and fired just below Skate's chin, sending off a mist of blood as it blew off his face.

Skate staggered back, the Sig plunking into the mud, his dogs watching the flat sheet of his face with their heads cocked inquisitively. He let out a pained grunt, and his breath bubbled through his former mouth, emitting a faint double whistle.

The release command.

The Dobermans fell on him, snapping and tearing.

Tim tugged the pepper spray from his belt and directed two blasts into the dogs' snouts and eyes. They whimpered and dropped, pawing their faces. Skate no longer moved. Tim could barely look at what was left of him.

He shouted for Bear and tried to get at Danner, but Cosmo lowered her head and growled at him, driving him back. He was radioing Miller by the time Bear, Thomas, and Freed stumbled over the granite crest. Letting them take over, he ran to the first corpse, sliding on his knees through the sludge. His hands scrabbled over the bloated face, bending the mud-slick hair aside.

Nancy Kramer.

He'd seen TD give the command to march her into the

woods. With the help of a forensic entomologist, a medical examiner could set the time of death, corroborate Tim's eyewitness account.

Bear was squatting, murmuring to Cosmo until she came forward and licked his hand. Thomas stood over the Dobermans, can of pepper spray at the ready.

Freed sat by Danner, who groaned and said, "Damnit."

Tim trudged over to the other corpse. Only a slender, muddy hand was visible, shoved up from the moist earth.

The long road to Leah had ended here—four fingers and a thumb sprouting from the ground.

Tannino might want to call Judge Seitel for a telephonic warrant before digging; Tim didn't want to take any chances.

His breath caught in his chest. He crouched over the small hand.

A metal ring glinted through the grime on one of the fingers. A gold signet, inscribed with the letters DK.

The initials floated through Tim's head before striking chimes. Danny Katanga. The first investigator Will had hired. *Short little nervous guy, the PI was.*

He moved back to Bear—already he could hear backup crashing through the growth.

Bear's stubbled face was heavy. "That her?"

Tim shook his head.

"We'll get more dogs out here, sweep some more."

Tim turned away, but he had nothing to look at behind him except the glittery remains of Skate's face, the thread of a necklace embedded in the meat of his neck.

He stared at the little silver key.

He pivoted on his heel, raising the portable to his lips. "Frankie, did you clear *all* the rooms in the treatment wing?"

A sputter of static, then Palton's voice—"*Negative. We just peeked in the windows, confirmed they were empty. We didn't want to step on the warrant.*"

Tim reached down, grabbing the chain against Skate's

torn-open Adam's apple and twisting. The key pulled loose.

He moved through the woods, barely hearing Bear's shouts behind him.

Branches whipped at his chest. Leaves tore his face.

He passed a sheriff's deputy carrying a come-along pole, two fire-department medics hustling with a stretcher. Deputy marshals filled the clearing now, bagging evidence and muttering into portables.

On the step, Denley scowled and said, "Computer's got Frisk all in a tangle."

Tannino's voice through the Racal—*"Bring me something to link Betters to those bodies."*

Tim's breath burned as he charged up the trail. The other deputies were chatting up the Pros like old friends. Tim blew by, handing off his MP5 to Miller, who called after him, puzzled, as he trotted up the hill.

Tim kicked down the treatment wing's door, the sound traveling down the tiled corridors and coming back at him. He made ragged progress now, his limp more pronounced.

He called out her name once, twice, but heard nothing save the hum of electric clocks and the tired refrigerator in Dev-Room C.

The tiny square of glass atop the Growth Room door looked in only on darkness, and he felt the optimism whoosh out of him, leaving him breathless. He fumbled the key, dropping it, and finally found the lock. The door stuck, so he kicked it open.

A triangle of light fell over his shoulders, his shadowed outline stretching across the floor and her crumpled form.

She stirred, shook her head as if to clear it.

The lightbulb blinked on, throwing an aquarium-blue glow that lent her flesh a pale, cadaverous tint. Her lips were cracked—white, rectangular segments of peeling skin. They moved soundlessly, then moved again.

Her voice was hoarse, little more than a whisper. "I knew you'd come."

He went to her. She was shivering, so he wrapped her in his raid jacket.

The Racal sputtered, and Denley said, *"Aside from the mail stuff, we're drawing a blank in here."*

Frisk's voice—*"I can't determine what's on the computer—everything's unreadable. I can see files and folders, but they're PGP-encrypted."*

Leah pulled herself to her feet. "All the good stuff is encrypted on the C drive..." She paused, leaning against the wall, catching her breath. Her voice was weak but clear. "I built a passphrase generator that creates hex values to reverse-engineer the hashing strings of the PGP. I hid it in the system file."

"I don't know what that means."

She reached for the portable. Tim keyed it to the right channel and handed it over. Leah walked Frisk through a few simple steps, and then he gave an excited bark of a laugh and said, *"I'm in."*

Leah clicked off, and Tim holstered the radio.

"I would have sent you all the stuff out, but I didn't want to keep dinging the access log, and encrypted files have too many megs to upload quickly anyway." Leah staggered a bit, and Tim threw an arm around her back to steady her. Her eyes were rimmed black with stress and exhaustion.

"How'd you get a phone cord to send out the e-mails?"

"I snuck in Skate's shed when he was sleeping, slid his necklace off. I took the copper wires out, twisted them to minimize inductance." A faint smile. "A makeshift phone cord. He caught me later." She shuddered.

Frisk's voice—*"Pay dirt. We've got the Dead Link files. And financials, surveillance shots—"*

Tim eased down the radio volume.

They walked up the hall, out the doors. The cold hit them fiercely; she turned her face into him, thin arms tightening around his waist.

They walked down the hill toward the staging point.

Night was squeezing in on dusk, cutting visibility.

By the guard station, TD glowered from the back of an unmarked car. A frayed wick protruded from the bottom of the closed door—the end of the nylon cord securing his ankles. When he spotted Leah, he blanched.

The car pulled away, clearing their field of vision to the staging point.

Will turned, his face red and chapped from crying, and did a pronounced double take. Tim and Leah high-stepped over the fallen gate. She stumbled a bit, weak on her feet.

Tannino grasped Dray's shoulder, and she turned. He saw the breath go out of her, saw her shoulders lower a good three inches with the exhale.

Will was wiping his face, already directing traffic as if he had jurisdiction. "Ambulance. We need an ambulance."

Three rescue vehicles sat parked and ready within ten feet of him, but he didn't seem to notice them. Rooch and Doug approached on either side of him.

Will stroked his daughter's cheek. His face crumbled, and then his hand spread over his eyes like a mask. He turned away, took a deep breath. "We need an ambulance."

Wheels crackled through the mud. Two doors slammed in unison, then the paramedics opened the back of the ambulance.

Rooch grasped Leah's shoulder, starting to guide her to the ambulance, but she wouldn't let go of Tim.

Tim started to move her, but she held him harder. He tried to pry her off gently. His throat was thick, but he managed the word "Go."

She gripped him tighter.

Will stepped between Rooch and Doug, splitting them. His arm slid alongside Tim's behind Leah's back. Tim leaned, shifting her sagging weight to Will.

She looked up at Tim, her green-gray eyes frightened, and he tried to steel her with his look.

"Go."

The arm around his waist relaxed.

Will pulled back, drawing her gently to him. The paramedics were at his side, helping them to the rear of the ambulance, reassuring her.

They loaded her up, and Will ducked into the back. The doors slammed. The tires churned mud and found their hold.

Tim watched the diminishing white square until it faded into darkness.

"Go," he said.

Dray was at his side, the wind whipping a band of hair across her forehead. Her curled fingers found it and tucked it behind an ear. The APC's headlights lit her eyes magnificent green, liquid emerald, a shade he'd never seen anywhere else in thirty-four years and counting.

He looked down at the faint bulge beneath her sweatshirt and felt his throat tighten up, the pressure building behind his eyes. She was stepping to him already, and he fell into her, his face bent to the side of her head, buried in silky hair and the scent of jasmine.

"Let's get you home," she said.

Acknowledgments

Guard Harris,

See that this listing reaches William Morrow Publishers, HarperCollins, 10 East 53rd, NY, NY 10022. Fulfillment of this duty will assure your position as cigarette supplier during Wednesday's Orae in the East Block chapel.

TD extends thanks to the following individuals for their commitment and contributions to the growth of The Program:

Michael Morrison—Silent Partner

Suzanne Balaban—beloved Program Publicist, for putting the Source Code's humble progenitor on the map. And elsewhere.

Meaghan Dowling, Lisa Gallagher, Libby Jordan, Debbie Stier—Program Ambassadors-at-Large

George Bick—Program Group Leader, Expansion

Gratitude must also be extended to Brian Grogan, Brian Mc-Sharry, Mike Spradlin, David Youngstrom, and Jeannette Zwart for getting the Source Code out there in their unrelenting quest to reach more Neos.

Sean Abbott, Julia Bannon, and Carol Topping—Program Electronic and Internet Outreach Coordinators

TD and the Pros welcome Rachel Fershleiser, Rome Quezada, and Diana Tynan to the Inner Circle.

Marc H. Glick and Stephen F. Breimer, Esqs.—Protectors, who, despite certain errors of judgment that directly or indirectly led to an undesirable outcome in a certain criminal trial, performed (for the most part) admirably

Jess Taylor—Director of Admissions, Southern Hemisphere, for his unflagging commitment to recruiting youthful Neos

Matthew Guma, Richard Pine, and Lori Andiman—the backbone of the Program Financial Department, for exalting strength

Richard Green and Howie Sanders—for Rejecting Old Programming, Taking Sole Responsibility, and Maximizing Growth in the service of expanding The Program's reach

Robert Crais—who, having spent some time on the "inside" himself, was able to offer this persecuted doctor advice on how to persist in the face of an ever-changing and occasionally threatening new environment

Booksellers and Librarians—whose dissemination of Program literature has proven indispensable

Melissa, Marge, and Al Hurwitz, and Gary and Karen Messing—who could not help but fall under the sway of the Source Code's Version 1.0 as embodied in a loquacious young visionary

Rosie—to whom, someday, the Source Code shall be passed. May she wield it wisely and dedicate herself (as did the Teacher before her) solely to the growth of others.

TD should like to direct his ill will and disdain at the Common-Censors listed below, who, corrupted by overriding negativity and petty envy, were responsible for undoing the first phase of TD's great work:

Richard Cheng—federal persecutor . . . er, *prosecutor*

Joan Freeman—turncoat, supposed federal defender, who lent her considerable talents to the dark side

Mike McCarthy—postal inspector, manufacturer of trumped-up charges

ACKNOWLEDGMENTS 441

Thomas Sendlenski of the Massachusetts State Police Crime Laboratory and Deputy Nicholas Razum, Canine Handler, Los Angeles County Sheriff's Department—for helping fraudulent officials in their campaign of planting and manipulating forensic evidence

Tony Perez, former U.S. marshal—for opening up the U.S. Marshal Service's considerable resources to a certain arrogant and overrated civilian writer with shady intentions

William Woolsey, formerly of the U.S. Marshal Service—for not letting well enough alone

Tim Miller, Supervisory Deputy of the hated Arrest Response Team and the equally loathsome Explosive Detection Canine Team—the sole purpose of which (as recent media accounts have made clear) is to trample individual rights in the pursuit of governmental zealotry

Deputies Chris Daniels and Sean Newlin—whose regrettably clever investigative talents enabled a frame-up of disgraceful proportions

Chris Scalia—who sat down when everyone else was standing. Were it not for his lack of commitment, inability to minimize his negativity, and obdurate nature, the whole crusade against TD might never have been launched.

If you enjoyed

THE PROGRAM

you'll love the following excerpt from

TROUBLESHOOTER

by Gregg Hurwitz,

available at bookstores now

from William Morrow,

an *Imprint of* HarperCollins*Publishers*

Den Laurey strained against the cuffs so his shoulders bulged under his jailhouse blues, sending ripples through the FTW tattooed above his collarbone. An amused smile, all gums at the corners, rode high on his face. In an additional security measure, the chain of his leg restraint had been knotted, narrowing the space between his ankles. Kaner sat beside him on the transport's bench seat, stooped so his head wouldn't strike the roof during freeway turbulence. Because he was too broad for his wrists to meet behind his back, Kaner's arms were secured with two sets of handcuffs linked together. A onetime sparring partner to Tyson—in prison—he'd snapped more than one set of cuff chains, so a second pair of restraints secured him at the forearms. Beneath a wild man's spray of black hair, a 22 tat on the back of his neck advertised his previous stint in the pen. Kaner had a broad, coarse face and prominent earlobes, fleshy tags that lay dimpled against his skull.

Den, president of the Laughing Sinners nomad chapter, and Kaner, the biker gang's national enforcer, were being driven under heavy guard directly from sentencing to San Bernardino County Jail, where they'd await Con Air transport to a federal penitentiary. They'd been convicted of the torture-killing of three members of the Cholos, in retaliation for the shooting of a Sinner. Den, renowned for his knife skills, had severed the victims' heads with surgical precision and set them in their laps. For good measure he'd removed their hearts and left them on the Cholos' clubhouse doorstep. The gesture marked another leap in the escalation between the Sinners and Cholos, a broad-ranging turf war for control over key arteries of Southern California's drug-trafficking network.

Deputy U.S. Marshal Hank Mancone, a fixture behind the wheel of the transport van, was the only nonprisoner in the three-vehicle convoy not a member of the Service's Arrest Response Team. Frankie Palton in the passenger's seat, the four deputy marshals in the armored Suburban behind them, and the two in the advance vehicle five miles up the road were all part of the district's ART squad, called in for tactical strikes and high-risk transports. Mancone was a deputy as well, but given his retirement age and contentment in grousing about his narrow bailiwick, he had little interest in the ARTists aside from giving them the occasional lift.

Palton pivoted in his seat, meeting Den's shit-eating grin through the steel security screen. "Nice tats."

"You can take our clothes, but you can't take our colors."

"What's 'FTW' stand for?"

"Fuck the World."

"We keep having these Hallmark moments, I might get dewy-eyed."

The radio crackled in from the chase car. Jim Denley—Palton's partner: "Eyes up on your right. We got some more bikers coming on."

Palton looked in the sideview. Two bikers rattled past, double-packing, their mamas reclining against sissy bars and offering the deputies languorous waves. Another three bikers zipped by on the right, flying colors, filthy club logos flapping on the backs of their leather jackets.

Mancone's grip on the steering wheel eased once the whine of the Harleys faded. "What's with all the bikers?"

"Relax, lawman," Den said. "It's the season. You got your Love Ride in Glendale, the Long Beach Swap, San Dog Run, Left Coast Rally in Truckee, Big Bear Ride, Mid-State Holiday Hog Run in Paso Robles, Squaw Rock Run, Desert Whirlybird Meet." His smirk bounced into sight in the rearview mirror. "All the wannabes on the move."

Kaner's three-pack-a-day voice emerged from the tangle of hair down over his face. "I'll still take it over you citizens driving around in your cages."

"Hear that, Mancone?" Palton said. "We got nothing to worry about. Just wannabes. And to think I was carrying this gun for no good reason."

Den said, "You want to get your shorts twisted over some weekend warriors, be my guest."

From the chase car: "Shit. Greaseball alert number two."

Two streams of bikers throttled by on either side of the van, their top rockers—the strips of stitched leather cresting the jackets' logos—announcing them as Cholos. Their bottom rockers showed their mother-chapter affiliation: PALM-DALE. A few minutes later, a beefy biker rolled past and did a double take at the prisoners. When he lingered to gloat and flip them a middle finger, Palton raised the stock of his MP5 into view. The Cholo opened the throttle, ponytail flicking, and his bottom rocker came visible: NOMAD.

Den laughed, scratching his cheek with a swipe of his shoulder. "Good ol' Meat Marquez. Now that his nomad buddies met their untimely demise, poor spic's gotta ride all by his lonesome."

They came around a bend in the 10 and were greeted by hundreds of brake lights. As Mancone cursed and slowed to a crawl, Palton got the advance car on the air. "What's with the traffic?"

"What traffic? We sailed through."

"Accident?"

"Probably, but stay alert. We'll exit and wait."

Once traffic ground to a standstill, a biker wearing a duster pulled a few lengths ahead of them, stopping where the space between idling cars narrowed. He was low in the seat, pint-size but exuding attitude. He turned and looked back, the van reflected in the silver blade of the helmet's faceplate. The distinctive Indian logo identified the motorcycle frame's maker, but the rest of the sleek bike seemed to be custom-built. It sported a leather saddlebag on the left side, but its mate was missing on the right. The biker revved the engine giving voice to 1,200 cubic centimeters of rage.

Jim's voice came through the radio again, and Palton replied, "Yeah, we got him. Looks to be unaffiliated—he's not flying colors."

A Harley white-lined through the traffic jam, easing up past the right side of the Suburban and van. The helmeted rider paused a few feet back from the other biker, across the lane, idling.

Hands tensing around his weapon, Palton checked the side mirror. Jim had the stock of his MP5 against his shoulder ready to be raised. Something was lying on the ground under the Suburban at the front left tire. Palton clicked the rearview controls, centering the object in the mirror.

A leather saddlebag.

Palton's eyes lifted, noting the bare right side of the Indian bike ahead. He raised his gun, spinning around. Den and Kaner were lying on the floor, braced against the seats, covering their heads. Palton grabbed for the radio. "Shit, get off the—"

The biker on the Harley raised a lighter-size initiator. His gloved hand tensed.

A low-register boom. The Suburban rose up on the fireball eruption, crashing on its side. The surrounding cars slid a few feet from the blast, doors caving in, windows shattering.

The transport van skidded forward on its front tires, its ass end lifted by the explosion under the trailing vehicle. It smashed the car in front and slammed down directly beside the Harley. Seat belts gut-checked Palton and Mancone, their weapons banging against the dash. The Indian's kick stand was down; the small biker sat backward on the seat, sighting with the AR-15 he'd produced from beneath his duster.

The two deputies raised their heads as the first volley of bullets punched into the window, degrading the armored glass. The inside layer fragged out, glass embedding in their faces. When the windshield gave, their bodies jiggled like marionettes.

The man on the Harley had dismounted and was firing into the van's side lock. When the door slid open, he threw down his gun and caught the bolt cutters his partner tossed him. Rolling to the edge of the van, Den offered up his arms, then his legs, the steel jaws of the cutters making short work of the connecting chains. He bounced out of the van and hopped onto the empty Harley, cuffs rattling like jewelry around his wrists and ankles, chains dangling. A jagged edge by the door lock caught Kaner's prison jumpsuit as he stood, ripping it from collar to tail. Kaner hopped on behind Den, their rescuer leapt on the back of the Indian, and the two bikes took off in opposite directions, splitting lanes.

The four deputies in the keeled-over Suburban strained against their seat belts, coughing out glass and bleeding from the ears. One set of motorcycle wheels zipped past, heading the wrong way. Innumerable car alarms bleated; someone's cry of anguish expired in a gurgle.

The wind picked up the severed chains dangling from Den's and Kaner's shackles, drawing them horizontal. Kaner's torn shirt flapped open, showing off his backpack, the club logo rendered on his flesh in orange and black. They sped off, the flaming skull screaming back from the receding bike at the dead and wounded.

Silver rattled on china as white-gloved waiters cleared the remains of the five-hundred-dollar-a-plate luncheon. Marshal Tannino stood milling with other Angeleno political luminaries, looking mildly out of place with his coiffed salt-and-pepper hair and his department-store suit. He tugged at his too-short shirtsleeves to bring his gold-star links into view and squinted up at the chardonnay-haired woman holding a glass of white wine.

"If we really are serious about committing resources—"

Across the vast ballroom of the Beverly Hills Hotel, some-one's beeper chirped—a cutesy electronic rendition of "Jin-gle Bells."

"—to fully secure the courts, we need to—"

Another pager added a discordant melody, and then a mul-titude chimed in. Tannino glanced down, frowning at his own beeper. "Excuse me, Your Honor."

State assemblymen and deputies alike scurried to the ball-room's exits, checking the reception levels on their cell phones. Tannino was halfway to the lobby when the city at-torney approached, holding out a Nextel. "It's the mayor."

Tannino snapped the phone to his ear, still moving. "Yes, sir. Uh-huh. Uh-huh." His face tightened. As he continued to listen, he fished his cell phone from his pocket and, holding it down at his waist, speed-dialed. "Right away, sir."

He handed back the Nextel and pressed his own phone to his ear. "Get Rackley."

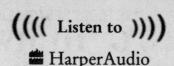